W9-DAM-098

AVENGER

FORGOTTEN REALMS

RICHARD BAKER

AVENGER

BLADES OF THE MOONSEA

BOOK III

WIZARDS OF THE COAST

Blades of the Moonsea
Book III
AVENGER

©2010 Wizards of the Coast LLC

All characters in this book are fictitious. Any resemblance to actual persons, living or dead, is purely coincidental.

This book is protected under the copyright laws of the United States of America. Any reproduction or unauthorized use of the material or artwork contained herein is prohibited without the express written permission of Wizards of the Coast LLC.

Published by Wizards of the Coast LLC

FORGOTTEN REALMS, WIZARDS OF THE COAST, and their respective logos are trademarks of Wizards of the Coast LLC in the U.S.A. and other countries.

Printed in the U.S.A.

Cover art by Raymond Swanland

First Printing: March 2010

9 8 7 6 5 4 3 2 1

ISBN: 978-0-7869-5393-6
620-25148000-001-EN

Library of Congress Cataloging-in-Publication Data

Baker, Richard (Lynn Richard)
  Avenger / by Richard Baker.
    p. cm. -- (Blades of the Moonsea ; bk. 3)
  ISBN 978-0-7869-5393-6
  I. Title.
  PS3602.A587A96 2010
  813'.6--dc22

                                                                2009046407

U.S., CANADA,   EUROPEAN HEADQUARTERS
ASIA, PACIFIC, & LATIN AMERICA   Hasbro UK Ltd
Wizards of the Coast LLC   Caswell Way
P.O. Box 707   Newport, Gwent NP9 0YH
Renton, WA 98057-0707   GREAT BRITAIN
+1-800-324-6496   Save this address for your records.

Visit our web site at www.wizards.com

For Hannah

You were right, and I was wrong.
The trail was too snowy.
Next time I'll listen better.

PROLOGUE

5 Nightal, the Year of the Heretic's Rampage (1473 DR)

When Geran Hulmaster heard the distant strains of song drifting through the evening air like the snow falling lightly on his shoulders, he knew he'd reached Myth Drannor. He could see nothing of the city yet, but he stopped on the old elven road that lay under the soft snow and stood listening, captivated by voices inhumanly pure and sweet lifted in ancient elven melodies. He knew only a few words of the Elvish tongue, but he *felt* the song's meaning in the deepest part of his heart. It was sad and beautiful and wise, a song about the winter sleep that had fallen over the land, a memory of the year that was fading and the longing for loved ones now far away . . . and yet in the countermelody he heard celebration of the winter's own beauty, the anticipation of spring soon to come, the hope for reunions long delayed. Snowflakes drifted silently down to coldly kiss his face and catch in his hair, and still he stood listening, heedless of the long chill that had crept into his limbs during days of travel from old Harrowdale into the heart of the elf kingdom. The city of the elves was near, and yet Geran could not bring himself to take another step for fear that he might lose the marvelous song that drifted faintly to his ears.

The dim golden glow of lanternlight in the winter sky waited ahead of him, as if the forest had somehow given way to a great hall pillared with slender silver trunks. Geran stood as quietly as the drowsing beeches in the gentle snow. He was a tall, lean man, twenty-five years of age, with raven-dark hair and eyes of steel gray, now half closed as he gave his full attention to the song. Beneath his weatherbeaten cloak and sodden hood, he wore a fine jacket of blue suede, a shirt of good Turmishan cotton, breeches of gray wool, and knee-high boots of chased Cormyrean leather—the clothing of a man of means, perhaps a noble born to rich estates or a merchant of great wealth. He was neither, having come by his fortune in a different fashion. Silver mail beneath his shirt glinted at his collar, and at his hip he wore a long sword enchanted in old Chondath five centuries earlier. It was the most valuable of the treasures he'd won in five years of adventuring across the lands of the Inner Sea.

He might have stood mesmerized for hours, but a new sound grew behind him—a faint jingling of bells, and muffled hoofbeats. Geran realized that he was standing in the middle of the road, and managed to rouse himself enough to step aside for the carriage or sled that was approaching. In human lands a fast-driving coachman might not take any great pains to avoid running down a fool in his path. He doubted that the Fair Folk were that callous, but who could say what elves might or might not do? They were a strange people, and sometimes proved dangerous in unexpected ways. He'd met a few in his travels, including one he'd come to regard as a comrade as true as any he'd ever known. But even after years of traveling, fighting, drinking, and competing alongside Sonnelor in the Company of the Dragon Shield, he'd hardly begun to glimpse the elf's depths. He liked to think that Sonnelor had regarded him as a friend, and perhaps not quite as foolish and shortsighted as most humans, but Geran still wasn't sure of it.

"I suppose I'll never know now," he muttered aloud. Sonnelor was dead a year or more now, and Geran's journey to Myth Drannor was something of a farewell to his fallen comrade. Sonnelor's kin had heard of his death many months before, but Geran thought that they deserved to hear the full story of the Dragon Shields' last adventure and the part Sonnelor had played. More to the point, Geran *owed* it to Sonnelor—and to himself. He'd never said as much to Hamil or any of his other friends in Tantras, but some part of him simply wasn't satisfied to carry on with his own affairs and leave the Company of the Dragon Shield behind him forever, not until he'd found a better way to say good-bye to those who'd fallen.

RICHARD BAKER

He glimpsed a shadow of white and gray overtaking him along the road, and stepped a little farther out of the way. Beneath the softly falling snow, a sleigh of white wood pulled by a single dappled horse came into view. The horse's harness was fixed with tiny silver bells, a merry sound as the animal pranced along the way. Two elves rode in the sleigh, a lord and lady draped in long robes against the chill of the evening. They were of the moon elf kindred, almost as pale as the snow themselves, with dark hair and dark eyes. Geran bowed politely as they approached, and waited for them to pass on by. But to his surprise, the elf woman drew up the reins and stopped the sleigh. He thought that her companion glanced sharply at her, perhaps annoyed, but he couldn't be sure.

"Well met, stranger," the woman said. She spoke Common with a light, lilting accent, and looked much like a slender human girl not much more than eighteen or nineteen years in age. Of course, it was difficult indeed for a human to guess at an elf's age. She had a fine-featured face, bewitching violet eyes, and a dancer's unconscious grace; Geran was smitten where he stood. "Have you lost your way in the snow?"

"No, my lady," he answered. "I only paused a moment to listen to the music."

She cocked her head to listen for a moment, and then laughed softly. "Then you might be here for some time. That is the *Miiraeth len Fhierren*, the Song of Winter's Turning, and it has only just begun. This is the longest night of the year, and it will not end until sunrise. Many would call you fortunate to hear it completely. But I imagine you would hear it much better if you paused somewhere a little closer."

Geran grimaced, wondering what sort of fool he looked like, standing out in the middle of the forest to catch the merest strain of an elven melody. The young woman's companion smiled at him, almost as if he sensed how ridiculous Geran felt, but his eyes held a hint of wariness. "Not all who roam these forests are friends, Alliere," he said. "It might be wise to find out who this fellow is, and what he is doing on our doorstep. What is your business in Myth Drannor, sir?"

Geran didn't care for the elf's manner, but it was a fair question. "I am Geran Hulmaster of the family Hulmaster. I intend to call on House Ysfierre, since I knew a kinsman of theirs." He shrugged. "After that . . .

I've heard that the coronal sometimes takes skilled blades into her service. I thought I might offer mine, if she'll have it."

"Oh, you're one of *those*, then," the elf replied with a laugh. "They seem to come from all corners of Faerûn to lay their swords at Ilsevele's feet, sometimes a dozen in a tenday. I regret to inform you that the Coronal Guard is adequately staffed at the moment. You've most likely walked a long way for nothing."

Geran bit back the retort that leaped to his lips. He doubted that this elf would believe him if he claimed to be a little more seasoned or skilled than most rootless dreamers who came this way. Instead he looked over to the beautiful elf woman, and inclined his head. "Not for nothing," he said evenly. "I've heard the Fair Folk singing the *Miiraeth len Fhierren* in the silver beeches of Cormanthor, and I'm the richer for it."

She smiled, and unlike her companion, her smile was warm and merry. "Well answered, Geran Hulmaster! Please, join us and allow me to drive you the rest of the way. I can see that you've had a long, cold journey, but at least we can ease the last mile for you. Tomorrow will bring what it brings."

Under most circumstances Geran would have declined, since it was clear to him that the woman's companion preferred to have her company for himself. But the fellow had enjoyed a laugh at his expense twice now, and Geran was in no hurry to lose sight of the elf woman—Alliere, that was her name, he told himself. "My thanks, dear lady," he said. Before he could change his mind, he climbed up into the sleigh and found a little space in the comfortable seat beside her, pointedly ignoring the flash of irritation that crossed her companion's face. "You are very kind."

She spread the blanket covering her lap over his as well, and flicked the reins lightly. The sleigh gave a little start as it began to move again, the bells on the horse ringing in the falling snow. "I am Alliere Morwain, of House Morwain," she said to him. "And this is Lord Rhovann Disarnnyl, of House Disarnnyl."

"Lady Alliere," Geran murmured. He looked past her to Rhovann, who managed a very sincere-looking smile that did not quite reach his eyes. Geran nodded. "My lord Rhovann. A pleasure to make your acquaintance. I shall not trouble you for long."

"Oh, nonsense," Alliere said. "The Ysfierres are dear friends of mine, and I will be happy to take you to their home. But I hope that you will tarry a little while in Morwain Tower and warm yourself first. I have never ventured outside Myth Drannor, and I love to hear travelers' tales of the lands beyond our forest."

"I'm at your disposal, my lady."

"Excellent!" Alliere turned to Rhovann. "You don't mind, do you, Rhovann?"

"Of course not, my dear," Rhovann answered. He slipped his arm through hers and patted her hand, drawing her a little closer. "I know how you can't resist caring for any lost little creatures of the forest you come across. I suppose it's your compassionate nature."

Alliere favored the elf lord with an arched eyebrow, and looked back to Geran. "Then let me be the first to welcome you to Myth Drannor, Geran Hulmaster. May you find whatever it is you seek in our fair city."

"I hope that I will," Geran answered her. He settled back in the seat, already enjoying the warmth of the blankets. The singing grew stronger as the sleigh glided onward through the soft wet snow, and he knew that he was lost no longer.

ONE

3 Hammer, the Year of Deep Water Drifting (1480 DR)

The lights of Thentia glimmered below Geran at dusk as he descended from the lonely moors to the settled lands ringing the old port. He rode past snow-covered fields, steep pastures bordered by crumbling stone walls, black orchards stretching barren branches to the darkening sky. Thentia's valley was wider and more gentle than Hulburg's, and its belt of farmland stretched for many miles from the city walls. He came to a cart track that ran northward, away from the city, and guided his weary mount into the muddy lane.

The cottages and barns of Thentia were not much different than those of Hulburg to Geran. The two cities enjoyed something of a mercantile rivalry, since they produced similar goods and had more or less the same wants, but their people came from the same stock, the sturdy Moonsea settlers who'd tamed this cold and bitter land in the days of old Thentur. Many Hulburgans had kin in Thentia; as a young man, Geran had always thought of Thentia as "the big city," looking for any excuse to visit. He knew the place almost as well as he knew Hulburg or Myth Drannor.

After another mile, he crested a small rise and started down toward an old manor house that lay within a deep hollow hard under the mistblown slopes ringing the city. Home, such as it is these days, he told himself. He tapped his heels to the tired gelding's flanks and picked up the pace, anxious to be in from the cold.

The manor known as Lasparhall was not quite a palace and not quite a castle. It was a large house with thick stone walls, sturdy barred doors, and rooftop battlements, standing in a lonely vale just under the eaves of the Highfells, a little more than four miles from Thentia's walls. In warmer seasons sheep grazed on the windy green hillsides that mounted up behind the old estate, but in the dark months of winter the manor's flocks were kept in fenced pastures and low stone barns just behind the great house. The old estate had come into Geran's family as a dowry when his grandfather Lendon Hulmaster married Artissa, cousin to Thentia's ruling prince. In the decades since Geran's grandparents had passed away, the Hulmasters had left the place to its caretakers for the most part, visiting every summer or two as the mood took them. As a child, Geran had spent many hours exploring the wide green pastures and wild moorland that waited just beyond a thin ring of apple orchards, or playing chase with the servants' children up and down the long hallways, thick with sunmotes and the redolent scent of the golden brown lasparwood beams that gave the old house its name. It was far from a wealthy estate—the meager rents paid by shepherds and orchard keepers hardly paid for the house's upkeep—but it was otherwise a comfortable home in exile for the Hulmaster family and those retainers loyal enough to follow them to Thentia.

How long before a home in exile simply becomes a home? Geran wondered tiredly. Three months earlier, the usurper Maroth Marstel and Geran's old rival Rhovann drove Harmach Grigor and the rest of the Hulmasters from the castle of Griffonwatch. Fall had faded into winter, and still they seemed no closer to reclaiming their home. The swordmage sighed as he studied the old house—a fine enough place in its own way, but a far cry from the great halls and lofty towers of Griffonwatch. Every day that Marstel remained in power, the borders of Lasparhall grew more familiar, more acceptable . . . and more cagelike to Geran.

He trotted into the courtyard before the manor house, dismounted, and led his horse to the stable nearby. After passing the animal to the care of a stablekeeper, he hoisted the saddlebags over his shoulder and walked to the manor's door. A pair of Shieldsworn guards in the blue and white surcoats of the harmach stood watch just inside, displaying to visitors that the Hulmasters in exile still commanded a small company of loyal armsmen—and were important enough to have enemies to be wary of.

"Welcome home, Lord Geran," said the Shieldsworn sergeant by the door.

"Home, Noram?" Geran snorted and shook his head. "Hardly *home*. But I'm glad enough to return, nonetheless."

Sergeant Noram flushed in embarrassment. He was a young soldier, new to his rank, having been promoted after the heavy losses in the fighting against the Bloody Skull horde nine months past. "Your pardon, my lord. I meant no offense," he stammered.

Geran winced. He hadn't meant to snap at the fellow. He paused in the doorway, and said, "It was nothing you said, Sergeant. Forgive me; it's been a long day."

Noram smiled nervously, and relaxed a little. "We'll see to your saddle-bags, Lord Geran," he said. "I think the harmach and the rest of the family are at their supper, if you've a mind to join them."

"My thanks," Geran said. He allowed the sergeant to take the heavy pouches from his shoulder, and shrugged off his damp cloak. He was hardly dressed for dinner at the harmach's table, but he was more than ready for a hot meal, and he figured that his uncle would forgive his informality. Working the stiffness from his neck, he crossed the manor's front hall to the doorway under the great stairs and headed toward the kitchens. Lasparhall had a fine old banquet hall that was more impressive, but it was too big and drafty for anything less than twenty or thirty at a seating; the harmach preferred the smaller dining room that stood in the back of the house. He passed a few of the serving staff, folk from Griffonwatch who'd followed the Hulmasters into exile, exchanging greetings as he went. Then he came to the dining-room door and let himself inside.

Harmach Grigor, his uncle, sat at the head of the table, a roasted quarter-chicken untouched on the platter before him. To his right sat Grigor's sister, Geran's aunt Terena, and next to her Geran's cousin Kara, who wore a simple dress of green wool instead of the armor she often wore during the day as the captain of the Hulmaster's Shieldsworn. On the other side of the table were Erna and young Natali and Kirr, the widow and children of Grigor's son Isolmar, dead almost five years now. Before Geran could even open his mouth to greet his family, Natali and Kirr scrambled out of their chairs and bolted around the table to launch themselves at his waist.

"Geran's back! Look, Geran's back!" the youngest Hulmasters shouted. "What happened, Geran? Is Marstel still calling himself the harmach? Did anyone recognize you? Did you see Mirya and Selsha? Can we go back to Griffonwatch now?"

"One at a time, one at a time! And who said anything about Hulburg?" Geran protested. He'd done his best to keep his travels secret, not wanting the children to worry about him while he was gone, but it seemed that the young Hulmasters had discovered his whereabouts anyway. He leaned down to hug his young cousins. Over their young lives Natali and Kirr had heard many stories about the Hulmaster who was off to see the world, and even after months of living under the same roof as Geran they still regarded him with appreciable wonder. Natali was the older of the pair, a clever, dark-haired girl of ten years with dark, thoughtful eyes. Kirr had his mother Erna's reddish gold hair and a rambunctious, inexhaustible energy to him that seemed enough to vex and bother half the adults in the manor, Hulmaster, Shieldsworn, and servant alike. The one good thing about the family's fortunes in the last few months, he reflected, was that he'd finally come to know Isolmar's children.

"Geran, my boy, good to see you again," Harmach Grigor said. He motioned to the far end of the table. "Please, sit down, have something to eat. I'll wager you've had a long ride today."

"Twenty-five miles by my guess. I just came in." Geran gave his uncle a tired smile, but he found himself surprised by how gaunt and pale the old man looked. In the tenday that Geran had been off to Hulburg and back he'd somehow forgotten just how fatigued his uncle was. The defeat at Marstel's hands and the subsequent flight into exile had taken a heavy toll on the harmach; Grigor was better than seventy-five years of age, and he hadn't enjoyed very good health to begin with. The swordmage shook himself free of his young cousins and ventured over to clasp his uncle's arm in greeting. The harmach's grip was shockingly weak.

"Well?" said Geran's Aunt Terena. She was Grigor's younger sister and Kara's mother, a woman who wore the wisdom of her years well. She had a kindly, gentle manner, but there was unmistakable firmness in her voice. Much of Kara's stubbornness came from her mother. "Since the secret of your journey's out, what news of Hulburg?"

"Things are much as they've been. Marstel is still holding court in Griffonwatch, I'm sorry to say, and his Council Guard holds the town in force." He moved around the table to kiss his Aunt Terena on her cheek, set a hand on Kara's shoulder, and then sat at the next place down. The kitchen servers quickly set a plate of roasted chicken and a goblet of warm mulled wine in front of him before retreating from the room again. Between mouthfuls of chicken, he recounted a carefully edited version of his journey to Hulburg and travels around the countryside, leaving out most of the names. Since his treacherous cousin Sergen's passing, there were no more Hulmasters he didn't trust, but the children were young and might say something where they shouldn't. If word got back to Rhovann that he'd been helped by the Sokols or had spoken with Mirya or the Tresterfins or any other old loyalists, lives might be in danger. But he made sure to exaggerate every conceivable hardship and moment of peril he faced for the sake of Natali and Kirr, so that the whole drab and wearying tenday became a hair-raising dance with death in the retelling.

By the time he'd finished, the eyes of both young Hulmasters were wide with astonishment. Erna frowned sternly at Geran, well aware that the truth had been stretched more than once. "They'll be up half the night with that tale in their heads," she said. "You should be ashamed of yourself, Geran!"

"Every word of it true," he answered. "Besides, Hamil isn't here to spin them their bedtime story. I did what I could in his place." Hamil Alderheart, Geran's old adventuring companion, was greatly beloved by the young Hulmasters. He'd sailed back to Tantras a month before to see to the business of the Red Sail Coster, his trading company.

"Every word true, indeed," Erna muttered. "Come, Natali, Kirr. It's to your lessons and then bed for the both of you, and I'll not hear a word of protest about it!" She gathered her children and shooed them out of the room. Terena excused herself and followed to give Erna a hand with the young Hulmasters, leaving just Kara and Harmach Grigor with Geran.

Kara looked at Geran, and raised an eyebrow. "I'm accounted one of the best trackers in the Moonsea North, and I have to say, I've never met any frost giant robbers or pixie bandits haunting the roads between here and Hulburg." Laughter danced in her brilliant blue eyes, touched years before by the azure fire of the Spellplague. "Natali saw through every word of that, you know."

"I know it," answered Geran. "I simply didn't want to say too much about my true business in Hulburg. Careless words may prove dangerous."

They fell silent for a time, listening to the receding sounds of the children retreating to their rooms. Harmach Grigor smiled sadly, and then returned his attention to his nephew and niece. "Speaking of dangerous, you were rash to return to Hulburg, Geran," he said. "We have other sources of information. It's not worth your life."

Geran shook his head. "I disagree. There's a difference between reading about what's happening in the town and seeing it with your own eyes. Besides, to have any hope of organizing resistance to Marstel's rule, we must have the trust and respect of old Hulburg. We will be asking people to run deadly risks on our behalf. They need to see that we haven't abandoned them."

"Geran is right, Uncle," Kara said firmly. "Even the most loyal hearts will lose hope if they come to believe we don't intend to return." With the brilliant azure of her eyes and her well-known spellscar, she could not disguise herself as easily as Geran. He knew it was hard for her to leave the dangerous spying to him, but as risky as it was for him to venture into Hulburg now, it would have been twice as risky for her. She looked over to Geran and asked, "So how do matters stand in Hulburg now?"

"It's hard on the folk who supported us," he admitted. "Marstel—well, Rhovann I suppose, I can't imagine this was Marstel's scheme—is taxing the old landowners and shopkeepers into penury. Then he's awarding their confiscated property to the outlander gangs to buy their support. Yarthin, Errolsk, Baudemar, they're all out of business."

"And the Cinderfists are staying bought?"

Geran nodded. "For now. Their priest Valdarsel now sits on the Harmach's Council as the so-called high prelate of Hulburg. Things might be different in a few months when Marstel's tax collectors run out of folk to rob and have no more gold or land to give to the Cinderfists, but that day isn't here yet."

"Who did you see?" Grigor asked.

"Mirya, of course. After her, Sarth, Burkel Tresterfin, Theron Nimstar, the Ostings, a couple of others. Nimessa Sokol likely knows I slipped into Hulburg in a Sokol caravan, but I didn't speak with her or any of her folk."

"How many of the Spearmeet are ready to fight for our cause?" asked Kara.

"If Tresterfin, Nimstar, and the Ostings are right, a couple of companies still. I'd guess ten score, altogether. More would join once the fighting began in earnest, I think. Few are willing to be the first to rise in opposition, but once some do, more would follow."

"No," said Harmach Grigor. "Not yet. Encouraging our loyalists would only bring down reprisals that we cannot shield our people against. If we cannot protect them, then we must make sure that they don't suffer on our behalf."

"Every day we wait, our loyalists grow weaker, and Rhovann adds to his own strength," Kara replied. "Wait too long, and we'll miss our chance altogether."

"I understand that, Kara. But this is not yet the time. Better to do nothing at all and let Marstel have his way with the town for now than to cause our folk any more suffering." Grigor pushed himself upright with a grunt and motioned to the door. "It's getting late. I believe I'll retire for the evening."

Geran frowned, unwilling to let the matter rest. Despite the hard day's travel in the cold weather, he was not yet ready for bed. Still, he was certainly in need of a change of clothing, and a warm bath wouldn't be amiss. The three Hulmasters said their good nights to each other, and parted ways—Kara to make her rounds of the manor and its grounds, seeing to the Shieldsworn guards, and Geran and Grigor to the wing of the manor where their rooms were. They climbed the stairs to the second floor, Grigor moving slowly and carefully as Geran tried to hover nearby as unobtrusively as possible.

At the top of the stairs Grigor paused to catch his breath. "The winters are growing harder every year," he said, leaning heavily on his cane. "The cold never leaves me, it seems. Ah, well, that's the price of seeing so many of them. It's good to have you back safe and sound, Geran. We worry about you when you're away."

"I try to be careful." Geran hesitated, weighing the question of whether to push again on the issue of more direct action against Marstel. He decided to try one more time. "About Marstel . . . I believe there's more we can do than you might think, Uncle. In a tenday Kara and I could muster a hundred riders to harry Marstel's frontier posts and borders. It might not be much, but it would show friends and foes alike that we're not beaten yet. Even just a show of resistance might be enough—"

"Not yet!" the harmach said sharply. He fixed his pale, watery eyes on the younger Hulmaster. "I have spoken on this matter, Geran. There is no point in spilling more blood if we don't yet have the strength to win."

Geran fell silent, meeting his uncle's gaze for a long moment before he reluctantly nodded. "I hear you, Uncle. There's to be no fighting for now."

"Good," Grigor said. He smiled again, and turned toward his chambers. "Good night, Geran. We'll speak again tomorrow."

"Good night, Uncle Grigor," Geran replied. He watched his uncle limp away on his cane, then headed for his own rooms.

TWO

4 Hammer, the Year of Deep Water Drifting (1480 DR)

Geran was sound asleep when the assassins came. Only the fact that he'd carelessly left his boots lying on the floor near the foot of his bed saved his life.

A soft stumble in the dark roused him from a dreamless slumber; he awoke just as iron-hard talons were reaching for his throat. Flailing wildly, he caught his attacker's arms in his hands. He felt rough, scaly skin that was as hot as a firepit's stone in his grasp, and heard a hiss of anger from the thing leaning over him. The air reeked of warm sulfur, acrid and strong enough to choke his cry of alarm.

"He wakes!" a second voice hissed from nearby. "Slay him swiftly!"

The first creature did not reply, but bent all its strength to seizing Geran in its talons. It was horribly strong, and it steadily pushed its claws closer to his neck. He saw carious yellow fangs gleaming in the shadows above his face, and a beard of thick tendrils that writhed and dripped inches from his chest. Wherever its saliva dripped on his bare flesh, his skin burned and smoked. He couldn't hold the creature's talons from his neck for much longer, and he was defenseless against its companion as long as he dared not let go of the creature's arms.

A desperate idea came to him, and before he could think better of it, Geran gambled on its success. Somehow he found a still center in the midst of his pain and panic, focusing on the arcane symbols of the spells locked away in his mind. The featherlight touch of magic gathering to him stirred the bedchamber's cold air and the sheets entangling his flailing limbs. "*Sieroch!*" he shouted, finishing the spell as he released his foe's arms. The creature's lethal claws lunged forward, but Geran was no longer there. His teleportation spell had carried him across the room. He scrambled to his feet as the monsters screeched in frustration and whirled to face him again.

"Clever, mortal," the first creature snarled. It was little more than a jagged shadow in the darkened room. "You would have been wiser to die in your sleep."

What in the Nine Hells is going on? Geran thought furiously. He blinked the last of the sleep from his eyes, coming fully awake. His hands throbbed from the heat and jagged scales of the creature's hide. The Nine Hells indeed—if these creatures weren't devils of some kind, he would have been astonished. Some enemy had summoned infernal assassins to slay him in his sleep. Other questions crowded in after that, but he thrust them aside. There would be time for answers later, if he managed to survive the next few heartbeats.

First, he needed to see better. "*Elos!*" Geran said, casting a minor light spell. A globe of pale gold shimmered into existence a few feet from him, its soft illumination filling the room. The two monsters facing him winced and recoiled, surprised by the sudden light. They were roughly man-sized, covered in dull reddish scales and sharp barbs of horn at knees, shoulders, and elbows. Their feet were great raptorlike talons, and they had long, lashing tails studded with more sharp barbs. Coiling tendrils of darker red jutted from their chins, giving them foul, twisting beards of a sort. Geran hadn't faced their like before, but he'd heard of them before—*barbazu,* or bearded devils, fierce and deadly foes. How they'd gotten into Lasparhall he couldn't imagine, but their purpose was all too clear.

"Rend him to pieces!" the second devil growled. The two launched themselves across the room in a sudden rush, claws stretching out for him. Geran looked past the monsters to the place where his sword hung in its scabbard by his bedstand.

He reached out his hand and called out a summoning spell of his own: "*Cuilledyr!*" His elven backsword shivered once in its scabbard before lurching free and soaring hiltfirst to his hand, just in time to meet the devils' furious charge. Dropping beneath the raking claws of the first devil, he drove the point of his blade into the center of its torso, just under the breastbone. The ancient sword rang shrilly as it pierced infernal flesh; long before in Myth Drannor's Weeping War its makers had enchanted it with spells of ruin against hellspawned monsters just such as these. The creature shrieked horribly, impaled on the blade, then burst apart in a noisome black cloud. But its companion hurled into Geran, its sharp claws raking him deeply across the chest and shoulders as it slammed him into the cold floor.

Sizzling venom from the devil's writhing beard-tendrils splattered Geran's cheek, and he howled in anguish. The monster pinned his sword arm with one talon and mauled him with the other. Somehow the swordmage found the strength to throw the barbazu to one side. The devil didn't release him, but with its weight off his chest he was able to roll to one side and seize the hilt of his sword in his left hand, which wasn't pinned. Before his assailant could seize that arm too, Geran dragged the gleaming edge across the devil's scaly flesh in a single long draw. The bearded devil hissed in pain and scrabbled back from the bright steel. Geran surged to his feet and set upon the creature with a furious hail of blows. Yet its scales resisted all but the surest of his attacks.

"Ah, how delicious." The creature sneered. "While we dance, the rest of your family dies. Perhaps I should let you go to them before I slay you."

"You lie!" Geran retorted automatically. He had to believe the monster was toying with him, trying to urge him into a rash attack. If more devils were loose in Lasparhall, stealing into the harmach's chambers—or worse yet, Natali's or Kirr's—then every moment he was delayed here might come with a horrible cost indeed.

He traded passes with the barbazu again, his steel striking sparks from its ironlike claws as they exchanged places. Quickly he cleared the welling fear for his family from his mind, and summoned up the calm for spell-casting. This time he charged his sword with a crackling aura of blue-white lightning that threw garish shadows against the walls as it danced along the edge. The bearded devil bared its fangs in defiance and leaped to meet him again, but this time its hard scales did not stop the sword's bite. Lightning seared its red flesh, freezing it in place with powerful convulsions. Before the monster could recover, Geran slashed it through the throat. It, too, vanished in a sudden burst of black smoke, and the bedchamber fell still for a moment.

Blood dripped from his raked flesh to the wooden floorboards. Geran gritted his teeth against the burning pain of the wounds, and staggered to the door. Pausing only a moment to summon a better spell-shield to defend himself, he threw open the door and hurried out into the passageway. Shouts of alarm, screams, and the ringing sound of blade meeting blade echoed throughout the old manor.

Someone means to eradicate the Hulmasters this night, he realized—all of us. It was the second time in half a year that someone had tried to destroy the Hulmasters in their home. His cousin Sergen had tried to murder the family during his coup attempt the preceding spring, attacking Griffonwatch with summoned wraiths while his mercenaries waited to cut down anyone fleeing the castle. Sergen was dead now, but someone else clearly wanted the Hulmasters out of the way. Rhovann? he wondered. His old rival certainly held no end of malice for him, but indiscriminate murder was not like Rhovann. The Verunas, perhaps? Or someone else who wanted to make sure the Hulmasters never returned to Hulburg?

"Damn it," he snarled into the darkened hallway. He whirled around, trying to make sense of the chaos. To the right were the rooms of the young Hulmasters. In the opposite direction lay Harmach Grigor's chamber. The harmach was certainly the first target of the attackers, but Geran knew what his uncle would want him to do. Grigor would want him to make sure that Natali and Kirr were saved from this slaughter, regardless of the cost.

A child's scream rang out in the darkness. "Natali," Geran murmured. Without another thought he turned to his right and sprinted down the hallway, his sword bared in his hand. The harmach probably had Shieldsworn bodyguards close to hand already; if fortune smiled just a little, they might be able to hold off the attack for a while. He turned the corner at the manor's grand stair, and found several men and women in the harmach's colors lying dead or unconscious at the top of the steps. Two men Geran had never seen before were crumpled on the steps by the guards. They wore no colors at all other than their well-worn leather jerkins and dark, hooded cloaks, the sort of nondescript garb that scores of sellswords in Thentia's dockside taverns wore every day. Whoever was behind the attack had likely hired any killers he could find for the task—or wanted it to appear that way—and then reinforced the common sellswords with summoned devils.

Geran did not pause to study the scene more closely, leaping over one of the fallen guards and continuing down the hallway. He came to Natali's chamber, found the door standing open, and burst inside.

Two more Hulmaster servants were dead on the floor before him. Over them stood three more sellswords, already turning toward the corner of the nursery, where Erna huddled with her children. One of the sellswords, a bald man with Theskian tattooes on his scalp, raised a cleaverlike blade and seized Kirr's arm to haul him away from his mother. Natali and Kirr both wailed, but Erna glimpsed Geran past her assailants. "*Geran!*" she shrieked. "*Help us!*"

The two mercenaries between him and the Theskian holding Kirr wheeled about at her cry. "One more step and we'll slay the lot!" the first snarled. "Drop the sword, and we'll let the small ones go!"

He hesitated a moment before realizing that the man had to be lying. They had no intention of leaving any Hulmasters alive this night. Instead of releasing his blade, he fixed his eye on Kirr and the mercenary who gripped his arm, and formed a spell of teleportation in his mind. "*Sierollanie dir mellar,*" he said in a clear voice.

An instant of utter darkness and icy cold flashed across his senses—then he was where Kirr had been standing, with the Theskian's hand locked on his left arm, while Kirr stood dumbfounded in the doorway where Geran had been a heartbeat before. He rarely found use for the spell of transposition, but in this situation it was exactly the surprise Geran needed. The Theskian mercenary's eyes opened wide in astonishment, and he opened his mouth to say something before the heavy basket hilt of Geran's backsword slammed between his eyes with a sickening crunch. The fellow staggered back and collapsed to the floor; Geran turned to engage the remaining two swordsmen. "Kirr, get out of the hallway and find a place to hide!" he cried. "Erna, get Natali into the washroom and barricade the door!" Then his blade met the hard parry of the first of the two enemies he now faced, and the fight was on in earnest.

Unlike the Theskian sellsword lying motionless on the floor, these two were now fully cognizant of his skill and magic. He had no more surpises for them, and they were good enough blades that he couldn't simply overwhelm them with a quick assault. He tried anyway, and succeeded in driving them back two steps toward the doorway, steel crashing against steel as their swords danced with his. Behind the two mercenaries, Kirr glanced left and right down the hallway. "More of them are coming, Geran!" he shouted. Then he darted out of sight to the left—Geran hoped to find some secure bolthole where the assassins couldn't find him. He risked a peek over his shoulder and saw Natali and her mother pushing the door of the garderobe closed behind them.

"A futile gesture," said one of the swordsmen dueling Geran. "We'll have all of them within a quarter hour anyway!"

"Not while I still stand here, you won't," Geran retorted. He resumed his attack, trying to beat down the assassin's guard, but now his two opponents were working together. Whichever he attacked gave ground and went on the defensive, while the other pressed hard and tried to catch him with his guard out of place. He grimaced, beginning to wonder if he'd been wise to transpose himself into the bedchamber after all. He'd caught the one holding Kirr off guard, but in doing so he'd put two good swordsmen between him and the door. His quick stroke had left him pinned in the childrens' chamber, unable to fight clear quickly or affect events anywhere else in the manor. The youngest Hulmaster was out in the dark hallway somewhere, all too likely in need of Geran's help, and he could hear more fighting echoing throughout Lasparhall's fragrant chambers.

Steel flickered and shrilled in another exchange, and Geran ground his teeth together in growing frustration. He had to get by these two and find out what else was happening! Pressing forward recklessly with a spell of attack on his lips, he managed to shock the sword out of one man's hand with another lightning-blade spell. The man yelped and moved back, holding his sword hand, but Geran paid for it with a shallow cut to his left calf as the fellow's comrade struck back at him. Then the doorway filled again, this time with two more assassins and the hot, sulfurous stink of another bearded devil.

"I've got Geran Hulmaster here!" the swordsman fighting him cried. "Two more of them are in the garderobe! Cut him down!"

"*Cuillen mhariel,*" Geran said, casting a spell in reply. Thin streamers of silver mist appeared around him, the best defense he could summon at the moment. He might be able to escape with a spell or two, but he couldn't abandon Erna and Natali. He settled into a fighting crouch, standing his ground in the middle of the bedchamber, teeth bared in a grimace of determination. Here he would stand and, if fate ordained it, die, but he would not give ground. Then the assassins and the grinning hellspawn rushed him all at once.

For a single impossible moment Geran stood without yielding, his elven blade a silver blur as he parried and countered as fast and furiously as he'd ever fought in his life. The assassins closed in from all sides, sword points weaving and darting like steel serpents eager for a taste of his flesh, while the bearded devil hissed and bulled straight at him, slashing wildly with its iron talons. A point grazed his ribs, another pinked him in the thick of his left thigh, and raking talons furrowed his chest. Despite himself Geran faltered a step, trying to use his foes as shields against the others, but there were simply too many to deal with at once in the close quarters. So be it, he thought grimly. He'd try to take as many with him as he could, and hope that any assassins he delayed here missed their chance to kill more of the Hulmasters.

The rearmost assassin suddenly cried out, back arching as his arms flew up in the air. He took two staggering steps and then pitched forward on his face. Behind him stood Kara Hulmaster in her mailed coat, her saber dripping blood from its point. Her spellscarred eyes blazed with azure light, and a snarl of rage twisted her face. "Murderers!" she snarled. "You'll not see the sunrise, that I promise you!" She leaped into the fray, driving against the two remaining swordsmen, who turned to meet her. Kara was almost as skilled with the sword as Geran, and two more Shieldsworn followed close behind her.

Geran took advantage of the sudden distraction Kara caused to duck beneath the slashing claws of the bearded devil and throw himself into the back of one of her opponents, driving the man into the wall. He seized the stunned assassin and threw him headlong back into the face of the bearded devil rushing after him, briefly tangling the two together. While the assassin struggled to get free, the swordmage snarled a spell of strength and drove his point through the man's torso and into the body of the devil behind him. With the power of the strength spell, Geran shoved both his impaled foes three steps to the nearest wall and drove his sword through until it grated on stone behind them. When he yanked the blade free, the assassin groaned and slid to the floor, while the bearded devil screamed in rage before vanishing in a foul cloud of smoke like the others had. He turned back around just in time to see Kara finish her last opponent with a graceful slash across the throat. A moment's calm settled over the room.

"Natali! Kirr! Are they safe?" Kara demanded.

"Natali's here. Kirr ran off to hide. I don't know where he is." Geran found that warm blood was dripping over his brow from a cut he didn't remember receiving. He wiped it away with the back of his left hand. "What of the harmach?"

Kara paled. "I'd hoped that you might know. I was making the rounds outside when I heard the fighting."

A terrible suspicion dawned in Geran's heart. He looked over to the Shieldsworn who followed Kara. "You two, stay here and guard Lady Erna and Natali," he ordered them. "Watch out for Kirr, too, if you see him. Kara and I are going to the harmach." He pushed past the soldiers into the dark hallway beyond, and hurried back in the direction from which he'd come. Kara raced along a half step behind him. They passed the door to Geran's quarters and continued into the short hallway leading to the harmach's chambers. There they found several more dead sellswords and Shieldsworn. Evidently there had been a fierce fight to defend the doors to Grigor's room, which now stood open. He could hear more sword play and the sinister hissing of another devil from inside. Without a moment's hesitation the swordmage stormed into the room, hoping he was not too late.

One Shieldsworn was still on his feet, doing his best to fight his way past two sellsword assassins at once. A pair of Hulmaster servants—stewards, not warriors—tried to fend off one of the bearded devils, flinching in terror from their infernal foe. Just behind them, Grigor Hulmaster struggled in the grip of a second devil, a wand clutched in his right hand. He fought to bring the implement to bear against his assailant, but the monster grinned in wicked amusement, its cruel talons clamped over the harmach's wrist as it held the wand toward the ceiling. Before the harmach and the devil pinning him stood a hooded woman in dark mail, with a cleric's black cassock over her armor. A long dagger glinted in her hand. She whirled as Geran and Kara burst into the room, baring her teeth in a fierce snarl.

"*Arochen nemmar!*" Grigor cried in a pained voice. "Unhand me, foul beast!" He had a little talent as a wizard, but not enough to deal with the monster that pinned him. The wand discharged a bright lance of dancing white motes, gouging the ceiling with its icy blast. The devil gripping him laughed aloud, a terrible sound like brazen saws grinding together.

"Release him!" Kara shouted. She rushed the cleric, but at that moment the last of the Shieldsworn fell, and the sellsword who'd been dueling the guard blocked her path. Her sword flickered like blue lightning as she tried to fight her way past.

"I hardly think so." The cleric sneered. She raised her dagger and turned to the harmach.

Geran started forward as well, only to realize his way was blocked by the devil who toyed with the harmach's stewards. In the space of an instant he summoned his teleportation spell to mind. "*Sieroch!*" he said, releasing the magic held in the symbols that danced in his mind. In a single instant he stood by the cleric in her black cassock, and lunged at her with his blade.

He was too slow.

As she struck at the harmach, her motion caught his point in the long sleeve of her cassock. Instead of running her through, the elven blade glanced from the mail under her robes. And the dagger she wielded plunged hilt-deep into Grigor Hulmaster's chest. The old man grunted and sagged; the dark priestess yanked her dagger from the awful wound and twisted away from Geran's grasp. "Destroy them! Destroy them all!" she shouted at the devils in the chamber.

"*Uncle Grigor!*" Kara screamed.

Black fury washed over Geran in an irresistible tide. He leaped after the cleric with murder in his eyes, but the devil holding Harmach Grigor contemptuously discarded the gray-faced harmach, tossing him aside like a broken toy as it slammed into Geran from the side. Geran was conscious of slashing claws and the burning touch of the stinging tendrils, and he answered with a furious burst of his own. Too close to use point or edge, he seized a handful of the beard-tendrils in his left hand, ignoring the acidic ooze burning his fist, and jerked the devil's face down into his hard-driven right knee. Needle-sharp fangs pierced his leg, but more snapped and splintered under the impact. He brought the rose-shaped pommel of his backsword down against the top of the devil's head with enough force to crack bone, and then rained down a second, a third, a fourth blow until the creature's skull gave way and it vanished in a belch of black smoke.

He looked up just in time to see the last of the assassins lining up a thrust at Kara's back while she fought the other devil in the room. But one of the wounded servants in the room—short, slight Dostin Hillnor, the harmach's chamberlain—snatched up a heavy wooden chair and threw it at the sellsword behind Kara. The blow knocked the mercenary to the ground, and an instant later, Kara finished her infernal opponent with a sweeping blow that took off most of its hideous face.

The cleric in the black robes retreated to the doorway, seeing her summoned devils and hired assassins losing ground. She looked back at Geran. "Greetings from Hulburg," she snarled. Then she darted down the hallway, disappearing from view.

Still in the grip of his dark fury, Geran dashed after her as Kara, Hillnor, and the other servants turned on the last of the hired blades. She ran for the stairs, a dozen steps ahead of him. In desperation, he shifted his grip on his sword and hurled it spinning ahead of him. By skill or chance, the whirling blade caught the cleric across her calves. The throw was far too awkward to do any real injury to her, but she stumbled and went down to her hands and knees, her dagger clattering to the flagstones ahead of her. She started to climb back to her feet, but Geran was upon her, slamming into her at a dead sprint. His momentum carried them to the rail overlooking the manor's grand stair.

"Let go!" the cleric hissed at him. She brandished her holy symbol, an amulet emblazoned with a silver skull, as Geran struggled to keep the symbol at bay and subdue her. He spun her around in a half circle, battering her against the lasparwood railing—and the railing gave way.

She flailed for balance before toppling over the edge to the hard flagstones twenty feet below. Geran caught himself an instant before following her over the side.

He found himself standing at the broken rail, glaring down at the cleric crumpled on the floor beneath him, her holy symbol caught in his fingers. He'd seen the silver skull design before. "Cyric," he spat. The god of lies and strife had a following among the foreign gangs infesting Hulburg. In fact, it was probably Valdarsel himself who'd sent the cleric and her infernal servants against Harmach Grigor.

His dark fury evaporated as he remembered his uncle. "The harmach!" he said. He turned back and hurried back to Grigor's chamber.

Kara kneeled by the harmach, holding a blood-soaked sheet to his chest as a makeshift bandage. Grigor's face was gray, and blood streaked the corner of his mouth. He breathed in small, wet gasps. Tears streaked Kara's cheeks. "Stay with us, Uncle!" she pleaded softly. "We'll find a healer, a curing potion. It's not your time yet!"

"Kara, my . . . dear child . . . I fear that you are mistaken," Grigor said weakly. He looked up at the two younger Hulmasters, and somehow found a small smile for them. "It is . . . for you and Geran . . . to carry on now."

"Don't say such things!" Kara cried.

Geran kneeled on Grigor's other side and met Kara's eyes. He slowly shook his head. He'd seen enough fighting to know a mortal wound, and so had she. He bowed his head, reaching down to grip Grigor's hand in his own. "Speak your mind," he said softly. "We're listening."

"Geran, my boy . . . I am glad . . . you came back from your travels." Grigor looked up at both of them, gasping for the breath to speak more. "You . . . and Kara . . . must decide who will be . . . harmach after me . . . if ever you win back Hulburg."

"We won't rest until we set things right, Uncle," he answered. "I promise you the Hulmasters will return to Hulburg. I promise it."

Grigor nodded, and fell silent for a long time. His breathing grew shallower. Geran blinked the tears from his eyes, and waited for the inevitable. Kara wept quietly, holding Grigor's other hand. Then, when Geran had started to think that he would not stir again, the harmach coughed weakly and said, "Come closer, Geran."

Geran bent low above the harmach's face, turning his ear to his uncle's mouth. "The King in Copper waits . . ." Grigor whispered. "There is . . . an oath . . . that must be kept . . . in Rivan's crypt . . ." He sighed, a long soft sound that trailed into nothingness.

"He's gone," Kara said in a small voice. She bowed her head a moment, wiping the tears from her cheeks with the heel of her hand.

"I know." Numbly Geran stood. He could hear no more fighting anywhere in the old manor, only the cries of the wounded, the jumbled orders and reports of Hulmaster soldiers searching for more attackers, and the keening wails of sudden grief as the living found someone dear to them among the dead. "Come, Kara. We'd better make sure that Natali and Kirr are safe, and your mother too. Master Hillnor can look after him for now."

Kara nodded, and rose to her feet. Her face was like iron as she picked up her sword again. "Who did this, Geran?"

He showed her the holy symbol he'd wrestled from the Cyricist. "The priestess is dead," he told her. "But I think we know who put her up to this."

THREE

6 Hammer, the Year of Deep Water Drifting (1480 DR)

A damp, cold fog clung to the Winterspear Vale as Mirya Erstenwold drove a wagon north along the Vale Road. Noon had already come and gone, but still the mist lingered, and Mirya decided that it was likely to last out the whole day. She'd spent her whole life in Hulburg and knew its winters well, but that didn't mean she liked them much. Snow, fog, wind, rain . . . today it was fog, clammy and dismal, dense enough that she couldn't see the high rocky hills that hemmed in Hulburg's valley or the rooftops and walls of the town half a mile behind her. With a small sigh, she drew her blanket closer around her shoulder, and took a moment to wrap it more closely around Selsha too. Her daughter glanced up at her face with a small smile, and snuggled closer to Mirya's side.

"Mama, how long will I have to stay with Niney and Auntie Elise?" Selsha asked. Nine years old, slight as a willow switch, with her mother's black hair and freckled nose, Selsha had a stubbornly independent streak in her that Mirya could only attribute to the girl's father—a nobleman of Phlan Selsha had never met, and never would. Under most circumstances Selsha would have argued for hours about having to go out to the country-side. The fact that she'd acquiesced to Mirya's decision without a debate was an indication of how worried Selsha was too.

She's wiser than her years, Mirya thought fondly. She decided against putting on any sort of brave front for the girl; Selsha would see through it. "I don't know, darling," she answered. "One way or the other, I've a feeling that things will be settled within a couple of months. By Greengrass we'll know more about what Marstel and his wizard have in mind for Hulburg. But until then, I think you'll be safer with the Tresterfins. They'll look after you just as well as I would, and I'll be out to visit every few days, I promise."

"Is Harmach Grigor ever coming back? And Geran?"

"I hope so, my darling. Hulburg's not the same without them." Mirya flicked the reins, turning the horse drawing the wagon into a wide lane heading west toward the far side of the vale. Here the Winterspear ran swift, cold, and hard under the steep western hills leading up to the Highfells; an old farm surrounded by apple orchards and walled pastures huddled against the river bend. The Tresterfin farm was only a couple of miles outside Hulburg proper, but Mirya hoped that was enough to put it well out of mind for the false harmach or his silver-handed wizard. She doubted that Rhovann would forget about her—the elf mage was far from stupid, after all—but in their brief interaction before the Black Moon raid she'd gotten the impression that his particular brand of malice was pragmatic, not vicious. He was not the sort to waste time on petty wickedness. On the other hand, the priest Valdarsel and the rabble who followed him were not so detached. She'd seen enough neighbors beaten and robbed by the Tailings-folk and the Cinderfists to know otherwise.

"Selsha, there's something more I want to say to you," said Mirya as they rolled into the Tresterfin's farmyard. "I hope it won't come to this, but if things keep on as they are, we might have to leave."

"Leave Hulburg?" Selsha sat up straight and fixed her bright gaze on Mirya.

"Aye. We've a little coin laid by, perhaps enough to make a start of things in Thentia or Phlan. It would be hard, but it might be better than staying here if things go badly this spring."

"I don't want to," Selsha said.

"Nor do I, but we might have to anyway." She found a small smile, and brushed Selsha's hair from her eyes. "Don't worry yourself about it for now. That day's not here yet, and it might never come. I just wanted you to know in case it did."

The door to the house opened, and the Tresterfins—Burkel, Elise, and their daughter Niamene—bustled out to greet them. The Tresterfins and Erstenwolds were both old Hulburg stock, but the two families were more than just neighbors. Burkel and Elise were the closest Mirya had to parents now that her own had passed on, and Niamene had been promised to her brother Jarad before he'd met his death out on the Highfells.

"Welcome, Mirya," Burkel said. "Welcome, Selsha. We're glad to see you." He was a stoop-shouldered, gray-haired man who wore a short, spade-like beard at his chin. Before Marstel's coup he'd sat on the Harmach's Council, but he'd never been comfortable as an adviser to the harmach.

"Well met, Da Burkel," Mirya replied. She set the wagon's brake, clambered down, and helped Selsha to the ground.

Selsha ran over to Niamene and hugged her. "Niney!" she cried.

"Selsha!" Niameme kneeled and returned Selsha's hug warmly. A pretty young woman of twenty-four years, she'd come to know Selsha well during the time she was betrothed to Jarad. Selsha looked on her as something of a big sister, which tickled Niamene. "I hope you'll like staying with us for a time."

"Come in out of this damp, both of you," Elise said. While Burkel retrieved a chest with Selsha's clothing from the wagon, his wife ushered the Erstenwolds inside. The farmhouse was warm and comfortable, with a cheerful fire in the hearth and the smell of a good stew rising from the kettle above it. In short order they were enjoying a hot midday meal of mutton stew and coarse bread, a rare treat for Mirya and Selsha—with Erstenwold's to mind, she never cooked for herself or Selsha in the middle of the day, so they usually made do with some cheese and smoked fish.

After they finished, Burkel glanced at Mirya, and then looked over to his daughter. "Niamene, I'd wager that Selsha would love to see more of the steading."

Niamene gave a nod of understanding. "Let me show you around the farm, Selsha," she said. "I'll show you all the places I loved to hide when I was your size."

"Really?" Selsha said. She bounced up from her place at the table, and followed Niamene to the door. They threw on cloaks and went outside.

Mirya watched her go, trying to still the pang in her heart. She knew she'd miss Selsha terribly, and in countless ways that she couldn't even begin to guess at yet. But she couldn't bear the idea of being the cause of any danger to her daughter, not again—the Black Moon misadventure had taught her everything she'd ever need to know about that. She looked over to Burkel and Elise, and sighed. "Thank you both for taking her in," she said. "I'll sleep better of nights, knowing that she's safe here with you."

Elise waved her hand. "Think nothing of it, Mirya. She's a darling girl. It'll be a pleasure to the both of us."

"She might be more of a handful than you think." Mirya smiled, and steeled herself for what she had to say next. Drawing an envelope from a pocket in her skirts, she handed it across the table. "Listen, if anything should befall me, this is for you to give to Selsha when the time's right. It's . . . it's about her father. She knows nothing about him now, but if worse comes to worst, she has kin in Phlan. She won't have much of a claim on them, but I'd hope that if she ever needed it, they might help her in some way."

The Tresterfins looked at each other. After a moment, Elise reached out to take the envelope. "Of course we'll see to it," she said. "But Mirya, what do you mean to do?"

"It would be better if you didn't know," she answered. She paused, gazing out the thick glass window in the house's kitchen door as she considered her next words. She could make out the barn behind the house, and a few skeletal apple trees, but blank gray fog hid the world beyond the Tresterfins' farm. "I mean to do what needs doing. Marstel, his wizard, the Verunas, the Chainsmen, the Cinderfists . . . they'll not stop until every decent person in Hulburg is coinless or enslaved. The Hulmasters haven't forgotten us, but this isn't their fight alone—it's ours too. I've a mind to do my part."

"That's a dangerous pastime," Burkel said. "You're already under suspicion because of your friendship with Geran. And even if you're not concerned for yourself, you know that if you—and any others of like mind—strike back at the conniving sellswords and thieves who are running things these days, the first thing they'll do is knock us all to the ground and put a foot on our necks. It'll be blood, Mirya."

"I know it," she said in a small voice. "But we've got a foot on our necks already, haven't we? It's a hard world out beyond the Highfells, and I don't fancy the idea of being driven out into it without a copper to my name. Better to make our stand here, and fight for the Hulburg we remember."

They fell silent for a long moment. Outside, Mirya heard Selsha laughing in delight at something Niamene had said. Burkel looked to his wife again, and sighed. "I can't say I haven't had thoughts like yours," he told Mirya. "Are the Hulmasters coming back? Do you know?"

"I've seen Geran," she replied. "I trust him, and Kara too. They'll not leave us to Marstel and his wizard one moment longer than they must."

"All right, then. What can I do?"

"You've got the hardest task of all: you're to do nothing other than keep Selsha safe and out of sight. In the days ahead we'll sorely need people we trust who aren't under any suspicion at all, people who can show their face in town without fear and pass messages without seeming to do so. Beyond that, I've no idea yet."

The Tresterfins exchanged one more look, and Elise gave Burkel a small nod. The former councilman tilted his head. "So be it. You know where to find us when you need us, Mirya. And don't have a worry for Selsha. We'll look after her like she was our own."

Mirya smiled. "I know it. That's why I asked you." She stood and went to the back door, opening it up to look outside. Selsha and Niamene were looking at the goats the Tresterfins kept in the pasture behind the house. "Selsha, come inside a moment! I'll be heading back into town!"

"Coming, Mama!" Selsha shouted. She ran to the door, breathless with excitement.

Mirya smiled at her and ushered her inside, determined not to let her daughter know that she had the slightest worry for either of them. "I want you to be your best for Aunt Elise and Uncle Burkel," she said. "Mind them as you'd mind me—no, *better* than you'd mind me. There's to be no arguing over chores or any such thing."

"I promise."

"Good. Then be a good guest, and don't forget your lessons!" She leaned down to catch Selsha in a fierce hug, squeezing until her daughter squeaked in protest, and kissed her cheek when she was done. "I'll be back to visit in three days. Fare you well till then."

"Fare well," Selsha answered. "I'll be fine, Mama."

Mirya sighed and straightened up. Leaving Selsha behind was harder than she'd thought, but she knew it was for the best. She'll only be three miles down the road, Mirya told herself. I can see her every day if I've a mind to. She turned to give Elise Tresterfin a quick embrace, and gave the older woman a grateful smile. Then she hurried out before any tears might appear. Burkel followed her out to lend a hand with the wagon.

After they said their good-byes, Mirya drove her wagon—now loaded with several casks of Tresterfin cider—slowly back to Hulburg. She passed a few travelers heading away from Hulburg, mostly Winterspear folk who'd come to town on some errand or other and were now heading back home. Most of the wagons hauling provisions up to the timber and mining camps in the Galena foothills were well on their way, having left early in the morning. About a mile outside town she passed by a small band of soldiers in Council Guard tabards riding out to patrol the road, but they didn't bother her. She guessed that most of the merchant company sellswords had orders to leave her be, since the Hulmasters were in exile. With Geran and the others out of sight, she wasn't of any special interest to them.

That might change soon enough, she reflected. It wouldn't be wise to count on being ignored for too much longer.

Another hour saw her safely back to Erstenwold's, where she had her clerks store the Tresterfin cider, stable the horse, and put away the wagon. The afternoon was drawing on, so she devoted herself to catching up with a dozen small tasks around the store—setting out the orders that would go out the next morning, totaling her ledgers, putting together her own orders to leatherworkers, blacksmiths, ropemakers, brewers, cheesemakers, and smokehouses all over the vale. Erstenwold's had seen better days, but for now she could still make a decent living from the store, and pay a half-dozen clerks too. At six bells she shut the storehouse doors, sent the last of her clerks home, and locked up the store.

"It's too quiet without Selsha about," she muttered to herself. The old store seemed still as a tomb without her daughter's sudden laughter or carefree footsteps pelting over the well-worn floorboards. She ate a cold meal made up from the pantry she kept in Erstenwold's back rooms, spent an hour tidying up, and then settled in to wait. When ten bells tolled over the city streets, she drew on a heavy cloak, tucked a dark hood in her pocket, and took the crossbow she kept under the counter. In one of the back storerooms she rolled a heavy barrel aside, and lifted up the trapdoor leading down into the cellars. She lit a lantern, and descended into the darkness.

The cellars were deep and empty. In another month or so, Mirya would hire workmen to cut blocks of ice from Lake Hul before the thaw and drag them into town on horse-drawn sledges. No one needed cold storage now, but with a little luck her ice cellars would last through the summer, and she'd turn a decent profit by selling it off a block at a time then. She headed for the far wall of the cellar, where a small, thick, double-barred door stood in the foundation wall. Drawing back the bolts, she pushed the door open and peered into the passageway beyond with lantern held high.

"Don't be a goose, Mirya," she told herself. "There's naught to fear down here but rats and dust." Drawing a deep breath, she headed into the passageway.

Hulburg was built atop the ruins of a much larger city. The town she knew had grown up only in the last hundred years or so, but the city beneath it was almost five times as old. It had been burned, razed, plundered, and reduced to rubble two or three times over its sad history, and each time folk had come back to rebuild from the ruins. Most of Hulburg's current wooden buildings stood atop stone foundations from the far older city. In many places, old cellars—and in a few cases, whole streets—had been filled in or covered over, leaving a dusty old labyrinth of forgotten cellars with no buildings above or blind passageways joined to the basements of businesses like Erstenwold's. Most of the old passages were sealed off, of course, but over the years quite a few folk had found it useful to have secret ways to move about just beneath the streets. In other cities, the shades of the dead might have haunted such places, making it terribly dangerous to wander through the hidden bones of the old Hulburg . . . but the harmachs of old had struck some bargain with the great lich Aesperus, the King in Copper, and undead creatures did not lurk beneath Hulburg's homes and workshops.

She set her foot in the stirrup of the crossbow and cocked the weapon, laying a bolt in on the string. There might not be any ghosts or ghouls to fear, but that didn't mean buried Hulburg was necessarily *safe*. Then Mirya set off through the old rubble-choked passages. From time to time she passed by doors leading into other cellars or basements, intersections where several tunnels met, even one open space where a whole taphouse had been buried in its entirety, with the great wooden tuns of ale standing dry and dusty. As a teenager she'd explored some of these passages with Jarad and Geran, nosing around in search of lost treasure or hidden smugglers' dens. She hadn't much liked the old passages then, and she didn't like them much now.

She turned a corner and let herself through a small door into a dusty old cellar beneath a cobbler's workshop, then climbed a flight of stone steps back up to the street. Carefully she shuttered her lantern and set it by the upper doorway, waiting a short time to let her eyes adjust to the darkness. Then she drew a simple sackcloth mask over her face before letting herself out into the cold night again.

The stairs emerged in a dark alley behind Gold Street, not far from the compound of the Iron Ring Coster. Several hooded figures waited in the shadows, their faces covered by masks like hers. She knew them all anyway, of course: Brun Osting, the strapping brewer who owned the Troll and Tankard; his cousin Halla Osting, a tall young woman who could bring down a rabbit with a slingstone at fifty paces; Senna Vannarshel, a half-elf woman of sixty years who was the best bowmaker in Hulburg; Rost Therndon, a carpenter and shipwright almost as big as Brun Osting; and the dwarf Lodharrun, whose smithy was the largest in Hulburg not owned by one of the foreign merchant companies. They tensed in sudden alarm as Mirya made her appearance, steel glinting in their hands before they recognized her.

Mirya looked about the dim alleyway, and allowed herself a humorless smile. "I thought you all had more sense than to carry on with this," she murmured. "Well, first things first—were any of you seen? Were any of you followed?"

They all shook their heads, but Brun spoke softly. "There are more of the gray guards by the Harmach's Foot and the Middle Bridge," he said. "I counted eight more of 'em tonight on the way here. They didn't see me, but if more of them show up in the streets, it'll be hard to avoid them."

"I'll make a note of them," Mirya replied unhappily. The gray guardians were some work of Rhovann's, she was sure of it. A month before the first of the tall, silent things had appeared on the battlements of Griffonwatch, armored warriors seven feet tall with thick, powerful limbs. Their faces were covered by black helms, and strange magical sigils were written in their gray flesh. Sometimes they accompanied the Council Guard on patrol, and other times they simply stood watch at street corners or doorways. Figuring out what they were and how Marstel's wizard was making them was clearly becoming more important every day . . . but that wasn't her mission tonight. As far as she knew, none of the gray guardians were nearby, and she and her small band of rebels had different work ahead of them. "Any word from Darsen?"

"Aye," Halla answered. "The Jannarsk sellsword's in the Black Gull, with two more mercenaries. Darsen's there."

Mirya nodded. It was one more foe than she'd hoped for, but she meant to carry things through anyway. Two days previous, one of the House Jannarsk sergeants and his squad had wrecked the shop of Perremon the cheesemaker, beating him severely when the Hulburgan had objected to their crude overtures to his daughter. It was time to draw some boundaries for the foreign mercenaries occupying Hulburg. She slid out to the mouth of the alleyway, looking up and down the street; a handful of passersby were still about, but no one nearby.

"Should we head for the Black Gull?" Rost Therndon said. "We could take them from the front and the back in one rush—"

"No, we'll wait for eleven bells," Mirya answered. That was the plan they'd worked out before, and she didn't want to throw it out over simple impatience. The night was cold and damp, with a thin wet fog brooding over the streets. She drew back into the alley's shadows, and wrapped herself more tightly in her cloak. The others in her small band did likewise, and they waited in silence for a time. Finally, the bell in the Council Hall struck eleven; Mirya shivered and straightened up, as did her companions.

Out of sight down the street, she heard a sudden distant burst of laughter and music as the taphouse door opened up. A few moments later, a single slender figure hurried by the mouth of the alleyway—Darsen Ilkur, the son of Deren Ilkur. The younger Ilkur worked as a clerk in the mercantile compounds, and was well placed to watch the foreigners' comings and goings. "Three right behind me," he murmured as he walked past, careful not to even turn his head toward the alleyway.

Mirya motioned to Brun, Rost, and Lodharrun. The three loyalists crept closer to the alley mouth. Heavy footsteps, the jingle of mail, and a coarse drunken jest announced the approaching Jannarsk men. The armsmen walked unsteadily past the alley mouth with hardly a glance at the shadows—and Mirya's fighters struck. A quick, stealthy rush brought the three Hulburgans into the street behind the mercenaries, with cudgels gripped in strong hands. Mirya, Halla, and Vannarshel followed after them, spreading out to cover the streets to either side.

"What is this?" the Jannarsk sergeant snarled, reaching for the sword at his belt.

"You're not welcome here," Mirya spat.

The other armsmen started to turn, reaching for their own weapons. They were too slow. In a dark, furious tide, the Hulburgans swarmed over them with their cudgels rising and falling. The sergeant managed to draw his sword, and stayed on his feet long enough to line up a thrust at Rost as the carpenter bludgeoned one of the other sellswords to the ground. Mirya raised her crossbow, sighting for a shot—but Brun Osting stepped close and neatly rapped the sergeant's sword from his hand with a sharp blow of his club that likely broke the man's thumb. Then all three of the sellswords were on the ground, and the Hulburgans fell to beating and kicking them furiously.

Mirya winced at the violent assault, but she refused to look away. There'd be worse than this if she meant to see things all the way through. "Leave them alive!" she hissed to her neighbors. "We'll not spill blood until we have to." She had no particular concern for sparing Hulburg's enemies, but she hoped that leaving the Jannarsks alive would bring less of a reprisal than cold-blooded murder.

In the space of ten heartbeats, it was over. Mirya motioned for Brun and Therndon to drag the mercenaries back into the alleyway, pausing for one more look up and down the street. No one was close enough to pay them any attention; the fog was their friend tonight, or so it seemed. She stooped by the battered mercenaries, searching for signs of life. All of them were breathing, but if she was any judge, they'd be in slings or casts for tendays. Well, it wasn't anything more than they'd inflicted on poor Perremon. "Take their weapons," she told Therndon. The carpenter quickly gathered up their swords and daggers in a sack, throwing it over his shoulder.

"Anything else for these villains?" Vannarshel asked.

"Leave them for their friends to find," Mirya answered. "We'll see if the lesson takes or not. Now, let's be on our way before the Council Guard or their gray guardians come by. We'll have more work soon enough." There was a Veruna supply train bound for their mining camps in a day or two; Mirya was already thinking of how she and her small company might waylay it.

"Not a word to anyone," Lodharrun grunted. The dwarf held out his thick fist; Mirya set her hand on top of his. The others joined them.

"Not a word," she repeated. "Now, away with all of you!" Briefly, the Hulburgans clasped hands before parting ways and silently vanishing into the night fog.

FOUR

10 Hammer, the Year of Deep Water Drifting (1480 DR)

Geran's mother arrived at Lasparhall the morning of the day before Grigor's funeral. A Hulmaster chamberlain summoned Geran from the garden where he'd been practicing his forms, a refuge of exercise that he'd used more than once over the last few days to lose himself for an hour without thought. Quickly toweling off, he drew on a dove gray doublet and hurried down to the manor's front hall, where two footmen waited to help Serise Hulmaster out of her heavy winter cloak and hood. Serise was a tall, sparely built woman of fifty-five years, graceful and reserved; Geran had gained much of his height and quickness from her. Beneath the furs she wore the rich blue gown and ivory corset of a Selûnite initiate, and a pearl-studded comb of silver to keep her long hair—still more black than gray—in its elegant coiffure. She'd retired to Moonsilver Hall, a temple of Selûne a few miles west of Thentia, several years earlier, having grown weary of Hulburg after Bernov Hulmaster's death and Geran's departure on his long travels.

"Mother!" Geran hurried over to clasp her hands in his and kiss her on the cheek. "How was your journey?"

"Fair enough, but colder than I would have liked," Serise answered with a shiver. The carriage ride from Moonsilver Hall was the better part of six or seven miles, and usually took well over an hour. With the bitter temperatures the roads were frozen hard and Geran knew from experience that a carriage ride on a hard-frozen road was likely a ride full of sharp jolts and painful bounces. "The high priestess insisted that I should use her coach, for which I'm grateful, since it was well supplied with blankets. I would have been much more uncomfortable if I'd had to hire a coach from town."

Geran extended his arm. "Well, come on inside. There's a fine fire in the great room, and I'm sure that Mistress Laren will be happy to find something warm for you to drink."

His mother took his arm and allowed him to guide her from the foyer. She looked around the hall with interest. "Lasparhall was empty for fifteen years or more," she said. "Strange to see the place with so many people keeping busy! Your father and I used to bring you here when you were just a lad, usually when your father was restless and took it into his head to get away from Hulburg for a few tendays."

"I remember."

"I'm sure you do. We never had more than a dozen people in this whole great house in those days. Now . . . so many people, so much going on!"

They came to the study, and Geran asked the first footman he saw to fetch some warm cider or mulled wine for his mother. They took seats in the chairs by the hearth, as close to the roaring fire as they could stand. "I'm glad you came," he said. "It's good to see you, Mother."

"And you, Geran. I only wish it was a happier occasion." Serise sighed, and leaned forward to peer critically at him. "Your neck is scored! Were you hurt in the fighting? Are you all right?"

He waved away her concern, glad that she couldn't see the mess of scabs and bandages under his shirt. "Scratched and cut in quite a few places, but nothing serious. Ilmater knows I've had worse. And I survived, which is more than many of the Shieldsworn can say. We lost eleven, not counting Uncle Grigor."

She paled. "That's terrible! I only heard that there'd been an attack, and that poor Grigor was dead. What happened, Geran?"

"A Cyricist priestess hired sellswords and conjured devils to attack Lasparhall," he answered. He recounted the awful events of the evening, making an effort to downplay the exact amount of danger he'd been in—Serise Hulmaster was no shrinking violet, but there was no point in giving her more cause to worry than she doubtless already had. "When we searched her body, we found correspondence from Valdarsel, the high prelate in Hulburg," he concluded. Of course, that could have been planted, but Geran doubted it; he'd seen the hateful fanaticism in the woman's eyes. "It seems that he directed the priestess to strike at us."

"I haven't heard much of this Valdarsel. Who is he?"

"A priest of Cyric. A few months earlier Mirya discovered that he was leading the Cinderfists—gangs of poor foreign folk who've fetched up in Hulburg over the last few years. Many of those are decent people simply trying to get by, but there are all too many criminals and slavers mixed up with them." He made a sour face. "Valdarsel's been stirring up the foreign folk and their gangs for months, although we didn't know it at the time. They backed Marstel when he overthrew Uncle Grigor. Marstel rewarded him by giving him a seat on the Harmach's Council."

Serise glanced toward the window, painted white by the heavy frost. "It's been six days now," she murmured, thinking aloud. "Counting three days to Hulburg for the hard weather, it seems likely that this Valdarsel—and Marstel, too, I suppose—knows by now that poor Grigor is dead, but he also knows that his attack was not completely successful. You'll have to be careful, Geran. They very well may try again."

"I know it. Kara and I have done everything we can think of to safeguard the house and protect the rest of the family."

"Good." Serise sipped at her cider. "Your uncle was a gentle soul, perhaps too gentle to rule a realm like Hulburg. He didn't deserve such an end."

Geran stood up to pace in front of the hearth. "It's my fault," he said bitterly. "Marstel never could have seized Griffonwatch without Rhovann's magic or his guile, and the only reason Rhovann came to Hulburg was to cause harm to me and those dear to me. And when I might have put a stop to it all by staying in Hulburg after the Black Moon raid, I took *Seadrake* and sailed off to rescue Mirya. I was warned about what would happen if I left Hulburg, but I chose not to listen. I've brought ruin on our House."

"Nonsense, Geran," Serise said sharply. "Perhaps Marstel's wizard followed you from Myth Drannor—you would know better than I. But I recall that last spring Sergen attempted to kill Grigor and all the rest of the family, and it was you who prevented him from succeeding. If you hadn't come back to Hulburg at all, none of the Hulmasters would be left today." She fixed a stern look on him. "You didn't murder your uncle, by action or inaction. The enemies of House Hulmaster did. All you did was to make the best choices you could at the time, and no one—not even the gods—can foresee all outcomes. To think you should have done so is simply indulging in self-pity."

He winced. His mother was far from stupid, and she'd never been one to mince words. He knew she was right, but it didn't mean that he couldn't have been more vigilant. Of course the harmach's blood was on the hands of their enemies . . . but Geran could imagine many things he might have done differently to safeguard his family against an attack. Grigor's death might not have been his fault, but it was something that he might have stopped, and he sorely regretted that he hadn't. "I understand," he finally admitted. "I can't even say that I truly regret my choice, because the Black Moon Brotherhood is no more, and Mirya and her daughter are alive and safe. But I wish the cost of my choices wasn't so dear."

"As do we all from time to time, although it's true that few people see consequences such as you've seen." Serise sipped again at her warm cider, and set down the cup. "I feel somewhat recovered now, and I'd dearly love to see young Natali and Kirr. Children have a way of raising spirits, you know."

"Is that a hint, Mother?"

"I wouldn't dream of wondering aloud when my son of thirty-one years might finally find a wife and present me with grandchildren."

"I've got a lot on my mind these days!" he protested. But he smiled and offered his arm again, escorting her to the family's living quarters.

They found Geran's Aunt Terena in the family's great room, assisting Erna as she tried to keep Natali and Kirr at the day's lessons, a task that was soon abandoned. Geran's mother hadn't seen the young Hulmasters in several years, and they were eager to make the acquaintance of a relation they'd all but forgotten. Geran passed an hour keeping them company and listening to Serise and Terena recall old stories about a younger, haler Grigor and the misadventures of their own departed husbands—in Terena's case, not Kamoth Kastelmar but instead her first husband, Kara's father Arvhun—in years when Geran was not much older than Kirr. He would have thought that the stories of happier days would have been too sad to bear with Grigor's funeral drawing near, but to his surprise he found himself laughing aloud more than once at stories he'd heard a dozen times as a young man.

After a midday meal of venison stew and fresh-baked bread, Geran excused himself with an idea of riding to Thentia to make some inquiries about the sellswords who'd been hired for the attack. But before he could don his riding furs against the weather, he was intercepted by Master Quillon—a halfling scribe who'd served as the harmach's private secretary for the better part of two decades—and his cousin Kara. "A moment, Geran," Kara called. "Master Quillon's brought something to my attention."

Geran paused and regarded the halfling. Quillon was a balding fellow with long sideburns and a thick pair of spectacles balanced on the end of his nose; he wore a tabard in the blue and white colors of the family Hulmaster with a matching cap. "Go on," he said.

Quillon held up a sheaf of letters in one inkstained hand. "We're beginning to receive correspondence addressed to the Harmach of Hulburg," he said. "Mostly, they're condolences, letters that simply express sympathy for our loss and outrage at Harmach Grigor's murder. This sort of thing is commonplace after the passing of a head of state, even a small state such as Hulburg. They come from various nobles and realms around the Moonsea. We've only received a handful so far, but there will be more over the next few tendays."

Geran glanced at Kara, and back to Quillon. "If it's typical correspondence, I'm not sure I understand what the problem is. How would we normally answer them?"

"Oh, I can see to *that*, Lord Geran. Answering them is not the difficulty—although there are some that should be read by a member of the family, and not just myself. The difficulty is that, well, I am not exactly certain who should *sign* them." The halfling pushed at his spectacles uncomfortably. "You see . . . well, ah . . . I am not certain who is to become harmach. I brought these letters to Lady Kara since she assisted Harmach Grigor with such things over the last few years, but she told me that no decision has been made yet."

"It's not just the correspondence," Kara added. "With the funeral tomorrow, there are questions of protocol too. We've avoided this discussion as long as we can."

He stood in silence, looking at the letters in Quillon's hand. Between the two of them, he and Kara had overseen the household for the last few days. But that was clearly a temporary arrangement. "Is there any decision to be made?" he finally asked. "I assume that Harmach Grigor left instructions for this. Or do the laws of succession simply dictate the answer?"

"I am afraid that Harmach Grigor named no one after Lord Isolmar died," Quillon replied. "And the laws of succession are unclear. I believe that it is a matter for the family to decide, my lord."

"I see." Geran frowned. "Kara, what do you make of this?"

"I think the best thing to do is to bring everyone together and discuss it. The sooner, the better."

He nodded. "Master Quillon, would you join us in the study at two bells? Your knowledge of the law may be helpful."

"Of course, Lord Geran. I'll fetch my pen and paper." Quillon bowed, and hurried away.

The two Hulmasters watched him go, and Geran allowed himself a grimace of apprehension. He knew he didn't want the throne—he wanted Grigor to be harmach, just as he'd been throughout the entirety of Geran's life. But an assassin's dagger had changed that, and Geran's wishes had no power to put things back in order. No, the question was not whether he wanted to be harmach. The question was whether he was willing to be harmach if that was the best thing for his family.

Kara watched him as he wrestled with his thoughts. "I know it can't be me, Geran," she said in a low voice. "Whatever you decide, I'll back you."

He nodded gratefully, even though he had no idea what was the right course. "I suppose we'd better gather everyone."

A little less than an hour later, the Hulmaster clan assembled in Lasparhall's study. Natali and Kirr were excused, but Erna was present to speak for her children if need be. Terena and Serise sat near the fire, and Geran stood by the window, paying little attention to the chill radiating from the frost-covered panes. Master Quillon took an unobtrusive place in the room's corner, his writing materials laid out before him.

Kara dismissed the servants from the room, closing the door behind them as she turned to face the Hulmasters. "I'm afraid there is a question that we must settle today," she said. "Scores of nobles from Thentia and ambassadors from other cities will be here tomorrow to attend Harmach Grigor's funeral rites. The question that will be on all their minds is simply this: who is to be the next harmach?"

"You and Geran have been looking after things since—well, over the last few days," Terena said. "What do the laws of succession say?"

"Very little, I'm afraid," Kara answered. She looked over to Master Quillon. "Have you found anything more?"

The halfling shook his head. "Regretfully, no. The difficulty is that Hulburg's laws provide little guidance. By tradition the harmach names his heir. Until four years ago, that was clearly Lord Isolmar, but Harmach Grigor never named a new heir after Isolmar's death. As far as I can determine, it's been more than a hundred and fifty years since a harmach died without a son who was ready and willing to take the title, so there is no obvious precedent to follow."

"Why didn't he simply choose someone?" Erna said sadly. "Then we would know better what to do now."

"He was worried that he would endanger whoever he named," Terena said. The others in the room looked at her in surprise; she shrugged. "We spoke of it once or twice. After all, Isolmar—his own son—had just been murdered, in all likelihood because he was close to the throne. I suspect that Sergen may have influenced his decision as well, either by advising him not to name anyone else, or perhaps by indicating that he wished to be considered as a potential heir. With Geran away on his travels, Isolmar's children hardly more than babes, and Kara's condition, there was no one else."

Geran glanced at Kara, who grimaced quickly but said nothing. The eerie azure of her spellscarred eyes and the blue serpentlike mark on her left hand shimmered in the room's dim light. She was undoubtedly the most qualified candidate, since she'd sat on the Harmach's Council and served as Grigor's right hand for years, but no one would suffer a harmach whose children might turn out to be monsters.

"I doubt that we can divine Grigor's intent," said Geran's mother. "Let us look at this another way. Neither Erna nor I are Hulmasters by blood.

That simply leaves Terena, Geran, Natali, and Kirr. Terena is, of course, the eldest Hulmaster remaining, and the daughter of a harmach herself. Geran is the eldest male Hulmaster. If we believe the succession should pass to the oldest child of Grigor's oldest child, that would be Natali of course, but she's only a child. She'd need a regent to rule for her."

"Excuse me. The law is unclear about whether the eldest Hulmaster or the eldest *male* Hulmaster is to be preferred," Quillon said. "Of course, by chance those have happened to be the same for a number of generations now."

"I have no desire to be harmach!" Terena said quickly. "In these circumstances, we need a war leader, someone with courage and vigor. I have little of either. Our friends—and our enemies—need to know that the Hulmasters have not relinquished our claim, but I wouldn't inspire confidence or fear in anybody."

Geran felt the gazes of the other Hulmasters shifting to him. He looked down at the table, considering the question. If he asserted his claim he had no doubt that his family would be content to support him. "I'll assume the title if I must," he said slowly, "but I would not be very well suited for it. I know nothing of statecraft."

"Geran, knowledge of statecraft is not a requirement," his mother said. "*Leadership* is. I think you underestimate yourself. Would Grigor have been content to see you become harmach? And is it something you are willing to do?"

"I've spent most of my adult life avoiding that sort of responsibility," he said.

"No one knows that better than I do. I know how restless you've always been. Still, you are the only choice if we seek a harmach who could rule today."

He shook his head. "I mean to go in harm's way. A harmach must be more careful than that. Let the throne pass to Isolmar's children, and appoint a regent. Kara's far and away the best qualified. She's commanded the Shieldsworn in battle, and she counseled Harmach Grigor for the better part of the last ten years. And—forgive me for saying so, Kara—her spellscar is no drawback for a regent. In fact, it might be seen as an advantage, since she'll be understood to have no dynastic ambitions of her own."

The room fell silent for a long time. Finally Kara spoke. "I'll do it if that is the consensus of the family. But there are two things I think we should consider. First, a harmach would be seen as a more powerful figure than a regent. After all, a regent by her nature would be someone whose reign is soon to end, but a harmach might hold the throne for decades. A harmach's promises carry more weight, as do his threats. Secondly it's just been demonstrated to us that our enemies are willing to strike at whoever is harmach. I would be very fearful about naming Natali or Kirr harmach now."

Erna paled. "Dear gods," she whispered. "I hadn't thought of that."

Geran folded his arms in front of his chest and scowled. He hadn't thought of it, either. Kara's point about appearances was one thing, but he couldn't stand the idea of endangering his young cousins simply because he was unwilling to shoulder the title. He looked over to Quillon and asked, "Is there any reason a harmach couldn't abdicate and appoint a regent for a young successor?"

The halfling scribe gazed upward in thought, considering the question. "No, Lord Geran. The law is generous about allowing a harmach to step down."

"Very well." He squared his shoulders and turned back to face his family. "Kara's convinced me; it's best that I should do it. But I won't name myself harmach, not until Hulburg is freed, and Marstel and Rhovann have answered for what they've done. Claiming a title we have no power to enforce would appear weaker than not claiming it at all. Someone must be the Lord Hulmaster in name, but we'll show the Moonsea by our actions, not our words, that we haven't waived our claim on Hulburg."

Quillon scribbled on his parchment, then cleared his throat. "I beg your pardon, Lord Geran, but in point of fact, you'd be known as the Baron Hulmaster, since that is the precedence accorded your family in other lands."

"Lord Hulmaster is good enough." He looked around the room; his mother nodded in approval, Terena appeared relieved, and Erna frowned but nodded as well. He could already feel their expectations settling around him; in the dark and chaotic days since Grigor's murder they'd all been caught up in the simple process of grieving and the automatic responses of dealing with a death in the family—something that the Hulmasters knew all too well. Geran's father, Kara's father, now Isolmar and Grigor both . . . he could almost believe that some dark curse had settled upon the Hulmaster line. "I still believe I'm not a very good choice to be harmach, but I'll do what I can to restore our family's birthright to the next harmach."

"Should you name a successor in case . . . ?" Erna asked.

"No, and for the same reasons that Uncle Grigor didn't. At least, I won't make any sort of formal announcement. Privately . . . well, if a successor is needed, I wouldn't be around, so you should do what you think best in my absence. But my recommendation would be that if something should happen to me, Natali becomes the next harmach, and Kara should be her regent." He waited in case anyone else wished to speak, and nodded to Quillon. "Master Quillon, does this all seem in order to you?"

"It does, my lord har—baron . . . er, Hulmaster. I'll have the proper patents and notices drawn up at once." The old halfling stood and shuffled his papers together. "And I have some correspondence that requires your attention."

"I'll be along shortly, Master Quillon," Geran replied. He waited for the halfling to let himself out of the room, weighing the iron resolve that was beginning to take shape in his heart. Serise, Terena, Erna, and Kara all watched him, perhaps measuring him against their expectations of what a harmach—in name or not—should do next. *I'd better begin to get used to that,* he realized. *Shieldsworn, servants, clerks, scribes, even my own close family, they'll all be watching to see how I meet each decision, each development, that comes our way.* He found himself shivering at the thought, his stomach growing unsettled, and he closed his eyes to gather himself. *I don't even have a kingdom to rule yet, and Hulburg's a small realm by any measure. How could someone become the King of Tethyr or the coronal of Myth Drannor and stand it?*

There's no sense in wishing for this to go away, he told himself. Before he could reconsider the intent growing in his thoughts, he faced the rest of House Hulmaster and spoke. "Tomorrow, we bury Uncle Grigor," he said. He let the words stand for a moment to let the others think on them. "But the day after, we begin the war to retake Hulburg. Mother, I think it might be a good idea to take Erna and her children into hiding in Selûne's temple—Aunt Terena too, if she's willing to go. Too many people know we're here, and we have enemies who command powerful magic. Natali and Kirr would be safer somewhere else. Kara, your task is to build the Shieldsworn and any exiled Hulburgans willing to join us into an army that can defeat Marstel's Council Guard. Hire sellswords, recruit adventuring companies, make deals with the merchant costers of the Moonsea, whatever is required. I want to be able to march in the spring."

Kara nodded, but a frown creased her brow. "You have some other purpose in mind, don't you?"

He met her eyes, and let the anger that had simmered in him for days put steel into his voice. "Vengeance," he said. "Before I do anything else, those who ordered Grigor's murder are going to die under my blade."

FIVE

17 Hammer, the Year of Deep Water Drifting (1480 DR)

Six days after Grigor Hulmaster's burial, Geran set foot in Hulburg again. He trudged alongside the mud-spattered wagons of a Double Moon caravan, playing the part of a Vastar sellsword. He'd signed on to escort the caravan from Thentia's crowded merchant yards to Hulburg for a half-dozen gold coins. While the winter ice held in Hulburg's harbor, the only commerce with the city consisted of a bare handful of overland wagon trains making their way along the windswept coastal road. It was a hard and uncomfortable trek in the depths of winter, but there was money to be made, and so the great trading companies sent their goods creaking along the trails as weather and opportunity permitted.

Geran's hair was bleached to a dark blond, and he wore a fringe of yellow-dyed beard on his face. A heavy coat of burgundy-colored leather sewn with steel studs hung down to his knees, and he wore a shapeless, baglike hat of the same color. He'd cultivated a relentless pipe habit, marching along from dawn to dusk with a pipestem clamped between his teeth and as often as not a wisp of aromatic smoke ringing his head. It had taken every bit of stubbornness he possessed to keep Kara from sending disguised Shieldsworn along with him. She'd argued that it was beyond foolish for him to venture into Hulburg alone, risking capture—and most likely a swift, unpleasant death—at the hands of Hulburg's enemies. He'd finally won his way by persuading Kara that a small number of Shieldsworn wouldn't substantially add to his safety, while a large number following him about would simply make it much more likely that his ruse would be noticed. Even then he'd had to threaten to renounce the lordship altogether if that was what it would take for her to agree that he could set out for Hulburg on his own.

At the Double Moon tradeyard, Geran stood in line with the other caravan guards to be paid off, complained a little about how little coin he'd actually earned, and asked whether he might be needed for a return trip any time soon, all the things a poor sellsword might be expected to do. Then he left the Double Moon yard and lost himself in the bustle of wagons and passersby moving through Hulburg's streets. After a few minor errands—purchasing more pipeweed, a new cloak, new stockings, and the like—to make sure that no one was following him or paying too much attention, he decided that it was safe to head to Erstenwold's.

He saw the first of the gray, helmed warriors at the foot of the Lower Bridge, where Bay Street crossed the mouth of the Winterspear. The creatures were tall, a good half a head taller than his own six feet and two inches, and they stood motionless without paying any attention to the bitter cold or the folk passing by. Their faces were hidden behind their blank metal visors, and he could glimpse strange runic markings on the claylike flesh that showed beneath their black breastplates and helms.

"What in the world are these?" he muttered to himself as he drew near. For a moment he considered reversing his course and retreating, but realized that might appear suspicious when other folk simply carried on right past the things. The people going by on the bridge eyed the things nervously and gave them a wide berth; Geran followed their example. If the gray warriors were aware of the stares and dark mutters they provoked from the people who passed by, they gave no sign of it. Some sort of conjured guardians? Constructs built to serve as warriors, supplementing the numbers of the Council Guard? He remembered hearing rumors about creatures such as these in Griffonwatch. Had Rhovann created or conjured more of the gray warriors in the last few tendays, enough to station them around the city? If so, what was their purpose? Protecting the city and castle from attack? Or were they simply intended to intimidate the greatest number of common folk possible?

At the far end of the bridge, he spied a driver waiting with his wagon by a cobbler's shop. On the spur of the moment he wandered over to the fellow, an old dwarf in a heavy hood of fur. Leaning close to the wagon seat, he said, "I'm new in town. Who are the gray warriors in the helms? What do they do? Should I mind myself around them?"

The dwarf scowled. "They're servants o' the harmach's wizard. For th' most part, they do naught but stand an' watch. But ye mind yer step 'round them nonetheless. I've heard it said they take note o' every soul that walks past and remember him or her. And if that's a person that the harmach's wizard suspects of something, they lay hold of him and drag the poor bastard on up to Griffonwatch, where the wizard steals their souls. It's no' right, but that's the way of it." He shook his head, muttering darkly. Geran took that as his opportunity to continue on his way, wondering how much of the old dwarf's story was idle rumor and how much was based in truth.

He came to Plank Street, and noticed another pair of the helmed constructs watching the crowds at the intersection of Cart Street—as busy as any corner in Hulburg. It would be a good place to set unsleeping eyes to watch over the people who came and went in town. There's probably nothing but empty speculation to the rumors, he told himself. Most folk knew little of magic or creatures made with magic, after all, and therefore assumed all sorts of things might be possible that weren't all that likely. But the old dwarf's story had planted a dark little seed of doubt in his mind. He paused, feigning interest in a tavern's bill of fare as he surreptitiously watched the gray-skinned creatures towering over most of the crowd. If the creatures really were made to remember all that they had seen, then Rhovann might know enchantments that called upon those memories to quickly find or follow any person in whom he took an interest. The anonymity of Hulburg's crowds could be much less protection than he'd assumed. How could you plot against a foe who might be aware of your every move?

"There's no need for that," he murmured to himself. If Rhovann was truly that capable, then his efforts would be doomed from the first. He might as well assume that Rhovann's creatures couldn't see what wasn't there to be seen, or he'd go mad from worry and suspicion. Still, it couldn't hurt to avoid the creatures as much as possible. With that in mind, he decided against moving in the open. Marstel—or more likely, Rhovann—would be sure to have Erstenwold's watched, just in case he showed up. He was confident enough in his simple disguise, but Rhovann was a patient and meticulous adversary; even if the elf mage hadn't placed his gray sentries by Mirya's door, he might have woven alarm spells in places where he was likely to make an appearance. Magical measures might easily see through a little hair coloring and spirit gum if he simply walked up to the front door.

Instead of turning up Plank Street toward Erstenwold's, he walked past Plank to Fish Street and turned north there. He could think of a few ways to get into Erstenwold's without being seen. If he remembered the neighborhood, the tinsmith's shop might have exactly what he needed. He hurried up a half block to the building where old Kettar had his workshop and house, only to find the place closed up with its windows dark.

"Now what?" he muttered, peering in the window. He could see empty worktables, a cold furnace, a few furnishings that had evidently been left behind. What happened to Kettar? he wondered. The tinsmith had been puttering away in his workshop on Fish Street since Geran had been a young boy. Had the tinsmith simply packed up and abandoned town? Had his store been seized through one of Marstel's newly enacted taxes? Or had some gang of Chainsmen or Cinderfists run him out of his own shop? He scowled into the dirty window, and took a couple of steps back to see if the private rooms behind the shop were occupied or not. A single slat of wood had been nailed across the door, and a tattered leather scroll tube hung by it; he looked inside and found a notice of confiscation from the Tower. Taxes, then, he thought to himself. Hopefully Kettar and his family had a roof over their heads and a little money to get by on, wherever they were.

He glanced up and down the street, decided that no one was paying him any special attention, and pried the slat loose enough to let himself inside. Kettar's misfortune provided him with a very handy bit of cover for what he had in mind next. It might look a little suspicious for an ordinary caravan guard to be skulking about in an empty property, but if anyone troubled him, he could just claim that he was looking for a place to set up shop and had a mind to buy the tinsmith's store if it came up for auction. He crossed to the rear of the store and peeked out a window that looked down the alleyway.

Thirty yards away stood the back of Erstenwold's. Fixing his eye on a small window in the rear of the Erstenwold's building, he built a mental picture of the storeroom beyond. Closing his eyes, he summoned the arcane sigils of the spell to his mind and said softly, "*Sieroch!*" An instant of darkness—

—and he stood in a dim, cluttered pantry. Hoping that Rhovann hadn't thought to ward the entirety of the storehouse, he let himself out into the hall beyond. From a short distance away he could hear the clatter and murmuring voices of the clerks and customers by the store's front counter. He smiled a little, and started down the hall.

Mirya suddenly bustled around the corner in one of the practical wool dresses she favored in the wintertime, this one a light blue in color. Her arms were full of blankets, and her dark hair was pulled back in a simple braid. An absent frown shadowed her wide blue eyes. Geran's heart lifted at the sight of her familiar features; he hadn't realized how much he missed her. Then Mirya caught sight of him and let out a startled gasp, dropping her armload as she suddenly recoiled. "What—you shouldn't be back here!" she spluttered. Then, before Geran could even get a word out, her eyes flew open wide in recognition. "Wait a moment—*Geran?*"

He motioned for her to lower her voice. "Yes, it's me," he said. "Forgive me for sneaking in, but I thought it better to avoid being seen."

"By the Dark Lady, but you gave me a fright! Never do that again!" She stooped to pick up the blankets; he kneeled beside her and helped her scoop them up. When they stood again, she scowled at him and said, "It's no help at all that you're dressed like an outlander and your hair's that awful color. I thought some Cinderfist ruffian had broken in to rob me."

"I am sorry, Mirya. Truly I didn't mean to startle you."

"Hmmph. Well, you can wait back in the counting room. I'll be along as soon as I tell Ferin to mind the counter for a time." She brushed past him with her blankets, carrying them out to whatever customer had asked for them. Geran suppressed a smile and ducked back into the store's back room, where Mirya kept her ledgers among a clutter of merchandise and knickknacks that had likely been moved from room to room in Erstenwold's for years. The store had been in her family for almost fifty years, beginning as a ramshackle chandlery and storehouse built by her grandfather. Geran made himself comfortable in an old leather armchair and waited. A few minutes later Mirya returned and took a seat on the edge of a small couch across from him with her mouth settled in its customary frown.

"Is this a good time?" he asked her. "If you've business to attend, I can wait."

"No, it's fine. I'm simply surprised to see you. I would have thought . . ." She paused, searching his face with her keen blue eyes before continuing. "Geran, it may be that you haven't heard, but word from Thentia arrived two days past that Harmach Grigor was killed by assassins."

He met her gaze and nodded. "I was there."

"Oh, Geran, I'm sorry for it, I truly am. He was a sweet old man who'd naught but kind words for me any time I spoke with him." She reached across to rest her hand on top of his. "Is the rest of your family well?"

"Yes. Natali and Kirr weren't hurt, thank the gods. Aunt Terena and Kara are fine too. But we lost a number of Shieldsworn and family retainers. It was a terrible scene." He frowned and looked around. Speaking of the young Hulmasters had reminded him . . . "Are you and Selsha well? Is she about?"

"Aye, we're well enough, I suppose, but I sent Selsha to stay with the Tresterfins for a time. I was worried that she might be caught up in some trouble here in town, and I thought she'd be safer in the countryside. I do miss her, though. I'm in the habit of listening for her footsteps or her voice." Mirya sighed, and drew back.

The trouble must be growing worse if she sent Selsha away, Geran reflected. Mirya was hardly the sort to panic, as he well knew. "I saw that old Kettar's workshop was empty," he said. "Have Marstel's tax collectors troubled you? Are you still able to make a living here?"

She made a dismissive gesture. "We've something laid by for hard times; we'll see it through, I think. But I worry about my neighbors."

"I do too. I won't let this stand a day longer than I have to. I promise you."

"I know it, Geran." She fell silent for a time, gazing down at her hands. He knew her well enough to see that she had something she wanted to say. After a moment she shook herself a little, and looked up at his face again. In a quiet voice she asked, "What happened in Thentia?"

"Your old friend Valdarsel sent a priestess from his order to organize an attack at Lasparhall," he said. "They struck in the middle of the night, when the household was asleep except for a few sentries. It was mere chance that I wasn't killed as I slept. Kara and I—and the Shieldsworn—managed to foil the worst of the attack. But we were too late to save Harmach Grigor."

Mirya covered her mouth in horror. "Oh, Geran," she whispered through her fingers.

He sighed and glanced at the small gray patch of sky visible in the counting room's tiny window. "Kara and I saw to it that the Cyricist and her mercenaries had no opportunity to enjoy their success. None of them got away."

"Who is harmach now?"

He shrugged. "I am, I suppose. Well, I won't take the title until Hulburg is free. But I'm the Lord Hulmaster."

"Then what are you doing here?" Mirya recoiled in horror. "You must be mad! If Marstel knew that you were alone in Hulburg, right here under his nose . . ."

"I'm here to kill Valdarsel. He's the one who ordered Harmach Grigor's death. There will be no more Hulmasters assassinated on his orders." The thought brought another flash of anger, and he clenched his jaw. "I don't doubt that Rhovann put him up to it, and I'll deal with him in good time. But for now I'll settle for delivering an unmistakable message to Rhovann and his pet harmach about sending monsters and murderers against my kin. There's a price to be paid."

Mirya pressed her lips together, thinking on Geran's words. A few months earlier she'd found herself on Valdarsel's bad side, and she had good reason to fear the priest. "I wouldn't miss him, and that's the truth of it, but I don't know if you'll be able to put him under your blade. He spends most of his time in his new temple, and he's got a strong guard with him whenever he leaves it."

"New temple? What new temple?"

"They call it the Temple of the Wronged Prince," Mirya replied. She shook her head. "I never thought I'd see the day when such a thing as a temple dedicated to Cyric might be built in Hulburg, but it's happened."

Geran frowned. Cyric was a dark god, but his doctrines embraced concepts such as ambition, change, and revolution—things that often appealed to folk who were poor and desperate. He suspected that Cyric's priests downplayed the darker aspects of their Black Sun when recruiting from the wretched masses. "Where is this place?"

"On Gold Street, near the Middle Bridge. There are guards in black mail who stand by its doors both night and day, and acolytes are always about the public rooms. The priests' quarters and the temple's inner sanctum aren't open to any but the servants of the Black Sun." Mirya paused, studying him. "I've heard that there may be other guardians inside—devils or demons or some other such things. If you mean to face him, it might be better to wait for him to come out, guards or not."

"That may be," Geran replied. "Still . . . are there any other entrances?"

"Aye, there's a small garden behind the building. A gate from the alleyway leads to the garden, and there's a door leading in from the garden. It's guarded by some sort of magical glyph."

"I might be able to deal with that . . ." Geran mused aloud. Then a sudden thought struck him, and he looked sharply at Mirya. "Wait a moment. How do you know so much about this Temple of the Wronged Prince? Did Valdarsel have his ruffians drag you in?"

"No, nothing like that!" Mirya answered. She hesitated, looking away from him. "I've some . . . friends . . . who help me to keep an eye on things about town. We looked over the place a few days past, thinking that we might cause some mischief there. But as I said, it seemed too well protected to us, so we decided to leave it be."

"Mirya, what have you been up to?"

"Marstel and his sellswords are running this town into ruin, Geran. We're doing something about it. Hulburg is our home too, you know."

"Do you have any idea how dangerous that sort of thing is?" he demanded. "Once you raise your hand against Marstel and his allies, you can never take it back. Didn't you learn anything from what happened when you put your nose in Valdarsel and Rhovann's business a few months ago? They'll hang you for a rebel if they catch you!"

"If they catch me?" she said, bristling. "You're the one skulking about in a disguise, and you're the one person in all Faerûn they'd most like to catch playing at spy! How can you tell me that what I'm doing is too dangerous?"

"This is different," he retorted. "I have experience at this sort of thing. I know what I'm doing."

"Maybe I know what I'm doing as well, Geran Hulmaster."

Geran rose to reply in anger, but bit back on his words. He'd never get her to see that he was right by shouting at her; Mirya could be exceptionally stubborn when she set her mind on something, and this seemed like one of those times. He decided to try another tack. "Mirya . . . I understand that you love this land as much as I do," he said. "But I beg you, don't take chances! I couldn't bear to see you hurt."

She stood as well, and folded her arms like a battlement in front of her. "And why is that?" she asked in a sharp voice. "Don't I have the right to choose my own risks?"

He retreated from her, pacing around the small room. "Don't be foolish," he said. "You know that you're dear to me."

"I know no such thing," she snapped. "Oh, I know that I matter to you. You followed me to the Tears of Selûne. But why, Geran? Ten years ago you loved me. It ended. What is it that you think you still owe me? Why is it so important to you what happens to me now?"

"Because I—" he began, and stopped himself, unable to finish. He'd been about to say *because I love you*. He stood in silence, stunned to find those words on the tip of his tongue, and aghast at the realization that he'd come within a breath of speaking them aloud. He had no right to say any such thing to her. Ten years before he'd been a young, callous fool who broke her heart when he set out to make some kind of mark in the world outside Hulburg. She could never trust him with her heart again, and he could never ask it of her. He drew a deep breath, and found something else to say. "Because I owe it to Jarad," he said instead. "He'd want me to look after you and Selsha. I failed him once when I left Hulburg to fall into the state it did while I was gone. I don't want to fail him a second time."

"Because you owe it to Jarad," Mirya repeated. She frowned, and finally shook her head, smoothing her skirts with her hands. "Very well, then. You can stay as long as you like, but I think you're wise to avoid being seen as you come or go. I don't know how, but I've a feeling that Erstenwold's is being watched. I can show you a path in the buried streets if that would help."

He looked down at the floor. Mirya was no fool. She knew that he hadn't been honest, although he hoped that she didn't know exactly how. "I thank you for the offer, but I think I'd better be going. I don't want to tempt fortune by hiding here, and I've got a few more errands today."

She paused by the door and looked back at him. "We're ready to do what needs to be done. I can pass the word to the folk who are still loyal to the Hulmasters."

He nodded. "My thanks. I'll remember that when the time comes." Her frown softened just a little, and she ducked back out into the hallway to return to her business. He stood in the storeroom for a moment, listening to her voice coming from the front counter as she resumed her day. Did I mean what I almost said? he wondered. He looked inward, and found nothing he could make sense of, only a tangle of old memories and new friendship. Shaking his head, angry at his own foolishness, he deliberately set them all aside. "I have no time for that sort of nonsense," he muttered. He moved over to the counting room's window, fixed his mind on the empty tinsmith's shop down the alleyway, and teleported himself out of Erstenwold's. In a matter of moments he slipped back out onto Fish Street and continued along his way.

The afternoon was drawing on, and he decided that he was hungry. He headed back toward the Winterspear along Market Street, and found a little smokehouse near Angar Square where he was able to buy a simple meal for a silver coin. When he finished, he turned his steps toward Gold Street and hurried past the Cyricist temple. It was much as Mirya had described it, a gaudy new structure rising from the middle of an old crafts-man's district on the edge of the Tailings. Black-clad guards stood by the open doors, doing their best to remain motionless and imposing despite the bitter weather. He was careful not to stare too closely as he walked past, giving the place what he hoped would seem like a cursory glance. He was tempted to wander in the open door and see what the public areas looked like, but decided against it; no doubt he'd be approached by someone if he did go in, and the whole point of a disguise was to avoid attracting atten-tion. Instead he went back over the Middle Bridge—this one was watched by the gray-skinned warriors too—and climbed up the Easthill toward the better homes that sat along the hillside of the headland that formed the eastern half of Hulburg's harbor. A few minutes' walk brought him in sight of his goal, a house that was anchored at one corner by a small round tower.

There was no other traffic along this street; these were the homes of the wealthy, people who had no reason to venture out in the cold unless they did so in blanket-filled carriages. He saw no signs of Rhovann's spies or Council Guards, and decided that a direct approach might be the best in this case. Squaring his shoulders, he marched up to the house's front door and rang the bell.

There was no response for quite a while. He rang again. This time he heard several quick footfalls, and the door opened a double handspan. In the dark foyer beyond Sarth Khul Riizar appeared, his deadly magical scepter pointed at Geran. The tiefling wore the splendid scarlet and gold robes he favored, and his face—brick red in hue, and graced with two large, swept horns—was set in a stern frown. "I do not know you," he said. "Explain this interruption at once!"

"Sarth, it's me! Geran!" the swordmage said, his voice low.

The tiefling frowned and peered more closely at him. "Oh, so it is," he muttered. "My apologies, Geran; it's a good disguise. I thought you were some merchant coster armsman, come to deliver yet another offer of employment." He lowered his scepter, and opened the door wide. "Come in, quickly. You'd best not be seen in the streets."

"My thanks. I'm sorry for barging in like this." Geran hurried inside, and Sarth closed the door behind him, bolting it with an absent wave of his hand. "I feared you weren't at home when you didn't answer."

"Ah, well, I forgot that I'd given Wrendt the afternoon off. I thought he was here to answer the door." Sarth set a hand on Geran's shoulder. "It is good to see you, my friend. When I heard what had happened in Thentia . . . it is a monstrous thing to seek the murder of the children and your older relations, cruel and monstrous. I cannot believe that your enemies stooped to such wicked efforts. If there is anything I can do . . ."

"In fact, I think there is," Geran replied. He gripped Sarth's shoulder in reply, the age-old warrior greeting. He had no call on Sarth's loyalty, no reason to expect that the sorcerer would be willing to make himself an outlaw and a rebel for the sake of a few shared moments of danger, but he hoped that he'd read the tiefling's character correctly in the months they'd known each other. "Valdarsel, the Cyricist priest, was behind the attack on my family. I mean to kill him for it, and I'm hoping that you'll lend me your help."

The tiefling grimaced, and glanced around at the comfortable house around him. "He sits on the Harmach's Council, you know. There will be unfortunate consequences." Then he sighed, and nodded. "Very well. Allow me a few hours to make some preparations, and we will see what can be done."

SIX

18 Hammer, the Year of Deep Water Drifting (1480 DR)

Early on a cold, gray morning, Kara Hulmaster stood holding the reins of her horse Dancer, and watched as her captains maneuvered their companies of Spearmeet and Shieldsworn through marching drills in the steep vale behind Lasparhall. A light snow flurry fell, and she wore a heavy cloak against the cold. Close-order drill was something normally reserved for masses of pikemen, but she'd always thought it handy for welding together newly formed companies and giving new officers practice at commanding their troops. Five days earlier she'd decided to combine the surviving Shieldsworn soldiers with the Spearmeet militia to form three new combined companies—or "shields," as they were called in Hulburg—for the campaign to come. The new units were still learning how to work together.

As she watched the captains maneuvering their shields, a dwarf riding on a thick-barreled mule came jogging down the lane leading back toward the manor. He was a black-bearded, broad-shouldered fellow even by the standards of his stoutly built kind, and he clenched the stem of a pipe between his teeth. When he drew up beside her, he reined in his mount and slid to the ground with a grunt. "Lady Kara," the dwarf said with a small nod. "The chamberlain o' the house told me I'd find you here."

"Master Ironthane," Kara replied. "My thanks for coming to call on me here. I'd have been happy to ride down to Thentia, you know."

Kendurkkel Ironthane shrugged. "It's the better part of two months now the Icehammers've been in winter quarters. I needed a reason to be out an' about. Besides, I wanted t' have a look at the Hulmaster army for myself."

"How have you been keeping?"

"Fair enough," he replied, watching the shields in their maneuvers. "Better'n you and yours, I'd say."

Kara winced. Many dwarves had a tendency to speak the truth and spare no feelings, and Kendurkkel was an excellent example. "I wish that weren't quite so true."

The dwarf raised an eyebrow. "Are ye wishin' hard times on me?" he said, but he smiled behind his pipe. Early the previous summer, the Icehammer mercenaries had stood side by side with the Shieldsworn and the Spearmeet to break the Bloody Skull horde at Lendon's Wall. Kendurkkel was a mercenary and owed allegiance to no one . . . but Kara had won his respect with her generalship in the desperate battle against the orcs, and respect was something that Kendurkkel was slow to give.

"No, better times for me and mine," Kara answered. She turned to face the mercenary and fixed her eyes on his. "We've got work for the Icehammers if you're willing, Master Ironthane."

"I'm always willin' t'talk business. What's it t'be, then?"

"I mean to retake Hulburg from Marstel and his supporters. We march at the end of next month. I'd like to hire the Icehammers to bolster our numbers."

"That soon, eh?" The dwarf drew on his pipe. "It'll no' be cheap, Lady Hulmaster. If that's what you've got in mind, well, there's a damn good chance of a field battle t'be fought. We'll no' shy from fightin', but it costs a good deal more, you see."

Steeling herself for the answer, Kara asked, "What's your price?"

"Well, the customary amount is two thousan' gold crowns up front, and a thousan' per month we're in your service. Add another six hundred if we provide our own quarters and board." The dwarf removed his pipe from his mouth and tapped it against his hand, emptying out the ashes. "We'll need a bonus of one thousan' per day o' skirmishin' or siegework, or five thousan' for a major battle."

Kara grimaced. That was frankly more than the Hulmaster fortune, such as it was, could manage, but she had to have the Icehammers. The winter weather meant that no other mercenary companies could be hired and brought to Thentia until late spring at the earliest, and that would pose its own problems—the Hulmaster treasury would be empty by then. More importantly, she couldn't take the risk that Marstel's agents might contact Kendurkkel and hire his company. All things being equal, she thought Kendurkkel would rather fight at her side than with her enemies, but it was hardly wise to count on such sentiments affecting a mercenary's business dealings. If Marstel offered to meet the Icehammers' price and she didn't, there would be two hundred more veteran soldiers lining up against her, enough to make an already difficult task next to impossible.

"All right," she finally said. "We can meet your hiring price and your monthly rates for several months, at least. We'll look after your quarters and provisions." Of course, that meant selling off almost all the jewelry she'd been able to scrape together from her mother's collection as well as that of Harmach Grigor's wife Silne, who'd died many years before. They'd fetch enough in the markets of Thentia to cover the Icehammers for a short season . . . she hoped.

"An' if there's fightin', can you pay?" Kendurkkel asked.

"It depends how much fighting you see. Is it possible that we could arrange to pay in installments once we see how much of a bonus you've earned?"

"That's no' the way 'tis done," he replied, shaking his head. "Usually our employer's t'set aside a provisional sum with some countinghouse or another. After all, if we fight an' lose, an employer might no' be able to pay the agreed upon bonus. An' if we fight an' win, employers sometimes forget that there's a bonus t'be paid."

"We don't have thousands of crowns to leave in a countinghouse right now, Master Ironthane."

The dwarf shrugged. "Then I don't see how t'help you, Lady Kara. I like you, I truly do. We've killed a lot o' orcs together, we have. But as I see it you've got long odds against you, and it's all too likely I'll no' see my pay."

Kara's stomach sank. She *needed* the Icehammers! She crossed her arms and paced away, trying to come up with some argument, some enticement, that might sway Ironthane. Beyond the troops drilling in the field before her, the false battlements of Lasparhall glistened under their dusting of new fallen snow. She gazed at the old manor, thinking furiously . . . and something came to her. She looked back to Kendurkkel and said, "How about Lasparhall? The manor and the land must be worth ten thousand crowns or more. It'll be our security for your fee."

The dwarf raised an eyebrow, but he turned to look at the house. "I'm no' certain what I might do with a manor," he muttered.

"Sell it, use it as quarters for your company, or keep it for your own. I imagine that someday you might want to retire comfortably," said Kara. Of course, if their attempt to retake Hulburg failed, that would leave the Hulmasters landless as well as penniless; there was literally nothing else to fall back on. Even Geran might have hesitated to make such an offer. Well, he wasn't here to offer some better answer to the challenge of securing the Icehammers for the spring campaign. This was the only thing she could think of that might hook Ironthane in the absence of hard coin waiting for him in some trusted countinghouse. "If we fail, the place is yours. If—*when*—we defeat Marstel, then I'd like the opportunity to buy the deed back from you. But if we can't, you'll have Lasparhall to show for your troubles."

Kendurkkel replaced his pipe between his teeth, studying the lay of the land around the field. "It's a fair piece o' land," he finally admitted. "I'll be needin' some assurance that th' lord o' Thentia would let the property change hands if it comes to it. But, if that's all well, then yes, I agree. We'll take your contract."

"Excellent!" Kara repressed a sigh of relief; she didn't need the mercenary captain to see anything but complete confidence on her part. "Your quarters will be ready in two or three days. I mean to drill hard for the next few tendays, so your soldiers'll be hard at it for a while."

"That's as it should be," Kendurkkel said. "A bored soldier's a trouble waitin' to happen. I'll have me boys begin the packin' up directly." He stuck out his hand, and Kara took it forearm-to-forearm in the dwarven manner. The mercenary nodded in approval and grinned around his pipe. "It'll be good t' work with you again, Lady Kara. I go."

"We'll speak again soon." Kara watched the dwarven mercenary climb back into his mule's saddle and ride off, then returned her attention to the companies wheeling and turning in the field before her. The sergeant's sharp voices carried over the snowy ground, and from time to time one company or another gave a sudden shout in response. They're good troops, far better than the foreign blades who make up Marstel's army, she told herself. The question was whether she had enough of them . . . and with the Icehammers, she thought she had an answer.

She motioned for her standard-bearer, a young Hulburgan soldier named Vossen, to join her. The sergeant trotted over, the Hulmaster banner fluttering from his stirrup. "Aye, Lady-Captain?" he said.

"My compliments to the captains of the shields, and Sergeant-Major Kolton. Carry on with the day's drills, and join me with the House War Council in the upper library at four bells this afternoon."

"Yes, my lady," Sergeant Vossen replied. The soldier saluted, striking his right fist to his breastplate, and rode down into the drillfield in search of the captains as Kara turned Dancer and cantered back up to the manor. She'd been thinking of the campaign to come since the day the Hulmasters and their Shieldsworn had been driven out of Hulburg. It was time to set events in motion.

A little before four bells, Kara waited for the House War Council to gather in Lasparhall's fine old library. It was a broad, sunlit room on the upper floor of the manor's west wing, and for the next few tendays, she intended to use it as her headquarters. A large map showing the lands lying between Thentia and Hulburg hung in the middle of one wall; a great table of gleaming dark mahogany was set up in the center of the room. The banquet hall in the middle of the manor was a larger room, but Kara preferred one that she could lock up and keep guarded without rendering half the house inaccessible.

She busied herself with reading through a small handful of correspondence that Master Quillon had given her earlier in the morning as the chief commanders of the Shieldsworn and the family's key advisors filed in. First came the shield-captain Merrith Darosti, a sturdy woman of thirty who wore mail much like Kara's and carried her bold red hair in a long braid. Sergeant Kolton, who looked distinctly uncomfortable at the idea of participating in the officers' council, followed a step behind her; since he was one of the most experienced sergeants remaining in the ranks of the Shieldsworn, Kara had promoted him to head of the House Guard.

Brother Larken, a tall young friar in a brown robe adorned with the yellow sunburst of Amaunator, filed into the room next. Behind Larken two former members of the Harmach's Council made their way into the room and took their places: Deren Ilkur—formerly the keeper of duties—and Theron Nimstar, who'd been Hulburg's high magistrate. Neither man was a fighter, but they had good minds and broad experience in running civic affairs. Bringing up the rear of the procession came the stockman Nils Wester, who'd brought more than a hundred Hulmaster loyalists from his Spearmeet company into exile rather than submit to Marstel's rule. The assorted clerks and seconds for the council members took their own places in the row of chairs along the wall.

"It seems we're all here," she observed to Quillon. She handed the letters back to the old halfling, and adjusted the saber hanging in its scabbard by her hip. Since the assassins' attack on Lasparhall, Kara had made a habit of wearing her arms almost every waking hour. Today she wore her light kit—a shirt of fine mail over a knee-length skirt of reinforced leather and half-greaves, all beneath a surcoat of quartered blue and white much like that worn by any Shieldsworn. She didn't intend to be caught off guard by Hulburg's enemies again. Unlike the soldiers' coats, Kara's featured a griffon of blue and gold embroidered on the upper left quadrant—the insignia of House Hulmaster, which was only worn by a member of the family under arms.

She approached her place at the head of the table. "Good day, gentlemen," she said. With a scraping of wooden chair legs on the flagstone floor, the men and women in the room rose to their feet as she took her seat. "Please, be seated." Her officers and advisors sat down again and turned their attention to her, waiting for her to speak.

Kara regarded them evenly as she organized her thoughts. This was more properly Geran's task, not hers; it was frankly reckless and irresponsible of him to hare off to Hulburg and play at being a spy or assassin when there was serious work for the head of the household to look after in Thentia. It wasn't entirely outside her experience—after all, Harmach Grigor had trusted her to lead Hulburg's small army with hardly any guidance at all— but as the only Hulmaster in Lasparhall, she was more than the commander of the Shieldsworn. All of House Hulmaster's interests and concerns were now in her hands, whether they were political, diplomatic, or simply administrative. She'd tried to convince Geran that she needed his help on those fronts, but her cousin had simply said, "I have complete confidence in you, Kara; you'll manage better than I would," as if that was sufficient answer to her worries. Part of her understood that Geran's work in Hulburg could very well be just as important as her work in Thentia, especially if it brought hundreds of oppressed Hulburgans into the loyalists' ranks. But it was even more clear to her that Geran was hazarding the fortunes of the whole Hulmaster family along with his own life by carrying on as if he were nothing more than the rootless adventurer he'd been for so long. If he managed to get himself killed, she'd be the only Hulmaster who could carry on the fight . . . and the burden of leadership would fall completely on her shoulders, with no hope of reprieve for decades.

No sense in returning to an argument already lost, she told herself. Especially not when Geran was already abroad, beyond her ability to recall or even contact for now. No, all she could do now was to throw herself into the challenge Geran had set out for her. She set her mouth in a determined frown and began to speak. "Today I struck a deal with Kendurkkel Ironthane of the Icehammer mercenaries," she began. "With the Icehammers, we have the strength we need to defeat the usurper Marstel's Council Guard wherever they meet us. On the tenth of Ches— fifty-two days from today—we march on Hulburg.

"For the next five tendays, we will be engaged in maneuvers and training, come good weather or bad. By the time we march, we will be fast, disciplined, organized, and aggressive—a well-balanced sword in the Lord Hulmaster's hand." She paused, measuring their reactions before continuing. "Fifty-two days may seem like a long time today, but it's not. If any here have doubts or questions about a spring campaign, now's the time to voice them." Kara held the rest of the room with her gaze for a moment more, and then leaned back in her chair.

No one spoke at first. Then Nils Wester cleared his throat. He was a wiry man of fifty years with a weatherbeaten face and dark, fierce eyes under bushy gray brows; before he'd rebelled against Marstel, he and his large clan had kept hundreds of sheep on their pastureland high on the hills west of the Winterspear Vale. "I've little learning in strategy," the wiry old stockman said, "but I suppose I don't see why we've got to give that fat old bastard Marstel fifty days to get ready for us, Lady Kara. My warriors could march by the end of the tenday! Why wait?"

"Because we need time to reequip and train," Kara answered. "Half the men from the old Spearmeet musters don't have any armor heavier than a leather coat or a weapon better than an old hunting spear. We might be a match for the Council Guard even so, but if you count the merchant coster armsmen in Hulburg, the Cinderfists, and whatever magic Marstel's master mage can employ, the odds are longer than I'd like. Trust me, we'll need the five tendays to make a field army out of the fighters we've got here."

"Marstel might find more sellswords by the time we march," the old magistrate Theron Nimstar pointed out.

"True enough," Deren Ilkur said, "but regardless of whether we wanted to strike quickly or not, we simply don't have the provisions or material to march now. It will take me some time to gather a supply train that could support our little army in the field for more than a few days."

"Do we need more?" Nils Wester asked. "Hulburg ain't more than forty miles from here—two days if you've a mind to hurry."

"In good weather," Kara pointed out. "And assuming no enemy force takes a position to contest our march. Imagine that we find we have to march another twenty or thirty miles out of our way to avoid some obstacle Marstel puts in our path, or that heavy rains make the tracks—such as they are—impassable. I don't care for the idea of marching back to Thentia for our supper three or four days into the campaign simply because we'd neglected to adequately provision ourselves."

Wester grimaced, but subsided. "Well enough," he replied. "I can see the reasonin' of it. But—no disrespect intended, Lady Kara—where's Lord Geran? If this whole campaign is a plan o' his, I'd like to know what part he aims to play in it."

A good question, Kara answered in the privacy of her own thoughts. She couldn't blame Wester for asking about exactly the same concern that she'd been worrying at for days now. On the other hand, the last thing her captains needed to hear were her own doubts about the wisdom of Geran's actions. Wester was a good man, and a fiery leader to the Spearmeet muster who'd followed him into exile, but he was a difficult subordinate. He'd quickly fall into the habit of questioning every order she gave him if she showed any signs of equivocation.

"Lord Geran is engaged in a secret mission," she replied. "I wish I could speak freely about what he's doing, but I can't rule out the possibility that Marstel's spies—or the scrying of his mage Rhovann—might unearth some report from Lasparhall. If our enemies learn what he's about, they might take steps to counter his efforts, and his life could very well be in danger. Suffice it to say that we have too few allies and too many enemies at the moment; Geran means to amend that before our campaign begins." All of that was, of course, true enough, which spared her conscience; she'd never been a good liar. But that might be anything from secret diplomacy in Melvaunt or Hillsfar to seeking out magical assistance to raising the common folk of Hulburg against their oppressors. Let Wester and the others guess at what exactly she meant. "Now, are there any other questions or concerns before we get to work?"

No one spoke for a long moment. Kara studied the faces of her captains; some were grinning in eagerness, anxious for a chance to redeem themselves, but others—mostly the older, more experienced men—harbored dark flickers of doubt. They understood well enough the disparity of numbers and the slender resources available to the Hulmasters for their campaign. The defeat Marstel and his Cinderfist allies had dealt them back in the fall was still all too fresh in their memories.

Without even realizing what she intended to do or say, Kara slowly rose and leaned her mailed fists on the great table. "Marstel's soldiers are growing fat and lazy in their comfortable winter barracks, bullying old graybeards and children," she said in a snarl, allowing her voice to rise. "We're the warriors who met the Bloody Skulls on Lendon's Wall and stopped those savages dead in their tracks. Marstel's sellswords caught us spread out all over Hulburg and surprised us with sudden treachery last time; they won't surprise us again. When next we meet the usurper's forces in the field, I promise you this: *we will cut them to pieces*! Now—are you with me, or not?"

Sergeant Kolton scrambled to his feet and struck his fist to his chest. "Aye!" he shouted. "I'm with you, Lady Kara!" Chairs scraped and mail rustled as the others in the room stood and spoke, filling the room with a chorus of "Ayes!" and "We're with you!" and even a few cries of "Death to the usurper!"

Kara straightened up and nodded to herself. She had them for now, at least. As the cacophony of replies faded, she spoke again. "Good!" she said, grinning fiercely. "Now let me tell you how we're going to smash Marstel's hired blades."

SEVEN

20 Hammer, the Year of Deep Water Drifting (1480 DR)

A soft snow was falling at three bells after midnight as Hulburg slept. Dawn was still almost five hours away, and even the most determined revelers had abandoned the streets and taverns. Geran and Sarth stood in the shadows by the garden gate of the Temple of the Wronged Prince, wrapped in the eerie silence of the snow and the sleeping town. It seemed they were the only two people awake in the whole of Hulburg, although Geran knew that was a misleading thought. They'd seen two or three patrols of Council Guards on their way to the temple and its grounds, and avoided at least one pair of the tireless helmed warriors with the gray skin. The constructs took no notice of passersby during the day, but that didn't mean they would ignore two armed men at an hour when no honest folk were out and about.

"I see no wardings over the garden," Sarth said in a low voice. "However, there is a glyph upon the door, as you said. I believe I can defeat it without making much noise."

"Good," said Geran. He drew his sword—a fine straight long sword with a modest enchantment upon it, borrowed from Sarth's collection since he'd left his elven blade in Thentia—and murmured the words of a spell to summon a faint veil of silvery mist around himself. The *cuillen mhariel*, or silversteel veil, was a potent defense against many forms of attack, including magic. "You know that you need go no farther. Once you strike a blow, you'll lose what remains of your neutrality. Marstel's men and Rhovann's helmed constructs will storm your house before the day's out."

The tiefling shrugged. "An unfortunate loss, since I rather like the place. But I've made arrangements for the things I value, and have no great concern for the rest." He hesitated just a moment, and added, "Geran . . . this is your chance to reconsider as well. There is no telling what sort of retaliation you may provoke."

The swordmage shook his head. In his mind's eye he saw the blood-splattered corridors of Lasparhall and the gray face of his uncle, dying with an assassin's knife in his heart. He knew that nothing could undo what had been done, but at the very least he could make sure that Grigor Hulmaster's murderers never had the chance to kill anyone else dear to him. "That may be true, but Valdarsel will have no part in it," he said. "Come on; we're wasting the night."

Sarth sighed, but he turned to the gate and murmured a minor spell of opening. The bolt on the far side rasped softly as it drew back under his magic, and the wrought-iron gate swung open. Geran pushed through and hurried across the snow-covered garden beyond. Most buildings in Hulburg were made of timber on strong stone footings, but the temple was made entirely of masonry. It did have windows, but they were narrow embrasures that stood a good ten feet above the ground, like a castle's arrow slits—far too narrow for anyone to scramble through, as Mirya had observed. He drew close to the temple's back door, and paused when the magical glyph guarding it became visible to his eyes. He could sense the baleful curse held within its faintly glowing lines and whorls. It was nothing he would care to tamper with, but Sarth was better with such things than he was.

Sarth studied the glyph closely for a moment, his eyes narrowed. "A competent effort, but I can defeat it," he murmured. In a low voice he began to whisper the words of a counterspell, gently gesturing with his hand as he traced the glyph's shape in the air with a fingertip. The glyph glowed brighter, its lines blazing a brilliant emerald green before they suddenly grew dark and vanished. "It is done."

Geran glided forward and set his hand on the handle, not without a small quiver of trepidation. Glyphs, symbols, and such things could be highly dangerous, after all, but he trusted Sarth. He opened the door as quietly as he could, and found himself looking into a stone-flagged hallway dimly lit by small oil lamps in wall sconces. Several doors opened off the hall before it turned out of sight. He slipped inside, and Sarth followed behind him, pulling the door closed after him.

"Seal the door," Geran whispered. "No one is to get out this way."

"We may trap ourselves," Sarth replied. But at a nod from Geran, he whispered the words of a locking spell to hold the door against anything short of destruction by a battering ram.

Geran moved down the hall, glancing at the doors as he went. This was the weakest part of his plan; he knew nothing about the layout of the priests' quarters behind the Cyricist's chapel. He simply hoped that Valdarsel's chambers would be obvious from a quick inspection. The temple was not a very large building, after all, and he doubted that there were more than six or seven rooms in the portion of it barred to the public. The hallway from the garden door met an intersecting hall in a **T**, and he paused to look left and right. To one side the new hall opened into a large antechamber that led to the great chapel, and to the left he saw two more doorways, including one that was lavishly gilded and carved into the skull-and-sunburst emblem of Cyric. He allowed himself a small smile at their good fortune; that was the first place they'd look.

He motioned for Sarth to follow, and turned left toward the ornamental doorway. But the sudden soft clicking of claws on stone and rapid foot-falls came from the antechamber behind him. Geran whirled, and found himself facing a terrible devil with greenish black scales and razorlike barbs jutting from shoulders, elbows, knees, and skull. The monster hissed in frustration as it realized that its stealthy rush had failed, and threw itself forward in a flurry of raking talons and stabbing spikes.

The swordmage gave a step or two, parrying the monster's claws with his blade. The steel rang shrilly under its iron-hard talons, and sparks flew. "Foolish mortal," the monster snarled. "Do you not know whose house this is? Did you think the servants of the Black Prince would leave their shrine unguarded?"

Geran said nothing in reply, still hoping to avoid making too much noise if he could. He fought back in grim silence, his blade leaping and darting to nick the barbed devil once, then twice. The creature's scales were as hard as a coat of mail, and he quickly realized that it could shrug off anything but the most solid thrusts or heaviest slashes. Sarth stepped out into the hallway behind the monster, his rune-carved scepter of gold leveled at the creature's back—and a second devil appeared in the archway to the antechamber at the far end of the hall, hurling itself toward the sorcerer.

"Sarth, behind you!" Geran cried.

Sarth spun to meet the new threat; the second devil was almost upon him, and he had no time for subtlety in his magic. "*Narva saizhal*!" he shouted, and from his outstretched fingers a half-dozen spears of blue-white ice took form and streaked toward his attacker. The monster screamed in rage and tried to leap out of the way, but two of the ice spears skewered its torso even as the rest streaked past and shattered loudly down the hallway. It staggered back and sank to the floor, but found the strength to conjure a ball of green hellfire and fling it at Sarth. The tiefling deflected the blazing ball with a motion of his scepter; it bounced back down the hall leading to the back door, scorching the flagstones.

Claws raked through Geran's spell-shield, and he hissed aloud as his adversary's hot talons scored the meat of his left arm. He returned his full attention to the monster in front of him, launching a furious attack of his own. Steel glittered and rang as the barbed devil batted the blade aside with its claws and spikes, and the monster grinned at Geran with a mouthful of yellow fangs. He could hear an uproar beginning in the temple as the Cyricists began to wake to the battle in their halls, shouting alarms to rouse the rest of their fellows or demanding to know what was happening. There's no point in trying to keep it quiet now, Geran realized. Time is more important than stealth. With that in mind, he cleared his mind for a sword spell and let the arcane words roll from his mouth. "*Sanhaer astelie*!" he shouted.

Supernatural strength flooded into his limbs. When his foe raked at him again, Geran caught its forearm in the grip of his left hand—gashing his palm badly on the monster's sharp scales in the process—and spun around to fling the creature into the wall as if it were a toy. Plaster cracked and the stone blocks of the wall shifted out of place under the impact. Before the monster could recover, he set the point of his sword against the barbed devil's side and rammed the blade through lungs and heart until the point burst through the opposite ribs. With the last of the strength spell's brutal power he wrenched his blade free and tossed aside the fiend's corpse, which collapsed into sulfur-tinged smoke.

The door with the skull-and-sunburst design opened. A black-robed man with straw-colored hair and a sandy goatee stopped on the threshold, momentarily taken aback. A holy symbol of Cyric hung from his neck by a silver chain. Two soldiers in black mail with curved half-sickle swords hurried out to take position between him and Geran. "What is the meaning of this?" the Cyricist demanded. "You dare to defile the house of the Wronged Prince?"

"Are you the one called Valdarsel?" Geran said to him. The man in the black robes met Mirya's description of the Cyricist well enough, but Geran had never actually laid eyes on him before; he'd happily kill all the Cyricists in the place, but he wanted to make sure that the so-called high prelate was among them.

The robed man's eyes narrowed. "Who are you?" he snarled.

"I am Geran Hulmaster, of the House Hulmaster, and you are a murderer and a coward. Your hand is on the letter calling for my uncle's death. For that, you'll not live to see another sunrise."

"Then you're a fool to challenge me here." Valdarsel sneered. He glanced to the armsmen at his side. "Slay him!" The two soldiers started forward, advancing on the swordmage.

"More are coming, Geran!" called Sarth. "Strike swiftly!"

Geran glanced over his shoulder. "Sarth, keep the others busy!" he replied. "Raze the place to the ground if you have to!"

Behind him, the sorcerer nodded and unleashed a great blast of golden fire that roared back down the hallway, shaking the building and filling the air with acrid smoke. Screams of pain and terror rang from the hall. Sarth shouted the words of another spell and flung a sizzling orb of green acid back at the antechamber from which the devils had come, catching several of the human temple guards as they rushed back in from their place by the front doors. The stone blackened and sizzled as the green acid ate into the walls and floor. Dark chants rose as lesser priests summoned their own magic against Sarth, and the very air crackled with the ripples of spell and counterspell. Then Valdarsel's bodyguards threw themselves at Geran, and the swordmage had no more time to concern himself with how his friend was faring in the hallway behind him.

The hallway was narrow enough that two enemies couldn't easily come at him at the same time, so one guard held back a step and allowed his companion to go ahead. The leading bodyguard gave voice to a shrill laugh, his eyes ablaze with a fanatic's reckless zeal. "Die, defiler!" he shrieked, and hacked down at Geran with an overhand cut. The sword-mage parried the hard blow with some difficulty—the oddly shaped sickle swords were unfamiliar to Geran, and he wasn't exactly sure where he wanted his own blade to meet his foe's weapon. The curved point passed over his shoulder as the black-clad guard bore down, pushing the crossed blades down toward Geran with a two-handed effort . . . and the instant the curve of his sword was around Geran's back, he suddenly leaned back and yanked with all his might. The sickle point wasn't quite curved in enough to pierce Geran's back, and it wasn't effective as a slash, but the Cyricist guard did manage to drag him stumbling forward off balance, right into range for his comrade to cut Geran down. Geran survived only by throwing himself to the right, getting inside the second man's swing and ramming his right elbow into his mouth. Then he stepped toward the guard who'd pulled him close so that his sword was no longer pinned against his body, and managed to smash the heavy pommel into the side of the second guard's head as he recoiled from the elbow smash. The guard groaned and sank against the wall, his hand clapped to his ear as blood streamed through his fingers. But the guard grappling Geran shoved the swordmage back and attacked again.

The two of them traded slashes and parries for three, perhaps four, passes of steel, and then Geran spied Valdarsel brandishing his skull-and-sunburst symbol, his voice raised in an unholy chant. Dark energy swirled around the wounded guard kneeling by the wall, drawing him back to his feet and staunching the blood that flowed from his fractured skull. Damn it all! Geran fumed. He'd put that fellow out of the fight, and Valdarsel had used his priestly magic to heal the man's injuries and return him to the fray. He caught another swing from the first guard on his blade and circled his point under his foe's, ending in a lightning slash that arced up and through the man's throat. "Heal that if you can!" he snarled at Valdarsel as this guard fell back to the flagstones.

"Now you will witness the might of the Black Sun!" the Cyricist answered. He stretched his hand over the dying man at his feet, and began another chant even as the soldier he'd healed first surged back into the fray. Geran met the man's assault with a furious counterattack of his own, trying to batter his way through the guard and get to the priest behind him, but the man had just enough skill—or caution—to stand his ground and foil the swordmage's attack.

Time for a different tactic, Geran decided. He backed away a step and wove his sword through an intricate series of precise motions, summoning the most powerful spell of offense he could manage. "*Nhareith syl shevaere!*" he chanted, timing the syllables to the movement of his blade. A corona of blue flame woke around the steel, trailing behind it as it danced through the air, and with the final gesture of the spell, Geran thrust the long sword straight ahead as if to fling the blue fire from the steel. A sheet of fierce blue flame roared out over the hall, catching the guard who'd been advancing to attack, the guard with the wounded throat as he rose to his feet, and even Valdarsel behind his bodyguards. Black surcoats and robes smoldered as a swordlike slash appeared where the plane of searing blue flame struck. The guards crumpled under the full fury of the deadly spell, but Valdarsel was shielded by their bodies; he staggered back, hunched over the shallow cut seared across his midsection.

"To me! To me!" the priest shouted. But none of his followers were nearby. More battle spells rocked the building in the hall behind Geran, and leaping flames danced across the wall hangings, the ceiling beams, even the plaster of the walls. Valdarsel looked around in disbelief, and sudden fury twisted his face into a hateful sneer as his gaze met Geran's. "I swear by the Dark Prince that you will never see the end of your suffering!" he hissed. Then he turned and bolted back through the doorway with the carved door.

Geran darted after the fleeing priest. The door slammed shut in his face and latched; he tried it and found it locked, but he'd caught a glimpse of the chamber beyond as the door closed. Fixing it in his mind, he brought the teleportation spell to his mind and snarled, "*Sieroch!*" In the blink of an eye, he stood in the chamber beyond, a lavishly appointed suite with ceiling-to-floor wall hangings in gold and rust red, opulent couches, and a gleaming wooden table. Valdarsel groped behind the arrases, evidently searching for a concealed door. He whirled to face Geran as the swordmage appeared in the room.

"Defend yourself, murderer," Geran said in a cold voice. "I'll run my sword between your shoulder blades if you lack the courage to face me."

"Your anger has brought you far, prince of Hulburg." The Cyricist priest sneered. "Are you so certain that you aren't serving the Black Sun's purposes even now? Perhaps Cyric has caused your thirst for vengeance to lead you to your destruction!" Clutching his amulet with his left hand, he chanted the words of another priestly spell. Geran leaped forward to strike him down before he could finish, but Valdarsel was quicker with his magic. Ghostly chains appeared around the swordmage, anchoring him to the ground in midstep. A dim purple radiance flickered over the spectral iron, its touch searing Geran's flesh and sapping his strength. Geran struggled to advance, but he could only shuffle another half step before the chains coalesced around him.

Valdarsel laughed shrilly. "See? Your determination is admirable, Lord Geran, but all your passion and skill are nothing in the face of Cyric's might." The priest drew a long dagger from the sleeve of his robe, and began to chant another spell.

Geran wriggled his sword arm free and readied a spell of his own. "*Haethellyn*," he breathed, infusing the long sword with a spell of defense. Valdarsel finished his dark prayer and directed a lance of dancing black fire straight at Geran's heart, but the swordmage spun his blade in a half circle and parried the priest's deadly strike directly back at him. Valdarsel's eyes widened in disbelief a split second before his own black fire melted his holy symbol and burned deep through robes, mail, and flesh beneath. With a choking cry, he staggered back and fell, leaving a trail of smoke behind him. The spectral chains pinning Geran where he stood suddenly wavered as the priest's concentration faltered and failed. He dragged a foot forward through the vanishing chains, then the other, and finally strode free to stand over the fallen priest.

Valdarsel glared up at him, blood and smoke escaping from his mouth.

Geran fixed his eyes on the cleric's. Another fiery blast rocked the hallway outside. "I should let you die slowly and savor every moment of it," he said, "but I can't spare the time. This is for my uncle Grigor Hulmaster, you bloody-handed bastard." Then he finished the Cyricist with a single fierce blow.

He stood and stared down at Valdarsel's corpse for a moment, vaguely surprised at the lack of satisfaction he felt in what he'd done. As much as the Cyricist had deserved to die, the fact remained that Geran's enemies still held his homeland in a grip of iron. He couldn't believe that Valdarsel would have struck against Harmach Grigor without the knowledge and approval of Maroth Marstel or Rhovann Disarnnyl. Is that it? he wondered. Do I have to slay them as well to set matters right in my mind? Or is it simply that there is so much more to be done, and this is only the start of it all?

A great crash of masonry shook him out of his reflections. Sarth was still battling outside, and likely needed his help. Besides, nothing more would be put right if he didn't take care with his life and freedom so that he could strike again. He turned on his heel and darted back to the door. With his sword in his hand, he drew back the bolt and hurried out into the hallway.

Roaring flames and thick smoke greeted him. Sarth's spells or the battle prayers of the Cyricists trying to stop him had set the Temple of the Wronged Prince afire. The building looked like it was already well beyond saving, and was likely to come down around their ears at any moment. "Sarth!" Geran called. "It's time to leave!"

There was no reponse at first, and Geran feared that Sarth had left already—or fallen in battle against the Cyricists. But then the tiefling sorcerer staggered through the smoke, coughing through the handkerchief he was using to cover his mouth. Blood streamed from a nasty cut above his knee, and his fine robes were peppered with blackened scorch marks as if he'd been caught under a shower of sparks. But Sarth's eyes glowed with the hellish wrath he was capable of unleashing when angered or hurt, and Geran could see a half-dozen Cyricists lying crumpled on the floor behind him.

"Is it done?" Sarth asked through his handkerchief.

"Valdarsel's dead," Geran replied. "Come, we'd better get away from here." He started down the hall leading to the back door, only to realize that a great collapse of the roof beams had made it impassable.

"Not that way, I fear!" Sarth shook his head and caught his arm, pulling him out toward the main shrine. "We must leave by the front door."

Geran grimaced, but assented with a nod. Together they hurried out through the antechamber into the smoke-filled shrine beyond. Here stood a large statue, showing the god Cyric seated on his great throne with a sword lying bare across his lap. Bas-reliefs along the walls showed scenes of Cyric's mortal life, telling the story of his fated birth and the trials through which he ascended to divinity. Geran hardly spared them a glance as the two hurried out through the gates into the cool, snowy streets outside, where a large knot of onlookers—mostly foreigners and Cinderfists, since the temple was not far from the Tailings and they made up most of Valdarsel's followers anyway—had gathered to watch the place burn. Behind them a half dozen of the helmed constructs he'd seen earlier stood mutely watching the crowd, the reflection of the flames shimmering across their blank visors.

"There they are!" shouted a singed-looking acolyte in black robes. He stood, pointing an accusing finger at Geran and Sarth. "There stand the defilers! Seize them!"

"By all nine screaming Hells," Geran muttered. "This is why I hoped to use the back door when we'd finished."

Uncertainly at first, and then with angry mutterings and shouted threats, the small crowd began to surge forward. Geran thought about standing his ground and teaching the Cinderfists a second lesson to go along with the destruction of the temple, but then his eye fell on the towering rune-marked warriors in their blank helms. The creatures fixed their empty gazes on the two comrades and swung into motion, striding straight for them with a direct quickness that Geran frankly wouldn't have expected of them. He hesitated a moment longer before glancing at Sarth. "I think we'd better be on our way."

"Agreed," the tiefling said. He stepped forward and locked his arms around Geran's torso. Then, with a muttered spell, he leaped up into the air, bearing the swordmage into the firelit night with his flying spell.

EIGHT

21 Hammer, the Year of Deep Water Drifting (1480 DR)

Rooftops reeled under Geran's feet as Sarth carried him away from the Temple of the Wronged Prince. Behind them, flames shot up into the night from the building's collapsing roof, and the fire's sound—a dull, shapeless roar, interspersed by the constant popping and crackling of combustibles igniting within—filled the night. He glanced down as Sarth narrowly cleared a chimney and winced in fear of a fall. The last time he'd been carried into the air in such a way, he'd been fighting for his life against a gargoyle. But Sarth managed to keep the both of them in the air, his teeth bared in the effort to carry Geran along with him. In the space of ten heartbeats the tiefling returned to the ground two blocks from the temple, out of the mob's sight, and released the swordmage.

"That . . . is much harder . . . than using the spell for myself alone," Sarth panted. He leaned over with his hands on his knees. "My apologies . . . for not asking . . . your permission before . . . carrying you into the air."

"Think nothing of it," Geran answered. "We were about to be set upon by a mob; I approve of your judgment."

"Shall we continue . . . as we'd planned?"

"I think so, and the sooner the better. I hadn't expected so many Cinderfists to respond to our attack on the temple. Then again, I hadn't expected to burn the place to the ground." Geran and Sarth had decided it would be wisest to make for Thentia as soon as possible after dealing with Valdarsel. Even though Geran wished to begin plotting against Rhovann next, he was afraid that if he remained in Hulburg, Marstel's men would tear the town to pieces to find him; if he allowed his return to Thentia to become widely known, the usurper's soldiers wouldn't waste any time trying to root him out of hiding.

"You wished to send a stern message to your enemies. The destruction of the temple certainly contributes to that." Sarth drew one more deep breath, and straightened up. "Lead the way."

"Our mounts are waiting." The swordmage looked around to fix his bearings; they were in the small alleyway between High Street and Plank Street, not that far from Erstenwold's. With a quick glance up and down the streets, he set out at a fast walk, figuring that would look less suspicious if they met any guardposts. Geran had prepared for their escape by purchasing a pair of riding horses the day before and stabling the animals with their tack, harness, and provisions in a disused storehouse near the intersection of Market Street and Keldon Way. With any luck they'd be mounted and on their way within a quarter hour, long before any pursuit could be organized. Of course, Marstel's soldiers would certainly expect them to flee along the westward roads, but Geran was confident that he could lose pursuers in the moors.

They turned west on Cart Street; Geran glanced behind them, where he could see the bright orange-glowing smoke rising from the burning temple above the rooftops. Dark figures milled around a couple of hundred yards farther down the street. He couldn't tell for certain from this distance, but it looked as if several parties of searchers were setting out to comb the streets. He quickened his pace, heading for Fish Street to cut over toward their waiting mounts and stay out of sight.

A muted clatter of steel came from the other direction, and four of the helmed gray warriors suddenly rounded the corner at a silent run, halberds clutched in their thick hands. Geran and Sarth froze in surprise; they'd been watching for pursuit from behind them, not ahead. For an instant Geran hoped that the creatures were simply hurrying to the scene of the fighting, but the gray monsters altered their course the instant they caught sight of the two fugitives, lowering their halberds to charge with the weapons' deadly spear points.

"Take them!" the swordmage said to his friend. "We can't let them follow us to the horses!" He drew his sword, and ran forward to meet the first of the helmed guardians. The creature drew back its thick arms and rammed the halberd point ahead in a powerful but clumsy thrust that might have driven the big weapon through the side of a house, but Geran simply stepped aside. In a single fluid motion he rolled in along the weapon haft, crouched, and drove his sword point up under the ribs on the thing's right side. Fifteen inches of steel vanished into its gray flesh. He drew out his sword and spun away, searching for the next foe—but the hulking creature he'd just stabbed planted its lead foot and pivoted to bring the halberd around in a massive sweep that Geran avoided only by throwing himself back on his seat. He scrambled to his feet, ducked to his left, and lunged forward to cleave his long sword through its lower torso, just below the armor plate guarding the center of its body. The steel sword smacked into the creature's flesh as if he'd hewed at a block of wet clay; when the blade passed through, it left a wide, thin-lipped cut, but only a few dark drops of ichor leaked from a wound that would have disemboweled any mortal foe. The creature raised its halberd for another strike, and this time Geran was obliged to scramble away from that attack as a second helmed guardian tried to skewer him from the side.

"They don't bleed!" he cried in frustration. "It's like hacking at mud!"

Sarth scorched another of the monsters with a jet of bright fire. Claylike flesh hardened under the heat and then broke away in fist-sized chunks as the construct advanced and swung its halberd at the tiefling. The sorcerer ducked and retreated. The construct paid no attention as huge slabs of its substance delaminated and fell to the snowy cobblestones, pressing after Sarth. "Nor do they burn very well," the tiefling snarled. "In fact, they seem difficult to harm."

We don't have time to carve these things to pieces or bake them into immobility, Geran decided. They could not afford much delay in their escape. He traded one quick glance with Sarth, and said, "Run! We'll lose them in the alleyways."

Dancing away from the slow-footed guardians, Geran sprinted up Fish Street to the first convenient alley and darted in. Sarth followed a step behind him. He led the way as they darted through one yard after another, vaulting fences and darting down each twist and turn they could manage. They quickly outdistanced the hulking helmed guardians; the creatures were fast enough in a straight sprint, but they fared poorly in quick turns and narrow places. Geran worked his way north and west toward the storehouse where he'd left their mounts, and after a hundred yards or so emerged onto Keldon Way across from the towers of glassy green stone known as the Spires. Breathing heavily, he paused to scan the streets for signs of pursuit.

Sarth halted alongside him, panting. Then the tiefling snarled and spat a curse in a harsh language that Geran didn't know. "Two more are coming from the right!"

"Damn the luck," Geran said. He looked in the direction Sarth was staring, and saw the hulking creatures hurrying toward them. That was unfortunately the direction in which their waiting mounts were hidden; that pair might have been stationed up by the foot of the Burned Bridge, or perhaps near the gates of Daggergard. He glanced back to his left to see if there was someplace they might hide from the approaching guardians, only to see *another* pair of the monsters hurrying up from that direction. And now he could hear the clatter of the creatures they'd skirmished with drawing close through the alleyways behind them. That's not ill luck, he realized with a sick sensation. That's *coordination*.

"They know where we are," he said to Sarth. "They've got some way to follow us!"

"And to communicate that knowledge to each other without speaking," Sarth replied. "A subtle and powerful enchantment, but a very useful one."

"Useful, indeed," Geran muttered. "So how do we elude them?"

"That has now become problematic."

Geran gave Sarth a black look. "Come on, we have to keep ahead of them. Perhaps if we open a wider lead we can circle back to our horses." They hurried over another building or two and cut back into the alleyways east of Keldon Way, dodging through more of the narrow lanes and cluttered yards of the homes and workshops in Hulburg's westerly districts. This part of the city was not heavily inhabited, and some of the rubble of the old city that had once stood on this site still lay in heaps between the buildings that had sprouted up here over the last few decades. As often as not Geran and Sarth slipped and scrambled through weed-grown mounds of old masonry as they tried to keep ahead of the helmed guardians. This time Geran worked his way as far east as the Middle Bridge and then turned south to cut all the way across town toward the waterfront, staying off the major streets; now it was not just the gray constructs they had to be wary of, but also the bands of armed Cinderfists who roamed the streets. Near the tradeyard of the Jannarsk Coster they finally paused to scan the nearby streets for any sign of the helmed constructs.

"That must have lost them," Geran said as they caught their breath.

"Perhaps," Sarth said. The tiefling glanced up at the sky. "Dawn is not far off now. We are losing our chance to reach our mounts tonight."

Geran nodded agreement. He looked up to gauge the hour by the lightening of the sky, and he caught a glimpse of a small, bat-winged shape momentarily silhouetted in the gap between two buildings. He frowned and let himself look away, but marked the spot. "Sarth, do you see something on the roof of that countinghouse to my right? Something like a large bat? Try not to look right at it."

The tiefling turned his head slightly and looked from under his brows. "There is something there . . ." he said in a low voice. "Ah, a homunculus. It is watching us. That would explain how we have been followed so easily, although I still wonder how the gray guardians know what it sees."

"It must be Rhovann's work. He is an expert in alchemical creatures."

"Their bodies may be formed by alchemy, but the animating force is another matter. There is magic at work here that I am not familiar with."

Geran frowned. He had some skill with arcane lore, of course, but his education in magic was fairly narrow. When they had more time, he'd have to question Sarth closely on the topic of his observations about Rhovann's magic. In the meantime, they had more pressing matters to deal with. "Can you destroy it?" he asked.

"Of course." The tiefling changed his grip on his scepter, hiding the magical weapon from the small thing watching from the rooftop. Then he spun and pointed the device, shouting the words for a powerful spell. A brilliant green ray darted out and struck the little creature; it let out a startled squawk before bursting apart in a gout of dank clay and dark ichor.

Geran clapped the tiefling on the shoulder. "That's one small spy who won't trouble us anymore. Now, while we're unobserved, I think it's time to split up. Our enemies are looking for the both of us together, and—forgive me for being blunt—you stand out much more than I do. If you take to the air without trying to carry me along, I very much doubt that anyone will be able to catch you. Make your way to Thentia as swiftly as you can, and see to it that Kara learns everything we've learned about Rhovann's guardians. I fear they'll be a formidable obstacle to our plans to liberate the town."

Sarth frowned, but he nodded. The tiefling was a very pragmatic man, when it came down to it. "Very well. What will you do?"

"I'm going to try for the mounts again." He took Sarth's arm in a warrior's clasp. "Now go. I'll see you in Thentia."

"Be careful, Geran," Sarth said. He glanced around, his eyes glowing crimson in the shadows, and murmured the words of his flying spell. In three heartbeats he shot up into the sky overhead, turned west, and arrowed away from Geran's sight.

Geran heard a commotion behind him. He peeked around the corner of a building and saw a gang of Cinderfists coming in his direction. Quickly he turned and ran in the opposite direction, doing his best to stay under overhangs and awnings just in case more of Rhovann's homunculi were about. He darted back into the nearest alleyway and began to work his way westward, looping back around toward the square by the Merchant Council's grand hall. He paused between a taphouse and a bakery on Cart Street just a stone's throw from the Merchant Council hall, and carefully risked another glance up and down the street.

To his right, a pair of the helmed guardians stood near the center of the small square, scanning the surrounding area behind their blank visors. To his left, another party of Cinderfists carrying lanterns hurried up from the waterfront. He muttered a curse and drew back out of sight, waiting for the foreign brigands to pass by. "At least the helmed creatures didn't come for me this time," he murmured to himself. Perhaps Sarth had managed to blind their pursuers for a time by destroying the winged spy.

Inside the bakery he leaned against, he could hear the clatter of firewood and pans as the baker and his helpers began to stoke their ovens. Dawn was approaching, and he didn't want to be caught slinking around Hulburg in broad daylight. He might be able to blend in among the crowds, but he wasn't at all certain that he could avoid Rhovann's monsters indefinitely. What was it the dwarf had told him the other day? The creatures sensed the presence of those Rhovann wanted found? If there was even the slightest chance that was true, he could find himself at the center of a rapidly closing net even if he managed to outdistance any helmed guardian he ran into.

The Cinderfists passed by his hiding place with no more than a cursory look down the narrow lane between the buildings. They're taking steps to seal the town, he realized. He looked to his left, toward the bay, where House Sokol's walled compound stood. For the moment the way was clear.

In the distance, he heard the clatter and shouts of a Council Guard patrol moving into the yards he'd just left. "Cinderfists, Rhovann's constructs, and now the false harmach's men," he muttered aloud. Simply escaping from Hulburg, with or without his mount and provisions, seemed less and less likely. He needed a place to hide for the day. It couldn't be Erstenwold's, it was far too likely that Marstel's men might look for him there. The tinsmith's shop might serve, but he might be spotted as he tried to slip through the net of searchers closing in. He needed someplace close by . . . he glanced again at the Sokol compound at the end of Keldon Way. It was close, and as a House represented on the Merchant Council, it enjoyed protections against the harmach's authority. And it was conveniently sited on the west side of town for when he did decide to attempt escape again. The question was: did he trust Nimessa Sokol with his life?

She didn't betray me when I spied out Hulburg a few tendays ago, he answered himself. Then again, there was quite a difference between turning a blind eye to his comings and goings and sheltering him from the harmach's soldiers after a brazen attack on the Cyricists' temple.

Before he could second-guess himself, he darted across the street and hurried down Keldon Way toward the Sokol compound. He was careful to stay out of sight of the yard's front gate, which would be guarded by Sokol armsmen; the fewer people who knew where he was, the better it would be for all concerned. Instead he headed down the lane that ran behind the walled yard, fixed his eye on the wall top, and used his teleportation spell to blink himself up to it. Quickly he dropped to the ground inside and made his way to Nimessa's comfortable house, knocking softly at the door.

There was no response at first, and Geran began to wonder if perhaps Nimessa might have returned to Phlan before the ice set in. But then he heard footsteps coming to the door. A moment later, a gray-haired valet in a nightcap opened a small spyhole to peer out at him. He looked at Geran and frowned. "Who are you?" he demanded in a hard whisper. "What business do you have here?"

Geran didn't particularly care to announce his identity unless he absolutely had to. "I have an urgent message for Lady Nimessa," he said. "Could you please wake her?"

"Do you have any idea of the hour?" the valet demanded.

"I know it's not yet four bells after midnight, but trust me, she'll want to hear what I've got to say."

The old valet scowled. "You'll have to be more forthcoming than that, young master. I'm not about to admit a stranger to my lady's house in the middle of the night, especially one who refuses to give his name. Now be off with you, before I summon our guards!"

Geran frowned, considering what he could say to convince the servant to rouse the lady of the house. But then he heard a small rustle behind the valet. "Who's at the door, Barrad?" Nimessa called from somewhere inside.

The valet glared at Geran, and looked away to answer. "An armsman who claims he has a message for you, m'lady," he replied. "He's not one of ours and he hasn't identified himself. I was about to tell him to come back in the morning."

"You might as well admit him," she replied. "I've already been roused twice tonight, after all." Geran heard light footfalls inside, a brief murmur of conversation, and then the valet Barrad opened the door and motioned for him to enter. He stepped into the house and found himself in a comfortable foyer with rich wood paneling; a sitting room lay through a doorway to his right, and a dining room to his left. On the stairs leading to the house's upper floor stood Nimessa Sokol, wearing a dressing gown with a warm blanket draped around her for warmth against the winter chill. Her long golden hair fell loose to her shoulders, and her eyes—an enchanting shade of greenish blue—settled on him with a mild curiosity. He noticed that she kept one hand tucked into the sleeve of the other arm. Dark wood gleamed in her fingers; she had a wand ready in case he turned out to be less innocuous than he claimed.

He pushed his hood back over his shoulders and looked up to meet her eyes. "I'm sorry to wake you, Nimessa, but I'm afraid I'm in need of your help," he said.

She looked more closely at him, and her eyes widened in surprise and recognition. "I can imagine," she replied. She tucked her wand back into her sleeve and hurried down the last few steps. "Are you hurt? Were you caught up in whatever trouble's afoot in town this night?"

Geran glanced down at himself. He noticed that he was scratched and bleeding in several places where the barbs of Valdarsel's spectral chains had caught in clothing or skin. His shoulder and back ached where the point of the guard's sickle sword had snagged him. *I look like a ruffian who's just come from a riot*, he realized. No wonder the valet hadn't liked the look of him. "Only scratches," he said. "Otherwise, I'm well enough." He cut his eyes toward Barrad before saying any more.

Nimessa took his meaning. She glanced to her servant and said, "Barrad, you can go back to bed. I'll be fine."

"As you wish, m'lady," Barrad answered. The valet looked at Geran dubiously, but he bowed and withdrew.

Nimessa waited for the old servant to leave before turning on Geran, a small frown fixed on her face. "What are you doing here?" she asked urgently. "You shouldn't be anywhere near Hulburg!"

"The Cyricists attacked my family in Thentia," he answered. "I had to settle a score with Valdarsel."

"We heard about that, of course, but I can't believe that you'd dare to come into Hulburg alone. You must be out of your mind." She leaned close to peer at his cuts and the torn clothing, and frowned. "This is no scratch. I'd better fetch some bandages."

"It's nothing," he said, but he grimaced when she poked at a bad cut on the back of his left hand. She raised an eyebrow at him, and hurried off to what he presumed was the kitchen. He heard cabinets creaking open and thumping shut. A moment later she returned with a basin of warm water and a roll of linen bandages.

"Are you behind the fire at the Temple of the Wronged Prince, then?" she asked. "My armsmen woke me an hour ago to tell me the place was burning to the ground." She took him by the arm and ushered him into the sitting room adjoining the foyer.

He nodded. "It wasn't my intent to burn the place down, but I'm not sorry to see it destroyed."

"For Selûne's sake, what have you done? Half the town's been turned upside down to find those who attacked the temple." She steered him to a couch, and sat close beside him, dipping a clean bandage into the water to begin washing his cuts. "Was Valdarsel there? What happened?"

"Valdarsel's dead," he said. "And more than a few of his guards and acolytes with him, I suppose."

"You killed the high prelate?" she asked in amazement. She frowned and looked away, quickly thinking through the consequences of his actions. After a moment she sighed and took his hands in hers. "You must flee Hulburg at once, Geran. It's far too dangerous for you to remain here after tonight."

"That was my intent. Unfortunately, I hadn't reckoned with the capabilities of Rhovann's gray guardians or the alertness of his spies. I couldn't reach the horse I'd left for my escape to Thentia. In fact, it's not possible to set out on foot at the moment." He made himself look into her eyes, bright with worry for him. "Listen, Nimessa . . . I know it puts you in a difficult position, but I need a safe place to lay low for a day or so before I attempt to set out again. I'll understand if you can't allow me to stay. But if that's the case, I'd better leave immediately."

"Did anyone see you come here?" she asked.

"Only your valet. I'm fairly confident about that."

"Barrad can be trusted to keep things to himself. Still, it would be wise to keep you out of sight. Most of our folk here are loyal enough, but I'd rather not take the chance on someone carrying tales to the Council Guard in hope of a reward, or simply saying something they shouldn't out in the town." She wrapped a strip of bandage around his hand, and turned her attention to another gouge by his left knee.

"All I need is a pallet in a dark corner of your storehouse," he said. He shifted and straightened out his leg so she could get at the minor wound more easily. He hadn't realized how weary he was; it felt good to sit for a time, and even better to watch Nimessa's deft hands at work, even if it stung fiercely at odd moments. "I'll wait out the day and see if things have improved by nightfall."

She smiled. "I'm afraid it'll be nothing quite so heroic as a bit of straw and a crust of bread as you hide out in an attic or basement. I've got a guest room that you can have as long as you need it. I carry out a fair bit of business here in the house, but no one goes upstairs except Barrad, the maid, and myself, and the maid's not due for another day or two. As long as you're quiet, no one'll know you're here."

"Are you certain you're fine with this?"

"I've chosen my side, Geran," she said. "Marstel is the wizard's puppet, and I don't trust Rhovann as far as I could throw him. I might have to conceal our sympathies in public for now, but if House Sokol can help you win back your realm, we will. I haven't forgotten that you risked your life to rescue me from Kamoth Kastelmar, or that you stamped out the pirates who murdered my kinfolk and robbed our ships." She stood, slender and graceful in her thin gown, and pulled him to his feet. "Come, I'll show you where you can wash up and sleep. You might as well rest if you plan to set out at sunset."

She took a small lamp from the mantle and led him to the house's upper floor. He followed after her, carrying his sword belt over his shoulder. The second floor was as well-appointed as the rooms below, its wide hallway graced by half-a-dozen fine portraits. Nimessa's house was no palace or grand manor, but it was a comfortable residence for the head of House Sokol's concession in Hulburg. The merchant nobles of the Moonsea looked after their own, Geran decided.

Nimessa opened a door at the end of the hall, revealing a small room with a large canopy bed. She went to draw the curtains and quickly check that the linens were fresh. "It's been a month or two since anyone's used this room," she explained. "I hope you don't mind if it's just a little bit musty."

"It's far better than a hayloft or an attic, which is how I thought I might spend my day." He dropped his sword belt into a chair by the room's hearth, slipped his cloak from his shoulders, and turned to face her. "Nimessa . . . thank you."

"I don't suppose I've ever properly thanked you for saving me from the Black Moon pirates," she said with a smile. She leaned close to brush her perfect lips against his; the delightful sensation made him shiver down to the toes before she drew away. "How can I do any less for my brave rescuer?"

She walked to the door, leaving the small lamp on a chest nearby, and paused to smile at him over her shoulder. Then, as she opened the door to let herself out, Geran found himself moving after her without consciously deciding to do so; his legs simply carried him to her. His arms circled her waist and he buried his face in the soft golden tresses by the nape of her neck, drawing her to him. She gasped, and began to say something, but he reached up to turn her chin toward his face and covered her mouth with his. She hesitated, shivering in his arms, and then she responded, her breath warm in his mouth, her soft figure melting into him.

Once upon a time I kissed Mirya like this, he thought. For a moment he hesitated, too, surprised to find those memories surfacing when Nimessa sighed in his arms. That was a long time ago, Geran, he told himself. Ten years before, Mirya had been his first love, but he'd wanted something more out of life than the narrow confines of a small town at the edge of the wilds and the love of a girl whose simple dream was to live her life in the place where she'd been born. The rational part of him knew that Mirya couldn't ever love him as she once had, not after he'd abandoned her once. Whatever it was that his heart hoped for now, it wasn't fair to Mirya—or himself—to imagine that she might come to feel the same way about him. And if that was true, what was the point of keeping himself for her any longer?

Nimessa glanced up to him, sensing his hesitation. Deliberately he reached past Nimessa to push the half-open door shut, and kissed her again. Closing his eyes, he banished Mirya's ghost from his memory, abandoning himself to the moment.

NINE

21 Hammer, the Year of Deep Water Drifting (1480 DR)

Little was left of the Cyricist shrine. The thick masonry that comprised its outer walls had survived the fire intact, if somewhat blackened and burned, but it was only a shell now. The wooden beams supporting the building's roof had given way, leaving a mound of smoking rubble in the temple's interior. Several black-robed acolytes supervised gangs of guards and Cinderfist loyalists as they sifted through the ashes and ruin, searching for anything that might be salvaged from the destruction.

"So passes the Temple of the Wronged Prince," Rhovann murmured to himself, amused by the irony of it. Followers of Cyric claimed that their god was misrepresented by other faiths and treated with a shameful lack of respect—a divine martyr who suffered the jealousy and resentment of all other gods. He'd always felt that the Cyricists were overly quick to claim insult and injustice from those who failed to bow to their demands; their credo, such as it was, made it easy to rationalize any sort of setback or obstacle as the action of a petty, hostile world determined to deny them their due. But here he stood in the ashes of Cyric's house, and he had to admit that the followers of the Black Sun for once had a wrong for which redress was due.

Captain Edelmark emerged from a blackened archway, his fine cloak streaked with soot. The soldier paid it no mind. Edelmark was a Mulmasterite of thirty-five years or so, not very tall, with the buff features and coarse manners of a common driver or woodcutter. He was a seasoned mercenary who'd fought for every city in the Moonsea at one point or another in his long career. "Lord Rhovann?" he said. "I think we've found him."

"Very good," Rhovann replied, even though nothing about this catastrophe was good at all. The tall moon elf absently adjusted the hood of his cloak with his hand of silver, shielding his fine-featured face from the freezing drizzle—not quite snow, and not quite rain—that sifted down from the sky. He noticed that his boots of fine gray suede were now almost black with wet ash, and sighed. His clothes would smell of the fire for tendays, no matter how many times he had them washed.

"Come, Bastion," he said, motioning to the golem that waited silently at his side. The mage followed the Council Guard's commander into the ruin, wrinkling his nose at the thick smell of smoke that hung over the place. The hulking golem in its vast brown cassock and hood padded after him, the rubble shifting and crumbling under the weight of its footfalls.

Some of the interior walls still stood, while others had collapsed. Edelmark led him through the doorway that had once separated the public shrine from the priests' quarters and down a short hallway—there were two bodies here, guards in blackened mail and charred harnesses—to what might have once been a large suite. Rhovann had never set foot in the place before, so he had no real idea of whether this room had been Valdarsel's living space, his office, a secret shrine, or a bordello for the privileged initiates. Regardless, several Council Guards and underpriests stood around a pile of masonry near the center of the room. From beneath the debris jutted a blackened, skeletal arm, its bony fingers clutching a tarnished medallion. Rhovann leaned closer and recognized the skull-and-sunburst design of Valdarsel's holy symbol, but there was no way to be certain otherwise.

"Stand back," he warned the others nearby. "Bastion, remove these beams and uncover this body—carefully, if you please."

The golem stepped forward and seized an eight-inch-square beam that must have weighed the better part of five hundred pounds. Without a sound it lifted the fallen rafter, swiveled, and tossed it to the other side of the room, where it raised a great puff of ash amid a horrific clatter. Bastion took a step, selected another beam, and discarded that one as well. Then the golem stooped to pick up a large section of charred roofing, stepped back, and threw it aside. Rhovann sensed the humans around him shrinking from the pure physical power of his unliving servant, but he paid it no mind; he knew exactly what Bastion was capable of, and was no longer surprised by such demonstrations.

Beneath the roof section, the rest of the body was revealed—burned, crushed, but not incinerated as Rhovann had feared. He could still make out Valdarsel's distinctive robes, although the face was unrecognizable. Still, it was intact enough for his purposes. He motioned at the guards and lesser priests standing about and said, "Leave me. I do not wish to be disturbed for the next quarter hour. Edelmark, you may stay." The others withdrew.

"Your satchel, Bastion," Rhovann said. The golem shrugged a large leather bag from its shoulder and set it down at Rhovann's feet. Frowning as he kneeled in the ashes, Rhovann opened it and quickly found the implements and components he needed. Working swiftly, he set several black candles in a ring around the dead priest's body, and then sprinkled a carefully mixed oil over the corpse with a small aspergillum. Then he took a small black book from the satchel, opened it up, and began to read the words of a long and somewhat involved spell.

The skies, already gray and dark, seemed to darken even more, and the air grew still. Edelmark shifted nervously, uncomfortable in the presence of Rhovann's magic, but Bastion simply watched impassively. Rhovann rarely had reason to perform this particular spell, but Valdarsel's mysterious death presented an ideal opportunity. As he neared the end of his invocation, he sensed an intangible doorway of sorts taking shape in the air above the corpse. With his left hand he made a beckoning motion. "Valdarsel, return! I have questions for you!" he called into the cold stillness.

A spectral shape—a simple outline of pale mist, hardly visible even to Rhovann's magically attuned senses—slowly emerged from the doorway and sank down into the corpse. It stirred sluggishly, its burned tendons creaking and skin crackling. "What do you want of me?" the corpse said in a thin, hissing voice. "Let me rest!"

Does Valdarsel enjoy the eternal rewards promised by his god, or is he disenchanted with how Cyric keeps his promises? the mage wondered. The dead priest was of course beyond his recall, but Valdarsel's soul was not required for the ritual; the minor spirit he'd summoned out of the deathly realms had nothing whatsoever to do with the dead man. It was merely an animus for the priest's remains, a way to give the dead body a voice. Only things known to Valdarsel in life could be drawn out with this spell. Rhovann considered the questions he desired answers for, then addressed the corpse. "Who slew you?" he asked.

The dead jaws worked in silence before the answer came. "Geran Hulmaster."

Geran? Rhovann had to force himself to stay silent despite his surprise. If he spoke aloud, the spirit animating the corpse might take it as another question, and simply repeat its answer. So it was no common sellsword or assassin his runehelms had pursued the night before—it was the impudent swordmage, his most bitter nemesis, challenging his power in a brazen act of mayhem! Not only had Geran visited Hulburg in defiance of his family's exile, he'd murdered a high-ranking member of the Harmach's Council and a useful, if somewhat unreliable, ally of Rhovann's. The elf ground his teeth together and mastered his anger before proceeding to his next question. "Who was with him?"

"The tiefling . . . Sarth Khul Riizar," the corpse groaned. "No others that I saw before I died."

"I should have known," Rhovann murmured to himself. He'd known that Sarth was almost certainly a Hulmaster sympathizer, given the amount of help he'd provided to Geran when Geran was hunting the Black Moon corsairs. I should have driven him off too, he fumed. But the sorcerer had simply kept to himself and hadn't done anything to provoke suspicion, at least not until the attack on the Temple of the Wronged Prince. Rhovann believed he was Sarth's better in the arcane arts, but he hadn't been so confident that he'd been willing to directly confront Geran's friend without evidence of conspiracy. Clearly, Sarth's participation in the attack on the Cyricists changed that; as soon as he finished here he'd see to Sarth Khul Riizar. But he suspected that he'd find nothing more than an empty house if the tiefling wasn't stupid.

He returned his attention to the burned corpse at his feet. "Why did Geran attack you?" This was a little trickier, since it called for speculation, but the mage hoped that Valdarsel's corpse might retain enough resentment toward his slayer to cooperate.

The grisly thing did not answer for a long time, but just as Rhovann was about to give up, it stirred. "Vengeance," it said. "I ordered Larisse to destroy the Hulmasters in Thentia, and gave her gold to hire sellswords and scrolls to summon devils. For that Geran Hulmaster slew me."

Rhovann frowned, wondering which of Valdarsel's followers Larisse was. She might have been one of the assassins who died in the attack, of course. He'd been almost certain that Valdarsel was behind the attack at Lasparhall, although he'd also suspected House Veruna and the Crimson Chains of involvement in the clumsy debacle. It seemed that Geran Hulmaster had uncovered Valdarsel's hand behind the attack too. If it had been anybody else, Rhovann might have savored the sheer justice of Valdarsel dying at the hand of an adversary he'd underestimated; after all, *he'd* been foiled by Geran Hulmaster before, and there was a grim satisfaction in measuring himself by the quality of his enemies. "Did Geran tell you anything about his plans when you met him here?" he asked the corpse.

The corpse groaned again. "No. He only spoke of vengeance. Now let me rest."

"Very well." The mage straightened and brushed the soot from his robe. With a gesture he ended the ritual, severing the tenuous thread that imbued the corpse with its animating force. It fell still at once, nothing more than a dead body again. Rhovann absently rubbed at his right wrist, thinking about what he'd learned.

Edelmark looked down on the corpse, frowning in distaste. He cleared his throat and asked, "Are you finished with the high prelate's remains, Lord Rhovann?"

"Hmm? Oh yes, I have no further use for poor Valdarsel here . . . no, wait. I may very well need to speak with him again. Inform the surviving clerics that we will see to the high prelate's burial, and have the remains sent back to the castle."

"Yes, m'lord." The mercenary motioned to one of the Council Guards hovering nearby, and glanced around at the wet, smoking ashes and rubble. "It seems that Geran Hulmaster has much to answer for. I can't believe that he would be so foolhardy as to defy the harmach's edict and wantonly murder his councilors."

"I can," Rhovann muttered. He knew all too well that Geran was a man with more determination than sense at times, and Valdarsel had certainly provoked him. "I must speak with the harmach about my findings here. Have word sent to the other members of the Harmach's Council; there is to be an emergency session at three bells this afternoon. We must weigh our response to this attack."

Edelmark bowed, then marched off, calling for his messengers and guards. Rhovann gestured for Bastion to follow him, and made his way back out to the street. He climbed into his carriage while the golem took its place at the running board across the back like a gigantic footman, its weight testing the wooden springs. "Back to Griffonwatch," Rhovann instructed the driver; the carriage set out with a small jerk, rocking side to side as it clattered through the mud, slush, and uneven cobblestones toward the castle.

As it so happened, the occasion of an emergency council gathering was convenient. For many tendays now, Rhovann had been working to create a Maroth Marstel that could look after himself without constant guidance. The old Hulburgan lord was failing swiftly, his body worn by age and heavy drinking, his mind broken by months of control under Rhovann's enchantments. Rhovann kept the harmach of Hulburg safely locked away in his own chambers, too ill to see to his duties . . . but that was about to change. In a vat in his laboratory an alchemical copy of Maroth Marstel was almost ready for its debut, and the council's meeting would make for an excellent test. As soon as the coach halted in Griffonwatch's courtyard, Rhovann returned to his laboratory to see to scores of the final details involved with his rituals and alchemical processes.

A little before three hours after noon, he left his laboratory—sealing and warding it behind him, as he always did—and descended from his working space to the castle's great hall, which served as the meeting place of the Harmach's Council. He was pleased to note that his fellow councilors were already assembled, waiting for him. Their conversations faltered and they turned astonished looks up at the stair leading down into the room from the castle's upper floors.

Rhovann smiled and gave a slight bow as he stepped to one side. "My lords and ladies, may I present Harmach Maroth Marstel?"

His simulacrum of Marstel limped forward, raising his hand in greeting. The thing was a perfect copy of Marstel—or, to be more precise, Marstel as he might have appeared had he been enjoying his first days of good health after a long and debilitating illness. To lend credence to the idea that the harmach had simply been indisposed for a time, Rhovann had carefully added a hint of dark circles under the eyes, a little looseness to the flesh to suggest a loss of weight, and a slight shuffle to the footsteps. But the false Marstel's eyes were clear, and his smile was genuine enough.

"Ah, my good friends!" the false Marstel said in something close to the booming voice of the old lord. "It's been far too long, it has. But I'm glad to report that I am finally feeling myself again."

Rhovann made a show of offering his hand, which the old lord's duplicate refused. He made his way down the stairs, leaning a little on the balustrade as the wizard followed, ready to aid him if he faltered. The waiting councilors stood and applauded as the harmach took his seat at the head of the table. The moon elf moved around the table to his own place, where the master mage customarily sat. The false Marstel inclined his snowy head, accepting the applause of the assembled councilors and guards. "Most kind, most kind," he said. "Good Rhovann informs me that I'm still recovering and shouldn't weary myself too much yet, so let's get to our business."

He waited as the council members took their seats again, and looked over to Rhovann. "You'd best let the council hear what you had to tell me about the murder of Valdarsel, Rhovann."

"Of course, my lord harmach," Rhovann replied. He made a mental note to instruct the simulacrum to act with more bluster and bluntness; he was perhaps just a little too reasonable and mild-spoken for Maroth Marstel. He turned to face the rest of the council. "I investigated the remains of the Temple of the Wronged Prince at length. My divinations and questionings are quite conclusive: High Prelate Valdarsel was killed by none other than Geran Hulmaster, with the aid of the sorcerer Sarth Khul Riizar. I have carefully reviewed the reports of those of my guardians who were involved in the pursuit as they fled the scene. Unfortunately, the murderers vanished somewhere near the waterfront, and I cannot conclusively determine if they have fled Hulburg or not. They may still be here, sheltered by Hulmaster loyalists." He paused to study the reactions of the merchant leaders around the table before adding, "I will, of course, begin a new course of divinations immediately. If Geran and Sarth are still here, we'll unearth them quickly enough."

"There is also the question of those who helped Geran Hulmaster to enter the city, or sheltered him before his attack on Valdarsel," Captain Edelmark said. "Any such actions amount to high treason against the rightful harmach. If we fail to catch Hulmaster and his half-devil accomplice, we can make sure that those who aided them are suitably punished."

"Indeed," Marstel said. He shifted in his seat, leaning forward with a determined frown on his face. "To that very point, I'm instructing the Council Guard to begin an immediate crackdown on all Hulmaster loyalists or sympathizers, known or suspected. This brutal assassination, this fiendish arson, have forced my hand! All persons of suspect allegiance are to be closely questioned regarding their activities over the last two tendays; I want to know where they've been, who they've associated with, and what they've been saying to each other. All arms and armor are to be confiscated. Personal wealth or property that can't be adequately accounted for are to be confiscated as well; we'll smother this little rebellion before it spreads any further."

Old Wulreth Keltor, the keeper of keys, looked stricken. He was the only member who'd also served on Harmach Grigor's council, and his duties pertained to the Tower's treasury and administration. "Forgive me, my lord harmach," he said, "but such an action simply isn't countenanced in Hulburg's body of law."

The false Marstel waved aside Wulreth's objections. "And well I know it. I'll issue a decree to set it all down in black and white. But to put it simply, old friend, these are extraordinary times and they demand extraordinary measures. No effort can be spared to secure Hulburg from lawlessness and anarchy!"

"I'm afraid I share Master Keltor's concerns," Nimessa Sokol said. "How many people of suspect allegiance do you intend to move against, my lord? As a member of the Merchant Council, I am frankly worried about the effect a widespread confiscation of property would have on our interests. House Sokol's business in Hulburg will be sorely damaged if our customers and suppliers are impoverished or run out of town arbitrarily."

"Speak for yourself," Captain Miskar Bann retorted. He was the ranking member of Mulmaster's House Veruna present in Hulburg, a big, round-faced mercenary who had a mouthful of gold teeth and wore an iron brace on one knee. The Verunas had been evicted from Hulburg after their role in Sergen Hulmaster's attempted coup, and they'd eagerly provided mercenaries to help Marstel and the Cinderfists seize control of Hulburg during the Black Moon troubles a few months later. Of course, they'd profited greatly by scavenging property confiscated from old Hulburg and awarded to Cinderfists. No doubt Captain Bann was already salivating at the new possibilities in Marstel's plan. "I'm a member of the Merchant Council too. Everyone knows you've got a soft spot for the Hulmasters, Lady Sokol. I think the harmach's men ought to begin by searching your compound."

Nimessa flushed. "The laws of concession prohibit any such intrusion."

"Do you have something to hide?" Bann taunted.

"Do you?" she retorted. "If Sokol opens its gates to the Council Guard, I'll insist that *every* coster in Hulburg does the same. I doubt that Geran Hulmaster is hiding in the Veruna compound, but I wonder whether you've got any stolen goods or slaves stashed away in your mistress's storehouses, Miskar. Trading in slaves is still against the harmach's law, is it not?"

Rhovann studied the half-elf thoughtfully. As Miskar Bann observed, it was certainly possible that Geran and his sorcerer friend had been aided by one of the other merchant costers. Clearly House Sokol was not without sympathies for the Hulmaster cause, but it was also possible that a neutral company such as the Double Moon Coster might have aided the Hulmasters in order to weaken the Cinderfists. Unfortunately Rhovann had to exercise care in making any such accusations against one of the great Houses, lest he drive the merchant costers into closing ranks and defending their precious laws of concession. On the other hand, he had means to quietly spy out the Sokol compound without any public accusation necessary.

Miskar Bann bristled, but Captain Edelmark cleared his throat and spoke before the merchant lord. "The Council Guard will, of course, implement the lord harmach's instructions immediately," he said.

"Disloyalty and sedition cannot be tolerated. But I fear that we are dealing with a symptom, not the disease. The ultimate source of this incipient rebellion is the Hulmaster enclave in Thentia. As long as the Hulmasters have a safe haven in Thentia to rebuild their army and foment trouble, we are threatened. If we want to put down this rebellion not just for this month but forever, we must deprive the Hulmasters of their refuge outside our borders!"

"What do you suggest, Captain?" the false Marstel asked.

"My lord, I propose that we muster the strongest army we can gather and march on Lasparhall. We can destroy the Hulmasters' army before it organizes, seize their supplies and arms, and raze their barracks and the old manor for good measure. The Hulmaster cause could never recover from such a blow."

Subtlety is not Edelmark's strong suit, Rhovann reflected. He caught Marstel's eye and gave an imperceptible shake of the head. Marstel frowned, weighing the captain's words, as Rhovann leaned forward to answer for him. "A bold plan, Captain," the elf said to Edelmark, "but I can't see a way to do what you suggest without making an enemy of High Lord Vasil and Thentia. Perhaps a show of strength would convince the high lord to stop coddling our enemies—but it might instead drive him to throw in with the Hulmasters entirely. For now Thentia is staying out of our quarrel, and that favors us far more than a Thentian intervention. Each day the Hulmasters remain in Thentia, their position grows weaker and ours grows stronger. We should be in no hurry to change that."

Marstel nodded. "Well said, Rhovann," he rumbled. "But, Edelmark, you are right to bring the threat of the Hulmaster army to our attention. We must be ready to strike and strike hard the moment they sally out from behind Thentia's skirts! I want you to make all necessary preparations to meet an attack from Thentia, no matter how improbable it may seem. And see if our agents can't spread a little gold around in Thentia's taverns to find out what the Hulmaster's soldiers think they're up to, as long as we're waiting."

Edelmark bowed. "As you wish, my lord harmach. I will review our defenses immediately, and redouble our efforts to hire more sellswords abroad." He smiled cruelly. "After all, we may have an unexpected windfall in the form of confiscations from those who are disloyal to the throne. I see no reason why they shouldn't contribute to the common defense."

Rhovann looked over to the simulacrum, and decided that it would not be wise to test it too aggressively in its debut. "My lord harmach, we should be mindful of your need for rest," he said. "You are still recovering, after all."

The false Marstel nodded. "Of course, of course," he said. "I confess that I am tiring already. I trust the council to work out all the necessary details of the decisions we've made today." He pushed himself to his feet, and the councilors around the table quickly stood as well, bowing as the old lord made his way to the stairs.

"The Harmach's Council is adjourned," Rhovann said. "Captain Edelmark, I'll speak with you soon." Then he hurried over to join his simulacrum and made a show of helping the harmach climb the stairs back toward the private quarters of the castle. Behind them, chairs scraped and voices murmured as the councilors and their various clerks and seconds began to leave or huddled together, discussing the harmach's decrees.

All in all, a very satisfactory debut, the mage reflected. The simulacrum had performed flawlessly with only the most minimal preparation and prompting. The real advantage of the creature was that it could incorporate his direction into its own reason and judgment, masquerading as Marstel while working toward the goals he specified without the constant enchantments and contest of will he'd had to endure in keeping the original Marstel under control.

"You are a much more tractable Marstel," he remarked as they came to the upper court. "Go about your business; I'll be in my quarters if you have need of me."

The false Marstel nodded once and set out for the library, which served as the harmach's office. Rhovann watched it leave, and glanced up across the castle's upper courtyard to the Harmach's Tower. Given the unqualified success of his simulacrum, a feeble old madman locked up in his chambers there had just become nothing more than a tedious liability. As long as Maroth Marstel remained alive, there was always a slight chance that someone might somehow stumble across the inconvenient fact that there were now *two* Harmach Marstels.

He allowed himself a small smile; after all, he'd been looking forward to this moment for months. "And now for a little bit of tidying up," he said to himself.

TEN

24 Hammer, the Year of Deep Water Drifting (1480 DR)

A winter fog hung heavily over Hulburg as Geran dressed himself for the journey to Thentia. A Sokol caravan was setting out along the Coastal Way in half an hour, and he intended to slip out of the town by playing the part of one of the caravan guards. Nimessa had provided him with a surcoat in Sokol's colors of blue and black, and the cold weather gave him the perfect excuse to cover most of his face with a scarf and hood. She'd quietly arranged with her arms-captain for him to join the caravan's mounted escort; the fellow didn't know who he was smuggling out of Hulburg, and Geran intended to keep it that way as long as possible. He checked his appearance one last time in the standing mirror in Nimessa's room, and decided that it was good enough for all but the closest inspection. Of course, that depended on whether they met any of Rhovann's constructs on the way out of town, and whether the helmed guardians had some means of seeing through common disguises or not.

In that case, I'll break ranks and make a gallop for it, he told himself. He adjusted his sword belt one last time, slung a pair of saddlebags with a typical sellsword's traveling kit stuffed inside over his shoulder, and trotted downstairs. Nimessa waited for him in the foyer, wearing a dress of green velvet with high boots—always a good idea in Hulburg's streets at this time of year—and a heavy fur mantle against the weather.

"It seems you're ready," she said. She glanced out the window toward the compound's courtyard, where the mule teams were being hitched to their wagons, and looked back to him. "Are you certain you want to leave today? You can stay longer if you feel you need to."

He sensed the unspoken invitation in her offer, and hesitated. He liked Nimessa very much, and it was certainly true that the last two days of hiding in her home had been very pleasant indeed . . . but strangely enough the time he'd spent with her had finally dispelled the mystery and confusion he'd wrestled with in his heart for months now. Nimessa Sokol wasn't the one he loved, no matter how desirable he found her, and he thought that her heart wasn't entirely given to him either. To stay longer and draw out their temporary entanglement would only make that more clear without changing the essential nature of his heart, or hers. Framing his answer in the simplest and most comfortable terms he could find, he said, "I'd better go while I can. You might not have another caravan setting out for a couple of tendays or more. And I don't want to endanger you any more than I already have. You've risked too much on my behalf already."

"I understand," she said, and her wry smile showed him that she did understand. She leaned forward to kiss him on the cheek, and drew a deep breath. "As for the question of danger, I'll be the judge of my own risks. I'll send word to our representatives in Thentia to extend you any help they can if you need to slip back into Hulburg again."

"I appreciate the offer," he said, "but the next time I return to Hulburg will be the last. There will be no more retreats. One way or the other, I'll settle with Rhovann and Marstel and put things right. I have to."

Nimessa nodded, and drew back. "We'll help as we can, then. A good journey to you, Geran."

He opened the door and stepped outside. The mists were cold and damp, the sort of weather that would slowly chill a traveler all day long until no fire or bedroll could warm him when he finally stopped. He made his way over to the mount waiting for him and swung himself up into the saddle as Nimessa went to have a few final words with the caravan master. Commerce in and out of Hulburg slowed to a trickle in the depths of winter, but the mines in the Galena foothills worked around the year, and so Hulburg's smelters did as well; the Sokol wagons were loaded with silver ingots, bar iron, and a few furs taken by trappers in the high country. With a jingle of harness and the nickering of the horses, the caravan passed under the gates to the Sokol tradeyard and into Hulburg's streets.

Geran watched carefully for any sign that Council Guards or helmed guardians were waiting to swoop down and seize him as he left the concession's shelter, but no enemies charged in as they left. The master turned the caravan toward the left and began to climb up Keldon Head toward the Coastal Way beyond, and still no hue or cry came. But up ahead in the fog Geran spotted two tall gray figures looming—a pair of the helmed guardians, standing motionless on either side of the road leaving the town. He surreptitiously drew his scarf up over the lower part of his face and tugged down on his hood. Slowly the caravan creaked and plodded ahead, and he found himself thinking again of the whispers he'd heard about the things and Sarth's speculations about the creatures speaking with each other. Do they see as men do through those blind helms of theirs? Geran wondered. Or do they somehow sense identity without recognizing facial features?

He tightened his grip on the reins, ready to spur his mount into a desperate gallop if the helmed guardians challenged him, and kept his eyes fixed on the back of the horse's head as he rode past the gray constructs. But they did not stir as he went by. Resisting the urge to look back, Geran breathed a small sigh of relief. Apparently the creatures weren't mind readers of some kind, which was a small comfort at least.

For the next four or five miles, Geran kept listening for the sound of galloping hoofbeats coming up the road behind the caravan, but no cries of pursuit or bands of Council Guard riders came. Finally he allowed himself to relax, and began to spend more time keeping an eye on the sodden landscape around them. Rhovann is clever and ruthless, but he's not omniscient, he reminded himself. He can be beaten . . . although how in the world the Hulmaster army could deal with scores of guardians that seemed almost impossible to hurt, Geran couldn't say.

He stayed with the caravan for two full days as it crept along the Coastal Way toward Thentia, just in case they met some far-ranging patrol of Council Guards or spies of Rhovann's. On the morning of the third day he informed the caravan master that he was departing, and rode on ahead to spare himself another day of plodding alongside the slow-moving wagons. An easy day's ride brought him to the gates of Lasparhall in the late afternoon, as the fog finally lifted and the weather began to grow cold again.

At the manor's front door, he swung himself down from his horse, and pushed his soaked hood back from his face. He rubbed at his back, glad to be done with the day's travel.

Two Shieldsworn stood guard by the front door. They came to attention as they recognized him. "The Lord Hulmaster's returned!" one called inside. He motioned for them to stand easy as stablehands trotted out to look after his mount and he climbed wearily up the steps to the door.

He was met there by a stocky, round-faced soldier. "Welcome back, Lord Geran," Sergeant Kolton said. The blunt old sergeant gave Geran a quick grin, and then turned to the younger warriors nearby. "Well, don't just stand there. Give the Lord Hulmaster a hand with his saddlebags!"

"It's good to be back, Sergeant Kolton," Geran answered. He paused. "I thought Kara was going to make a captain of you."

"Beggin' my lord's pardon, but I turned her down. I've spent the last thirty years complainin' about gentlemen of rank. It wouldn't be a decent thing to do to an old veteran like me. So Lady Kara decided to make me sergeant-major instead, and give me command o' the House Guard."

Geran smiled, and set a sympathetic hand on Kolton's armored shoulder. He'd known that Kara intended to reorganize the Shieldsworn and make some promotions. "Congratulations, Sergeant-Major. I'll sleep easier knowing that you've got the watch." He looked around the manor's front hall, and asked, "Have you had any word of Sarth Khul Riizar yet?"

"Aye, m'lord. He arrived three days ago." Kolton's expression grew fierce. "We heard from the sorcerer how the two of you dealt with the Cyricist behind the harmach's murder. That was well done, Lord Geran. Your da would've been proud."

"My thanks, Kolton. Is Kara around?"

"She's down at the encampment drilling the field companies. I expect she'll be back within the hour, though. Mistress Siever usually sets out dinner at six bells."

"Good. I'll see her then. In the meantime, I'm going to bathe and change. It's a hard ride from Hulburg at this time of year."

He went to his chambers and rewarded himself with a long soak in a warm bathtub, letting the hot water take away the bone-deep chill of the winter road. When he finished, he dressed and went down to the Hulmasters' private dining room, anticipating his first good meal in three days. The manor was quieter without Natali and Kirr around, and he decided that he missed his young cousins; he hoped they were faring well in the Selûnite temple where they'd been sent for safekeeping. He arrived just as the servants were beginning to set the board with a roast of beef, a carved goose, and all the trimmings. His resolve weakened from a long day in the saddle, he headed over to help himself to a slice of beef even though the dinner hadn't been announced yet.

"Now why is it that you can get away with that?" a familiar voice asked. "I've tried that two or three times in the last couple of days, and Mistress Siever has threatened me with bodily harm on each occasion."

Geran looked around, setting down his purloined plate. "Hamil! I wasn't expecting to see you here!"

The halfling stood up from where he'd been sitting by the room's great fireside (he fairly well vanished in the human-sized armchair, so Geran forgave himself for not having noticed someone sitting there) and eyed the spread the Hulmaster cooks were setting out. He was a lean, wiry fellow a smidgen over four feet in height, dressed in a fine burgundy doublet, cream-colored breeches, and a wide-brimmed hat capped by a bright feather; Hamil had always prided himself on his sartorial splendor. "I arrived two days after you'd set out for Hulburg again. I thought about chasing after you, but decided that you'd probably be hard to find. Besides, this Moonsea winter is no fit weather for any reasonable man to fare abroad."

Geran recovered his plate, added a wedge of cheese and some bread for Hamil, and joined his friend at the fireside. "How go things in Tantras?" he asked.

"Well enough. There's a newly organized coster down in Turmish that's buying up all the damned cotton, which is making it hard for us to place our own orders without paying twice what it's worth, but I might just let 'em keep it this year and see if they've got any idea of how to get it to the northern markets. Business as usual, in other words." He looked over to Geran, and his expression grew serious. "I was sorry to hear about the harmach. I set out from Tantras as soon as I heard about his murder, but travel's slow in winter, and I couldn't make it here in time for the funeral. Your uncle was a fine old fellow; I liked him a lot."

"I know it," Geran answered. "He didn't deserve to die under an assassin's knife."

"I hear that you've already delivered something of a reply."

"I did. I asked Sarth for his help, and together we paid a small visit to the Temple of the Wronged Prince." Geran rubbed at his right fist, remembering the sensation of the steel shuddering in his grip as he drove it through the cleric's black heart. "Valdarsel won't trouble my family again, nor anyone else."

"Good," Hamil replied, a fierce smile crossing his face. He'd always been quick to answer an insult with a blade or blood with blood; he wasn't about to lecture Geran on the hollowness of revenge. "I'm sorry I missed the chance to help you gut that murdering bastard. In fact, now that I think about it, I'm a little angry with you for killing him without me."

Geran offered the halfling the plate he'd filled from the sideboard by way of an apology. He knew Hamil would have gone to Hulburg without a word of complaint. They'd first met almost ten years earlier, when Geran—then a footloose freebooter just setting out from Hulburg—had fallen in with the Company of the Dragon Shield, an adventuring band traveling through the Vast. After the Dragon Shields had parted ways, the two of them had bought shares in the Red Sail Coster in Tantras, working together until Geran's travels had carried him to Myth Drannor . . . and after he'd been exiled from the realm of the elves, Hamil had cheerfully made room for him with the Red Sail again until Jarad Erstenwold's murder had brought him back to Hulburg. "You can help me deal with Rhovann, then," he said. "I can't believe that Valdarsel would have moved against us here without Marstel's consent, and from what I hear, Marstel can't count to five without Rhovann's help."

"Ah, there you are." Sarth appeared at the door, and gave Geran a stern look. "You certainly took your time in escaping. We have all been very anxious about your fate."

"I found myself boxed in after we parted," the swordmage answered. "I had to hide for a couple of days before slipping out of town, and then I joined a Sokol caravan on the Coastal Way for cover."

"Hmmph. I exhausted my flying spell a few miles outside Hulburg and walked the rest of the way with no provisions or bedroll, very nearly freezing to death before I reached civilization again." The tiefling scowled at Geran. "I sincerely hope you were hiding in some cold, dank hayloft with nothing to eat while I was trudging back to Thentia."

Geran shrugged. "It was something like that," he said carefully. Hamil must have sensed his evasions, for the halfling snorted and regarded Geran skeptically. Fortunately the swordmage was saved from explaining his escape from Hulburg in more detail by the arrival of his cousin Kara, who bustled into the room, doffing her heavy cloak and shaking off the water that had beaded over it.

Geran rose and went to greet her, giving her a quick embrace. "It's good to see you, Kara," he said. "It seems that you've got things well in hand here."

"Not so well that you can plan to run off again and leave it all on my shoulders," she replied. But she gave him a lopsided smile as she said it. "It's good that you're back. We have a lot to talk about."

"After dinner," he promised. "I'm sorely in need of a good hot meal, and I'd wager that you are too if you've been outside with the troops all day."

"Go ahead and start. I want to dry off and change first."

"You don't have to say that twice," Hamil remarked. He jumped to his feet and made a beeline for the smorgasbord. Geran and Sarth followed suit. Geran helped himself to a heaping plate—it always amazed him how hungry being outside on a cold day could make one—and Hamil did likewise on general halfling principle. After a short time Kara rejoined them, wearing a riding dress with a tailored leather jacket instead of the heavy armor she'd had on before. Over their dinner Geran related a somewhat abridged version of his visit to Hulburg, including his conversation with Mirya, his strike against the Temple of the Wronged Prince with Sarth, and their efforts to evade Rhovann's constructs afterward. He admitted to taking shelter in the Sokol compound—which brought a grumble from Sarth, and a raised eyebrow from Hamil even though he left out any hint of the hours he'd passed with Nimessa—and finished by recounting how the helmed guardians seemed to be watching the roads out of Hulburg now. When he finished, the four of them helped themselves to mugs of mulled wine and retired to the seats close by the fireplace.

Geran propped his feet up on a stool and sipped at the warm wine. *If I mean to get anything more done before morning, I'd better do it soon,* he realized. He was more than ready to retire for the evening. "You've heard the tale of my visit to Hulburg," he said to Kara. "How are matters proceeding here?"

"Well enough," she replied, "but our purse isn't deep enough to keep our men fed and quartered much longer. We *have* to march in Ches or Tarsakh, because by Mirtul I doubt we'll have an army any longer. On the bright side, I secured the Icehammers for a couple of months." She made a face. "I'm afraid that will probably cost us Lasparhall. I had to promise the manor and the grounds to Kendurkkel Ironthane as security against the contract's fighting bonuses."

Geran winced. He wished she hadn't done that; if their throw of the dice failed, Lasparhall would have at least provided a modest inheritance for Natali and Kirr, a minor title for the family to cling to in generations to come. *There's no point arguing it,* he told himself. *I told Kara to do as she must in order to raise an army and then left it all in her hands, so I've got no cause to complain with how she does what I ask.*

"How does your army compare against Marstel's forces?" Hamil asked.

"With the Icehammers included, we'll march with a little less than eight hundred soldiers," Kara answered. "That's a fair match for the Council Guard and any merchant detachments that Marstel can muster. If we count the Cinderfist gangs, I guess we'd be a little outnumbered, but I'm confident in our ability to beat the Council Guard and a hodgepodge of mercenary companies and ruffians in any kind of open battle."

"You're forgetting about Rhovann's helmed guardians," said Geran. "We didn't take them into account before, but I think we have to now. If Marstel's sellswords have enough of the guardians backing them up, we might not be able to beat them."

Sarth nodded in agreement. "The constructs would be formidable foes on the field of battle."

Kara leaned forward, looking from Geran to Sarth. "How many of these helmed guardians are there?"

Geran thought for a moment. He'd seen as many as ten at one time, counting the group that he and Sarth had skirmished with as others were closing in. Others had been posted in pairs at each of the bridges, by the Council Hall, and likely in other strategic spots throughout the town, and Mirya had mentioned that there were more in Griffonwatch. Presumably the creatures didn't sleep or rest; they were automatons, and wouldn't need to be rotated on or off duty. "My *guess* is that Rhovann's got at least twenty of the creatures scattered throughout the town, and I wouldn't be surprised if he has that many more guarding the castle. He might have as many as fifty or sixty."

"That matches my estimate," Sarth said.

"How did they fight?" Hamil asked.

"They're not quick or skillful, but they're as strong as ogres, and they're damned hard to kill," Geran replied. "Nothing seems to hurt them much. They don't even bother to defend themselves, really. I think they'd cover ground fast too—they're likely tireless, or close to it."

"So, in other words, we'd better assume that the Council Guard is backed up by fifty trolls, or creatures that fight much like trolls?" said Kara.

Geran grimaced. He hadn't thought of it in such a way, but Kara's comparison was fairly accurate. Trolls were big, strong, slow, and likewise damned difficult to kill. And they knew it, of course, so they wouldn't hesitate to throw themselves into a hedge of spears to win a fight. By most measures a single troll was worth five human footsoldiers in a battle, which meant that even twenty or thirty of Rhovann's monsters could be a very formidable force in the field. "Yes," he said. "They'd be a lot like trolls."

Sarth shook his head. "Perhaps physically," he said, "but I think you would be wise to remember that the helmed guards seem to act in concert. They might prove even more dangerous on the battlefield than their sheer strength and resilience would indicate. For example, they might relay messages over great distances, or react far more swiftly to orders than simple trolls would."

"If that's the case, I don't see how we can risk a pitched battle without *some* way to deal with these helmed guardians," Kara said. "It would be foolish to march out just to put ourselves where Marstel and Rhovann can finish us off. Maybe we could draw them out with skirmishing, or drive Marstel out of power by blocking commerce long enough . . ."

"There must be some weakness you can exploit," Hamil offered. "Trolls fear fire; it's one of the few things that can hurt them. If you think you might have to deal with trolls, you make certain you've got the means to burn them. Sarth, isn't there some magic you could employ against them? A counterspell or disjunction to remove their animating force?"

The tiefling spread his hands. "Given time, I am confident I could find a spell that could disable one physically. If nothing else, I might disintegrate enough of its mass to render it useless. But I know nothing about the magic that animates them and bends them to Rhovann's will. My own arts simply do not deal in necromancy or shadowstuff, and that is precisely what powers the helmed guardians."

"I don't suppose we know any necromancers?" Hamil remarked. No one answered, and he gave a small shrug. "Well, in the absence of a magical counter, I'd wager that you could immobilize one of Rhovann's creatures if you cut it apart. Zombies ignore pain and don't bleed, but it's simple enough, if a little messy, to make sure their limbs don't work anymore. These helmed guardians must have the same sort of mechanical connection of muscle to bone—or whatever they use in place of muscle and bone—that living creatures would have, or they couldn't move. It's not like they're specters or ghosts."

Ghosts and necromancers . . . Geran stared into the wine in his goblet, thinking. He found himself remembering the desperate night when Sergen Hulmaster had summoned an army of spectral warriors—servants of the lich Aesperus, the King in Copper—to attack Griffonwatch in a bid to wipe out the rest of the family and seize power. An undead mage of dreadful power, Aesperus had claimed dominion over the barrowfields of the Highfells between Thentia and Hulburg for centuries. Geran had met the lich once on a cold night out in the barrowfields, and Aesperus had recognized him as a Hulmaster. And later on, the lich had used the slain crewmen of the luckless *Moonshark* to deliver a cryptic warning to Geran about the doom approaching the House of the harmach.

Harmach Grigor said something about Aesperus before he died, he recalled. "An oath to be kept in Rivan's crypt," he murmured aloud, frowning into his wine. What had Grigor meant by that?

The others looked at him strangely. "What did you say?" Kara asked.

He looked up, and spoke more clearly. "I think we do know a necromancer. The question is whether or not he'd help us . . . and at what price."

ELEVEN

1 Alturiak, the Year of Deep Water Drifting (1480 DR)

For the next few days, Geran worried at the mystery of Grigor Hulmaster's final words. He'd all but forgotten them in those confusing days as the family had struggled with the questions of how to carry on after Grigor's death. Immediately after the funeral he'd fixed his mind on his need to avenge the harmach's murder, focusing all his attention on the deadly dangerous game of threading his way through Hulburg's streets and shadows without making some error or blundering into his enemies' hands. And finally he'd been more than a little distracted by his interlude with Nimessa Sokol and the indecipherable yearnings in his own heart as he made his way back home. Now, for the first time in half a month, he found himself looking past the exigencies of the moment toward the confrontation looming ahead . . . and every time he closed his eyes and tried to envision the reckoning that drew closer each day, he couldn't shake the nagging sense that Grigor's words about the King in Copper were important.

Part of the riddle was fairly obvious to Geran; Rivan was the first lord of the Hulmaster line. He'd come to power in Hulburg almost four hundred years earlier, right around the time that Aesperus had ruled over his short-lived kingdom of Thentur. Unfortunately, he had little idea what Grigor had meant about an oath, or any idea of where Rivan's crypt might lie. Much of old Hulburg had been destroyed by the sackings early in the fourteenth century, and further damaged by the catastrophic emergence of changeland in the form of the Arches or the Spires later in that century. There was an excellent chance that Rivan Hulmaster's burial place simply didn't exist anymore, which would seem to be an insuperable obstacle to keeping any oath there, unless it was a clue not intended to be taken literally.

Geran prowled the warm hallways of Lasparhall, he rode over the snow-covered hills that surrounded the manor, he sparred with Kara and Hamil, he debated with Sarth a dozen magical theories about the powers of Rhovann's construct army and ways the things might be defeated. He even spent a few hours with Sarth at the tower of the mage's guild in Thentia, paying a handsome fee for the privilege of poring through musty old spellbooks and tomes of arcane lore in the hope of learning more about their foe's defenses. He returned to Lasparhall little wiser for the effort; nothing he'd found about Aesperus in the guild's stacks made any mention of an oath or hinted at anything more about Rivan Hulmaster than he'd already known. He lay awake for an hour or more that night, replaying again and again the last few things his uncle had said to him.

The next morning, he found his steps leading him up to the suite Grigor had used. The rooms were still unoccupied; the chamberlain Dostin Hillnor had urged Geran to take the suite, as he was the head of the family now, but Geran hadn't wanted to yet. He looked around at the room, made up neatly but still palpably empty, and frowned as he recalled that last desperate struggle against the Cyricist assassins and their summoned devils. He sighed and sat in an armchair by one of the windows.

"Still stumped?" Hamil leaned in the doorway, looking over the room.

Geran nodded. "It's important, I can feel it. But I can't make any more sense of what my uncle meant."

"It might have been nothing, Geran. He was mortally wounded when he spoke, wasn't he?"

"He was. But I think he was trying to tell me something about Aesperus. There's an old bargain between the harmachs and the King in Copper, you know. That's why the harmach's law was so stringent about opening barrows or crypts in the Hulmaster domains. But I don't know the details of the arrangement."

"If you want to speak to Aesperus, you could go out and break into a barrow or two," Hamil pointed out. "Sooner or later he'd respond, wouldn't he?"

"Possibly," Geran admitted. "But I'd rather not bring him to me by doing something that offends him. If my uncle knew something about the King in Copper that I don't, I'd like to figure out what it was before I risk drawing his attention to me again."

"I don't suppose I understand why it's so important to deal with Aesperus," Hamil replied. "You and Sarth know enough about Rhovann's creations to take them into account. Assume they're trouble and lay your plans around the idea of avoiding them or drawing them away from the crux of the fight. Wouldn't that be sufficient?"

"That assumes the helmed guardians are the only surprise that Rhovann's prepared for us," Geran said. "Rhovann's magic is the single most formidable threat to our plans to retake Hulburg. The more I think about it, the more certain I am that any attack we launch without some counter to his defenses will fail."

"Sarth's a very competent sorcerer," Hamil pointed out. "Are you sure that he couldn't defeat Rhovann in a spell duel?"

Geran shook his head. "No, that's not what I'm worried about. I think Sarth could very well defeat Rhovann in a straightforward contest. After all, I defeated Rhovann once in a duel. But he's grown more powerful than he was a couple of years ago in Myth Drannor—or revealed more of the power he already wielded. Besides, his true strength doesn't necessarily lie in simply flinging battle spells. His power lies in subtle enchantment and spells that might take him months to weave. He's had half a year to prepare for an attack exactly like the one we're launching in a few tendays. I think we have to do something he doesn't expect."

"So you seriously propose to call on that dreadful old King in Copper for help?" Hamil shuddered. "I was there when you met him, Geran. He isn't a friendly sort. Why do you think he'd consent to help us instead of slaying you with some awful curse just for the temerity of asking?"

"Because Sergen managed to strike a bargain with him." Geran stood over the spot where Grigor had breathed his last, looking down at the cold flagstones. They'd been scrubbed clean, of course, but those last moments were starkly clear in his memory. The harmach had been lying on his back, his head near the corner of the trunk against the wall. He'd looked off past Geran, reaching out weakly with his hand . . . "Somehow he summoned Aesperus and convinced the lich to hear him out. He knew about the *Infiernadex* because Darsi Veruna told him that Sarth was looking for it, so Sergen knew that he had a chance to get his hands on something that Aesperus might value. And Aesperus honored his end of that bargain when the book finally fell into his hands."

"So how did Sergen summon Aesperus?"

"I think that might have been what Uncle Grigor was trying to tell me at the end," Geran answered. "I know he trusted Sergen implicitly before Sergen's true colors became obvious, but still, I doubt that Grigor would have *told* Sergen what he knew. After all, he didn't choose to tell Kara or me at any point in the last few months until he was within moments of death, even though he *knew* that Sergen had dealt with the King in Copper."

Hamil frowned in thought. "You think Sergen figured out something or stole something your uncle intended to keep secret until he passed it to the next harmach?"

"Exactly. And if it was that important, I think Grigor would have brought it out of Griffonwatch when he fled, and kept it somewhere close by here in Lasparhall." Geran's eye rested on the trunk again. Could it be that simple? He took two steps over to the small chest, dragged it a little way out from the foot of the bed, and kneeled by it, but when he tried the latch, he found that it was locked. "Hmmm. Hamil, I don't suppose you'd have a look at this for me?"

The halfling sighed. "It's a misuse of my talents to have me break into your uncle's nightshirts," he muttered. But he fished a small pick out of a pocket in his waistcoat, and kneeled in front of the old chest as Geran moved aside. A moment's deft probing in the lock released the catch with an audible click. "I think we can safely assume your uncle didn't fit his trunks with spring-loaded daggers or poisoned needles," he remarked, but Geran noticed that he stood up and moved just a little to one side before he opened the lid—the hard lessons of a long past adventuring career remained with him, or so it seemed. Nothing but folded blankets greeted their eyes.

Hamil gave Geran a pained look, but Geran began to empty the chest, setting the blankets aside. Near the bottom of the chest he found a muslin-wrapped book; he lifted it out and carefully unwrapped it. The thing was musty with age, its vellum pages stiff and yellowed, and it was bound in thick black leather. On the cover small Dethek runes of tarnished silver had been hammered into the leather. Geran brushed his fingertips over the old tome, and he raised an eyebrow at his halfling friend.

"Fine. If you'd been truly clever, it wouldn't have taken you two tendays to figure out that your uncle wanted you to look in there," Hamil said. "I don't read Dwarvish. What's the cover say?"

"It's not Dwarvish. It's old Damaran, which used the Dwarvish runes. It says 'The Book of the Harmachs, Lords of Hulburg.' It's something of a family history."

"You've seen it before?"

"Yes, on several occasions. It was one of my uncle's prized possessions. When I was a lad he'd sometimes show me different parts of it." He smiled a little at the old memories; he'd been very impressed as a small boy by the size and age of the tome, and the care with which his uncle handled it. He flipped it open, turning the pages gently. It was a disorganized collection of old letters, genealogies, records of procla-mations and patents of nobility, illustrations and maps, essays on the family history . . . whatever the harmachs of old had seen fit to save or write down for those who would follow. He noticed that many pages toward the book's end were written on new vellum in his uncle's hand, including a fairly extensive index. "Books were his great love. He should have been a scholar," he murmured.

"Are there any spells in there? Rituals? Other things that might explain why your uncle thought it was so important?" Hamil asked.

"I'll tell you if I find any," Geran replied. He closed the book with care, and carried it to the door. "Excuse me, Hamil—I think I've got some reading to do."

He retreated to the house's library, threw a couple of logs on the fire, and settled down in one of the armchairs by the fireplace to carefully peruse the Book of the Harmachs. One of his old tutors had taught him long before that the best way to read a book was to start with the first page, proceeding through introductions and prefaces with the same care he'd spend in the body of the book, and Geran had never abandoned the habit; he was a very deliberate reader. He spent the rest of the afternoon engaged in his task, losing himself in the stories of people dead for centuries, the glimpses of a Hulburg in the days when it had been a great city several times the size of the realm Grigor had ruled over, the records of old tragedies and lost wars that had reduced the harmachs' domain to a desolate ruin in the decades before the Spellplague and its gradual resettlement. Dinnertime came and went, and Geran absently ate a little bread and sliced roast that the mistress of the kitchens had sent to him.

An hour before midnight, he found what he was looking for in a chapter added by his great-grandfather, Angar Hulmaster. A hundred years earlier, Angar had been forced to open the crypt of the old Hulmasters by tomb robbers, and he'd visited the crypt of Rivan, learning the truth of the family's origins. Not long after that he'd encountered Aesperus the lich, the first Hulmaster to do so in centuries. Geran read his great-grandfather's account in amazement, then immediately reread it to make sure he'd understood it correctly. When he finished, he set the book down and went to stand by the fireplace, gazing into the flames as he grappled with what he'd learned.

The Hulmasters were the only living kin of Aesperus, the King in Copper. And the lich permitted Hulburg to exist only because Angar had promised to keep the places of the dead in the Highfells unspoiled.

In the margins of a drawing next to Angar's account—a drawing of Rivan's sarcophagus—an invocation was scrawled in a shaky hand. "An oath that must be kept in Rivan's crypt," Geran murmured. He took a blank piece of parchment and carefully copied down the words of the invocation, deliberately avoiding speaking them aloud. When he finished, he tucked it into his pocket, closed the Book of the Harmachs, and protected it with a minor warding spell before returning it to its wrappings and locking it in one of the library cabinets.

Two hours before sunset on the following day, he took a mount from the Lasparhall stables and rode up into the Highfells. Kara, Hamil, and Sarth accompanied him. The afternoon was clear, windy, and cold, and a rippled overcast of steel gray like the serried scales of a dragon roofed the moorland. Bright sunbreaks lingered in the west, where the sun was slowly sinking toward the horizon.

"I have misgivings about this, Geran," Sarth said as they left the wide fields of Lasparhall below them. "It is a reckless thing you intend!"

"Aesperus offered me counsel once before," the swordmage answered. He drew his hood over his head, shivering against the cold. "He might not care much about the living, but I think he's absorbed in his own legacy. That's why the troubles of our family interest him; the only thing that he fears is that he might be forgotten. He'll come if we call him."

"That is exactly what concerns me," the tiefling replied. He frowned deeply, but he fell silent as they continued to ride deeper into the Highfells.

Geran had grown up riding, hunting, and sometimes skirmishing in these wild lands, and he knew them well. Much like Hulburg, Thentia lay under the verge of the wild and desolate moorland of Thar, a hundred miles or more of wiry moorgrass, ribs of wet stone, gorse-filled hollows, and meandering streams winding through hidden channels that were often ten or fifteen feet below the plain, posing a considerable hazard to an unwary rider. Wind-blown mists often rolled in without warning to hide landmarks and confuse travelers; in wintertime, heavy snow only lingered in low places or along the lee side of hills and ridges, since the ever-present winds usually scoured the level ground clear. Yet, despite all that, Geran had always found the moorlands beautiful in their wild desolation. The vast distances and stone-crowned hills could be spectacular on a clear day, beckoning to his native wanderlust with the promise of lands few people had ever seen.

Geran thought he sensed a whisper of peril in the biting wind, a hint of supernatural malice gathering as night drew near. He said nothing, but Hamil narrowed his eyes and shifted in the saddle. "Do you feel it?" he said aloud. "Something's stirring in the wind."

Kara nodded. She knew the Highfells even better than Geran, having spent most of her life crisscrossing the wilds as a scout and hunter. "Sometimes the spirits of the dead roam abroad in the wild places after the sun sets. I think this will be one of those nights," she said. She looked at

Geran, a crease of worry marking her brow. "Will that help or hinder you in what you intend to do?"

"Help, I think. I don't know how far King Aesperus's domain extends toward Thentia, but I've got a feeling that if the dead are restless *here*, he'll hear us."

"We are well within the borders of Aesperus's old domain, so he can certainly answer if he is willing," Sarth said. "However, I still advise against proceeding. Drawing Aesperus's attention may very well be the last thing any of us do. And even if he deigns to treat with you, Geran, he may not see any reason to aid you—or may offer you assistance that fails you at the crucial moment."

"He aided Sergen," Geran replied. "And he kept his bargain. But I'll agree that we must be very careful in what we promise him." The dying sun finally broke through the clouds in the west, throwing long orange rays across the moorland; their shadows stretched out long and dark before them. Ahead, Geran spied a row of small, regular hummocks marching across a gentle hillside—a line of old barrows, completely covered in moor-grass. He turned his horse toward the ancient grave mounds. One didn't have to ride far in the Highfells to find an old grave, but he was gratified to find that this small group was more or less where he remembered it from his days of exploring the country around Lasparhall as a young lad. "There, I think those will do," he said.

Distances could be deceiving on the open moor, and the barrows were the better part of a mile off. By the time they reached the old graves, only the last limb of the sun remained above the horizon, and the wind was growing viciously cold. They picketed the horses a hundred yards away in a small jumble of boulders, and as the day slowly faded Sarth picked out a spot near the middle barrow and fashioned a ring of fist-sized stones around it, muttering wards and protections over each one as he put it in place. Before he emplaced the last stone, he motioned for the others to step within. When Geran did so, he felt the palpable menace of the evening drawing back, as if it had been pushed away by some great unseen hand.

"Are you finished?" he asked Sarth.

"Only if you are certain that no argument of mine can dissuade you," the tiefling answered unhappily.

Geran nodded. "I'd better do most of the talking. He knows me," he said. Reaching into his pocket, he pulled out the piece of parchment and read aloud:

> Dark the night and cold the stone,
> Silent grave and barren throne,
> Empty halls, a crown of mold,
> Deathless dreams the king of old.
>
> Long the dark and brief the light,
> An hour's play, and then the night,
> Beauty fails and all grows cold,
> Still awaits the king of old.

For a long time, nothing happened. Hamil glanced at him and said silently, *Perhaps you didn't do it right?*

A circle of mist abruptly appeared on the ground a short distance in front of Geran, bubbling upward as if fed by some dark spring. He took a step back as icy dread congealed in his heart. The mist rose higher, taking on a hunched, humanlike shape, and began to darken and thicken. In five heartbeats it was mist no longer, but instead a figure of nightmare—a skeletal corpse clad in the tatters of kingly robes. Evil green flames flickered in its empty sockets, and it clasped a great iron staff in its bony fingers. Its bones were sheathed in strips of hammered copper, each incised with tiny arcane runes. It regarded the four of them for a moment with its horrible lipless grin; Geran could barely stand to look at the thing, and he kept his eyes fixed on its breastbone rather than gazing full into its emerald gaze.

"As you have called, so I have come," the lich said in a dry, crackling voice. "What is it that you wish of me?"

"We desire your counsel," Geran answered. "The enemies of House Hulmaster have seized Hulburg, King Aesperus."

"That is hardly any concern of mine."

Geran winced, but he pressed on. "We mean to take back our realm, but the false harmach's wizard—an elf named Rhovann Disarnnyl—has created a small army of constructs animated through powerful necromancy.

If we could neutralize or destroy the helmed guardians, we could meet the rest of the usurper's forces on equal footing and win back Hulburg for the Hulmasters. Do you know how Rhovann created his guardians and how we might defeat them?"

"Of course I do," the King in Copper grated. "I perceive many things, young fool; how could I fail to notice the elf's forging of such a spell? Once upon a time I made *legions* of such things to serve me. Your adversary's efforts are clever in their own little way, but he has outwitted himself in his handiwork."

"Outwitted himself? How?" Kara asked.

Aesperus turned to regard her with his horrible gaze. "Ah, another Hulmaster," the lich said. "Daughter of Terena, daughter of Lendon, son of Angar. Yes, I know who you are, Kara, altered though you might be by the Spellplague's curse. I should destroy you to ensure the curse dies in your generation . . . or perhaps it might be excised, although the damage would be severe at this stage of your life." Kara paled and swallowed, but she stood her ground.

"Do not harm her," Geran said firmly. "We're the last kin of yours left in this world, King Aesperus. Cursed or not, she is a Hulmaster, and you are sworn not to raise your hand against any of Angar's line. Kara knows what might become of her children. You needn't worry about that."

The lich's eyes blazed angrily as he turned back to Geran. "Do not presume too much on Rivan's blood, young fool. Rivan was a worthless traitor who turned against me when I was at the height of my power! Do you think that I would hesitate for the merest moment to extinguish the last of his wretched line? I could destroy you both with a word!"

"In which case, Maroth Marstel remains harmach of Hulburg, dancing on Rhovann's strings until the end of his days," Hamil interjected. "And the surviving few Hulmasters live out their lives in poverty and exile. Hardly a fitting fate for a family fortunate enough to share your noble blood, mighty King."

Aesperus glanced at Hamil but did not deign to answer. Geran decided that it might be wise to engage the ancient lich again. "How has Rhovann outwitted himself?" he asked carefully.

"His creations all share a single masterful enchantment," the lich answered. "This is their great strength, since each additional runehelm he creates multiplies the power, resilience, and reasoning ability of all the runehelms he has so far created. But this is also their vulnerability. To share their senses with one another, to act in such perfect concert, they necessarily share a single animus. Sever that, and you could destroy them all at once."

"What animus? How can it be severed?"

Aesperus made a low whistling sound deep in his bony chest, and Geran realized that he was laughing after a fashion. "My counsel is not without cost," he said. "No more will I say until you meet my price."

Geran felt the worried glances of his friends, but he did not look away. "What do you wish, King Aesperus?" he asked.

"Last spring, you delivered to me an old tome I have sought for centuries." The lich's jaws moved, smiling horribly at his own ironic wit; Geran had in fact done everything in his power to keep the *Infiernadex* from Aesperus's bony claws, only to have the spellbook ripped from his hands at the lich's mere gesture. "Unfortunately, it is incomplete. Do not fear, young one, I know that you did not maim my prize; the damage was done long before you stumbled across it. A number of pages were removed from the *Infiernadex* before it was hidden by the accursed Lathanderians. Complete the *Infiernadex* for me, and I will give you what you need to defeat Rhovann's runehelms."

"It is too high a cost, Geran," Sarth said. "If he holds only part of the tome, then it would be better to leave it at that. We will find some other way to best Rhovann."

"I am not speaking with you, devilspawn," Aesperus snapped. "You gainsay me at your peril!"

Sarth fell silent, although he gave Geran a warning glance. Geran thought swiftly, considering the lich's offer. His cousin Sergen had bargained with Aesperus a year prior, and the *Infiernadex* was the price the lich had named. The King in Copper had dealt honestly with Sergen and the House Veruna armsmen; Geran and Hamil had watched the lich hand Anfel Urdinger, the Veruna arms-captain, the amulet by which he paid for the book's recovery. Aesperus hadn't agreed to slay the Hulmasters out of hand; the lich had simply armed Sergen with the means to do so, which seemed a fine line to walk in terms of honoring his old promise not to raise his hand against any of Angar's line. But even that suggested that Aesperus valued his word enough to take pains not to violate the exact wording of a promise.

"If we get the rest of the *Infiernadex* for you, will you promise not to employ its powers against Hulburg or its folk?" he asked.

The lich made a small snorting sound. "Done. I have far more important concerns than your miserable little flyspeck of a realm."

"Then I agree. We'll find the book's missing pages if it lies within our power." Geran felt Sarth's discomfort, but the tiefling did not speak; he hoped that he was not making a terrible blunder. Of course, there was no telling where in Faerûn any pages removed from the book centuries before might then lie. Perhaps Sarth would be able to divine their location, assuming that his friend would be willing to help.

I hope you know what you're doing, Hamil told him silently. The half-ling looked up at the lich and said, "I don't suppose you know where the missing pages are, do you?"

The lich looked down at Hamil, his jaw clicking. "I have known for centuries, but potent countermeasures obstruct me. They should pose less of an obstacle for the living. The missing pages lie in the vaults of the Irithlium in Myth Drannor."

Geran stared at the lich, dumbfounded. Myth Drannor was the one place in the world he could never go again, but before he could begin to frame a protest, Aesperus raised his iron staff, silently regarding each of Geran's companions in turn, and dissolved back into mist again. "Summon me when you have brought the pages I seek. Do not long delay, young Geran. Doom draws near, and you will need my aid."

The lich vanished, and silence fell over the barrowfields.

TWELVE

3 Alturiak, the Year of Deep Water Drifting (1480 DR)

The Council Guard soldiers came for Mirya in the middle of the night. She was awakened from a fitful sleep by the sound of her cottage's door breaking open, the angry shouts of the harmach's soldiers, and their heavy, armored footsteps thundering over the old floorboards. She sat up and started to swing her legs out of the bed with some half-formed notion of fleeing out the back door, but the bedroom door flew open and several soldiers with bared steel in their hands surged forward to seize her. She was dragged stumbling from the bed to the kitchen, where a Council Guard sergeant she didn't know waited by the banked fire.

"Who are you? What's this all about?" Mirya managed.

"Shut up, you!" one of the soldiers holding her snarled. He cuffed her across the mouth with the back of his mailed gauntlet—not with his full strength, since no bones broke and her teeth all stayed where they belonged, but still hard enough to buckle her knees and split her lip. Dizzy, she sagged in the soldiers' grip until they stood her upright again.

"Mirya Erstenwold, we've got a writ for your arrest," the sergeant said. "You're accused of conspiracy, harborin' spies, and committin' acts of rebellion 'gainst the harmach."

"No—" she began to protest, but a hard look from the soldier who'd hit her brought her protest to a quick end. Then the Council Guards marched her out the door to a waiting wagon and shoved her inside, slamming the door of iron bars shut behind her. In the space of a few heartbeats the wagon was jouncing and rocking as it rolled down the lane back toward the center of town. Mirya huddled inside her night-shirt, trying to make sense of what had happened and where they might be taking her. The night air was cold and dank, and a sour old smell clung to the wagon's interior. She could hear the clatter of hoofbeats on cobblestones from the team drawing the wagon, the harsh commands of the driver and the sharp flick of the lash, the creaking and jingling of the soldiers' armor and the wagon's springs.

Thank the gods that Selsha wasn't home, she thought dully. She didn't think the soldiers would have dragged in a girl not even ten years of age yet, but the whole scene would have terrified her daughter beyond words. She had no idea what was about to become of her, but at least Selsha was safe with the Tresterfins.

The wagon finally rattled to a stop. Two more Council Guards unlocked the door and dragged her out. She caught a single glimpse of their surroundings, and recognized the silhouette of the Council Hall's decorated eaves in the dim orange light of the streetlamps. Then she was ushered inside and down a flight of stairs to the guardrooms below the hall proper. She'd been this way once before, when Geran had been arrested at his cousin Sergen's order and held here. The guards led her past several cells that were already occupied; she recognized half a dozen of her neighbors, including the bearlike Brun Osting, who was stretched out unconscious on his cell floor. She doubted that they'd brought him in without a fight. The young brewer's face was a mass of blood and bruises, but two of his kinfolk—fortunately Halla was not among them—were tending to him in the cell. Torm guard us all, she thought. Marstel's soldiers have caught half the resistance tonight!

The guards came to an empty cell and shoved her in. "Enjoy your stay," one snarled at her. Then the door slammed shut, its heavy iron bolt sliding shut. Mirya picked herself up off the flagstones, and crawled off to curl up in one corner of the cold stone chamber. Her mouth ached where she'd been struck, and she touched her lip gingerly. I'll count myself lucky if that's the worst I have to show for this, she thought.

Hours passed as she waited in the cold cell. To judge by the sounds she heard echoing down the halls, the council dungeons were bustling with activity this night. Doors creaked open and slammed shut, guards moved around with heavy footsteps and jingling mail, voices shouted in protest or suddenly cried out in pain. She found herself cringing at each new outburst, wondering who'd been caught and what was happening to them. Just when Mirya was beginning to wonder if she'd simply been forgotten, she was roused by the sound of keys turning in the lock of her cell. A pair of Council Guards let themselves in, and without speaking a word to her, simply grabbed her by the arms and hustled her out the door.

"What is it?" Mirya asked. "Where are we going?" But her jailers didn't answer. They showed her into a small, windowless room, sat her down in a sturdy wooden chair in its center with her arms behind her back, and bolted her manacles to a shackle in the floor. Then the two of them took station behind her.

A short time after that, the room's door opened again, and a short, broad-shouldered officer with sandy hair and a stern frown fixed over his small goatee entered the room. She recognized him as Edelmark, the captain of the Council Guard; they'd never met, but she'd seen him a few times. A clerk followed him in, taking a seat in the corner and laying out a quill and parchment by a small writing desk there.

Edelmark regarded her in silence for a moment before taking a seat behind a wooden table and setting his helm—the brow marked by a device of a golden stag—on top. "Well, what are we to do with you?" he finally said.

Mirya wasn't entirely sure that the question was meant for her, but she did her best to meet his steely eyes without cringing. "I suppose that depends on what you think I've done," she replied. If Edelmark knew about her involvement in the resistance, then he had ample reason to have her executed at once. She and her small band had struck several times in the last few tendays, and blood had been spilled more than once. On the other hand, it was just barely possible that she'd been swept up with the rest on suspicion alone, and that she might still walk free.

Edelmark studied her without expression. "I *think* that you're one of the people behind some of the little troubles we've seen of late, which makes you quite possibly a rebel, a murderer, and a traitor. Any one of those things would be ample grounds for me to have you hanged at dawn. On the other hand, I'm a reasonable fellow. If you're honest with me and simply explain what part you've played in some of these events, I'll urge Harmach Marstel to exercise leniency in your case. You have an opportunity to make up for whatever misjudgments you might have made lately. I sincerely suggest that you take it."

A chill ran down Mirya's spine. A small, frightened part of her whimpered and begged to throw herself on Edelmark's mercy, hoping that she might save herself by doing as he asked. But she guessed that Edelmark's definition of "mercy" probably did not extend to letting her go, not after the part she'd played in Hulburg's incipient resistance. And she'd never be able to live with herself if she offered someone else to face justice—well, Harmach Marstel's so-called justice—in her place. She simply shook her head. "I've done nothing wrong," she told him.

Edelmark allowed himself a small smile. "Indeed," he said. "Two days ago, someone shot half-a-dozen crossbow bolts at a Council Guard patrol on the Vale Road. One man was badly wounded, and two more injured. It was a carefully planned ambush by someone who knew the woods in that area quite well. Do you know anything about that?"

"No," she answered, doing her best to lie with a straight face. She'd put Brun and Senna up to it a tenday earlier; they'd spent days choosing the right spot. It had been a risky attack, but she wanted the Council Guards to think twice about where they went and in what numbers.

"An attack on the harmach's soldiers is a capital offense. The *only* way you'd avoid execution for involvement in something like that is by admitting your guilt and showing you sincerely regretted your actions by helping us to locate everyone involved."

Mirya said nothing. Edelmark waited, simply watching her. Then he sighed and continued. "Two Iron Ring armsmen were murdered in an alleyway behind the Siren Song festhall three nights ago. They were seen to leave the place in the company of a dark-haired woman who'd apparently promised them her favors."

"It certainly wasn't me!" Mirya snapped, and she meant it. "I wouldn't set foot in such a place."

"Of course not," Edelmark replied, but his eyes remained as cold as a drawn blade. He leaned back, drumming his fingers on the tabletop. "A little more than three tendays ago—on the 8th of Hammer, to be precise—a House Veruna supply caravan bound for the Galena camps was attacked by ten masked bandits. They killed five Veruna armsmen and pillaged the wagons, but they spared the drivers. Do you know who might have been involved in that?"

Keep calm, Mirya! she admonished herself. She allowed herself a frown of disapproval. "So far you've suggested I might be involved in prostitution, murder, and now brigandage," Mirya answered. "Have there been any kidnappings or rapes lately? We might as well go through those as well."

"Mind your manners, Mistress Erstenwold," Edelmark replied. He nodded at the soldiers standing behind Mirya. She heard two quick footsteps and a rattle of chain before her arms—still bound behind her—were jerked upward sharply by the manacles between her wrists. Twin stabs of pain in her shoulders brought a cry from her throat, and her face was forced down toward her knees. Then the pressure was gone, and her arms fell back into their natural place. "Would you like to rephrase your answer?"

Mirya winced. "Captain Edelmark, I've no idea who's behind the attacks."

The captain studied her for a long time. She expected him to nod at the soldiers behind her again, and found herself tensing for the sudden jerk and sharp pain again, but instead he frowned and leaned back in his chair. "Have you seen Geran Hulmaster since his exile?"

Everybody knows that Geran attacked the Temple of the Wronged Prince, she thought swiftly. He must know that Geran's looked out for me before. And it might make other things I've said ring more true if I show a little honesty now. Carefully, she nodded. "Yes. I saw him the day before the temple burned down."

Edelmark raised an eyebrow. "So you consorted with an avowed enemy of the harmach?"

"It was no idea of mine," Mirya replied. "He simply appeared at my storehouse—how, I couldn't say—and he didn't stay long. He was gone again within half an hour."

"And you made no report of this to the Council Guard?"

Mirya scowled. "Geran saved my daughter and me from slavery at the hands of the Black Moon pirates. All of Hulburg knows the tale by now. No, I didn't see fit to tell the Council Guard that I'd seen him."

"What did you talk about?"

"He stopped by to see how I was getting along."

"Did he say anything about his intentions?"

"He blamed Valdarsel for Harmach Grigor's murder in Thentia. I guessed that he meant to do something about it. But I'd no idea that he'd attack the Cyricists as he did."

"Do you know where he is, or what he might be planning next?"

Mirya shook her head. "Away from Hulburg by now, I would guess. As for what he intends to do now, I couldn't say."

Edelmark paused. He stood slowly, folding his hands behind his back, and paced away, evidently thinking over what she'd said. Mirya watched him, wondering if he was merely making a show of careful consideration or truly digesting the very little she'd actually told him. Absently he motioned to the guards behind her, and she squeezed her eyes shut in anticipation of the pain to come—but this time the guards unlocked her manacles, and freed her wrists. She frowned and rubbed at her bruises.

"I suspect that you haven't been completely honest with me, Mistress Erstenwold," the captain said. "However, I can't easily prove it—at the moment. You may go, but I'll send you with a warning. If you see or hear from Geran Hulmaster again, you will tell us *immediately*, or I will charge you with conspiring against the harmach, and that will lead to a short drop and a sudden stop very soon thereafter. Do you understand me?"

"Aye, I understand you," she answered.

Edelmark looked to the soldiers behind her. "Show her out." He picked up his helm from the table and left; the clerk followed after him, gathering his parchment. The soldiers behind Mirya came forward and helped her to her feet—somewhat less roughly this time—and quickly ushered her out of the council dungeons. Before she knew it, she was standing on the front steps of the Council Hall, still dressed in her nightclothes, blinking at the sunlight. The guards returned inside without a word, leaving her there.

"Now what was that all about?" she muttered aloud. If Marstel's men suspected her enough to bring her in, they certainly had reason enough to jail her or hang her. But perhaps Edelmark's suspicions were as thinly founded as he claimed, and he didn't want to risk making a martyr of her for the rest of the loyalists to rally around. She shivered in the cold air, drew her robe around her, and hurried toward Erstenwold's. The first thing she meant to do was to get properly dressed; fortunately she had several changes of clothes at the store and wouldn't have to walk all the way back home in her stocking feet.

When she reached the store, she found that her clerks had opened without her, but it was a quiet day and nothing had needed her immediate attention. She stayed only long enough to send word to the Therndons that she needed a woodworker to have a look at her door, and then made her way back home.

As she'd thought, the front door was well and truly ruined; the harmach's men had simply stood it up in the doorway, but it was no longer attached. She sighed and worked her way inside, pausing to take in the damage to her cottage. As she'd expected, it had been searched violently and thoroughly. Many of her best plates were broken on the kitchen floor, the cupboards were bare, the sheets and blankets were dumped on the floor . . . "What a mess," she muttered. If she weren't so angry about the senselessness of it, she would've thrown herself down in one of the chairs and cried.

She looked around, trying to determine the best place to start, but an envelope on top of her mantle caught her eye. Frowning, she went and took it down. It was addressed simply "Mirya" in a graceful, feminine hand. Somehow she doubted that the soldiers would have bothered to leave her a letter; they'd delivered their message by ransacking the house. Curious, she broke the plain wax seal and drew out a short note:

> *Dearest Mirya,*
> *It is imperative that we speak at once.*
>
> *– S.*

"Sennifyr," Mirya breathed. She frowned at the note, wondering what to do. Once upon a time she would have answered such a summons without a moment's hesitation; junior initiates in the Sisterhood of the Black Veil were expected to obey. But she'd parted ways with the Sisterhood years earlier, until the troubles plaguing Hulburg in the last few months had led her to seek Mistress Sennifyr's counsel again. The

First Sister was very well informed about events in Hulburg. Every devotee of Shar in the town—many of them women who were well-placed to see and hear many of the town's secrets—owed Sennifyr fealty, and reported to her a myriad of rumors, gossip, and observations. Mirya no longer devoted herself to the goddess of secrets and sorrow, but that didn't mean Sennifyr wouldn't help her if it suited her purposes to do so. Of course, Sennifyr meant to draw her back into the Sisterhood's orbit, so Mirya would have to be on her guard.

"What is it Sennifyr thinks I should know?" Mirya murmured to herself. She frowned, trying to decide whether to answer or not. Finally she sighed, drew a warm hooded cloak around her shoulders, and hurried back out into the cold. A quarter-hour's walk brought her around the foot of Griffonwatch and then up Hill Street toward the houses of the wealthy that dotted the higher slopes of Easthead. The houses were grand old places with gated drives and manicured gardens, although those were brown and bare with winter.

She found the house she was looking for, a fine mansion that stood amid wind-swept cedars. Before she could reconsider, she let herself in the wrought-iron gate, climbed the stone steps to the door, and gave the pull chain for the bell a deliberate tug. Chimes echoed inside. After a short time, she heard light footsteps approaching, and a young woman with long dark hair opened the door—the same attendant who'd greeted Mirya the last time she had called on Sennifyr. "The mistress is expecting you," she said. "This way, if you please."

Mirya followed the young woman to the mansion's parlor, where she found Sennifyr reading a book by the fire. Sennifyr was a woman of forty-five years or so, but her face possessed an almost ageless serenity, and no gray touched her light brown hair, piled high above her head in an elegant coiffure. Sennifyr smiled and set down her book, rising smoothly to her feet. "Ah, Mirya, how good of you to come! I was afraid that you might not see the note Lana left in your house amid all the dreadful mess she found there. Tell me, are you all right?"

"I'm well enough," Mirya replied. At Sennifyr's gesture, she took the other seat by the fire as the young woman—Lana, or so Mirya supposed—stepped forward to take her hood.

Sennifyr returned to her seat, but she leaned forward, peering at Mirya. "Oh, by the Lady," the noblewoman said, her hand rising to her mouth. "Mirya, your face! Why, they've beaten you black-and-blue!" She made several small *tsk*ing sounds, leaning across to gently caress Mirya's cheek. Mirya steeled herself not to draw away; she did not intend to let Sennifyr see anything that might be taken as fear or weakness on her part. "I should tend to that!"

"It's not so bad as it looks," Mirya replied. "A few hours' rest and I'll be right as rain."

"You must have been terrified, my dear. Tell me, what happened?" Sennifyr nodded to Lana; the young woman rolled a small teacart close, and began to arrange the cups and saucers.

Mirya suspected that Sennifyr already knew quite well what had happened, but she answered anyway. "The Council Guard stormed my house and dragged me out in the middle of the night," she said. "I spent the rest of the night and most of the morning in the Council Hall's dungeons. Edelmark questioned me about loyalist attacks of late, but he decided he lacked any reason to keep me imprisoned and set me free."

"Indeed," the noblewoman breathed. "That seems rather . . . generous of him."

"I was surprised too," Mirya said. Sennifyr simply studied her without saying anything. Mirya frowned, wondering what it was that Sennifyr thought she'd missed. An ugly suspicion dawned in her mind. "You believe that he had some other reason to let me go?"

Sennifyr smiled thinly. "Mirya, if *I* wanted to find out who was loyal and who was disloyal, I would certainly think about letting at least a few of my catches go and watching to see who they spoke with after I released them. I imagine it might be quite instructive."

"I shouldn't have come here," Mirya murmured. "Now you'll be under suspicion too."

The noblewoman laughed softly. "Oh, I think I am safe enough. Unlike you, I have no suspicious activities to answer for and no special connection to House Hulmaster. You are my only flirtation with sedition, and I will of course be very careful to behave myself. But you, on the other hand, you are being watched very closely indeed. You must take great care not to bring suspicion to anyone who might in fact be involved with this show of resistance to Marstel's reign."

"How do you know this?" Mirya asked.

Sennifyr shrugged. "One of our Sisters is the mistress of a high-ranking officer in the Council Guard. She hears much of what Edelmark shares with his lieutenants. But even without her reports, I would have been suspicious of your release. For that matter, you must also be careful of any friends you have who are engaged in any . . . disloyal activities. They may also wonder why you were released, and they may come to their own conclusions."

"What a fool I am," Mirya growled at herself. Of course Edelmark wouldn't have let her go simply because he lacked any proof of her wrong-doing. Lack of evidence hadn't stopped him for months; a suspicion was all the captain of the Council Guard needed to have someone dragged off to the dungeons and kept there indefinitely.

"I have only your best interests at heart, Mirya. I was not about to let a sister—even one who has gone her own way for a time—walk unwittingly into Edelmark's little trap."

Mirya doubted very much whether that was Sennifyr's only concern, but whatever the noblewoman's motivation, she might very well have saved her from a very dangerous blunder. "I thank you, Mistress Sennifyr."

Sennifyr inclined her head, and leaned back in her seat. "Have you any news of Geran Hulmaster? I confess that I am very curious as to what he might do next after that terrible business at the temple of Cyric."

Now things become clear, Mirya reflected. Sennifyr hadn't offered her help out of the goodness of her own heart; she knew well enough that Sennifyr didn't have one. The Sharran hoped that Mirya knew something more than she did about the Hulmasters and their plans. "I'm afraid I haven't," she replied. "We spoke briefly before he and Sarth struck at the temple. Geran isn't done fighting for Hulburg, and he means to challenge Marstel soon enough. But where he is now, I've no idea."

The noblewoman studied her in silence. Then she carefully asked, "Would you like news of him? I will perform a divination for you if you wish. My own viewings are indistinct, but you are much more closely connected to Geran Hulmaster; I believe the results would be much more definitive for you."

Mirya hesitated, weighing her decision. She feared to accept more of Sennifyr's help, but on the other hand, she found that she was anxious to know whether Geran had escaped Hulburg or not. Marstel would have trumpeted the news from one end of town to the other if his soldiers had caught or killed Geran, but it was possible that Geran was in hiding and unable to leave now that the harmach's forces were sweeping up loyalists. He could very well need assistance of some kind . . . "Very well," she finally said. "I'm willing."

Sennifyr nodded. She turned to the teacart, poured a cup, then drew a tiny vial from her sleeve and added a drop or two of a dark liquid to the tea. Murmuring the words of a spell, she carefully stirred the tea. Mirya sensed something taking shape in the darkened room, a stretching of the shadows or simply a dimming of the light; she'd never had much talent for magic herself. Then the noblewoman lifted the cup and offered it to Mirya. "Here, drink this. You will *see* for a short time."

Mirya took the cup, and drank deeply of the sweet black tea. It had a faint oily taste, and it seemed to cling to her tongue and teeth. The vapors filled her nose, and she felt a mild dizziness. "Good," Sennifyr said softly. "Now close your eyes, dear, and think of your handsome lordling. Fix your mind's eye on Geran's face, the sound of his voice, the color of his eyes, the shape of his mouth."

She did as Sennifyr instructed, bringing to mind Geran's features as she thought of him standing in front of the counter at Erstenwold's on a sunny afternoon, a small smile touching the corner of his mouth as he listened to her recount some story of Selsha's doings. It was a memory from a few tendays after he'd foiled his cousin's plots, a brief carefree time in the summer when it seemed that all that was wrong in Hulburg had been set right. Then she felt the power of Sennifyr's magic begin to take hold; the memory simply drew away into darkness, and she groped blindly after it. Instead, she found a confusing jumble of images, Geran as seen in dozens of brief moments, each lasting for only the blink of an eye before it vanished again into the next. She shook her head and tried to fix the flickering visions in her mind.

Geran was making love with a golden-haired woman, their limbs entwined in the candlelight as they lay together in a darkened room.

Stunned, Mirya could only stare; as he shifted and drew back for a moment, she saw Nimessa Sokol, her eyes half closed. Somehow Mirya *knew* she was seeing something that had happened not long before—the divination's magic at work, she guessed. He slept with Nimessa? she thought dully. How could he do that? A familiar ache welled up under her breastbone, and Mirya hugged her arms close to her body. She wrenched her eyes away, horrified to have stumbled into such an intimate moment, and the vision complied by vanishing from her view. Then she caught a glimpse of Geran dressed in the colors of a Sokol armsman, jogging along on a horse as he rode alongside a creaking caravan leaving Hulburg along the Coastal Way. Two of the gray guardians watched impassively as he rode by, but they did not stir. "He escaped Hulburg," she murmured aloud. Sennifyr did not reply.

Now she saw Geran standing by the rail of a merchant caravel that plunged and pitched over a sea of leaden gray, bitter spray blowing back from each dip of the bow, his tattered cloak flapping around him. This time she sensed that she saw something that was happening as she watched. "He is at sea," she said, "but I can't tell where he is bound." Hulburg's port was still icebound, so he had to be on his way to another Moonsea city. A gray coast loomed ahead in the mists and rain, but before she could make out any more, the vision fell away to be replaced by another.

This time she saw Geran fighting in some strange, shadowy place, a great chamber of stone where ghostly warriors streamed from the darkness to beset him. He wielded a black sword in one hand, and his mouth moved silently as he shouted the words of a spell. "Now he's fighting in a dark place," she said. Mirya reached out to him, sensing the danger that he was in, but then she realized that what she was seeing hadn't yet come to pass. The image began to flicker, and she called out, hoping to see just a little more. "Geran! Wait!"

"He does not hear you, my dear," Sennifyr said.

Mirya blinked her eyes, realizing the visions were over. She surged to her feet, still trying to make sense of what she'd seen. Geran was safe, for now, although terrible danger waited for him soon enough . . . but the vision that she couldn't drive out of her mind was the image of Geran lying in

Nimessa's arms. It's none of my business! she fumed at herself. Why should I care? I have no claim on him, nor does he have any on me. But if that was true, then why did her heart ache as if she'd been pierced with a knife? Mirya, you foolish girl, she told herself. You've fallen for him again, and that's why your heart is breaking. You foolish, foolish girl!

Sennifyr watched her carefully. "Mirya, my dear, what is it? What's wrong?"

"I—I have to go," Mirya replied. She took her cloak from the peg where Lana had hung it and hurried out of the mansion into the clean, cold air.

THIRTEEN

13 Alturiak, the Year of Deep Water Drifting (1480 DR)

Nine days of hard travel brought Geran, Hamil, and Sarth to the outskirts of Myth Drannor. They'd sailed from Thentia aboard a Double Moon merchantman; unlike Hulburg, Thentia's port remained ice-free through the winter. Still, it was enduring a difficult three-day Moonsea crossing against the westerly winds. In the city of Hillsfar, they bought riding horses and provisions for an overland journey, setting out southward along the Moonsea Ride. Deep snow and cold, damp weather had made the hundred-mile ride far more tiring than Geran remembered it, but at least they'd run into no trouble with bandits or monsters; it seemed the bad weather had driven them into their lairs, leaving the roads open to any who were foolish enough to travel in such conditions. They spent their nights huddling around campfires beneath the forest's mighty boles, trying to keep dry and warm.

In the middle of the afternoon on the ninth day of their journey, Geran found that the endless woods around the elven road they followed had begun to take on a familiar character. The stirring of long-buried memories washed over him. He shortened his reins and brought his horse, a big gray gelding, to a stop on the snow-covered elven road, sitting motionless in the saddle as the wet snow floated down, sticking to his woolen cloak and the horse's mane. The woods were still, and the snow muffled the hoofbeats of his companions' horses, leaving no sound but the faint creaking of leather and the animals' heavy breaths. Without even realizing it, he leaned forward, listening with all his might for something that stirred at the very edge of his awareness.

"What is it?" Hamil asked, reining in beside him. Sarth, a little way ahead of them both, glanced over his shoulder and halted as well.

Geran gazed at the snowy forest that surrounded them. He recognized this place. "I first met Alliere and Rhovann at this very spot," he said. "A little more than seven years ago, I suppose. It was winter then too—Midwinter's Eve—and I could hear the elves singing the *Miiraeth len Fhierren*." He shook himself, raising a hand to brush the snow from his eyelashes and the memories from his sight. "It's only a mile more to the city."

"Good!" Hamil replied. "I'm more than ready for a hot meal and a warm bed tonight."

"As am I," Sarth said. The sorcerer had argued vehemently against completing Aesperus's task, but once Geran made his decision, he'd grudgingly agreed to go with Geran and Hamil so that he could view the missing pages of the *Infiernadex* himself before the lich took possession of them. Geran had agreed that if the pages held some lore or ritual that seemed too dangerous to hand over, he'd destroy them rather than deal with the King in Copper—an alternative that he sincerely hoped he wouldn't have to exercise. There was no telling how Aesperus might react to such a refusal.

Hamil tapped his heels to his mount's flanks and started again, but Geran hesitated a moment. This was the point of no return; if he continued forward, he'd be in defiance of the coronal's judgment. He was not quite ready to discount all his misgivings yet.

Sarth glanced around the woods to make sure of their privacy, and then spoke to Geran. "You need not go any farther," he said. "Hamil and I can find the pages Aesperus requires. There is no need for you to risk the coronal's displeasure."

The swordmage shook his head. "It might take you months to win the trust of the right people, and we can't afford much delay. I still have friends here—I think. But from this point forward, my name is Aram, and I'm only a Red Sail armsman here to guard Master Hamil from any trouble on the road." He was dressed the part, with an armsman's scale coat, the red surcoat with its yellow slash, a little pigment to darken the eyesockets and make them appear deeper than they were, and a thick goatee in the Vastar style. His elven sword was disguised in a false scabbard, its hilt of mithral wire covered with a simple leather wrap; it likely would have been better to leave the weapon in Lasparhall, but once upon a time it had been bestowed on Geran by Coronal Ilsevele herself, and if things went poorly, he hoped that it might serve to remind the elves of the service he'd rendered their queen in years gone by.

Hamil noticed that he was not following yet, and reined in again. He glanced at Sarth, and then twisted in the saddle to look back at the sword-mage. "You've never spoken much of your years in Myth Drannor," he said to Geran. "I think now might be time to tell your tale. What happened to you here?"

Geran sat his horse in silence for a moment, wrestling with the question of whether to answer. For many months he'd done his best to forget about the life he'd made for himself in the elf realm, unwilling to torment himself with the memories. But Hamil and Sarth certainly deserved to know whether their association with him entailed any risk in the City of Song. And it might be possible that he was finally ready to unburden himself of the tale, dragging it out from the dark recesses of his heart into daylight again.

He felt his companions waiting for his answer, and sighed. "I came here in Nightal of the Year of the Heretic's Rampage," he began. "It was a year and a half or so after the Company of the Dragon Shield parted ways and Hamil and I took over the Red Sail Coster. I'd been feeling restless in Tantras. I suppose my heart wasn't in the merchant trade—I missed the Dragon Shields, and I felt like I was still searching for a cause worthy of my sword. Anyway, some Red Sail business brought me to Harrowdale, and while there I intervened in a fight between an elf—a bladesinger—and a band of Netherese assassins. The bladesinger was as good as anyone I've ever seen, but the odds were long, and the Netherese fought with dark spells and shadowy blades. I was a good swordsman at the time, better than most, but I was out of my depth in that fight, and I knew it. Still, I timed things well, and my appearance tipped the balance of the fight. The bladesinger and I killed or drove off the Netherese.

"Afterward I spoke at length with the fellow I'd aided. He was a sun elf named Daried Selsherryn, a master bladesinger of Myth Drannor. He told me that he thought I had *potential*, especially since I'd had a little arcane study during my time with the Dragon Shields. Daried offered to teach me more of his art by way of thanking me for my help." Geran smiled as he recalled the evening. "I thought I'd pretty much figured out everything I needed to know about sword play, and I was a little offended by the idea that I might not measure up. But I'd sensed the magic Daried and his Netherese foes wielded against each other—I've always had a knack for it, I guess—and I was intrigued despite myself. Besides, I'd wanted to see Myth Drannor since I was a young lad. When I finished up with my Red Sail business, I sent a note back to Hamil explaining I might be a tenday or two late—"

"Five years late, as it turned out," Hamil muttered.

"—and I rode west into the forest, with nothing more than a vague notion of studying a few days with Daried and taking in the sights. Of course, the forest is a dark and wild place in its eastern marches, and I lost my mount to a hungry bulette. I finally arrived on foot, cold and hungry from days of walking."

"Here, on this very spot, I stopped to listen to the sound of elven singing that I could hear through the trees." Geran nodded at the small clearing around them. "And while I was standing here listening, I met the most beautiful woman I'd ever laid eyes on—Alliere Morwain, of House Morwain. She and Rhovann Disarnnyl, who was courting her, were out for a sleigh ride in the snowy woods. Alliere took pity on my weatherbeaten state and offered me the hospitality of her family's home. She showed me around the city, and of course, I'd never seen anything like it. I found Daried again soon enough, and within three days learned that I didn't know a thing about sword play or magic."

"Did Daried teach you your swordmagic, then?" Sarth asked.

Geran nodded. "I studied under him every day for months. In the evenings, I explored the city at Alliere's side, listening to the master bards reciting in the lanternlit glens, dancing on the tavern greens, watching plays and wandering through the shops of the city's merchants. When I'd learned enough swordmagic to regain some of my self-confidence and enough Elvish to avoid embarrassing myself, I went to the court of the coronal and offered her my sword. She accepted, and I became a member of the Coronal Guard. They don't choose many folk of other races, but Daried and Alliere spoke well of me, and I come from a noble line—such as it is. My experience of the lands outside the forest made me useful as a scout and spy, so I often went abroad when the guards found something that needed doing outside Myth Drannor. And during those days, I fell in love with Alliere." Geran paused, lost in the memories.

"I think I finally understand why you stayed so long," said Hamil.

Geran shrugged. "Myth Drannor is a strangely timeless place. Time doesn't touch the elves the same way it does the rest of us, of course, but there's something more to it than that. It's like living in a waking dream. The lords are so splendid, the ladies so fair, the songs so beautiful . . . there are days of toil and grief, but they're few and far between. The longer you remain, the more deeply you lose yourself in the dream. And I was lost here for years."

"How did it end?" Sarth asked quietly.

Geran's mouth tightened with old pain. "A duel," he said. "Rhovann and I grew into rivals for Alliere's affections. She cared more for me, I think, but they'd known each other since before I'd even been born, and their families desired a marriage between them. Perhaps she didn't really know her own heart. In any event, Rhovann became jealous of me, and I of course didn't like him much either. Whether he truly loved Alliere or simply regarded her as something that belonged to him, I couldn't say, but he never missed a chance to let me know what he thought of me. I challenged him to meet me in a tournament, and he agreed.

"It was supposed to be a contest of skill, but from the first we meant to hurt each other. I got the better of Rhovann and struck his wand from his hand, but he wouldn't yield." Geran closed his eyes, remembering the frost-covered leaves under his feet, the clash and thunder of spells striking spell-shields and steel gleaming in his hand. "Something came over me then, a black rage like I've felt only once or twice in my life. Rhovann reached for his wand again, and I struck off his hand, knowing full well what I was doing. And I would have done worse to him if Daried hadn't stopped me.

"For dueling Rhovann and deliberately maiming him, Coronal Ilsevele banished me. I found out later that Rhovann was banished a few tendays after me, since it turned out that he'd been studying magical arts banned in Myth Drannor. But Alliere was horrified. She couldn't bear to look on me after I'd maimed Rhovann." He sighed and opened his eyes, fixing his gaze on the snow-covered road ahead of him. "That's the tale. I haven't seen Alliere since that day. I returned to Tantras six years after I'd left, and Hamil was kind enough to make a little room for me with the Red Sails again."

He tapped his horse's flanks, and rode forward at an easy walk. Hamil and Sarth fell in with him, and the three companions rode in silence for a time. After a little while Hamil asked, "Exactly how banished are you?"

"I'm not supposed to be within the coronal's domain, which includes the city and the forests around it. Customarily that's held to be anything within a day's ride of the coronal's palace. What judgment Ilsevele would pronounce on me for violating my exile, I couldn't say. Imprisonment? A geas?" He shrugged. "I hope to avoid the coronal's notice, to be honest."

The road rounded a low hill and met a wide lake, running along the shore. Unlike much of the city behind it, the lake and the strong outbuildings were less than a century old, new defenses added to protect the great old city. Geran had heard that the elves hadn't cut a single tree to clear the wide open space of the beautiful lakes that now girdled the city; they'd used some sort of forest magic to move the trees, root and bole, to new places, creating a moat of sorts a good bowshot in width to protect the city from any attacking army. The isthmuses joining the city to the surrounding lands were guarded by white barbicans, their walls fashioned in the form of delicately pointed arches filled with carvings of forest scenes, but the city was unwalled otherwise. Many of the elves Geran knew regretted the fact that the city had been separated from the surrounding forest by its defenses, but he'd always found the lakes to be a very beautiful city wall indeed; on still days the city's wondrous spires and domes were mirrored perfectly in the reflecting ring.

"A wonder," Sarth breathed softly, taking in the sight of the slender towers.

Geran nodded in agreement. "I wish I could show both of you more of it; it's a shame to visit Myth Drannor in haste. But I suppose that might be for the best, since I should probably avoid my old haunts." Even though he'd lived in this city for years, familiarity hadn't diminished its beauty. They continued along the road as it turned toward the city again, now passing along a slender point of land dividing two of the reflecting lakes, and came to one of the city's barbicans—a freestanding gatehouse guarded by elf soldiers in long coats of silver mail.

"Last chance," Hamil remarked under his breath. "Just so you know, I intend to completely disavow you if you get caught."

One of the elves stepped forward, raising his hand as the travelers approached. "Halt and name yourselves," he said in a clear voice. "Who are you, and what is your business in Myth Drannor?"

Geran stared at the guard-captain in horror. It was Caellen Disarnnyl, a kinsman of Rhovann's. He wasn't anyone that Geran had known very well, but he'd certainly known Geran by name, especially after Geran's rivalry with Rhovann had turned ugly. He fought down the urge to immediately tug his hood down over his features or keep his face turned away from the captain; the last thing he wanted to do was *look* as nervous as he felt. He hasn't seen me in years, he reminded himself. I was clean shaven before, I dressed in elven garb, and I didn't wear bulky armor like this scale coat. Before the captain glanced at him, Geran turned his attention to the barbican and the towers behind, making a show of gawking just a little at the elven city. Either Caellen would recognize him, or not; nothing he could think of at the moment would make that less likely without also drawing the captain's attention to him.

"I'm Hamil Alderheart of Tantras," Hamil answered the captain. "You might say I speculate in antiquities and enchantments. This is Sarth Khul Riizar, a sorcerer in my employ, and my bodyguard Aram Kost. I've come to Myth Drannor to consult with your sages about some magical devices that have come to my attention."

"Antiquities, you say?" The captain frowned at Hamil. "In my experience, that is a euphemism for pillaging the old palaces and treasuries of my people. You understand that you may not enter any of the old ruins or vaults in Myth Drannor without a writ of permission from the coronal's agent?"

"Oh, of course!" said Hamil. "I don't risk my own neck in such foolishness, I pay others to do it for me. I'm simply here for research. The libraries of Myth Drannor are the finest north of the Sea of Fallen Stars; I'm hoping that they might contain lore pertaining to the items I mentioned. It would save me a great deal of time and trouble if they do."

Caellen studied Hamil's face for a moment, and then looked at Sarth with a small frown. Tieflings were hardly commonplace in most lands; Sarth's brick red skin, swept horns, and barbed tail certainly suggested a dark disposition. "There are potent wards against creatures native to other planes protecting the city," the captain said to the tiefling. "I am simply warning you that I do not know what might happen if you should enter the city."

Sarth nodded to the captain. "I am familiar with such measures. In my case, I am several generations removed from my . . . forebears, and share little with them other than a passing resemblance. I shouldn't provoke any response from your city's mythal."

Caellen shrugged, as if to say *we'll see in a moment*, and turned his attention to Geran. A brief frown creased his brow, and Geran wondered if he saw a glimmer of recognition in the captain's eyes. But at that moment Hamil cleared his throat and said, "This is the first time I've visited your city. Can you recommend a comfortable inn that isn't too costly for a few days' stay?"

Caellen glanced back to the halfling, forgetting Geran for the moment. The swordmage allowed himself a tiny sigh of relief. "Many travelers speak well of the Swan House," he answered. "You'll find it about two hundred yards ahead, on the right-hand side of the avenue. Madame Yisiere can also arrange to introduce you to the librarians at the mage's college."

"Excellent!" Hamil said. The elf captain stepped back and inclined his head; Hamil tapped his heels to his pony's flanks and rode on through the gate. Sarth followed after him, and Geran brought up the rear. He noticed that Caellen and the other guards were watching closely as he rode into the tree-shadowed lanes, but then he realized they were observing Sarth to see if the tiefling experienced any difficulties in entering the city's magical wardings. Well, that's one way to deflect suspicions, he thought. Travel with a tiefling, and no one will give you a second look.

Hamil glanced over his shoulder at Geran and spoke mind-to-mind, in the manner of his kind. *Is this Swan House where you want to go?* he asked.

It will do, he answered, keeping his eyes on Hamil's—it was the only way the halfling could read his answer. *It's the sort of place a traveling merchant would stay, although it's not easy on the coinpurse if I remember it rightly.*

The halfling nodded and returned his attention to the city ahead. Myth Drannor seemed more like a great noble's villa than a city; the streets were shaded by trees centuries old, and the buildings they passed—graceful towers, majestic manors flanked by slender colonnades, and elegant homes—were set well back from the street amid the trees and gardens. Even the workshops and mercantile establishments were open arcades of white stone, decorated with delicate carvings in the shape of leaves and flowers. Geran knew of no city in Faerûn that was as beautiful, and he sensed the growing wonder of his companions as they rode deeper into the city of the elves. A number of people were out and about, engaged in their day's errands, but the streets were hardly crowded. Most passersby were moon elves or sun elves who generally greeted the travelers with a polite nod or a small smile, but a few folk of other races were mixed among the elves—humans, halflings, even a dwarf or two. The elves welcomed the merchants, artists, and students of other races, although they kept a close eye on such visitors, and very few were permitted to settle in Myth Drannor. After winding along for a short distance, they came to a fine villa overlooking the ringing lake on the north side of the city. A stone slab by the lane was chiseled in Espruar glyphs beneath the image of a swimming swan. "This is it," Geran told his companions.

The Swan House was expensive as Geran remembered, but the three companions took a suite by the lakeside and left their mounts in the house's small stable. There were other places Geran could have guided his friends to, but they were places where he was better known, and he knew it would be wiser to avoid his old haunts. They changed out of their muddy, travel-worn clothes into better dress, and availed themselves of the midday meal provided by the house: a light repast of fruit, cheese, and bread.

"So far, so good," Hamil remarked when they'd finished. A good meal usually did marvels for his disposition. "Now how do we go about getting our hands on the bit of manuscript we're looking for? Do you know the place Aesperus mentioned?"

"No, I don't," Geran answered. "Many of the old ruins in the city have been covered over by newer buildings, and I suspect that the Irithlium might be one. We'll have to determine where it lies, and then see if we can slip into the ruins without notice."

"Correct me if I am wrong," Sarth said, frowning, "but I seem to recall that the captain at the gate specifically warned us that we were to rummage around in no old ruins without the coronal's permission. I would feel much better about this if we observed the legalities."

"Unfortunately, I doubt that we can," said Geran. "First, it could very well take tendays to obtain a writ—there are dangerous things still sealed in some of the vaults below the city, and the elves are very careful to make sure no one breaks wardings they've created to lock them in. Second, and perhaps more importantly, the Coronal Guard very well might confiscate anything that we remove, such as the *Infiernadex* pages."

The tiefling frowned, but subsided. Hamil helped himself to another slice of apple from the depleted dinner tray, and looked back up to Geran. "I don't like this idea of dangerous things sealed in vaults, but other than that, your reasoning seems sound. What are the odds that we can do what you say without being caught in the act? And how do we go about finding this Irithlium place, anyway?"

"The odds depend on where exactly the Irithlium lies. If it's in the outskirts of the city, we have an excellent chance to avoid being seen. If not, we might have to rely on Sarth's invisibility spell or some other means to get in and out," Geran replied. "As for finding out where the vault lies, well, I intend to ask."

He took a slip of parchment from a writing desk that stood in the suite's front hall and scratched out a short note with the quill and ink. He blew on it to dry the ink, then rolled the note into a tiny tube and pinched it closed with a little candle wax. Then he walked over to the suite's window, opened the clear glass, and gave a long, trilling whistle. Sarth and Hamil stared at him as if he'd lost his mind, but he just smiled at them and repeated the whistle. A moment later, there was a sudden flurry of wingbeats at the sill, and a small blue-feathered songbird appeared. It chirped once at him.

Gently, Geran pressed the tightly rolled slip of paper into the bird's talon. In Elvish he said, "Please, take this to Daried Selsherryn. You will likely find him in House Selsherryn or at Swordstar Hall." The bird chirped again, and flew off with the note in its grasp.

"Did you just *speak* to that songbird?" Hamil asked in amazement. "When in the world did you learn to do *that*?"

"It's not what I learned to say. It's the birds that have been taught to listen." Geran gazed out the window until the bird disappeared from view, enjoying a smile at his friends' expense. Then he turned away and reached for his cloak. "Come on. We've got a little bit of a walk ahead of us."

FOURTEEN

13 Alturiak, the Year of Deep Water Drifting (1480 DR)

A cold mist clung to the waters of Lake Glaerryl at dusk. The soft snow-fall of the day had finally ended, replaced by dense fog; from time to time the towering treetops of the lake's far shore emerged from the drifting vapors like the battlements of some vast castle. Geran, Sarth, and Hamil waited in the shelter of an elegant pergola that stood on a small islet amid the dark waters, linked to the shore behind them by a slender bridge. In the fading light, the spires and domes of the elven city behind them were invisible; for all they could tell they weren't within a hundred miles of Myth Drannor.

Hamil drew his cloak closer around his small frame and shivered. He hailed from the lands south of the Sea of Fallen Stars, and he did not care at all for northerly winters. He scowled at Geran, who stood wrapped in his own cloak a short distance away, and said, "You realize that there's no retreat from this little island? If your friend has an attack of conscience, we'll be trapped here like foxes in their den."

"I didn't give away much in the note I sent him," Geran answered. He doubted that Daried would turn him over to the Coronal Guard without seeing him first, but he could understand that Hamil wouldn't be reassured by his confidence in his old mentor. "But if we were found out, well, our chances to escape Myth Drannor wouldn't be terribly good anyway. Given that, I thought we might as well choose a spot where we can speak in privacy."

"Someone is coming," Sarth said. Geran exchanged a look with his friends, and the three of them turned toward the bridge; he stepped back to hide himself behind Sarth in case it was somebody other than Daried who might recognize him. He heard a light footfall on the wooden boards, and a tall, slender figure in white and pearl gray appeared through the mists—a golden-haired elf swordsman whose clothes were embroidered with leaf and vine designs in silver thread.

The sun elf paused, his eyes bright and sharp as he studied Sarth and then Hamil. "I do not know you," he said aloud. "Who are you, and why did you ask for me?"

Geran stepped forward, lowering his hood from his head. "Well met, Daried," he said. "I see my note found you. My apologies for not giving my name, but it seemed better to remain anonymous."

Daried's eyebrows rose in astonishment. "*Geran?*" he said. "What are you doing here? You're still under the coronal's judgment! Are you mad?"

"No, only desperate. I'm afraid we need your help." Geran indicated Hamil, then Sarth. "This is my old Dragon Shields colleague, Hamil Alderheart. You might remember that I spoke of him sometimes. And this is Sarth Khul Riizar, a sorcerer of no mean skill and a new friend. We've shared many dangers together in the Moonsea over the last few months. Hamil, Sarth, allow me to introduce Lord Daried Selsherryn, my tutor in swordmagic."

"A pleasure," the sun elf said politely, nodding briefly to Hamil and Sarth. But his eyes swiftly returned to Geran's face. "Geran, you must leave at once. If you are caught defying the coronal's law, the consequences will be drastic. You risk your life merely by setting foot here! And you place me in a very difficult position."

"I know it. I don't intend to stay an hour longer than I must. But, as I said, I've got an urgent errand in Myth Drannor."

The elf frowned. "What could possibly be urgent enough for you to flout the coronal's will?"

"There's a fragment of a magical tome hidden somewhere in the city ruins. It's become vitally important to retrieve it—the sooner, the better."

"So you intend to break the coronal's laws against pillaging the old ruins as well as defying her edict of exile?"

Geran shrugged. "I can hardly get in any more trouble with the coronal by adding the second offense."

"No, but your friends could," Daried pointed out. He put a hand to his brow and moved over to the balustrade overlooking the lake. Geran waited, allowing the sun elf to think. After a long moment, Daried sighed and glanced back to him. "What do you need this tome for?"

"To defeat Rhovann."

"Both of you are in exile, but still you indulge your enmity?" Daried shook his head. "Is there no end to it?"

"No, you misunderstand me," Geran answered. "When I left Myth Drannor, I wanted nothing more to do with Rhovann. I would've been happy to never lay eyes on him again. But Rhovann came to Hulburg in secret five months ago, and arranged the overthrow of my uncle, the harmach. He now rules Hulburg through a puppet, while my family and I have been banished." Geran's gaze fell to the wet flagstones of the pergola, but he forced himself to finish. "My feud with Rhovann has cost my family the realm they've ruled for centuries. I have to undo what Rhovann's done to Hulburg to set things right. And I'll need the missing pages of the tome to do that."

"It's true," Hamil added. "Rhovann allied himself with the enemies of Hulburg—mercenaries, pirates, slavers, even priests of Cyric. Geran didn't even know that Rhovann was moving against him until he deposed Harmach Grigor."

"I believe it, Master Hamil," Daried replied. "I have never known Geran to be untruthful. And there was always a spirit of spitefulness in Rhovann Disarnnyl that must have been sharpened tenfold by the indignity of exile, no matter how well it was earned. But some truths are hard to hear, and I have little liking for this one." The elf glanced back at the misty shore behind them, reassuring himself that no one else was near, and looked back to Geran. "Very well. What do you know about this tome you seek?"

"It's a piece of a book called the *Infiernadex*, which was once the property of Aesperus, the wizard-king of Thentur. We've been told that it lies in the vaults below the Irithlium. I've never heard of that, but I hoped that you might know more."

The sun elf nodded. "It was once a wizard's school, back in the days before the Weeping War. It was in ruins when we retook the city from the daemonfey in the Year of Lightning Storms, but the old ruin was rebuilt—you would know it as the building that houses the Celestrian Theater, Geran. Whether there is anything in the vaults below, I couldn't say."

"Why would Aesperus have told us to look in the Irithlium?" Hamil wondered. "If he meant the theater, he should have said so."

"His information about Myth Drannor is likely dated," Sarth replied. "He might have divined the location of the pages by using an old map of the city."

The elf glanced sharply at Sarth. "Any king of Thentur should be long dead. You are retrieving this tome for some ghost or lich?"

The tiefling grimaced. "Against my counsel, yes. However, Geran feels strongly that we will need the aid Aesperus can lend us against Rhovann's servants."

"Rhovann's created an army of constructs, animated with shadow magic of some sort," Geran explained. "Sarth and I encountered them a couple of tendays ago; they're an impossible obstacle to any attempt to retake Hulburg from Rhovann. Aesperus knows their vulnerabilities, but he demands the fragment of the tome as his payment for aiding us." He paused, watching Daried's concern deepening in his face.

"You trust this Aesperus?" Daried asked.

"Not entirely, but I wouldn't be here if I didn't believe him in this," Geran replied. "Do you know of any access to the ruins of the Irithlium? Is there some connection between the Celestrian's foundations and the older building?"

"There are scores of old doorways, cellars, stairwells, and such scattered all over the city. I can think of a couple near the Irithlium that *might* lead you in the right direction." Daried fell silent, considering the challenge.

Hamil shivered in his cloak again, and folded his arms over his chest. "Something about this confuses me," he remarked. "This wizard's school would have been destroyed in the Weeping War, which was about seven centuries ago, correct? So how did any spellbook of Aesperus wind up in the Irithlium, when he ruled over Thentur two hundred and fifty years later? Did someone try to hide his book in the *past*? Is that even possible?"

"It is, but such magic is incredibly difficult," Sarth replied. "It's more likely that simple accidents of fortune and coincidence conspired to bring the book to this spot. Things such as spellbooks might change hands dozens of times over a couple of hundred years, leaving a long and confusing trail across time and distance. I have followed such trails before. In all likelihood, the pages removed from the *Infiernadex* were sent from Rosestone Abbey to some center of scholarship, from which they were lost or stolen, only to pass through the hands of one wizard after another. Hundreds of adventurers came to this city in the years that it was abandoned. My guess would be that some unfortunate mage came to Myth Drannor with the pages we seek stuffed into his own spellbook, and met his end in the chambers below the Irithlium."

"A plausible explanation, Master Sarth," Daried said. "Before the Crusade, the Irithlium was infested with powerful devils. Before that, it was within the territory claimed by the phaerimm nest that haunted the ruins. Either would have recognized the value of a powerful spellbook and preserved it." He turned his attention to Geran. "Allow me to look into the question of how to gain access to the Irithlium. I know elves who are much more familiar with the ruins than I am; I'll see what I can learn with a discreet inquiry or two, and send word to you."

"Thank you," Geran said. "We're staying in the Swan House."

"I advise you to remain in your rooms. Each time you go abroad you risk discovery." The bladesinger hesitated a moment, and then asked, "Do you mean to see Alliere while you are here?"

Geran felt his heart skip. He'd longed for Alliere for the better part of two years after his exile; in fact, his banishment from the city had been nothing compared to the sudden ending of their love. Her perfect face had haunted his dreams, driving him almost half mad with heartbreak, and he couldn't deny that he'd spent more than a few hours during the long journey to Myth Drannor playing out in his mind what he might say or do if he were to meet her again. Would she still shy away from the violence, the black anger, that was lurking in him? Did she miss him as much as he'd missed her? Part of him still ached to find answers to those questions; he supposed that perhaps it always would. "How is she?" he asked Daried. "Is she well?"

"She is. She still lives in the tower of the Morwains, tending her gardens." He allowed himself a small smile. "It seems that half the young lords of the court are falling over each other, hoping to catch her eye."

"Good," Geran answered, and he meant it. He'd come to realize as he neared the city of the elves that, despite the old longings, his heart was hers no longer. Each time he'd conjured Alliere's face from his memories, he'd soon found Mirya coming to his mind. When he wondered how Alliere might greet him, he worried constantly for Mirya and anxiously awaited the day when he'd return to her. I've had strange fortune in my loves, he reflected. Alliere, Nimessa, Mirya . . . yet of all of them it was the strength and sincerity of Mirya that had captured him. "Is she happy?"

"It was difficult for her after you left, but now she fares better. The shadow on her heart has finally lifted. I think she would like to see you, if it could be arranged."

"I'd like to see her too, but I don't want to make trouble for her. It's enough that I've put you at risk of the coronal's displeasure. Better to keep Alliere out of this for now."

Daried rested his hand on Geran's shoulder briefly. "Perhaps you've learned a little wisdom since you left, then. I will send word to you when I learn something." The elf nodded to Hamil and Sarth before he turned and hurried off into the cold mists.

Geran and his companions waited a short time, so that anyone who'd noticed Daried leaving wouldn't associate him with the three of them. Then they made their way back to the Swan House on the city's north shore. The weather gave Geran a perfect excuse to hide under his hood, but he still felt a shiver of nervousness each time they passed elves in the streets. When they reached their inn, he settled himself by the fire to wait, and encouraged his friends to go enjoy the city's winerooms and taverns for the evening. He would have much preferred to show them some of the places he remembered in person, but it was simply out of the question.

The three travelers passed the next day and a half in much the same manner; Geran stayed in the Swan House, while Hamil made a show of looking through the wares of various craftsmen and merchants with Sarth at his side, playing the part he'd given himself. Then, late on the second day, Geran was startled by the appearance of a blue songbird by their room's window. He rose quickly and let the small creature in; it landed on the table and held still while he carefully retrieved the tightly rolled scrap of paper it carried from its talon. It read:

Meet me in the woods south of the Celestrian at midnight. I have learned that there is an entrance there.

"My thanks, Daried," Geran breathed softly. He scribbled a quick reply, and gave it to the same bird to carry back to his old mentor. Then he turned his attention to studying his spells, waiting for night to come.

FIFTEEN

14 Alturiak, the Year of Deep Water Drifting (1480 DR)

The Warlock Knight Kardhel Terov stood by his bedchamber's narrow windows, gazing out at the gray winter morning and the snowy landscape. He'd conjured his small fortress atop a bare hilltop on the shores of Lake Hul, a little more than four miles from Hulburg. The magical tower was his prized possession, a stronghold significantly more spacious on the inside than it appeared. With an hour's preparation, he could dismiss it into a distant dimension, only to summon it again wherever and whenever he happened to find himself in need of it. Not only did the iron tower provide him and his entourage with excellent protection against brigands, raiders, monsters, and other ill chances of the road, it also ensured a certain level of comfort in his frequent journeys. Terov was no stranger to privation, but he saw no particular virtue in it either.

He was interrupted in his reflections by a knock at the chamber door. "Enter," he called, absently cinching his sleeping robes closer around his waist.

A tall, red-haired woman in gray robes let herself into the chamber. She wore a dark veil over her eyes—the emblem of the *nishaadhri*, the Bound Ones. In Vaasa, mages were permitted their studies only if they swore lifelong fealty to the Warlock Knights; Terov's order was jealous of its power and had no intention of permitting anyone to wield arcane magic that they did not control in some manner. The Bound One bowed deeply before speaking, strictly formal even though she often shared Terov's bed at his command. "We have word from Griffonwatch, my liege," she said. "The harmach will receive us at noon."

"Good," Terov answered. "Have an escort of six armsmen made ready, Saavi. We will ride in an hour." The veiled sorceress bowed and withdrew; a moment later Terov's valets entered to assist him in dressing. That was another advantage offered by the tower—it could accommodate an entourage of a score or more, which only befitted a fellthane of his rank. They fitted him in his armor of black plate, chased with arcane sigils rendered in gold filigree, and then helped him don the long surcoat and surplice of red and black that went over the armor. A heavy broadsword was belted to his hip, and next to that a wand of black wood. As a rule, Warlock Knights did not appear in public unless armed and ready for battle.

When he was ready, Terov descended the iron stairs that circled the tower's interior and emerged into the cold, clean air. His soldier escorts were already mounted and waiting for him, along with Saavi. He mounted, and settled his black helm over his short-cropped hair of iron gray. Without a word, he tapped his spurs to his horse's flanks and rode off toward the road leading south to Hulburg. His bound sorceress and his soldiers took their places behind him.

The Vaasan lord set an easy pace, taking advantage of the ride to consider the challenge posed by Hulburg. A year before he'd secured the allegiance of the Bloody Skull orcs to sweep the Moonsea clear of obstacles to Vaasa's expansion . . . but the small realm of Hulburg had proved more resilient than he expected. Not far from this very spot, the defenders of Hulburg had stopped Warchief Mhurren and his Bloodskull horde at the old dike known as Lendon's Wall. Checked in his first move, Terov changed his tactics and dispatched the Cyricist Valdarsel to build up a faction loyal to Vaasa from the foreign laborers and gangs who thronged Hulburg's poorer quarters. Yet that stratagem too hadn't yet secured control of the city for Vaasa, mostly because the wizard Rhovann Disarnnyl had very ably seized the apparatus of power after the Hulmasters had been defeated. It seemed unfortunately possible that the mage Rhovann might prove even tougher to dislodge than the old harmach . . . which was why Terov had decided once again that a change in tactics might be in order.

For once, it was neither raining nor snowing, even though the skies were full of heavy gray clouds. A little less than an hour after setting out from his temporary stronghold, Terov led his small entourage up the causeway to Hulburg's old castle, dismounting in the courtyard before the great hall. Several footmen in scarlet and yellow, the colors of Harmach Maroth's family, hurried out to take the Vaasan delegation's horses.

"Lord Terov?" A short, stocky officer waited on the steps leading inside. "I am Edelmark, captain of the Council Guard. Please allow me to show you inside. The master mage will see you soon."

"Very well." Motioning for his retainers to dismount and wait for him, Terov followed the mercenary captain inside, Saavi trailing a step behind him. Edelmark showed them to an antechamber first and allowed the Vaasans a quarter hour to shed their muddy outer garments, warm themselves from their ride, and take some refreshment. Then he returned to lead Terov through the castle's maze of interior passageways and up several flights of stairs to a parlor whose windows looked out over the rooftops of the town below. Two council guards stood in front of the door, and saluted him as he approached before opening the door for the Vaasans and their captain.

The elf mage Rhovann stood by the large iron hearth in the parlor, glancing through several pieces of correspondence. Terov noticed that his right hand was covered by a glove, while his left was bare. Beneath his scarlet mantle, Rhovann wore a white tunic of elven graysilk embroidered with golden trees. As the Vaasans were shown in, the wizard set a piece of parchment down on a small writing desk littered with correspondence, and gave Terov a small bow. "A good morning to you, Lord Terov," he said. "I am Rhovann Disarnnyl, master mage of Hulburg and chief counselor to the harmach. Captain Edelmark I see you have already met. I must say, this is something of an unexpected pleasure."

"I thank you for agreeing to receive me on such short notice," Terov answered. He motioned to his sorceress. "My *nishaadhri*, Saavi. You might think of her as a bodyguard and advisor."

Edelmark studied the veiled sorceress more closely, while Rhovann gave her a mere nod; she was, after all, his servant. "Come, let's sit down," the mage said. He indicated several comfortable chairs arranged to face the fire.

Terov took the chair opposite, and motioned for Saavi to sit beside him. He glanced around the room, and frowned. "Forgive me, but will the harmach be joining us?"

"Possibly. He is but lately recovered from a long and severe illness and I am afraid that he must take care not to overexert himself. It falls on me to shoulder what duties I can to spare Harmach Maroth's health."

Terov frowned. He'd thought that he would be meeting the harmach today . . . but it seemed that would not be the case. *It seems that our reports were accurate enough,* he thought. *The mage was clearly the power behind the throne.* He considered insisting on speaking with the harmach, but decided that the most direct path to his goals likely led through his master mage anyway. "Perhaps later, then," he said. "I have heard that he has been slowly resuming his public offices."

"He has." Rhovann allowed himself a small smile. "I will, of course, arrange a formal reception of your embassy before the harmach's seat soon enough. But first I would like to get to the business of your visit, so that Harmach Maroth can be spared unnecessary details. Tell me, what brings a lord of Vaasa to Hulburg?"

"Hulburg has been much on my mind of late," Terov began. "We have followed events here with interest over the last year. Harmach Grigor was too weak to assert control over Hulburg's affairs, but your able administration offers the greatest promise we've seen from Hulburg in many years. We are pleased to see an end to Hulburg's disorders, but we believe that some of your other neighbors are much less pleased. Under Grigor Hulmaster, Hulburg could be safely ignored. Under Maroth Marstel"—Terov's crimson gaze did not waver from Rhovann's face, tacitly acknowledging the mage's evident influence—"Hulburg is now a potential rival to cities such as Thentia or Mulmaster, and a power to be reckoned with."

"We're flattered by your estimation of our talents, Lord Terov," Rhovann added in a dry voice. "However, I am not entirely certain I see your point."

"Only this, Master Mage: you lack friends. Thentia has blood ties, albeit distant ones, to the old Hulmasters. Hillsfar and Melvaunt see you as a rising rival. Mulmaster simply lusts after the land and resources of the north coast. Recent events have swept Hulburg into dangerous new waters." Terov clenched a fist, cupping it in the palm of his other hand. "It would be well for Hulburg to have a strong ally. Vaasa can guarantee Hulburg's security against any Moonsea state."

Rhovann leaned forward in his chair. "I see that Hulburg would gain the shield of Vaasan power against our Moonsea rivals," the mage replied. "But I am not sure what interest Vaasa has in Hulburg's security, Lord Terov."

"We seek a window on the west, Lord Rhovann. We are hemmed in by hostile lands to our east and south, and to the north lies nothing but unendurable ice. However, we believe that a trade road could be established through the Galenas to Hulburg's fine port. Naturally, the cost of driving a road through the mountains—and clearing a dozen orc chiefs and goblin kings out of our path—would be considerable. We're not willing to undertake it unless we know that Hulburg will welcome Vaasan trade, and the forces necessary to protect that trade. There must be certain guarantees on Hulburg's part."

"What sort of guarantees?" Rhovann asked mildly.

"A sworn alliance with the harmach. We place great importance on an oath freely sworn. It rightfully binds both giver and recipient. There must be no possibility of evasion."

"Your iron rings, of course," Rhovann murmured, steepling his fingertips before him. Terov was not surprised that the mage understood what Vaasa's lords required. Most folk in the lands near Vaasa knew the story of the Warlock Knights' rings, devices that were often enchanted to make oaths sworn to their wearers—and oaths their wearers swore—inescapable. He thought the question over for a long moment. "You ask much, Lord Terov. The harmach has little interest in providing himself with strict and attentive masters, oaths or no oaths."

Terov frowned. "I think you overlook the advantages of the arrangement," the Warlock Knight replied. "Needless to say, tolls and tariffs alone stand to greatly enrich the rulers of Hulburg. There would be a need for more laborers to unload ships, drivers to muster and guide caravans, more armsmen to guard them . . . within five years Hulburg would be the richest city on the north shore. In ten you might eclipse Mulmaster and Hillsfar as well."

"Few of our merchant costers would care to find Vaasan traders pushing them out of Hulburg," Edelmark remarked. "Whatever we gained in new commerce, we'd lose from costers such as House Veruna or the Iron Ring.

And Mulmaster's fleet is a lot closer to Hulburg than promises of Vaasan assistance."

Rhovann held up a hand, motioning Edelmark to silence. "I am not unaware of that, Captain. But it hurts nothing to hear Lord Terov out. What terms does Vaasa suggest, my lord?"

"In exchange for hosting a Vaasan trade concession, we can place a garrison of five hundred Vaasan soldiers at the harmach's service. And, as I said, the harmach would be entitled to collect tolls on trade bound to and from Vaasa. I am sure the exact details of trade arrangements can be worked out. Do you agree in principle?"

"The final decision will be the harmach's, of course. I must consult with him. As you have pointed out, agreements with Vaasa are not to be entered into lightly." Rhovann shrugged. "It is a serious decision, and we must weigh your proposal with care."

"As you wish. Take all the time to consider the question that you like." The Vaasan lord's lips twitched in a small smile at the notion of consultations with the harmach. Rhovann seemed to think that he could toy with him as long as he liked, dallying with Vaasa at his own convenience. Well, Terov was not accustomed to being ignored. He decided that the master mage of Hulburg could use a small reminder that he was not to be trifled with. "Of course, you will understand that if Harmach Maroth fails to come to an understanding with Vaasa in a timely manner, we will have no choice but to consider other alternatives. We are already engaged in certain preliminary steps to ensure that our interests are well looked after."

Rhovann narrowed his eyes. "Such as the bungled assassination in Thentia?" The mage paused, studying the effect of his words; Edelmark scowled at Terov, but said nothing. "Yes, I am quite well informed about Vaasa's machinations in Hulburg. You see, I have had several revealing conversations with High Prelate Valdarsel—well, his corpse—in the last tenday. I know now that he was a Vaasan agent who reported to you. And I know that he commissioned the attack on the Hulmasters in Thentia at your direction, a provocative act to say the least. So spare me your threats, Lord Terov."

"You should not have left the Hulmasters alive in the first place," Terov retorted. "I had no choice but to direct Valdarsel to eliminate the Hulmasters in exile. Any other Moonsea power—say, Melvaunt or Hillsfar—looking for an excuse to take control of Hulburg might do so under the pretense of 'restoring' the Hulmasters to their throne. Vaasa could not permit it."

"My reasons for leaving the Hulmasters alive are my own," Rhovann replied. "I wonder if you realize how much sympathy you created for the Hulmaster cause with your ill-considered attack."

An angry reply came to Terov's lips, but with iron effort he swallowed his annoyance. "Valdarsel's failure was regrettable," he admitted. "Had he succeeded, all the sympathy in the world wouldn't have mattered for the Hulmasters. Unfortunately for both of us, the Hulmasters still live, and the possibility that some other kingdom might intervene on their behalf still exists. The best way to avert it is for the harmach to align himself with Vaasa—sooner rather than later. Your hold on power depends on it."

Rhovann, on the other hand, frowned thoughtfully, weighing Terov's point at length. "I am not so sure of that." He stood, and gestured toward the door. "Accompany me for a moment, my lord. I want to show you something."

"As you wish," Terov replied. He rose to his feet and followed Rhovann; Saavi glided along a step behind him, and then Edelmark a few paces to the rear. The elf wizard led Terov through the castle halls to a broad staircase, descending to the floor below—halls and chambers built up around the living rock of Griffonwatch's hilltop, if he had his bearings straight. They came to a long hallway with windows on one side looking out the sheer face of the crag. At the end of the hallway stood two towering, black-armored creatures whose faces were hidden behind grim iron visors. They guarded a door at the end of the hallway, halberds held motionless in their thick gray hands. Beneath their breastplates, their rune-marked flesh was sculpted into textureless slabs of claylike muscle.

Rhovann paused by the two guardians, turning to face the Vaasans again. "My runehelms," he said, indicating the warriors with an absent wave. "Strong, fearless, nearly impossible to overwhelm through force of arms, and absolutely loyal to me. Very useful, as you might imagine."

"We have observed your creatures garrisoning the town," Terov replied. "As you say, a useful magic indeed. But a handful of battle constructs won't deter Mulmaster or Melvaunt should they decide to land an army on your shores. They'd likely bring war machines of their own."

"Not like these," the wizard replied with a small smile. He motioned the runehelms aside, and murmured the words of a passage spell to unlock the door they guarded. The room inside had been converted from a small banquet hall into a great laboratory. Cluttered tables lined the walls, covered with a fortune in imported glassware and urns full of alchemical reagents. A row of leaded-glass windows across the room offered little in the way of a view, but was sufficient to illuminate the room. To the left, eight great copper vats were arranged in a row along the near wall. "Come, Bastion," Rhovann said. "I need your assistance."

A hulking creature even larger than the runehelms outside stirred and silently stood. "Yes," it said in a deep, rumbling voice. Terov studied the creature with interest; he hadn't ever seen a golem imbued with the power of speech, no matter how limited. Clearly Rhovann was quite skilled in the creation of such devices. At the mage's gesture, the golem moved to the first of the copper vats, lifted its heavy lid, and began to pour a gray powder from a large wooden cask into the dark fluid inside.

"As much as I might like to create more servants such as Bastion, it simply isn't practical," Rhovann remarked as he observed the golem adding the powder to the vat. The hooded golem moved on to the next vat, opened it, and began to pour out more powder. "Instead, I devised my runehelms. As you can see, they are grown in these vessels."

Terov looked into the vats as the wizard's golem servant opened them one by one to add the reagents. In every one, the powerful form of a new runehelm floated in a bath of dark ichor, each progressively larger and more intact. The last was not animated yet, but it seemed to the Warlock Knight that it was otherwise complete, except for one detail: it possessed no facial features at all, only a blank visage of damp gray clay. "How long does it take you to grow one of your alchemical warriors?" he asked.

"Twelve days from start to finish. With eight vessels, I can manufacture twenty or so a month." Rhovann briefly inspected the creatures taking shape in the vats, and nodded to Bastion. The hooded golem closed each vat one by one, locking the lid with a heavy bar.

Terov glanced to his bound sorceress. Saavi replied with an imperceptible shrug, admitting that this was something outside her experience. She glanced at the complicated equipment filling the room, and said, "Fashioning the bodies is one thing, Lord Rhovann, but I am curious as to how you instill them with the semblance of life. That is no simple enchantment."

The elf laughed softly. "That is a professional secret, I fear. For now, all you need know is that animating the runehelms presents me with no great difficulties." He motioned to the door. "I think we are done here for now."

"I thank you for the interesting demonstration, Lord Rhovann," Terov said. "However, I am not sure I understand why you shared this with me."

"I want you to understand that I am very confident in the defenses I have woven around Hulburg, my lord Terov. You will have to offer me something more substantial than dark hints about foreign adventures if you wish me to support a Vaasan presence in Hulburg . . . something very substantial indeed if you intend to bring Hulburg entirely within Vaasa's orbit."

Terov's eerily crimson eyes flickered, but he made no other show of disappointment. "I see. What sort of incentive do you have in mind?"

"For a start, I believe that the priests of Cyric and their Cinderfist allies have outlived their usefulness. They were helpful in the overthrow of the Hulmasters, but now they are something of a liability. Before the harmach agrees to any Vaasan concession, we would have to be guaranteed that no more Vaasan gold or arms will go toward our dissatisfied citizenry."

Terov considered the question in silence for a long time. He had little liking for the elf, but he could not deny that Rhovann appeared to be very well entrenched in Hulburg. His best chance to bring Hulburg within Vaasa's influence was most probably by working with Rhovann, and not against him. After all, Rhovann was the power currently in possession of Hulburg. The Warlock Knights would hardly need to throw gold and mercenaries at Rhovann to keep him in power, but they'd have to spend, and spend dearly, to support his overthrow.

"It might be that we could exercise our influence with the clergy of Cyric and see to it that your request is met," he finally said.

"Good. And we would also need some guarantee that you are not supporting the Hulmasters in any way."

The Warlock Knight snorted in amusement. "Having gone to some trouble to allow our sympathizers in Hulburg to help Lord Marstel in his coup, it would seem counterproductive to then begin dealing with the Hulmasters now." Unless the Hulmasters came to Vaasa in a position of extreme need, in which case Terov might indeed have considered reversing course. Of course, Rhovann did not need to know that.

"I take that to mean that you do not object to giving me some guarantee on that score," Rhovann replied. "Very well: if you withdraw your support for the Cinderfists and remain disengaged from the Hulmasters, I will allow a Vaasan concession, subject to our normal laws of concession—which limit the size of your garrison, I should note. Is that agreeable to you?"

"It is," Terov said. A mercantile concession was only a small part of what he wished from Hulburg, but it was a useful first step. In time, that narrow opening might be widened. He held up his fist; the iron ring all Warlock Knights wore gleamed on his right ring finger. "Swear to it on my iron ring, and I will swear too."

Rhovann shook his head. "I will not place myself under your geas, no matter how specific or limited. You will simply have to trust me, and I in turn will trust you. We both stand to gain from our bargain; most people in the world make do with that."

Terov studied Rhovann's face for a long moment. It seemed that the master mage of Hulburg would not be so easily ensnared. "So be it. As a gesture of goodwill, allow me to add this word of warning: you can expect the Hulmasters to march in the second tenday of Ches. Kara Hulmaster hasn't been as careful in her hiring of sellswords as she should be. A few of her armsmen are sworn"—he held up his ring again—"to our service, and have provided agents of ours in Thentia with some insight into the Hulmaster plans."

"That agrees with what I have observed with my own spies, although I hadn't expected them to march quite that early," Rhovann said. "My thanks, Lord Terov. I look forward to our next meeting. Now, when would you like to be introduced to Harmach Maroth? I think you'll find him quite reasonable."

SIXTEEN

15 Alturiak, the Year of Deep Water Drifting (1480 DR)

The night in Myth Drannor was cold and fogbound. The silver lanterns that served as the city's streetlamps were few and far between in the chill mists; weak halos of light surrounded each, quickly giving way to the heavy murk. Geran regarded the weather as a great stroke of luck; not even elves cared to linger out in the streets, and the mists would make it much harder for any patrolling guards to notice him and his friends while they were in places they weren't supposed to be. As midnight approached, the streets fell still.

A half hour before their appointed meeting, Geran and his comrades slipped out of the Swan House into the fog. Hamil glanced up and down the deserted street, and shivered in his cloak. "I thought the nights were always starry and clear in Myth Drannor," he muttered. "This is no different from a sea fog in Tantras. Where are the faerie lamps and the dancing nymphs?"

"Some of the many stories about the city have grown in the telling in other lands," Geran replied. "Myth Drannor isn't impervious to foul weather and ill chance, which is something we should remember tonight. Besides, in Tantras the fog would reek of the harbor flats and smoke. Come on, let's be on our way."

He led Sarth and Hamil on a circuitous route that kept them in the city's public districts, approaching the old Irithlium carefully—the Celestrian stood in a quarter of the city where visitors weren't normally welcome without an escort. A few of Myth Drannor's winerooms and taverns remained open, but most folk had retired to their homes early. It might have been better to wait for the small hours, but Geran decided that Daried had chosen the hour so that he and his companions could pretend to be making their way home from enjoying the city's entertainments instead of skulking about on the streets when no honest person would fare abroad.

They came up on the wide wooded area where Daried was supposed to be waiting from its far side. He spied a path leading into the shadows, and took a careful look around. No one was in sight, although a faint lilting song spilled from a wineroom's door a good half block away. "This way," Geran said to his friends, and they followed him away from the deserted avenue and into the dark woods.

Myth Drannor was checkered with large copses and groves of living trees; there was nearly as much wild forest within the city's ring of lakes as there were streets and buildings. Many of the areas that had been reduced to rubble in the city's destruction long before had not been rebuilt when the elves reclaimed the city in Seiveril's Crusade, and the large area of ruins near the Irithlium's old location was an excellent example. Within the shadows of the trees, moss-covered stones of old walls and fallen buildings gleamed in the faint light. Geran felt his way forward, hardly able to see anything in the darkness.

"Ah, there you are." Daried Selsherryn materialized out of the shadows, holding a silver lantern dimmed to only a sliver of light. "A good night for scofflaws; few folk will be abroad in the fog. Come, the door you seek is this way."

Geran and his friends followed the sun elf into the shell of an old building, its foundations bare to the sky. Daried led them down a steep stone stair to what would have been the floor of its cellar; a dark archway loomed before them. "We are in the foundations of the Tower of Nythlum," Daried said softly. "There is no direct access from the Celestrian to the passages that were under the Irithlium, since the upper portions were largely filled in when the building was rebuilt. This tower belonged to a wizard who left it to the college on his death, and the foundations were joined by a new passage—this one before us. It leads to the passages that were covered up when the Irithlium was rebuilt."

Geran nodded to his old mentor. "I'm in your debt, Daried."

The sun elf shook his head. "Nonsense, since I was never here," he said. "Good luck, and if I do not see you again before you set out, sweet water and light laughter until we meet again." He dimmed his lantern and retreated, leaving Geran and his companions alone in the old foundation.

Hamil looked dubiously at the doorway. "Do you have any idea what might be sealed in this vault other than the harmless old manuscript we're looking for?"

Geran shook his head. "I couldn't begin to guess." He drew his sword and ventured into the dark doorway.

Sarth and Hamil joined him; carefully he picked his way down broken steps to a large chamber below the tower foundations, murmuring the words of a light spell to give him something to see by. The passageway continued to the north, back in the direction of the old Irithlium if Geran's bearings were correct, dropping a few steps as it went. After fifty paces or so, another archway loomed ahead, with a large door of stone filling the passageway.

Sarth set a hand on his shoulder to stop him. "There is an old warding here," the sorcerer said. "I will see if I can craft a brief opening so that we may pass through without destroying it." The sorcerer murmured a spell that Geran did not recognize, gesturing carefully with his hand. Geran was conscious of a subtle change in the cold air of the ancient halls, as subtle threads of magic drew taut and quivered under Sarth's careful weaving. A brooding menace seemed to gather form beyond the door; Sarth shot Geran a look of warning and continued with his spell.

Geran summoned a spell of his own. "*Cuillen mhariel*," he murmured, shaping the arcane syllables into the form of a misty shield, thin and silvery. Hamil glanced up at him and frowned; he lacked the magical training of the sorcerer or the swordmage, but he could tell from their tenseness that trouble was not far off. The halfling drew a pair of daggers and moved to one side, making sure he was out of the way.

What could endure a century in this vault? Geran thought. Some sort of undead? Or perhaps a demon or devil? That was unfortunately quite possible; in the days before the crusade had reclaimed Myth Drannor, the ruined city was full of such things. "Be ready," he whispered to Hamil. "I think there's a powerful fiend in here."

Perhaps we should stop what we're doing and leave it in peace? Hamil suggested. *After all, Aesperus might have been mistaken.*

Geran shook his head. "Unlikely." There was no doubt about it; something trapped within the old temple was straining at the portal that Sarth was carefully working open.

Sarth neared the end of his spell, but halted before he spoke the last words. He drew back a pace and looked at Geran and Hamil. "This is our last chance to reconsider," the tiefling said. "There is an infernal presence sealed behind this door. Once we pass within, we will be in its power."

"We didn't come all the way to Myth Drannor to leave empty-handed," Geran answered. "Aesperus is the key to defeating Rhovann's gray warriors, and the key to Aesperus is the bargain for the missing pages from his tome. I *have* to make the attempt; I can't see any other way to bring the pages out. But you two don't have to follow me."

"Not too likely now," Hamil muttered. "Let's get this over with."

Sarth nodded, and readied his scepter in one hand. He faced the archway at the bottom of the stairs, and spoke the last words of his passage spell: *"Anak zyrsha saigesh!"*

The stone portal blocking the passage ahead groaned open. In the space of an instant, the subtle menace waiting for them grew tenfold. Exchanging glances, they advanced into the chamber below the old school. It was a great vaulted cellar dominated by old sepulchers carved with the images of long-dead mages, most of them elves. Several other corridors led off into darkness. Geran paused, and murmured an elven finding charm he'd learned years before when he began his studies in magic, fixing in his mind the *Infiernadex* as he remembered it—he'd briefly handled the tome a few months back, and any pages that had once been a part of it likely retained a faint impression of the whole. The passage to the left immediately leaped to his attention, and he nodded toward it. "That way, I think," he said to his companions.

They were only three paces from the archway when the malevolence lingering in the temple's catacombs suddenly coalesced into a knot of living darkness behind them. They whirled to face the threat, watching as the inky blot took on a tall, manlike shape and became real and substantial. In the space of a few moments a gaunt, scaled, winged devil crouched in the center of the chamber, its wings flexing, its fangs bared in an evil grin. A chain of iron links glowing cherry red with heat dangled from its clawed hands.

"Foolish halfblood," it hissed at Sarth. "You have delivered me the keys to my freedom by weakening the warding above. When I slay you, I will at last be able to leave this place!" The creature hurled itself at the tiefling with sudden ferocity.

Geran leaped into its path, interposing himself between the devil and his friend. He struck with a crackling bolt of lightning that leaped from his blade, singeing the creature's belly scales in a smoking black crease. It wheeled on him, lashing with its burning chain, and for a moment overwhelmed Geran with the sheer frenzy of its wrath—snapping fangs, raking claws, battering wings, and goring horns, all the while flailing wildly at him with its infernal iron. He parried, ducked, countered—to no avail. A powerful wing knocked him off balance, and a raking claw under his guard caught him on the side and threw him headlong into the nearest sarcophagus. His magical wardings saved him from being gutted on the spot, but the impact against the cold stone knocked him senseless for a moment.

"Geran!" shouted Hamil. The halfling darted in beneath the monster's slashing claws, stabbing and cutting at its legs as he tried to stay inside its reach. Geran hardly noticed. Slowly he shook his head and rolled to all fours, wincing. Get up, Geran! he told himself. Distantly he was aware of a brilliant bolt of lightning searing the shadows of the catacomb, followed by a thunderclap that brought a rain of dust from the ceiling. With one hand on the sarcophagus next to him, he pulled himself to his feet and took two deep breaths to steady himself. Warm blood ran down his shirt and splattered the damp old stone. With a cry of challenge he charged at the monster's back and struck it deeply between its wings.

The infernal creature shrieked in pain, whirling to face Geran. He leaped over its lashing tail, and deflected a strike of its chain that was powerful enough to rip chunks of stone from the wall when it passed over his head. The monster surged toward him in fury, but at that moment Sarth—who was sprawled on the floor a good ten feet back from the creature—raised himself up on his elbow and shouted, "*Raizha ektaimu!*"

From his scepter, a bright green ray shot out, catching the devil in its side. Instantly a great gory bite appeared in its flesh as the disintegrating spell gouged a horrible wound in the creature. The monster shrieked again, so loud that Geran winced in pain, and then sank to all fours under the spell's power. In a moment nothing was left but a half-eaten corpse, its wound smoking with an eerie green vapor.

"I sincerely hope we see nothing more like that in here," Hamil said.

"As do I," Sarth admitted. "That was my only spell of disintegration."

Geran stood waiting, stretching out with his senses for any hint that more of the devil's kind were nearby. The aura of supernatural evil had diminished noticeably, but he couldn't be certain if it was entirely gone. "We'd better keep on," he finally said. "The sooner this is done, the better."

He limped toward the archway he'd sensed before with his finding charm, one hand clamped over his badly scored side, his sword in the other. Sarth and Hamil followed after him, weapons at the ready. The passage ran only a few feet before it ended in a large conjury. The summoning circle in the center of the room was defunct, its wardings broken by masonry debris that had fallen from the ceiling at some point in the past. Geran wondered if the devil they'd just battled had been confined within until the debris set it free to roam the vault, or if it had fled into the vault from outside to hide itself from the elves when they retook the city. He decided that it was irrelevant now, and looked around the room for any sign of the tome he sought.

A dusty old bookshelf leaned against the far wall. "Aha," he breathed. He hurried over to examine it more closely. Most of its contents had long since fallen to pieces, littering the floor with rotted coverings and scraps of yellow parchment, but one book seemed to be in better shape. Carefully he removed it, carrying it over to a worktable nearby.

"Is that it, Geran?" Hamil asked.

"I'm not sure," he replied. He blew gently over the cover, and found glyphs in Espruar gleaming under the dust: *The Book of Denithys*. He started to turn away in disappointment, but then it occurred to him that he was looking for a fragment, not a complete tome. He opened the book carefully, and found between its pages a folio of parchment that was a little larger and darker than the rest of the book. He closed the book, turned it over, and opened it by the back cover, and there, right in front of him, were markings to match the ones he'd seen on the rest of the *Infiernadex* months earlier in the tomb of the priestess Terlannis. "Wait, yes—yes, this is it! We've got it!"

His comrades hurried over to his side, peering at the ancient paper. "That's all there is?" Hamil said. "It can't be more than five or six pages. What does Aesperus want with them?"

"Allow me an hour to inspect them, and I will have an answer for you," Sarth replied.

"I suggest that we can inspect the pages later," Geran said. "I don't want to linger here a moment longer than we have to." He took a couple of endplates from the ruined books left on the shelf, brushed them clean, and placed the old *Infiernadex* pages between them as a makeshift protection for the old tome. Then he put the covered manuscript into his satchel, and led the way as they retraced their steps. They passed through the chamber of the wizards' tombs again, and back up the long passageway toward the tower foundations.

"Do we set out tomorrow?" Hamil asked. "Or should we wait a day, and make sure we've got what we came for?"

"Tomorrow," Geran decided. "Sarth can inspect the manuscript while you and I retrieve our mounts and reprovision. With luck, we'll be on our way by noon." He dimmed his light spell as they emerged into the tower foundation, turning toward the stair climbing back up to the ground level—and then he stopped midstep.

Elves in the fine mail and coats of the Coronal Guard stood waiting on the steps above Geran and his companions, their faces grim. Several held arrows on their bowstrings, half-drawn and pointed at the adventurers below. At the head of the patrol stood Caellen Disarnnyl, his sword bared in his hand.

"I am sorely disappointed in you, Master Alderheart," the moon elf said in a cold voice. "I warned you quite clearly against venturing into our ruins without a writ of permission. Apparently my words lingered with you for something less than a day and a half before you forgot them."

Ah, damn it, Hamil said to Geran. The halfling raised his hands in a placating gesture. "I think there's been a small misunderstanding," he began. "I believe we actually possess the proper permissions." Not a word of that last part was true, of course, but Geran thought it at least seemed plausible.

"Unlikely, as I happened to speak with the city warden not more than two hours ago before commencing my patrol, and I specifically asked him whether anyone had applied for a writ." Caellen smiled humorlessly. "He told me that no one had. Imagine my surprise when we heard reports of strange lights and sounds in this area! Now, I will only say this once: lay down your weapons and surrender yourselves, or we will slay you where you stand."

Sarth's eyes flashed in anger, but he did not move. He glanced to Geran and said in a low voice, "Well?"

We might be able to fight our way out, Hamil said to Geran. *The whole patrol is there on the stairs, so we'd have a chance to get by them and escape into the city.* His eyes flicked to Sarth, and Geran guessed that he was telling the tiefling the same thing.

Geran thought about it for a heartbeat. It was just possible that they might be able to do as Hamil suggested without being killed . . . but that would mean leaving Caellen and his guards dead, and after that, they'd have a hundred miles of forest to cross with the full wrath of Myth Drannor following after them. Even with that in mind he might have chanced it, but when it came down to it, he couldn't bring himself to spill elf blood to avoid capture. There was a difference between fighting for one's freedom and simple murder, and he knew it. *We have friends here*, he told Hamil. *We'll have a chance to beg forgiveness, to appeal to reason. But if we kill anyone, there'll be no help for us. Tell Sarth to yield!*

You tell him, Hamil replied, but he looked back up to Sarth and relayed the message.

"Surrender!" Caellen snapped. "I will not ask again!"

Moving slowly, Geran unbuckled his sword belt and let the weapon drop to the ground. He backed away from the sword. Beside him, Hamil snorted in disgust, but he began to divest himself of his daggers, dropping several of the weapons to the ground. Sarth shot Geran a murderous look, but he laid his scepter on the flagstones and likewise backed away. Caellen motioned to his soldiers. Some hurried forward to scoop up the weapons, while others approached to take Geran and bind his arms behind his back. He winced, but made no effort to resist; Hamil and Sarth were treated in the same way.

"This is not necessary," Sarth grumbled to the elves. "We have hurt none of your folk."

"That will be for the coronal to decide," Caellen replied.

In Elvish, the soldier who'd picked up Geran's weapon addressed Caellen. "Captain, have a look at this," he said. He drew Geran's sword from its scabbard, unwrapping the false leather grip from the hilt. The gleam of the elven steel was bright in the dim vault.

Caellen peered at the sword for a moment, and his eyes narrowed. "I know this blade," he murmured. He spun and closed on Geran, reaching up to jerk the hood from Geran's shoulders. For a moment he stared at Geran in astonishment, and then his lips twisted in a cold sneer. "Geran Hulmaster. I should have known! The coronal shows you mercy by banishing you when she might have ordered your death, and you repay her by defying her law? Oh, you will have much to answer for, my friend—and your companions as well."

"They're not guilty of defying my banishment," Geran answered.

"At the moment, I care not," the captain said. He stepped back and nodded to the guards. "Take them all away!"

SEVENTEEN

20 Alturiak, the Year of Deep Water Drifting (1480 DR)

Of all the prisons that Geran had been in—and he regretfully had to admit that that was a substantial number—the Jailer's Tower of Castle Cormanthor was certainly the least unpleasant. The furnishings were reasonably comfortable and there were no vermin at all. He was confined with Sarth and Hamil in the same roomy cell, which took up most of one floor of the tower. They even had a pair of slitlike windows that offered an excellent view over Myth Drannor's treetops and spires. Unfortunately, it was still a cell, and Geran and his friends were not likely to leave it any time soon.

When their jailers locked them in and left them to their devices, Sarth sat down on one of the bunks, holding his horned head in his hands. "Far be it from me to say I warned you against acting in haste," he growled at Geran, "but I seem to be in a prison because of your rashness. Do you have any idea how difficult it is for someone of my appearance to obtain even the slightest hope of a fair hearing? It will be years before I am released!"

"This was not how I hoped it would turn out, Sarth," Geran replied. He threw himself down in the opposite bunk. "It might have helped if you'd avoided the earth-shaking thunderclaps and dazzling flashes of lightning when we were trying to slip in and out of the Irithlium ruins without being noticed."

"You would rather I'd allowed the cornugon to slay you?" Sarth demanded. The tiefling glared at Geran, red anger flashing in his eyes.

For a moment Geran wondered if he'd presumed too much on the sorcerer's friendship; he doubted very much that Sarth was used to being spoken to in such a manner. In the last few tendays, he'd persuaded Sarth to become a renegade, ignored his counsel about dealing with Aesperus, and finally disregarded the danger his friend worried about—rightly, as it turned out. He sighed and shook his head. "No, I suppose not. Forgive me. I haven't listened well of late."

The tiefling glowered a moment longer before his anger faded. "You've had many things on your mind," he admitted. "I know this isn't your fault alone."

"Good," Hamil interjected. The halfling looked from Geran to Sarth, and back again. "It would have been damned annoying to be locked up with the two of you not speaking to each other. Now somebody magic us out of here, and we'll be on our way."

"It's not that simple, I'm afraid," Geran said. He gestured at the chamber around them. "These cells suppress most forms of magic. I can't speak for Sarth, but I know I couldn't light a candle in here without a match."

Sarth nodded glumly. "I will investigate carefully, but I fear it is the same for me."

The three companions passed a good deal of time in the next day or two by searching for any weakness in their confinement. Castle guards came by to check on them frequently; Hamil prevailed on them for a deck of playing cards, which helped to alleviate the tedium. Neither Geran nor Sarth could muster anything more than a cantrip in the cell, while the bars and walls seemed to be in excellent repair. Geran finally had to admit that there would be no quick escape from the coronal's palace. He'd have to hope that their hearing, when it came, would offer the opportunity to beg for leniency and perhaps get at least Sarth and Hamil released.

On their third day of confinement, the tedium was interrupted by the arrival of several Coronal Guards, who climbed swiftly up the steps to their cell. "Ho in there! You have a visitor," the first guard cried. "Make yourselves presentable!" Geran exchanged glances with his companions, and stood to face the hallway outside the cell. A moment later, a slender elf woman in a dress of green and gold appeared. Her hair, a glorious autumn red in color, was bound at the brow by a gold fillet, and flowed to the middle of her back like a river of molten copper.

"The coronal," Geran whispered to his friends. He lowered his head and dropped to one knee. Sarth and Hamil looked at him, more than a little surprised. Then Sarth put his arm across his waist and bowed stiffly, while Hamil swept his hat from his head and gave an extravagant flourish.

Coronal Ilsevele Miritar studied the three of them through the bars of the cell, and raised an eyebrow. "I am flattered by your courtesy, Geran Hulmaster," she said in the Common tongue, "but I seem to recall that you are no subject of mine."

Geran rose, and his friends straightened from their bows. "Old habits die hard, my lady," he said simply. As a Coronal Guard, he'd pledged his sword to the coronal and served her to the best of his ability for more than four years. He would still be in her service to this day if his duel with Rhovann hadn't happened.

The coronal regarded him coolly for a long time, and he did his best to meet the measuring gaze of those emerald green eyes without flinching. Finally she sighed and said, "What am I to do with you? I have to confess that it never crossed my mind that you would simply defy my banishment. On those few occasions in which I have had to impose that punishment, it was understood quite clearly that there was to be no return. And I know that you are well acquainted with the laws against delving into the ruins without permission. Do you have so little regard for my authority that you feel free to do as you please in my realm?"

He winced; having attended Ilsevele's court even for the brief time he'd been in Myth Drannor, he recognized that she was about as angry as he'd ever seen her. "I only did so in desperation, my lady," he said. "My homeland is in grave danger, and the key to setting matters right happened to be here."

"I am familiar with your reasons. Daried Selsherryn has already come before me to argue for you. Unfortunately, your belief in the necessity of your actions does not free you of my judgment—or free me to set aside the laws of the realm."

"I am sorry for the trouble I've caused, but I promise you this: Release my friends and me, and I'll never set foot in Cormanthor again. Or allow us to go our way now, and I'll return to face your judgment when Hulburg is no longer in peril. If you can't release me, then at least release Hamil and Sarth, and let them finish my errand for me. I led them to the Irithlium; it's my fault that they broke Myth Drannor's law." He met her eyes, hoping that she could see the sincerity in his words. "Please, don't delay us here."

Noble of you, but I don't care for the idea of whistling up Aesperus without you around, Hamil observed. *You're the one he bargained with, and I think he keeps track of things like that.*

"It is not as simple as that, I fear." Ilsevele sighed. "If matters were truly so desperate, you should have sent word to me. Some arrangement might have been possible. Now, my hands are tied."

Geran fell silent. He hadn't really thought it would be as simple as asking, but he had to try. As he searched for another argument, Sarth cleared his throat and spoke. "I am not familiar with your customs, my lady," he said to Ilsevele. "What is to be our fate?"

"Our Council of Justice will deliberate on that when next they meet," the coronal answered. "That will be on Greengrass. You and Master Hamil will likely be sentenced to a year and a day of service in restitution for your offense. Geran's fate is more problematic."

Sarth gave Geran a sidelong glance, but said nothing more. Greengrass was a little more than two months away; even if they were released with nothing more than a stern warning, they'd miss Kara's march against Marstel's soldiers.

"Is there anything else?" Ilsevele asked. Geran stopped himself from trying once more to beg for release; it would only annoy her even more. The coronal nodded to the guards and left, leading her small entourage down the stairs again. The heavy door at the base of the stairs clanged shut and locked.

"What do you know about this Council of Justice, Geran?" Hamil said. "Are they likely to be reasonable? Can they be bribed?"

Geran shook his head. "It's hard to say. I'll have friends on the council. I'll have enemies too. I would guess that the Disarnnyls and their allies are more than a little embarrassed by Rhovann's actions. I doubt they like being reminded of the dishonor he's brought on their House, and they may judge me accordingly."

"So we just wait?" the halfling demanded.

"What else can we do?" the swordmage answered. He returned to his bunk and stretched out, trying to imagine some ploy or stratagem that might win back their freedom, but nothing came to him.

Two nights later, Geran was lying awake, still brooding over the impossible situation, when a stealthy footfall on the steps outside their cell caught his attention. He sat up quickly, peering into the gloom; it was not completely beyond possibility that the Disarnnyls or some other rival from his days in Ilsevele's service might strike at him while he was held in the coronal's tower. But he saw only a slender gray-cloaked figure stealing softly into the chamber. The visitor hesitated a moment, as if uncertain whether or not to go any farther. Geran glanced across the cell; both Sarth and Hamil were asleep. Slowly he swung his feet to the floor and stood up. "Who's there?" he called softly into the shadows.

The visitor did not answer at first. But then she approached the bars, pushing back her hood to reveal long hair of raven black and eyes that gleamed a rich violet hue in the dim light. "It is I, Alliere," she whispered in Elvish.

"Alliere?" Geran repeated in amazement. She was the last person he would have expected to call on him during his imprisonment. After all, he'd been certain that she would never wish to lay eyes on him again, but here she was. He'd forgotten how beautiful she was; her fine, delicate features were simply flawless, and her eyes were entrancing. In fact, she looked exactly the same as the last time he'd seen her, but that was no surprise—a couple of years were nothing to one of the Fair Folk. He moved to the cell door, gripping the iron bars in his fists. He slipped back into Elvish without even realizing it. "What are you doing here?"

"I wanted to see you. We never spoke before you had to leave Myth Drannor. That was my doing, and I've come to regret it."

He shook his head in the darkness. "It might have been for the best," he said softly. Losing Myth Drannor had been hard, but losing Alliere had almost destroyed him. Before he'd returned to Hulburg, he would have done anything to see Alliere again and beg her to come away with him into his exile. Now he realized that perhaps fate had been kind to separate him from her so completely and quickly. The wound to his heart had been swift, giving him time to begin his healing. If he'd had some reason to cling to the idea that they might be together again, he never would have been able to leave her behind—or find another heart as dear to him as hers.

She looked down at the floor. "Still, you deserved better of me. Words of parting, at the very least, but I could not bring myself to face you."

"It was never my intention to hurt you."

She stood in silence for a time before she spoke again. "Daried told me what you'd told him about Rhovann's vendetta against you, about how he's ruined your homeland. I bear much of the responsibility for that." She sighed. "My indecision, my confusion, led Rhovann to hope for things that were not in my heart. He came to believe that you had in some way stolen me away from him. There must have been something I could have done to avert the feud that grew between the two of you."

He nodded. "I played my part in it, too, and I'm sorry for it." She reached over to rest her hand on his. After a long moment, Geran stirred and smiled. "As far as I know, I'm permitted visitors. You didn't have to sneak in to see me in the middle of the night."

Alliere laughed softly. "I'm sure you're allowed to have visitors, but I doubt you're allowed to have assistance for your escape." She reached into the folds of her cloak to draw out a small jar and a stylus with a slip of paper rolled tightly around it. "Daried gave these to me to give to you. The guards would never allow you to have them if they knew, so hide them well."

He took the jar and the stylus from her, frowning in puzzlement. "I don't understand. What am I to do with them?"

"The jar contains a magical pigment. With it, you can create a moon-door. Simply use the stylus to scribe the diagram shown on the paper upon one of the walls, and when the moon appears in the proper phase, the magic of the door awakens. It will become a portal that you can use to escape." She nodded at the small slip of paper in Geran's hand. "As I understand it, the next opportunity is the night after next, a little after midnight."

"Where will this portal lead us?"

"To a clearing a couple of miles outside the city borders. I will cache your belongings for you there tomorrow, and have mounts waiting."

He grimaced. "We can't leave without the manuscript we removed from the Irithlium."

"Daried said that you would say that." Alliere glanced about, listening for any sign of guards approaching before continuing. "It's with the rest of your belongings. I've already removed them from the guards' vault and replaced them with illusory copies. With any luck, you'll be many miles away by the time anyone discovers that you are missing."

He looked down at the jar, paper, and stylus in his hands. An ember of hope arose in his heart, and for the first time in nearly a tenday, he allowed himself to consider the possibility that his foolish quest hadn't been so foolish after all. *I told Hamil and Sarth I still had friends here,* he reminded himself. It seemed he had even more than he'd thought. "What will happen to you when we escape with your help?" he finally asked.

"I hope no one will be able to prove that I had anything to do with it," she replied. "Daried is under suspicion, of course, so he couldn't do anything openly, but no one knows I slipped into the guard's vault, and no one knows I'm here now. But I cannot stay long—I would much prefer not to be caught at this."

"Alliere . . . thank you."

Alliere started to reply, but she heard something below and started. "I must go," she whispered. She gave his hand a quick squeeze, then she hurried out of sight. Geran realized that he was standing by the bars with the jar and stylus in his hands, and quickly returned to his bunk. He hid the items under the pillow and climbed back into bed. A moment later two elves in mail entered the hall outside the cell door, one carrying a silver lantern with a soft blue glow. He closed his eyes and feigned sleep as best he could. The guards peered into the cell for a long time, until he was certain that somehow they'd realized he was hiding something from them . . . but just when he thought he couldn't bear it for another moment, he heard the rustle of mail and light footfalls descending again. The faint blue light receded, leaving the cell still and dark again.

Mind telling me what that was all about? Hamil asked him silently.

Geran flinched, startled by his friend's thoughts. He glanced over, and saw Hamil propped up on one elbow, looking across the cell at him. "I think we may have a way out," he whispered.

It's about time, Hamil replied. *When do we make our excuses to the coronal?*

"Two nights from now, if all goes well."

It's likely a plot to murder us while we're trying to escape, the halfling answered with a snort. *Oh, well, I hate waiting.* He shook his head and burrowed under his covers again.

The next two days passed with agonizing slowness. Geran had Hamil explain to Sarth everything he could recall of Alliere's instructions, keeping their speech silent to the greatest extent possible just in case they were being listened to in secret. The prospect of freedom dramatically improved the tiefling's spirits, and for the first time he days he managed to look at Geran without glowering or scowling. As opportunity allowed, Geran did his best to describe Myth Drannor's surroundings and the various roads and trails that crisscrossed Cormanthor to his friends, mulling over their options for flight once they got away from the city proper.

Finally the sun began to sink toward the horizon on the afternoon of the second day. As soon as their dinner plates were taken away, Hamil went to take up a post by the cell door, keeping an eye open for the guards who periodically came by to check on them. Geran and Sarth picked out the wall of an alcove leading to one of their window slits as the best place to draw their door. It was nearly perpendicular to the cell door, so even if their guards came to the bars they'd have a hard time seeing the painted diagram taking shape on the wall. Geran unrolled the parchment, and studied the design carefully. Then he passed it to Sarth, and let the sorcerer have a look as well.

I thought you two couldn't work magic in here, Hamil observed.

"We can't, but in this case, the magic is contained in the paint," Geran answered. He looked over to Sarth and offered the stylus. "Do you want to render it?"

"No, I think you had better do it," Sarth replied. "Your Elvish is much better than mine, and this is an elven spell. I wouldn't want to misdraw one of these symbols and send us all into some monster-haunted crypt unarmed, or strand us in some forgotten forest."

"At least we'd be out of our cell," Geran observed. Sarth's mouth twisted in a sardonic smile, but he smoothed the parchment out carefully and held it flat against the wall so that Geran could copy it more easily. Drawing a deep breath to steady his hand, Geran opened the jar, dipped the stylus into the thick silvery paint inside, and began to copy the diagram onto the wall, only much larger. It proved trickier than he would have thought—the magical pigment dried to a faint line of silver glitter within moments of its application, and he soon realized that some of the symbols he had to draw were very intricate indeed. He glanced at Sarth and said, "Watch me carefully to make sure I draw these glyphs correctly."

The tiefling nodded, and Geran focused on his task. He drew a tall oval frame four feet high and two wide, and a second oval within the first. In the space between the parallel lines he painted the words of the spell, struggling to make out the faint lines as they faded from view.

He was three quarters done when Hamil's voice lashed silently at him. *Guards coming*! the halfling said. Geran swore to himself and took a moment to mark his place as carefully as he could; then he tucked the stylus into his sleeve, capped the jar, and hid it in his pillow as he threw himself down on his bunk, making a show of folding his hands behind his head and staring up at the ceiling. Sarth joined Hamil at the table, where the halfling had already laid out two hands of playing cards. The tiefling looked across at his small opponent and said, "It's your play."

"So it is," Hamil agreed. He ruffled through his hand and was still studying the cards as two Coronal Guards appeared. The elven warriors checked the door and peered into the cell; Geran's heart raced as he waited for the outcry announcing that their half drawn escape had been noticed. But after a long pause, the guards continued on their way, and he allowed himself a sigh of relief. Their footsteps receded, and Hamil leaned out from his seat to watch them.

They're gone, he finally reported.

Hurriedly, Geran retrieved his jar and returned to the drawing. His heart sank as he studied his working space; the work he'd already done had faded to near invisibility. "Sarth, I don't know if I can see where I've been!" he hissed to the sorcerer.

Sarth grimaced. "Take your best guess," he said. "It may still function even with some amount of imprecision."

The swordmage daubed the stylus in the pigment again, and leaned close to begin again before pausing. He couldn't even tell if he was about to draw the next sign inside the door's frame, on the blank surface of the door, or somewhere outside the bounds of his work altogether. He made himself touch the brush to the wall in the spot he *thought* was right . . . and then, from the narrow window beside him, a faint silver radiance broke through the overcast. As the faint moonlight brightened the treetops and spires outside, the markings he'd already painted for the moon-door also began to grow brighter. Invisible lines and glyphs gleamed with a pale radiance as if they were made of molten silver, stark and beautiful.

"Hurry, Geran!" Sarth whispered. "Finish it while the break in the clouds lasts!"

The swordmage nodded and quickly began to draw and letter with confidence. In a few moments more he finished with it, and sat back on his heels to study the diagram on the parchment and the larger one he'd painted on the wall. "Do you see any mistakes?" he asked Sarth.

The tiefling studied the drawing as intently as he had. "No. I think it is done."

"Then let's see where it leads." Geran waited for Hamil to join them in the alcove, and focused on the last set of words he'd drawn, the activating phrase of the portal. With one more glance at his comrades, he read them aloud: "*Illieloch ser Selûnarr adhiarran!*"

The silvery runes glowed even brighter. Geran reached out to set his hand squarely in the center of the diagram, and willed himself forward; the light grew blindingly bright, a cool silver curtain that poured down over him as if he'd stepped under a waterfall of moonlight. Then, in the blink of an eye, he staggered forward into a dark clearing and stumbled to all fours, his eyes still filled with the brilliant radiance. I'm not in the cell anymore, he realized. But am I where I'm supposed to be? He tried to blink the bright afterimage from his eyes and started to stand, only to stumble again as Sarth and Hamil piled into him. When he finally regained his feet, he found that he and his friends were standing in a small open space before an old elven ruin. A complicated design of silver lines and Elvish lettering glowed brightly within an arch of white stone, one of several arches that made up the ruin's wall. He looked around, searching for something familiar.

A quick elf laugh interrupted him. "You succeeded!" Alliere said. He turned and found her in the moonlit clearing opposite the doorway they'd just come through. Daried Selsherryn sat on a log close by, smiling broadly. Alliere came forward to embrace him, and quickly drew back. "Well done, Geran! I knew you'd manage it!"

He shrugged awkwardly. "I couldn't have done it without your help. Thank you for aiding us—both of you. I sincerely hope that you don't wind up taking our places in the tower."

Daried stood. "I suspect that the coronal won't be unhappy with your escape. She did not care for the idea of Rhovann Disarnnyl causing mischief in other lands after she'd banished him from her realm. We shall see." He clasped Geran's arm, and nodded to Sarth and Hamil. "Come, you cannot linger here. I will seal the moon-door to bar pursuit, but the coronal's mages will be able to discern the door's destination easily enough, and we are only a couple of miles from Myth Drannor. You'd better go while you can."

Alliere took Geran's hand and led him and his friends to a trio of horses picketed in the shelter of an old courtyard, while Daried began to chant words of closing, interrupting the doorway behind them. As she'd promised, their belongings were gathered in tidy bundles by the horses; Geran belted his sword to his hip as Sarth tested his rune-marked scepter and Hamil rearmed himself with his seemingly endless store of daggers. When they'd finished, she handed Geran a wooden tube. "The manuscript you brought from the Irithlium," she explained.

Daried returned from the moon-door. "That should suffice for now," the bladesinger said. He nodded at the forest outside their small clearing. "There is an old road that strikes the Moonsea Ride not far from here, but if you'll heed my advice, you won't go that way. Any who pursue you will certainly expect you to fly in that direction. I would instead suggest that you make for the Silverleaf Trail and head due north, through the woods. Three to four days of hard riding should bring you to the Hillsfar–Yûlash road, a day's ride west of Hillsfar."

"Sound advice that I think I'll follow," Geran answered. He set his hand on Daried's shoulder. "How can I ever repay you for the help you've given us?"

"Give Rhovann my warm regards," the bladesinger said. His smile didn't reach his eyes. "Our paths will cross again before too long, I think."

The swordmage released his old mentor, and turned to Alliere. Strange, he thought. Only a year ago, and I would never have been able to turn my back and ride away from her, yet now he meant to do exactly that . . . and his heart was content. He took her hands in his, and looked into her face. "I am truly sorry for what I did before," he said to her. "But I'm glad that we part in friendship now. Sweet water and light laughter until we meet again."

She held his gaze for a moment before she nodded. "And to you, dear Geran," she answered. Then she released him and stepped away.

Sarth and Hamil were already mounted and waiting for him. He quickly swung himself up into the saddle, turning his mount's head toward the forest. "Follow me!" he said to his companions. He kicked the horse's flanks and led the way as they sped off into the night.

EIGHTEEN

23 Alturiak, the Year of Deep Water Drifting (1480 DR)

Shortly after sunset, a clatter at his window startled Rhovann from his meticulous record keeping in his laboratory. A small gray shape scratched at the thick glass; the mage set down his quill and hurried over to open the window and let in one of his homunculus spies. The creature croaked once and flopped inside, collapsing on the windowsill.

"What is this?" the mage muttered to himself. The homunculus was dying. Something had raked its body with deep claw marks, and dark fluid dripped slowly from the wounds. He frowned and examined the number scribed at the back of its neck, trying to determine which of his minions this was. After a moment, he nodded to himself. This homunculus he'd sent to Thentia several days before. The injuries were severe, but it was quite likely that the tiny creature had spent itself in the wearying flight. The creatures were not made to endure days of travel in the harsh winds and weather of the Moonsea North.

He sighed, closing the window against the wind-driven hail and icy rain that beat against the panes of his workshop. "Well, let us see what you have found," he said aloud. The creature could not understand that, of course, but the mage was speaking to himself, not the homunculus. He carried the small monster from the windowsill where it had collapsed to a worktable nearby. Murmuring the words of a spell, he set his hand—the living one—upon the tiny creature's head, summoning up its recollection of what it had seen during its long flight.

Endless miles of moorland and barren, stony hillsides reeled by beneath him; Rhovann ignored it and shifted the creature's recollection to something of significance. The image blurred, and then steadied again; now he seemed to hover above an encampment of wooden barracks and tents. Hundreds of soldiers in surcoats of blue and white marched and wheeled in some sort of mock battle. Rhovann blinked in surprise; that was certainly more than he would have expected the Hulmasters to gather in exile. They must have had more success reorganizing their Shieldsworn than he'd anticipated . . . or perhaps, as the Vaasans feared, some other Moonsea power had chosen to support the Hulmaster cause with gold and sellswords. It wouldn't be the first time such a thing had happened.

"A matter for concern, but not panic," he decided. No doubt Geran and Kara Hulmaster would get the most from the troops under their command, but the Council Guard still held an edge in sheer numbers— and that was not counting his own runehelms, who were far stronger and more resilient than merely human combatants anyway. "Show me more," he commanded the homunculus, and the picture in his mind's eye shifted again. Now he peered in a window at a large room where many captains gathered. He could clearly make out Kara Hulmaster, speaking at the head of the table. A tall young cleric in the robes of an Amaunatori friar stood listening nearby beside a black-bearded dwarf in heavy armor who smoked a pipe. Rhovann frowned, recognizing Kendurkkel Ironthane. He still didn't understand why the Icehammers had joined the Hulmaster cause; it didn't seem like the mercenaries to take on speculative work. There was a map on the table, and Rhovann strained to make out the details on it. Unfortunately, this vision only lasted a few more heartbeats before the homunculus was obliged to flit away from the window in order to avoid the attention of a nearby guard.

"What is your plan, Kara?" he wondered aloud. "You are outnumbered, but you prepare to attack regardless. What is it you know that I do not?" Geran and his cousin might be counting on more aid from friendly cities . . . or perhaps they hoped to combine forces with the rebels who'd been causing so much trouble in Hulburg. Yes, that might be it; they had a different appreciation of the numbers than he did.

Rhovann willed the homunculus to its next memory. He found himself flying over a field behind the manor, heading for one of the barracks. A solitary man on horseback sat back in the tree line, with something on his arm. He threw his arm forward with a sharp cry—and a large falcon leaped into the air, its wings beating with power and grace as it arrowed up toward the homunculus. There was a confused tumble of sky and ground, flashing talons . . . Rhovann snatched back his hand, unwilling to share in his small servant's mortal agony. It was just as well—the broken thing expired an instant after he severed their connection.

"A falcon," he murmured, pursing his lips in thought. Kara Hulmaster's doing, no doubt. Evidently she'd decided to guard her camp against airborne spies; she was damnably clever about such things. If she was cautious enough to post falconers, she might very well be cautious enough to anticipate his spying and make a point of showing him things she wanted him to see . . . in which case, he could not be confident of any report his minions brought back from the Hulmaster camp. Well, he would just have to find another way to keep an eye on the so-called Hulmaster army.

He closed his eyes, thinking hard about what the homunculus had seen . . . and not seen. There was no glimpse of Geran Hulmaster anywhere. Of course, the odds of his homunculus spotting one specific person in a manor crowded with many hundreds were low, but Rhovann had instructed his small spies to seek out Geran, and for tendays now, they'd found nothing. For that matter, the human spies he employed in Thentia couldn't confirm Geran's location, either.

The mage scowled as he realized that some of his calm confidence about the coming conflict had eroded away. Still weighing the homunculus's last vision, he closed his journal and secured the laboratory with the customary wardings. Then he went in search of Edelmark.

He found the Council Guard captain in the castle's rain-splattered courtyard, observing the drill of one of his companies. "Come, Edelmark," he said. "I want a word with you."

"Of course, my lord mage," the captain replied. He nodded to a subordinate to take over, and fell in a half step behind Rhovann as the elf mage led him into the dry interior of a turret overlooking the castle gate. A murmured spell and a simple gesture guaranteed their privacy.

"I have just received a report from Thentia," Rhovann said to his captain. "The Hulmasters are drilling and maneuvering their army every day. And it seems that our initial reports were correct, and the Icehammers are marching under the Hulmaster banner."

Edelmark nodded. "Do you know when they plan to march, my lord?" he asked.

"I haven't been able to discover that with my observations," Rhovann admitted. "If you were in command of the Hulmaster forces, what would you do?"

Edelmark frowned and considered his answer. "A winter campaign would be difficult. There's no shelter to be had in the Highfells. Given my choice, I'd wait for the weather to turn . . . but time doesn't favor them. If they wait for the spring thaw, the reopening of our port would give us the opportunity to bring more mercenaries into the city any time we liked."

"It would also give me the opportunity to manufacture more rune-helms," Rhovann observed. He hoped that the number and strength of the constructs he'd created would come as a very ugly surprise to any Hulmaster loyalists marching on Hulburg. Geran and his cousin might understand that, or they might not. On the other hand, they probably wouldn't overlook the significance of Hulburg's port reopening. "If the Hulmaster army comes before the thaw, could your Council Guard defeat them?"

"With the Icehammers, they've got about eight hundred armsmen. That is close to matching the strength of the Council Guard and the allied merchant companies." Edelmark shrugged. "Of course, many of the Hulmaster troops are ill-equipped militia and wouldn't stand up well to our professional armsmen. But we have to assume that any loyalists remaining in Hulburg would rise in support of a Hulmaster army, possibly shifting the odds against us."

Rhovann thought that his captain was a little too quick to dismiss the quality of the Hulmaster troops, but he didn't want the man starting at phantoms. "My runehelms are nearly a hundred strong now. They would make our victory certain, would they not?"

The mercenary captain twisted his mouth into a small smile. "Nothing is certain in war, my lord mage. But I have a hard time imagining how the Hulmasters could beat that many of your gray warriors. They're formidable opponents. Could you commit so many to the field?"

"What else would I do with them?" Rhovann asked.

"Some forces must be left to protect Griffonwatch and Daggergard, and keep order in the town. I don't trust the Cinderfists, regardless of what the Vaasans might promise. Valdarsel seemed to be the only one who could keep them in check, and now that he's dead, they're all too likely to riot and start looting the town as soon as our backs are turned. For that matter, I'm not sure that we've completely suppressed the Hulmaster loyalists. There may be more of them than we've seen so far."

"The Cinderfists do not concern me." An unruly mob in Hulburg's poorer quarters was troublesome, but without the priests of Cyric directing their efforts, they were simply ruffians, and didn't pose a lasting threat to Rhovann's control of the city. In fact, leaving them to roam unchecked might prove useful, since they'd likely harass native Hulburgans who might otherwise rise in support of the Hulmasters. Despite all of the plunder the Cinderfists had been allowed to strip from the native loyalists, they still clamored for more. "Who else might side with the Hulmasters?"

"The Thentians might take a more active role," Edelmark answered. "Some of the merchant companies are unreliable. And it's possible that a third party like the Mulmasterites might attempt to seize the city while we're busy fending off the Hulmasters. But that isn't likely until the ice is gone and the port opens again."

At least the Vaasans are dealing with me instead of the Hulmasters, Rhovann reflected. He gazed out of the arrow slit overlooking the gray-shrouded town below the castle, flexing his metal hand unconsciously. Geran's army didn't frighten him since he was clearly in the stronger position for now, but there were many interests colliding in Hulburg, and he couldn't guarantee that some of them wouldn't align against him if the right circumstances arose. If enough of them did so, it was far from inconceivable that Geran and his wretched family might unseat him. All things considered, Rhovann much preferred to deal in certainties. Perhaps he could take steps to fix some of the unknowns Edelmark feared, and eliminate variables that might otherwise provide the Hulmasters with a chance to succeed in their desperate gambit.

"Thank you, Captain. That is all," he said. Edelmark touched his knuckle to his brow and went back to his duties; Rhovann stood on the battlements, gazing out at the town—his domain, to order and arrange as he saw fit—for a short time before returning to his laboratory to work on the next group of runehelms.

For the next few hours, he weighed Edelmark's advice and the reports of his spies as he labored. It seemed likely that he'd have to commit many of his runehelms to meet the Hulmaster attack when it came, and that of course would leave the city vulnerable to the threats posed by the Cinderfists or the Hulmaster loyalists. The Cinderfists were in hand, or so he thought; it depended on whether he could trust Terov. But his mind kept turning to the unanswered question of Geran Hulmaster's whereabouts. Geran had already demonstrated the ability to slip into Hulburg whenever it pleased him. He'd be wise to come up with a counter to that potential threat.

"Bastion, I have an errand for you," he said, making his decision. "Bring me Mirya Erstenwold—alive and unharmed. I wish to have a word with her. If she is not at her home, return for further instructions."

The golem inclined its head, then turned and padded away. Rhovann put Bastion out of his mind, and turned his attention to the work at hand. The latest group of runehelms was almost finished; he had one more crucial step to see to. He went to a circle of silver runes inlaid in the workroom floor, and began to chant an incantation. The room around him began to grow dim, the shadows lengthening and taking on strange new shapes, and the air grew cold; light and warmth had little power in this place. Dark currents of power that Rhovann could barely perceive under most circumstances suddenly twisted into sharply defined focus, ready to his hand. He bared his teeth in a cold smile; here, in this realm, he was at his strongest. The spell of transference complete, he stepped from his silver circle into the Plane of Shadow.

The shadow workroom resembled his own workroom in the harmach's castle, but that was the way of the Shadowfell. It had little true existence of its own, and merely imitated the daylight world—although never perfectly. Many of the furnishings and accoutrements from his workroom weren't present here, or stood in the wrong place. Likewise, there were things present in the Shadow that didn't exist in the living world version of this chamber. Before him, a complicated apparatus of silver coils and dark glass seethed slowly with a thick black substance. Rhovann approached the device, placed a rune-carved mold of silver beneath it, and carefully decanted eight marble-sized drops of liquid ebon into the impressions. Within moments the drops congealed into lustrous shadowy pearls, fixed in their form. "Good," he murmured aloud. Then he returned to the silver circle and reversed his incantation, shifting himself back to the normal world. The shadows faded, and the air grew warm again.

Rhovann looked down at his shadow pearls, studying them for any imperfections. He found none. Satisfied, he carried them over to the great copper vats in which his runehelms grew. Murmuring potent spells, he took a shadow pearl and pressed it into the damp gray clay of each runehelm's uncovered face, otherwise devoid of any features at all. Setting his mold aside, he took blank visors and affixed them to the empty faces of each of his new creations, whispering more words of power over the creatures to awaken the shadow pearls that would animate them.

A small commotion by the door of his laboratory caught his attention. He ignored it until he finished the last of the spells required. Then he brushed off his hands and looked up; Bastion stood waiting with Mirya Erstenwold, one great hand clamped around her upper arm. Rhovann noticed that her hands were bound behind her back and she'd been gagged, but her eyes were bright and furious. "Ah, there you are," he said. "You may remove her gag, Bastion."

The golem obediently undid the gag. Mirya spluttered as it came free, working her jaw with a wince of pain. "What do you want of me?" she demanded. "You've no right to send your monster off to fetch me whenever you feel like it!"

"I thought we might have a brief chat, Mistress Erstenwold," he answered.

"You sold my daughter and me to pirates, you black-hearted bastard. I've nothing to say to you!"

Rhovann shrugged. "It would have been easier to have the two of you killed, Mistress Erstenwold; it was a matter of some inconvenience to spare your lives. I did so because I take little pleasure in wanton killing." She glared at him, but he thought there was a shadow of fear behind her anger now. He sighed, and went on. "You have seen Geran Hulmaster since his exile, haven't you?"

"You know that I have," she replied. "As I told Edelmark, he wanted to see how I was getting along. He didn't share any of his plans with me."

"I'm sure. Well, let me come to the point. I expect that sometime within the next few tendays Geran may slip into Hulburg and contact you again. You will inform me at once should he do so."

"Edelmark's already threatened me, Rhovann."

"Oh, you don't understand. This is not a threat. It is a statement of fact." Rhovann stepped close, and drew his wand with his silver hand. Mirya's eyes widened in fright, but he touched the tip of his wand to her forehead and began a spell of domination. She shuddered in sudden panic and tried to pull away, but Bastion held her motionless, unable to retreat. The mage locked his eyes with hers, and bent the full power of his magic against her. She fought, and fought hard, her will surprisingly strong for someone untrained in the magical arts. For sixty heartbeats or more they struggled in silence, until finally her defenses crumbled under the relentless pressure of his enchantment. Her eyes, blazing in anger before, suddenly went blank and glassy, and her chin drooped toward the floor.

"When next you see Geran Hulmaster, you will do everything in your power to betray him to me," Rhovann whispered in her ear. "Delay him in your home, lure him into meeting you in a specific place, seduce him—whatever you must do in order to keep him or maneuver him to a place where he can be caught. All you need do to summon me is to tell any runehelm—the helmed guardians in the streets—to tell me that you have Geran. Do you understand so far?"

"Yes, I understand," Mirya said in a weak voice.

"Good. Now you will forget that we have spoken today, and carry on about your business as you normally would until you meet Geran Hulmaster again. Give no sign or indication to anybody what you intend, and do your best to conceal what you have done until I tell you otherwise. Do you understand?"

"I understand," Mirya repeated.

"Very well. Bastion, unbind her." Rhovann waited for the golem to free her wrists before finishing. "Now return home. If anyone asks what you were doing at the castle, you will say that you were questioned about Geran's expedition against the Black Moon pirates. Supply whatever details are necessary to allay suspicion. You may go."

Mirya's eyes cleared, and she frowned. Without another word to Rhovann, she let herself out of the laboratory and hurried away. Rhovann returned his wand to his belt, feeling quite pleased with his own cleverness. Whatever else the next few tendays brought, Geran's days of skulking around unnoticed in Hulburg were at end.

NINETEEN

27 Alturiak, the Year of Deep Water Drifting (1480 DR)

For days, Geran, Hamil, and Sarth rode as hard as they dared to push their mounts, hoping to outdistance any possible pursuit from Myth Drannor. Geran didn't believe that the coronal's warriors had any special reason to pursue them with a vengeance, but he couldn't rule out the possibility that the Disarnnyls would make every effort to keep him from escaping justice. If he allowed himself to be recaptured, there would be no leniency from the coronal—of that much he was certain. Ilsevele might have been able to arrange matters with the Council of Justice given time, but he couldn't see that she'd entertain any pleas for understanding after he'd gone to such lengths to flee her authority. Deciding that it would be better all around to leave Myth Drannor as swiftly as possible, Geran urged his companions to the best speed they could make, hoping that no guard companies were in position to intercept them.

Early on the morning of the third day, they emerged from the great forest of Cormanthor into the open lands along the southeast coast of the Moonsea. These lands had been settled long before, but large parts of the countryside had fallen into ruin in the last century, pillaged in wars between the surrounding cities and finally swept clean by the Spellplague. Sarth reined in and rubbed at his back with a small groan. He was not a good rider, and the last few days had been a sore trial for him. "I would not have believed it possible, but we seem to have gained our freedom," the tiefling said. "Which way now? To Hillsfar?"

Geran brought his horse to a halt alongside Sarth. "I'm afraid we can't slow down yet. Myth Drannor might not claim any land beyond the forest, but that doesn't mean her warriors wouldn't pursue us beyond the woods."

"Do you really think they're chasing us?" Hamil asked.

"The coronal doesn't have a choice. She has to show that she won't play favorites, and letting us go when she might still catch us wouldn't look good at all. We might have fooled them by coming through the woods, but I think it's wisest to assume they're close behind us until we know they aren't." Geran glanced at the dark line of forest behind them.

"So, as Sarth said a moment ago: Which way now?" Hamil asked. "Do we head for Hillsfar anyway, or do we ride around the Moonsea and strike for Phlan?"

Geran thought it over for a moment. "Hillsfar. But let's stay off the roads and stick to the countryside as much as we can."

They continued on their way, heading northeast across the empty countryside. Keeping the dark edge of the forest a few miles to their right, they rode through long-abandoned fields divided by crumbling stone walls and hedgerows, and a little before noon the next day they spotted the walls and rooftops of Hillsfar. Geran allowed himself a long sigh of relief; Myth Drannor's agents might soon learn where they'd gone, but taking them into custody would be another matter altogether—the city's authorities would never permit the elves to arrest fugitives who hadn't broken any Hillsfarian laws. Geran and his friends went to the city's docks and booked passage on the first vessel bound for Thentia, then returned to the city's mercantile district to sell their mounts and await their sailing in a comfortable inn.

With a day and a half to pass before their ship sailed, Sarth retired to one of the inn's private rooms and made a careful study of their *Infiernadex* fragment, something he'd been unable to do during their brief rests during the flight from Myth Drannor. Geran left him to it for several hours, busying himself with several minor errands around the city. When he returned, he found Sarth busily copying the fragment to fresh parchment.

"What have you learned from Aesperus's spellbook?" Geran asked him.

"First of all, it is *not* Aesperus's spellbook," Sarth answered. "Rather, it is an older spellbook that was in Aesperus's possession for a time. Much of what I know about the complete manuscript comes from the writings of mages who had an opportunity to examine the tome before it fell into Aesperus's hands. That is what led me to Hulburg in the first place. In any event, the *Infiernadex* is the work of one of my forebears from ancient Narfell, recording several rituals and spells not found anywhere else. Many of those are diabolic in nature, and too dangerous even for one of my blood to wield safely. Others are simply rare and powerful; those I hoped to master." The tiefling managed an awkward shrug. "I have spent most of my life in search of greater command over the arcane arts. Perhaps I have not given much thought to the question of what I intend to *do* with such power once I hold it."

"You've chosen to save Hulburg at least two or three times in the last few months. That seems a good use for the power you wield." Geran looked over Sarth's shoulder at the cryptic pages spread out before him. They meant little to him; he'd been schooled in the elven tradition of magic, and the *Infiernadex* was based on another tradition, written in another language altogether. Even if he could read it, it might not make much sense to him. "Can we safely give it to Aesperus?" he asked.

The sorcerer looked down at the old parchment, thinking. "Yes," he finally said. "I am not happy about the prospect, but I've learned all I can from this. What does it matter if this knowledge is perilous? Aesperus is a perilous power already. But I must warn you, Geran, that the day may come when the King in Copper must be dealt with."

"I hear you," Geran replied. He set a hand on Sarth's shoulder, and left the sorcerer to finish copying the manuscript.

They sailed for Thentia aboard an Iron Ring tradesman the next day. The crossing was much easier than their last one; the westerly winds were on their quarter instead of their bow, which made for a swifter and easier trip. On the evening of the 6th of Ches, the ninth day since their escape from the coronal's tower, Geran and his companions set foot in Thentia again. For the first time in a tenday he allowed himself to believe that he wouldn't spend the next decade or two as a prisoner in Myth Drannor, and began to breathe easier.

They hired a coach to drive them out to Lasparhall, and arrived in the Hulmasters' manor an hour after sunset. Geran was pleased to see that things looked much as he'd left them. He allowed the guards at the door to relieve him and his friends of their sparse baggage, and went straight to the family's private hall to see if anything remained of dinner. While the three of them helped themselves to a late supper laid out by the kitchen staff, Kara Hulmaster appeared in the doorway. The Hulmaster captain threw off the heavy mantle she wore over her armored shoulders and hurried in to catch Geran in a bone-cracking hug. "Geran!" she cried. "I was worried about you. Where have you been?"

"Well met, Kara," he replied. "We landed in Thentia a couple of hours ago. As for the delay, well, I'm afraid we ran into some difficulties in Myth Drannor."

"We managed to get pinched, he means," Hamil said. "We spent a charming seven days as guests of the coronal before escaping her jail and absenting ourselves from the realm as quickly as possible. Fortunately Geran had friends willing to help spring us free, or we'd be there still."

"I should have known that you'd find trouble wherever you went." Kara released Geran and moved on to Hamil, leaning down to give him a warm embrace before moving on to take Sarth's hand. "Did you find the tome that Aesperus asked you to retrieve?"

The swordmage nodded. "Yes, we've got it." He glanced out the window; the evening was already well on. "I'll go out on the Highfells and summon him tomorrow night. We're tired from days of hard travel, and I want to be well rested and clearheaded when we speak again, just in case there's some misunderstanding. But right now I need a hot meal and a few hours of sleep in a warm bed before I do anything else."

"That much I think we can provide," Kara said with a smile. "It's good to have you back, Geran. All three of you, in truth. It seems that every time I turn around there's something else that needs the Hulmaster's attention, and while you've been away, that's been me."

"How are things proceeding here?" Geran asked. "Any more trouble with spies or assassins from Hulburg?"

"Some trouble with spies. We've caught a few of Rhovann's creatures lurking about. And I suspect that some of the drivers and provisioners in Thentia are paid to report on what they see of our encampment or hear from our soldiers."

That didn't surprise Geran. There were simply too many keen-eyed folk in and around Thentia who wouldn't think twice about taking a few coins to tell stories. He hadn't really imagined that he'd be able to keep all their preparations secret from Marstel and Rhovann. "Will we be ready to march when we planned?"

Kara hesitated. "We're as ready as we can be, I suppose. Another month of drilling and stockpiling supplies wouldn't hurt, but it would sorely stretch our treasury and we'd lose some of our sellswords. But there's troubling news from Hulburg. I've heard reports that Marstel's struck a bargain with the Warlock Knights. He's granted the Vaasans a trading concession, and it's rumored that strong companies of armsmen will soon arrive from Vaasa to reinforce his Council Guard."

"The Warlock Knights?" Geran muttered. The Vaasans had allied themselves with the Bloody Skull orcs a year previous. He'd briefly dueled a Warlock Knight in the Battle of Lendon's Dike, trading blows with the human sorcerer before the tide of battle had swept them apart. And there'd been plenty of stories of Vaasan magic playing a crucial role in the orcs' attack on the town of Glister at the northern margin of Thar. The Warlock Knights had disappeared quickly enough once the threat of the Bloody Skull horde had been smashed, and as far as Geran knew they'd played no role in the Black Moon troubles or the Cinderfist unrest . . . or had they? Had his traitorous cousin Sergen sold out Hulburg to the Vaasans after he'd failed to sell out the town to the merchant lords of Melvaunt and Mulmaster? "What's their concern in this?"

"If you're asking for my guess, I'd say that they put the Cyricists up to their mischief with the Cinderfists," Kara answered. "Before we were driven out of Hulburg, I'd turned up a few hints that the priests of Cyric were paid in Vaasan gold, but I never caught them at it. The Black Moon troubles drew all of my attention. What exactly they hope to gain from meddling in Hulburg, I couldn't say."

"How many Vaasans are coming? When will they arrive?"

Kara shook her head. "I've got scouts ringing the Highfells and the moorland now. They haven't run across any Vaasans yet, but then again, the Galena passes are still snowed in and likely to stay that way for another month or more. I doubt we'll see any large numbers of Vaasan soldiers in

Hulburg before the end of Tarsakh, at the earliest. Even then, it would be a hard crossing."

"That is another argument for striking at Marstel soon," Sarth observed. "It would seem better to attack before Vaasan soldiers reinforce the Council Guard."

As if we needed another reason to move with haste, Geran reflected. He didn't like the idea of the Vaasans choosing sides, but he couldn't see that it changed the essential facts of their situation. Every day that went by with Marstel in control of Hulburg was another day for the usurper to tighten his grip on his stolen realm, another day for Rhovann to devise arcane defenses and create deadly new soldiers, another day for the foreign mercenaries and brigands to plunder the honest folk of the town. "We should see to it that High Lord Vasil knows what we know about the Vaasan meddling," he mused aloud. "Thentia won't want to see another power gaining influence in Hulburg. It might buy us some additional help."

"I'll have Master Quillon speak to his counterpart in the high lord's palace," Kara said. "Now, for more important matters . . . what in the world did you do to end up in the coronal's dungeons? Other than you, Geran, of course I expected you to be imprisoned. I want to know how Hamil and Sarth got on Ilsevele's bad side."

"You *expected* me to be imprisoned?" Geran protested, but he was too late; Hamil was already embarking on the story of their brief sojourn in Myth Drannor. Instead, he shrugged and sat back to listen to his friend's version of the tale, which featured more than a few colorful exaggerations.

That night, he slept soundly for what seemed the first time in months. The following day was bright, clear, cold, and windy—a typically raw early spring day in the Moonsea. Geran spent it doing his best to catch up with scores of important details and decisions that Kara and her officers had settled on during his absence, but ultimately he simply concurred with everything that had been done already. He saw no reason to second-guess a decision arrived at over hours of dedicated thought with his own quick impressions, and he knew that his next task waited for him on the Highfells after sundown.

Late in the day, Geran took an hour to refresh his wardings and arm himself with the most powerful spells he could manage. A little before sunset, he rode up to the Highfells again, with Kara, Sarth, and Hamil at his side. The howling wind drove the moorgrass first one way and then another, an invisible serpent writhing and hissing its way across the landscape. The four riders huddled closer within their heavy cloaks against the biting cold and the sheer wild loneliness of the empty hills.

An hour's ride brought them to the line of barrows on the broad hillside where they'd met the King in Copper before. "This is the spot," Hamil said. He shivered. "The sooner this is over, the better."

Geran nodded. He closed his eyes, searching for the words to summon the lich, and began to recite:

> *Dark the night and cold the stone,*
> *Silent grave and barren throne,*
> *Empty halls, a crown of mold,*
> *Deathless dreams the king of old.*

> *Long the dark and brief the light,*
> *An hour's play, and then the night,*
> *Beauty fails and all grows cold,*
> *Still awaits the king of old.*

The wind grew stronger as he spoke, seeming to snatch away his words even before he spoke them. A chill began to gather in his bones, and he shivered; he could feel the King in Copper's presence. In the barrow's entrance, windblown mist began to stream and sink into the low doorway, pooling like water poured into a basin. From the gathering mist, the tattered robes and tarnished crown of Aesperus took form. An evil green light kindled in his black eye sockets, and his yellowed bones with their copper rivets took shape within his robes of black. Despite himself, Geran retreated a couple of steps; Sarth and Hamil did likewise.

"Have you brought the rest of my book?" the lich hissed.

"Aye, I have it," Geran replied. "I wouldn't have summoned you without completing my part of our bargain, King Aesperus." He drew the scroll tube from Myth Drannor from under his cloak, opened it, and carefully drew out the old parchment within. The wind, which had been howling with such bitter fury only a few moments before, had fallen still with the lich's arrival. With a conscious act of will he forced his feet forward and extended the pages to the lich.

Aesperus took them with surprising care, immediately turning his attention to the parchment in his bony hands. His jawbone worked silently as he read, examining the prize. "Ahhh, so I thought," he murmured to himself. "At last the ritual can be completed . . ." The lich's voice trailed off as he eagerly read on, studying the ancient pages with his eyes burning brighter.

Hamil gave Geran a sharp glance. *Remind him that we're waiting?* the halfling suggested.

"Is that everything you expected us to find, King Aesperus?" Geran asked.

The lich ignored him, reading further. Geran felt his companions' eyes on him, but he forced himself to keep his peace a little longer. He did not want to annoy the King in Copper, of that much he was certain. He waited until the lich raised one hand and began to chant in his horrible, cracking voice. For a moment Geran feared that Aesperus was simply going to enact whatever spell had been interrupted four hundred years earlier, or teleport away without another word . . . but instead the pages glowed briefly with a violet light, and vanished. "The manuscript is complete," Aesperus finally said. "I have sent the pages you brought me to rejoin the tome from which they were torn. I have much study ahead of me now."

Geran took a breath. "How do I defeat Rhovann's runehelms?"

"With the proper weapon, of course." The lich stretched his hand over the bare ground and rasped the words of another spell. There was a burst of mist from the spot beneath his hand. Then a black, dull shape seemed to rise up out of the ground in answer to his magic. It was a sword, long and straight, a double-edged broadsword with a blade of some unreflective black metal Geran did not recognize. Its hilt was wrapped in dark, pebbled leather, and its pommel was a flat disk in which small glyphs were inscribed around a large onyx gemstone. "This is *Umbrach Nyth*, the Sword of Shadows, forged of shadow to dispel shadow. Long ago I enchanted this black steel for your ancestor Rivan. He later attempted to slay me with it, the ungrateful fool. You will find that it carries a bitter sting for creatures infused with the power of shadow—and most others, for that matter. The runehelms will not ignore its bite. Take its hilt."

Trying not to flinch, Geran reached for the sword's hilt and drew it clear of the ground. It was lighter than it looked, not much heavier than his Myth Drannan backsword, and it was balanced quite well. He could sense the potent enchantments on the weapon as he brandished it. A matching scabbard appeared from the ground; he took it in his left hand, and sheathed the dark blade. "I can believe that this would be a better weapon against Rhovann's constructs than my own sword," he said, "but am I supposed to personally defeat each and every one of them? There may be hundreds by now."

"You forget what I told you about Rhovann's enchantment the last time we spoke," Aesperus replied. "A single animus unites the runehelms, equally present in each one of the constructs. A pearl of shadow lies within each of Rhovann's creatures, linking it to its fellows—and to a single great pearl or stone, a master sphere from which the others are drawn. Destroy the master stone, and all of the shadow pearls created from it will be destroyed. Without their shadow pearls, the runehelms are bereft of intelligence, purpose, resilience . . . they are little more than unthinking automatons. Your warriors will easily sweep them aside."

"Where would we find this master stone?" Hamil asked.

"It almost certainly lies in the Plane of Shadow. It must constantly draw in the energies of the Shadowfell to empower the runehelms, especially if this elf mage is creating many lesser pearls from it." Aesperus shrugged, and the copper bands of his shoulder blades creaked in protest. "Unless Rhovann is a great fool, it will be well guarded. Look for a place of strength in the Plane of Shadow's analogue of Hulburg. The runehelms will be stronger the nearer they are to the master stone, so he will not scatter them far."

"We've only seen the runehelms in Hulburg itself, so it seems likely that Rhovann keeps the stone somewhere in or near Griffonwatch," Sarth observed in a low voice.

Geran frowned, digesting Aesperus's advice. He had little personal experience of the planes of existence that echoed Faerûn's mundane landscape, but he'd studied them in his arcane training. The Shadowfell was a sort of dark twin or duplicate of the daylight world, an echo of reality that was only a step away—if one knew the proper magic to employ. With a little study, he thought he could manage it when the time came. But there was something else that Aesperus had said that caught his interest. "King Aesperus, how far can the runehelms go from their master stone?"

The lich considered the question for a moment. "It depends on the nuances of their maker's skill and the power he draws upon," he finally said. "I doubt that the minions of Rhovann can go more than a few leagues from the master stone without suffering degradation."

A few leagues . . . Geran's eyes narrowed in thought. That meant the runehelms would serve as a potent defense for the city proper, but they couldn't contest the Shieldsworn march. The beginnings of a plan took shape in his mind. "Does Rhovann have any other defenses?" he asked. "Besides the runehelms, how else could he strike at us with his magic?"

"Such knowledge was not part of our bargain." Aesperus laughed softly, his voice rasping in his empty throat. "You asked for the weapon and understanding necessary to defeat your enemy's magical constructs, and my promise to stay my hand against Hulburg. These I have given you. Do not presume upon my generosity, Geran Hulmaster. I find your circumstances interesting . . . but I care little whether you succeed or fail. In the end, your struggles are meaningless. All come to my realm in time." The lich folded his arms across his empty chest, and the wind began to blow again, a wild gale that tore at their cloaks and drove the four of them back several steps. Aesperus laughed scornfully, his ragged robes flapping around his yellowed bones, before he seemed to erode away like sand driven before a storm. In a moment the oppressive dread of the lich's presence was gone, leaving nothing but the bitter wind howling over the dark hillside.

"I take it our discussion is complete!" Hamil said, almost shouting to make his voice heard above the wind.

"So it would seem," Geran replied. He looked down at the black sword in his hands, and shivered with more than cold. "No prophecies of doom no matter what we do this time. I take that as a good sign."

"Does this change your plans at all?" Kara asked.

"Yes. It sounds like I'll need to slip into Hulburg and shift into the shadow to deal with Rhovann's monsters," Geran replied. He thought for a long time, ignoring the bitterly cold wind as it arose again and whipped his cloak behind him. "I wanted an answer to the runehelms before we risked meeting the Council Guard in open battle. Now I'm not so sure. If the creatures can't go very far from their base, we could bring the Shieldsworn to the outskirts of Hulburg before we'd have to worry about the creatures. In fact . . . I'm sorely tempted to see if we can lure them out, and then cut their strings with one swift stroke."

"There's something else," Hamil pointed out. "The threat posed by the Shieldsworn might serve as an excellent distraction for any skullduggery in Rhovann's shadow redoubt, wherever it is."

Despite the wild wind and the bonechilling cold, Geran smiled. It could work . . . it *would* work, if he could arrange it. "Come on, let's be on our way," he said to his friends. "This is no good place to linger, and we've got a lot to do in the next few days."

TWENTY

14 Ches, the Year of Deep Water Drifting (1480 DR)

From the moment he crested Keldon Head on the old coastal track, Geran sensed Hulburg's change of mood. Storm clouds were gathering, despite the cold, clear weather and the empty blue skies. He allowed his mount, a sturdy black gelding, to pick its way down the road unguided as he peered sharply at the town below, trying to determine what was different. He could still make out the clatter and bustle of the town's commerce . . . but there was definitely a different tenor to the activity.

From his vantage, he could look along Bay Street all the way to the mouth of the Winterspear. Even with the harbor ice unbroken, Bay Street should have been crowded with wagons and folks going about their business—after all, the mercantile concessions and their storehouses lined the harborside street. But instead of teeming throngs of carters and porters and clerks, he saw nothing but the occasional wagon or clerk hurrying on some errand or another. Small knots of idle workers gathered on the streets before the various taverns and taphouses, and the smelters whose chimneys would normally have been belching smoke instead emitted only a few thin wisps.

"Where is everybody?" said Hamil, studying the scene below. He jogged along on a baggage-laden pony a few paces behind Geran, dressed in the very ordinary garb of a poorly paid manservant. "Has Marstel declared a holiday for the war?"

"I'd guess that most folk are laying low to see what comes of Kara's march, or maybe getting ready to flee if it looks like the town might come under attack," Geran answered. "Either way, I think it'll make our work easier. It seems that no one is going to care much about two more travelers." He glanced over his shoulder at the sun, now sinking toward the west. If things had gone as he'd expected, then his cousin and her army would be drawing near to Hulburg. She planned to encamp near Rosestone Abbey and await events; they'd decided that it was far enough from the town to discourage Rhovann from marching out to meet the Hulmaster army, but close enough for Kara to strike quickly once the runehelms had been dealt with.

Sentries ahead, Hamil said silently. *Look sharp now!*

At the foot of the road that became the Coastal Way, very near the place where Geran had passed a pair of runehelms in the Sokol caravan a few tendays before, a half-dozen runehelms now stood guard. There hadn't been that many here the last time he'd left Hulburg. He frowned, hoping that his disguise was sound. This time he was dressed as an itinerant mage for hire, wearing a scarlet robe embroidered with arcane glyphs over a high-collared shirt of black silk and matching breeches. A great cowl-like cape protected him from the bitter weather, and he carried a staff across his saddlebow—although *Umbrach Nyth* was belted to his hip too. His hair he'd cropped brutally short, and he now wore a full goatee and an eyepatch. As they approached the runehelms, he made a point of giving them a casual glance, just as any newly arriving traveler might.

They were almost past the creatures when one on the right swiveled its visored face toward them and said, "Halt. Identify yourselves."

They speak? Hamil remarked.

The first I've seen of it, Geran answered. He reined in and turned his one "good" eye on the creature. "I am called Jhormun. This is my manservant, Pirr."

"What is your business here?" the runehelm said. Its voice was deep and oddly inflected, but still intelligible.

"I am a mage for hire. I have heard that some of the merchant Houses in Hulburg are willing to pay a wizard of my skill quite handsomely."

There was a long silence, and Geran quietly tensed, ready to draw his blade or cast a spell as he needed to. Then another one of the runehelms spoke. "You may go," it said.

Do you think they're speaking to Rhovann? Hamil asked as they rode on past. *Or are they simply following his directions and exercising their own judgment?*

"Neither possibility is very reassuring," Geran muttered under his breath. The sooner they dealt with Rhovann's monstrous creations, the better. In an inner pocket of his robe he carried twin scrolls, carefully prepared days ago in Thentia, that held a ritual of shadowcrossing to carry him into the Shadowfell at the proper time. Sarth was also capable of performing the transition, but Geran couldn't be certain that the sorcerer would be able to rejoin them by the appointed hour—in this case, midnight. That was still eight or nine hours off, and Geran had things to do before then.

Leaving the guardpost behind, he turned right on Keldon Way and headed for the Sokol compound. Hopefully anyone or anything watching wouldn't be surprised to see a mage for hire presenting himself at the first mercantile establishment he came to. At the gate he informed the Sokol guards that he wished to speak with the mistress of the establishment, and he and Hamil were shown to the sitting room of Nimessa's house. They waited for a short time before Nimessa bustled in, followed by one of her clerks.

"My apologies, Master Jhormun," she began. "There is a fair bit of trouble in Hulburg today—"

"I know it," Geran interrupted. He stood and removed his eyepatch, meeting Nimessa's gaze.

She drew back in surprise, and stopped. Then she glanced to her clerk. "Allow us a few moments," she said. The clerk raised an eyebrow, but gathered up his ledgers and let himself out. Nimessa waited until the door was firmly shut before she turned back to face Geran. "Master Jhormun, indeed. I would've thought you'd be with your army up on the moors! What in the world are you doing here?"

"Dealing with Rhovann and Marstel, once and for all," he replied. He nodded at Hamil. "You remember my old comrade Hamil?"

"Of course, but I thought he had more sense than to follow you into Hulburg with the Council Guard and merchant costers and Rhovann's awful constructs all watching for you."

"My mother warned me to choose my friends wisely," Hamil answered.

He jumped to his feet and took Nimessa's hand, brushing his lips to her fingers with a sigh. "She was always so disappointed in me." Nimessa smiled, and inclined her head to Hamil.

"I hope to do something about Rhovann's constructs soon enough," Geran told her. "Did the Council Guard march to meet our army? Hamil and I parted ways with Kara yesterday morning, and we haven't had any word of Marstel's movements since."

"Marstel's soldiers are assembling on the field by Daggergard," Nimessa said. "He's also ordered the merchant companies to put their armsmen under his command and send them to the muster. No one knows what he intends to do with them."

"What of Sokol's armsmen?" asked Hamil.

Nimessa smiled. "Regretfully, a serious flu has left most of my soldiers too ill to leave their barracks."

Geran nodded, trying to imagine what he'd do in Rhovann's place. After a moment, he decided that it didn't matter; he intended to carry on with his task of dealing with Rhovann's constructs. "House Sokol's been a good friend to my family over the last few months," he told Nimessa. "Tomorrow we find out if that was a wise decision for you or not. Do you think your armsmen might recover any time soon?"

"Yes—when I'm confident that we won't be caught out all alone by taking your side. We've only got a couple of dozen blades to offer."

"My thanks." Geran looked over to Hamil. "We'd better be on our way. We have a lot to do this evening."

"No rest for the wicked," Hamil lamented. He bowed again to Nimessa, and made his way outside.

Geran followed after him, but Nimessa caught his arm at the door. She leaned forward to kiss him on the cheek. "For luck," she murmured. "Keep yourself safe."

He paused. He didn't want to say what was on his mind, but it was important to him that Nimessa understood his motives, especially if things did not go well in the next day or so. "Nimessa, the last time I was here, I shouldn't have—I shouldn't have taken advantage of you the way I did, and I'm sorry for it. My heart's given to another. It's just taken me a long time to see it."

Nimessa looked down at the floor, and sighed. "You have no cause to apologize to me, Geran. You're in love with Mirya Erstenwold, even if you forgot it for a time. I know it was selfish of me, but I can't say I regret what happened." She gave herself a small shake, and met his eyes again with a small smile. "I don't suppose you've told Mirya how you feel, have you?"

He was silent for a long time before he finally said, "I don't know how."

She rolled her eyes. "Say what's in your heart. The rest is up to her."

"It seems so easy when you put it like that." He laughed softly at his own foolishness, and caught her hands in his before turning and heading out the door.

Hamil was waiting for him outside. The halfling glanced at Nimessa, who stood watching from the doorway, and back to Geran. *If I were a suspicious fellow,* he said silently, *I'd wonder what just passed between the two of you.*

"It's a good thing you're not a suspicious fellow, then," Geran said to him. "Come on, let's get to it."

"Suit yourself," Hamil replied. They mounted and rode slowly out of the Sokol tradeyard, heading up Bay Street. The street was eerily quiet; every so often they passed groups of merchant companies folk huddled together, trading rumors and speculation about the Hulmasters' army and whether or not Marstel's Council Guard would march out to meet it or stand their ground in Hulburg. In one of the wilder rumors Geran came across, Kamoth Kastelmar was due to arrive in a new pirate fleet at any moment to raze the town, even though the harbor ice still hadn't broken up enough for ships to reach Hulburg's wharves. He wondered briefly what the bystanders would do if he suddenly revealed himself before deciding that it probably wasn't a good idea.

They reached the gates of the Double Moon Coster, and paused briefly. Geran looked down at his small friend. "Do you still want to give it a try?" he asked.

Hamil nodded. "The Double Moons might surprise you," he said. "I'm on good terms with a number of their folk. I think I can convince them to discover a barracks full of sick mercenaries at the very least. Of course, you might have to remember their help when it comes time to negotiate their rents and terms of concession."

"If I have my way, the Jannarsks and the Iron Ring will be out along with the Verunas when things are settled. The Double Moons are more than welcome to some of those leavings if they help us now." Geran glanced around, looking for any sign of someone paying too much attention to them, and decided that Rhovann and Marstel were likely occupied with Kara. "I'll see you at midnight. You know how to find everyone on your list?"

The halfling snorted. "It's not that big a town. I'm sure I'll manage." Between them, Geran and Hamil hoped to visit a dozen or more loyalists, passing word to be ready to strike. Geran would have liked Hamil's blade at his side if he ran into trouble, but there were far too many people who knew that Hamil was one of his close companions—a human and a halfling together might easily spark a suspicion that wouldn't rise if they separated while wandering the town.

"Good luck, then," Geran said. He rode off without a second look, fixing an ill-tempered glare on his face and taking the middle of the street to play the part of a mercenary mage to its hilt. Turning up High Street, he crossed the Winterspear at the Middle Bridge—guarded by more runehelms, although they continued to ignore him—and headed north on the Vale Road, intending to visit Burkel Tresterfin and a few other loyalists whose homes were a little ways out of town. But he was turned back a little past the Troll and Tankard by Council Guards, who were halting all travel up the Winterspear Vale. Giving up on the idea of calling on Tresterfin, he turned back southward and headed for Mirya's house.

He rode once past the lane leading to Mirya's house, looking for any sign of Rhovann's spies or guards while feigning an interest in the nearby shops. Nothing seemed out of the ordinary, so he followed the road toward the Harmach's Foot and turned into the woods that surrounded the base of Griffonwatch's hill when he reached a bend in the lane. Mirya's house was just on the other side of the woods; after eighty yards or so he emerged from the belt of trees in Mirya's backyard. Dismounting, he looped his reins over a hitching rail and knocked at the door.

There was a small clatter inside, and the sound of swift footsteps on the floorboards. Then Mirya drew back the bolt and opened the door, a frown creasing her brow. "Yes, what——?" she began, and then recognition widened her eyes. "Geran! You're here!"

"So much for the disguise," he observed. Well, that wasn't the fairest test. Mirya knew his face better than almost anyone, and she'd learned to look twice at strangers on her doorstep. "May I come in?"

"Of course, come in! I don't think there are any spies about, but I can't be sure of it." She opened the door the rest of the way and stood aside as he hurried in.

"Thank you," he answered. He took a seat on a stool by the fire, warming his hands. It was a raw, cold day even with the spring sunshine, and he'd been outside for most of it. Geran noticed that the doorjamb was splintered, and several pieces of furniture and crockery were missing; apparently the house had been broken into and searched not too long ago, but she'd tidied up since. "It seems you've had some more trouble with Marstel's thugs. Are you all right?"

"Well enough. Selsha's still at the Tresterfins, but Erstenwold's is scraping by." Mirya put a kettle on a hook by the fire, and sat down on the stool opposite his. "We've heard that the Hulmaster army's on their way. Why aren't you with your soldiers?"

"I left them in Kara's hands so that I could slip into Hulburg and see to things here."

"What in the world is more important than beating Marstel's army?"

"Defeating Rhovann's runehelms, and raising the loyalists against Marstel," Geran answered. "Kara I trust to handle Marstel's Council Guard without my help, but the runehelms I mean to deal with tonight. Sarth and Hamil are meeting me at the Burned Bridge at midnight to help with that. I was hoping that you could help me with the loyalists."

"I thought you didn't want me risking my neck in any such foolishness."

He shrugged. "I didn't, but I've got a feeling that you're a little too stubborn to give it up simply because I asked you to."

She gave him a wry smile. "You know me too well, Geran Hulmaster. As it so happens, I know a few stouthearted folk who might help. But I'll warn you that many of my friends have had a hard time of it. It's a wonder I've stayed out of Marstel's prison."

"I guessed as much." He leaned forward. "If I do what I mean to tonight,

Kara'll have the Shieldsworn here by noon tomorrow. I want to raise the loyalists and seize all the strongpoints we can while the Council Guard's busy."

She frowned deeply, no doubt anticipating the fighting that would cause. "Can you really defeat Rhovann's gray guardians?" she asked.

"I've got good reason to think so. But if I'm wrong, I suppose we'll call off Kara's attack and retire toward Thentia." He paused, imagining what that would mean. "I guess that would be the end of it for our cause. One way or the other, this war will be decided tomorrow."

"It'll be hard on those of us who are left if you fail."

"I know it. In fact . . . after we arrange things with the loyalists, I want you to go on up to Tresterfin's tonight, and make ready to flee Hulburg if worse comes to worst. I'd like you and Selsha to stay there until everything's decided. I think I can see you past the Council Guard roadblock and still meet Sarth and Hamil later on."

She scowled stubbornly. "Because you don't want to fret about me?"

"Yes, because I don't want to fret about you." Geran looked down at his hands. "It will make things easier for me if I know that you and your daughter are out of harm's way. Please, stay at Tresterfin's, and keep out of the fighting tomorrow."

"Jarad would understand that I've just as much at stake in Hulburg as you do. How do you think I would feel, hiding in the countryside and wondering if everything and everyone I care for might not see out the day? How can I stand aside and let others fight my fight?"

"I'm not asking for Jarad. I'm asking for myself." He reached out to take her hands in his, and looked into her face. For a moment he struggled with his old hesitation, his fear of hurting her again, but this time he did not stop himself from saying what he wanted to. "I love you, Mirya," he said. "My heart's full of you, and I don't ever want to be parted from you again. Please—for me—promise that you'll keep yourself safe through what's to come?"

She stared at him, her face stricken. "Geran . . . don't do this to me again," she said weakly. "I can't bear it. Besides, it's Nimessa Sokol that you love."

"No, it's not, Mirya. It's you."

She rubbed the back of her hand across her eyes, damp with tears. "You've slept with her, haven't you?"

He winced. *I should have known she'd guess at that,* he told himself. *Mirya was far from stupid, after all.* With a sigh, he looked her in the face and said, "Nimessa and I have been together, yes. It was a passion of the moment months ago, and it's over now. She's not the one I see when I close my eyes at night, or the one I worry for when I'm away, or the one whose words I want to hear when I'm troubled and alone. You are, Mirya. So please, I beg of you—stay out of Hulburg tomorrow, because my enemies may hurt you or Selsha to strike at me, and that would ruin me."

"So I'm supposed to wait like a widow for news of whether you lived or died?" she demanded. "Can't you understand how it tears the heart out of me to wonder where you are and whether you're safe too? Because I do. Against every ounce of common sense I should have by now, I love you, and I'm a fool for it. Tonight you're laying your heart at my feet, and I can't say no to you. But where will you be tomorrow? What will it be that takes you away from me the day after? I've no strength to live like that."

He fell silent for a long time. Somehow he'd never understood until this moment that she could love him, and still be unable to let herself give in to what she felt. Without any idea of what else he could say, he shook his head helplessly. "I'm not the man I once was, Mirya. I can't love anyone but you. When we're done with all this, I want to marry you. Will you have me for your husband?"

"Damn you, Geran Hulmaster, why would you say something like that?" Mirya drew a deep breath, and stood up to pace away from him. She said nothing more for a long time, as Geran watched her. Finally she turned back to meet his eyes again. "It's some apology you owe me—not the least for that little bit about Nimessa Sokol—and I won't be easy on you, but that's for the day after tomorrow. This isn't the time for either of us to be foolish. If we see out the next few days, we'll talk of this later."

He stood as well. "Later," he said softly. *She didn't say no!* he told himself. She hadn't said yes, either, but she didn't say no. "You're right, Mirya."

"Get used to saying that," she answered. "Now, what must you do tonight?"

"I'd thought I'd call on one or two more loyalists before I meet up with Sarth and Hamil. It's still a few hours shy of midnight."

Mirya cocked her head, struck by a sudden thought. She frowned, gazing off into space as she gave it her full attention.

"What is it?" he asked.

"I have a better idea," she finally answered, still seemingly distracted by her thought. "We'll go to Erstenwold's, and I'll bring whoever you need to see to you. For that matter, I'm in contact with a few loyalists. If I call for them, they'll carry messages for you. You'll be able to stay out of sight."

Geran weighed the idea quickly. Erstenwold's might be watched, of course, but it was centrally located—and it had access to Hulburg's buried streets, which might prove very useful. She's got an instinct for skullduggery, he reminded himself. "Very well," he replied. "Let me leave my horse in the barn, and we'll do as you suggest. Time's growing short."

TWENTY-ONE

14 Ches, the Year of Deep Water Drifting (1480 DR)

Kara Hulmaster sat in her saddle at the edge of the Hulmaster encampment in the Highfells, watching as Maroth Marstel's army marched to meet her. "Well, then," she murmured aloud. A blustery wind out of the south held the banners and pennants of her small army aloft, fluttering and snapping in the breeze. The afternoon was waning, and the half-ruined silhouette of Rosestone Abbey was a jagged stump against the southern sky; heavy gray clouds marched in serried ranks to the Moonsea, a few miles away. It would rain soon, a cold hard rain, and she wondered which side the weather favored more.

For the last four days she'd led the Hulmaster army eastward over the Highfells, intending to take up a position within striking distance of Hulburg in accordance with the plan she'd worked out with Geran. But instead of waiting in camp for events to develop, it seemed she had a battle on her hands. Along the line of the old abbey walls her Shieldsworn stood to arms, watching as company after company of the Council Guard and their merchant allies formed up across the moorland a thousand yards distant.

"It seems that Marstel dislikes waiting," Sarth observed. The tiefling sat awkwardly on his own mount close by Kara, gazing at the ranks of the Council Guard marshaling a half mile away. "You expected him to stand on the defensive in Hulburg, did you not?"

"I did," Kara answered, frowning unhappily. Rosestone Abbey was a little less than ten miles from Hulburg, and its ruined outbuildings offered good defensive ground and shelter against the elements for a camp. If she needed to, she could hold her army in position for a month right where she was; Rosestone was in a good position to cut off Hulburg from the overland trade routes, but not so close that Marstel could attack her without leaving Hulburg uncovered—or so she'd thought. "It seems that Marstel's captains have a different view of the situation than we do."

"Marstel's captains might be worried about loyalists joining your ranks if he allows you to come any closer," Sarth guessed. "Or it may simply be impatience, or a concern for the perception of weakness. Maroth Marstel's motives do not necessarily have to make sense to you."

I hope Geran knows what he's doing, Kara thought as she studied the enemy ranks. The warriors in Marstel's Council Guard wore surcoats of red and yellow, but they weren't the only formation facing her. Behind the ranks of footsoldiers small companies of merchant company armsmen sat on horseback, each in their own colors. There were House Jannarsk riders beneath a banner of dun and red, Iron Ring Coster mercenaries in brown and black, and even a large band of House Veruna armsmen in their coats of green and white. She pursed her lips in anger at that sight; the Verunas had done their best to help her stepbrother Sergen in his bloody-handed coup attempt of a year past, and she'd taken great pleasure in watching them abandon their position in Hulburg when Sergen's plots came to nothing. But here they were again, restored to at least some of their former holdings by Marstel. We'll set that right soon enough if things go well, she promised herself. But most worrying of all, she could make out the towering shapes of scores of runehelms in a tight knot around Marstel's banner.

Kendurkkel Ironthane strolled up to where Kara and Sarth sat their horses, a battle-axe leaning on his shoulder. "They've got us in numbers by a wee bit," the dwarf observed. "Can't say as I'm happy t' see those big gray ones over yon. I'd hoped the wizard would keep 'em close t' home."

"I'm not worried about their numbers," Kara replied. "The merchant coster men aren't going to be in any hurry to die for Maroth Marstel. As for the runehelms, we'll see what we see. We've got reason to believe they might not be as formidable as we fear—at least, not here." She looked over to Sarth. "I think it's time, Sarth. I doubt we'll have much to say, but I suppose we should offer parley anyway."

"Very well," the sorcerer said. "Please excuse me for a moment." He dismounted, handing the reins to a soldier, and ducked into a doorway of the outlying abbey ruins. Kara thought she heard a whisper of arcane words and felt a tug of the unseen forces around her; the spellscar she carried made her more sensitive to such things than any but a trained practitioner of the arcane arts. A few moments later, there was a rustling in the doorway of the outbuilding—and Geran Hulmaster emerged, dressed in a light coat of elven mail, a fine cape of dark blue fluttering behind him and a plumed helm tucked under his arm.

"Sarth will be preoccupied for a time with important divinations," he said. "He suggests that we continue without him."

Kara hid a smile behind a small cough. The likeness was almost perfect. If she hadn't known that it was Sarth wearing her cousin's appearance, she never would have guessed the truth. There were a few details that weren't quite correct—Sarth's gait wasn't quite right, the voice was subtly off, and he didn't carry himself with the same unconscious ease and physical readiness Geran had gained through years of study in swordsmanship. But she knew that she was an exceptionally keen observer of such things, and she was of course very well acquainted with her cousin. People who knew Geran casually would never guess that he wasn't who he seemed to be, especially if Sarth was careful to avoid speaking too much.

"Very good," she replied. "Let's go." Tapping her heels to her mount's flanks, she trotted out into the open field ahead of the massed Shieldsworn. Her standard-bearer Vossen rode out behind her, carrying the blue griffon banner of the Hulmasters. Sarth, in his magical guise, rode on the other side of the banner, and Kendurkkel Ironthane jogged along on a stout pony just beside him. They reached a point about halfway between the two armies, and halted. Kara eyed the enemy ranks carefully; there were a handful of arbalesters mixed in with the Council Guard infantry, but none of them seemed to be thinking of trying their luck at a long-range shot. There was a small stir among the riders grouped under the banners at the center of the council army, and then a small knot of riders trotted ahead, riding slowly to meet them.

"What is the point of this exercise again?" Sarth asked quietly.

"Traditionally, it's done to issue challenges, to set terms for the ransom of prisoners, or to convince someone in a difficult position to retire without a fight," Kara answered. "I don't have any such notions on my mind today. My purpose is to make sure that Marstel and his captains see *you* here. I don't see any harm in misleading them as to Geran's whereabouts."

Kendurkkel chuckled into his beard. "Well, now I confess I'm wonderin' myself," he said. " 'Course, Laird Hulmaster might not want me t'be knowin'. I hogtied him and dropped him on the Council Hall steps the first time we met."

Kara smiled uncertainly at that. Was that intended as a jest, she wondered, or was Kendurkkel reminding her that his loyalties were for sale? She *thought* she'd won more of the dwarf mercenary's respect than most, and that just maybe he'd feel a little more allegiance to the Hulmaster cause than some other employer, but the fact remained that the Icehammers were mercenaries. Mercenaries had a bad habit of following the gold, and more than one battle had been lost by a company switching sides because of a better offer, or simply deciding to stand down while a contract was "renegotiated" to their liking. She'd never heard any such story of the Icehammers, but there was a first time for everything. She glanced at the dwarf, trying to gauge his mood.

"Well, it's old Marstel himself," Kendurkkel said in surprise, nodding at the riders approaching from the council army. "Hadn't expected that. And that captain next t' him is Edelmark of Mulmaster, I think. Dun't think I know the big fellow with them. No sign o' the wizard."

"I think that's Miskar Bann, the chief of the Veruna concession," Kara said. She frowned and studied the approaching riders. Marstel looked vaguely ridiculous in a plumed helm and a parade-ground suit of half-plate that was fitted around his broad belly, but he rode better than she would have expected. In fact, he looked in better health than she'd seen him in years. His eyes were bright above his stiff white mustache, and he wore an expression of bluff confidence as he reined in his heavy charger ten feet short of Kara's party. Marstel's followers lined up alongside him.

Marstel studied Kara, Sarth in his likeness of Geran, and Kendurkkel

Ironthane. Then he snorted. "Well?" he said. "You have something you wish to say to me?"

Kara fixed a stern look on him. "Maroth Marstel, you are a murderer and a usurper. I call on you to lay down your arms and surrender yourself to the rightful lord of Hulburg. All who have oppressed and harmed the people of Hulburg will be held to account, but we will spare the lives of your warriors and your captains if you surrender. This is your opportunity to make answer to the charges against you." She paused, then added, "I don't much care if you find your death on this field today, but your armsmen follow a fat old fool, and they deserve a chance to make restitution for what they've done. They won't be able to do that when they're dead."

Marstel flushed in anger, but it was Edelmark who spoke next. "Bold words," he said to Kara. "We'll see how far your righteous indignation carries you when our cavalry's cutting you to pieces and our runehelms are smashing your lines." He looked over to Kendurkkel, and smiled coldly. "You would've been wiser to pass on this contract, Master Ironthane. It's not too late to reconsider."

"It's been a long walk from Thentia," the dwarf answered. "Hardly makes sense t' turn back wi'out havin' a go at ye, Edelmark."

"Good," said Miskar Bann. He glared at Sarth in his magical disguise, and slapped his left knee, which was encased in a brace of leather and iron. "I came here for a fight, anyway. I owe you for this limp, my lord Hulmaster. I'll be looking for you on the field!"

Sarth shot Kara a quick look before he answered the Veruna captain. Clearly Bann knew Geran and had some grievance with him, although the tiefling had no idea what it might be. Sarth fixed an angry glare on Bann and snarled, "Then I'll give you one to match on your other leg, if you insist!"

"I'm waiting for an answer," Kara said.

"To that ridiculous ultimatum?" Marstel snarled. "You'll have it soon enough, my dear. Your tired little rebellion ends today. No quarter, asked nor given."

"Fine," Kara said flatly. "No quarter asked, no quarter given." She nodded sharply to Sarth and the standard-bearer, and the Hulmaster party wheeled their horses and cantered toward their own lines. Behind them, Marstel and his officers galloped off as well.

"I suppose we'll be earnin' our keep today," Kendurkkel said as they rode back.

"So it seems," Kara answered.

"Who was that Veruna captain?" Sarth asked.

"I wasn't there, but I seem to recall that Geran crossed swords with a couple of Veruna armsmen at Erstenwold's last year, just before his duel with Anfel Urdinger," Kara replied. "He carved them up pretty badly. I think Bann might've been one of them." She took a moment to study her dispositions from the front as they rode back. The tents and wagons of the Hulmaster encampment lay within the wide expanse of ruins that adjoined Rosestone, but all three shields of her army, and the Icehammers as well, now stood to arms along the remnants of the wall that had once encircled the abbey's large outer bailey. The ruined walls weren't much of an obstacle, but they offered some amount of cover, and the attacking force would be channeled toward the open spaces between the remaining wall sections. The old abbey building itself anchored their right flank; the Icehammers held that end of the Hulmaster line. Captain Wester's First Shield waited in the center of their lines, and Captain Merrith's Third Shield in a tangle of ruined outbuildings at the left flank. Larken's Second Shield guarded the rearward approaches to the old bailey. The Amaunatori friars who still lived in the abbey's intact portions had retreated to their chapel, hoping to stay out of the way.

The Shieldsworn cheered as they passed back into the lines. Kara nodded to Sarth, who slid down from his mount and hurried back out of sight in the abbey ruins again, and signaled for the shield-captains to join her. In a moment, Wester, Brother Larken, Merrith, and Kolton gathered around.

"I take it Marstel refused to kiss his own fat arse when you told him to?" Wester asked.

"No, he politely declined." Kara smiled, but her eyes were fixed on the field in front of her. She studied distances, imagined maneuvers, and considered countermoves, all in the space of a few moments. "Larken, I want your shield to stand back off the line. You're my reserve. As for the rest, we'll stand our ground and let them come to us. We've got more bows than they do, and we'll make them pay in the open ground." She glanced around behind her, studying the lay of the land behind the Hulmaster camp. "I don't think it's likely, but if for some reason we're driven out of the camp, fall back on the round hill there. That will be our rallying point."

"Aye, Lady-Captain," her captains answered.

"All right, get to your shields. No one's to move from our lines without my signal. May Tempus favor you all." Kara waited as the captains galloped off to their own companies, and quickly set their ranks in order. She rode over to take up a place near Brother Larken's company, where she could keep an eye on the whole battle and choose the right time and place to commit the reserve.

Across the space between the armies, she could see the standards of the various merchant detachments riding away from Marstel's banner, returning to their own companies. It seemed that the false harmach's forces had finished with their own deliberations and were ready to advance. Several trumpets sounded from Marstel's banner; the Council Guard ranks murmured and stirred, marching forward. The wind rose, making their banners ripple and snap in the breeze; the distance between the armies began to shrink.

"The enemy cavalry's on the move," Sergeant Kolton said from beside her. The old veteran was in charge of the small knot of bodyguards who stayed close to Kara and Sarth.

"I see them," Kara replied. Between the Jannarsks, the Iron Ring, and the Verunas, there were close to two hundred enemy horsemen to keep an eye on; they rode out from behind the enemy left and positioned themselves to harass her right flank, where the Icehammers were posted. "Kendurkkel can hold them at bay."

"Shall we open fire?" Larken asked her.

Kara shook her head, waiting for Marstel's soldiers to march closer. She didn't want her soldiers wasting arrows, and more importantly she wanted her enemies well within the killing ground when the first blows began to fall. When the distance between the ranks was half a bowshot, she nodded to her standard-bearer. "Vossen, signal the shield-captains: volley fire!"

The Hulmaster banner dipped and straightened; Shieldsworn trumpeters sounded the signal for Kara's command. As one, the archers in each of the shields on the line bent their bows, held a moment, and then loosed their arrows. Almost a third of the Hulmaster soldiers carried heavy bows, and hundreds of arrows streaked through the gray skies. Council Guards reeled and fell beneath the deadly rain; distant screams echoed across the open moorland, and the approaching ranks seemed to ripple and writhe like a great, wounded serpent. Ten heartbeats later, a second volley took flight, and more of Marstel's soldiers dropped. But now bolts and arrows arced out of Marstel's formation in reply. The Hulmaster troops were tough targets for Marstel's archers; most were armored in mail, and those not plying their bows carried large shields they now raised against the enemy fire. Some missiles found their mark anyway, and Hulmaster soldiers began to fall by ones and twos with cries of pain or choking screams. Then a third Hulmaster volley followed, raking Marstel's ranks again.

"The runehelms," Sarth murmured. Kara looked to the center of the enemy line, and scowled. The sleet of arrows seemed to make no impression at all on Rhovann's gray constructs. The things marched straight ahead without breaking step, gathering arrow after arrow with little effect.

"Let's hope that swords and axes work better," she answered. Nils Wester's First Shield held the center of the Hulmaster line; they'd be the ones to meet the runehelm assault. The enemy fire grew heavier, and now fiery bolts and jagged lances of lightning shot out from wizards and sorcerers scattered through the enemy ranks. Roars of fire and deafening thunderclaps pealed over the moor. The Hulmaster army had no spell-casters to speak of beside Sarth. Kara glanced toward the Icehammers' end of the battle; the merchant cavalry darted and feinted at the merce-naries' flanks, but they held their distance, waiting for the Hulmaster army to break.

"Archers! Fire as you will!" Kara called. Horns and trumpets sounded again, and regular flights of arrows became a steady hail of hissing shafts. The Hulmaster captain set her eyes on the cluster of banner-bearers where Marstel and his officers watched the unfolding battle behind the ominous formation of runehelms. She was sorely tempted to lead a charge against the enemy captains, but until she knew exactly how dangerous Rhovann's toys were, she didn't dare risk it.

Goaded by the deadly missiles, the Council Guard broke into a jogging charge, while the Shieldsworn raised a great chorus of war cries. With an awful sound of clattering steel and shouting warriors, the two armies finally met along the Shieldsworn line. To the left and right, the Shieldsworn wavered under the assault, but held the line; man-for-man, they were more heavily armored and better trained than the Council Guard, and Marstel's advantage in numbers wasn't enough to overwhelm them. But in the center, the Shieldsworn didn't face Marstel's hired soldiers; they faced Rhovann's runehelms.

"Here they come," she breathed, and allowed herself a humorless smile. She'd soon see whether the creatures were as dangerous as Geran feared, or not.

The runehelms, sixty or seventy strong, marched into Wester's line. Black halberds rose high, and then fell with sickening power. No shield or mail could withstand the blow of weapons that heavy driven with such remorseless power; in a matter of moments, two score Hulmaster soldiers were cut down by the hideous strength of the creatures. The constructs advanced a few more steps, drawing back for another blow. Brave Shieldsworn darted inside their reach, driving spears into gray claylike flesh or hacking furiously with axe or sword, but the runehelms seemed almost impervious to their attacks. One of the monsters staggered as a big Shieldsworn fighter flung aside his shield and hewed at its knee with his war axe in a two-handed grip, carving a notch in the creature's leg as if he had a mind to fell a tree. But the runehelm he attacked struck him a back-hand blow with its left hand and sent him flying through the air. Before he could rise again, the monster buried the blade of its halberd in his chest and wrenched it free. The center of the Hulmaster line buckled under the runehelm's inexorable assault.

So much for the hope that they might be easier to kill a few miles from Hulburg, Kara thought darkly. The only defense against the things was to not be standing wherever that halberd was coming down.

"Damn it all," she snarled. Her Shieldsworn weren't giving an inch to the Council Guard on either flank, but the runehelms were destroying her center before her eyes. If Wester's shield broke, the battle might be lost. In desperation, Kara motioned to her standard-bearer and Brother Larken behind her. "To the center!" she cried. "Follow me!"

Spurring Dancer forward, she rode up into the furious melee where Wester's shield struggled to stop foes that seemed unstoppable. Then the chaos of battle engulfed her and her bodyguards. In the space of five heartbeats, Kara found herself in the thick of the fray, unable to think about anything more than the enemies immediately around her. Her sword darted and flashed, batting away massive halberds, leaping out to find a gray throat, blurring in a brutal arc as it took a council soldier's arm at the elbow. Dancer's hooves lashed and struck as the big mare plunged through the fighting.

A few steps behind her, Sarth abandoned his horse and took to the air, shielding himself with a golden halo that deflected the occasional bolt or spear hurled in his direction. The sorcerer had no skill for fighting from horseback, and he knew it. From his vantage he scoured the enemy ranks with great blasts of fire, only to catch the attention of several merchant company wizards. A furious spell battle erupted in the air over the confused melee as the tiefling traded lightning bolts and brilliant darts of magical force with his adversaries. A gray-bearded mage in the colors of the Jannarsks lashed out at Sarth with a rainbow-colored ray that shattered into individual beams when it struck his spell-shield; a glancing touch of the orange ray singed a path across Sarth's chest, blackening his robes and raising a wisp of smoke from his smoldering garb. Sarth shrugged it off, as his race was little affected by fire of any sort, and replied with a barrage of deadly ice darts that skewered the Jannarsk mage several times through and cut down a number of the Jannarsk soldiers near him as well.

Kara wheeled around, trying to assess whether she'd downed any of the runehelms in her countercharge, but the automatons still pressed forward. No blood seeped from opened throats or deep stabs in their gray flesh. "How in the Nine Hells do you slay these things?" she growled to herself. The warrior who'd chopped at its knees might have had the right idea—a shield wouldn't help anyway, and if the things could be immobilized by cutting their legs out from under them, they'd pose little threat.

"Strike at their legs!" she shouted to her soldiers. "Give ground and slow them down by hacking at their legs!"

She decided to put her own advice into action, spurring back to meet the nearest of the creatures. She guided Dancer away from a monstrous sweep of the runehelm's halberd, and then spurred past the creature, leaning down from the saddle to hew at its thick leg. She felt the hard shock of her steel meeting bone—or something much like bone—just above the monster's knee, and bounded out of its reach as it turned awkwardly and lunged at her. Her standard-bearer darted in from the other side and distracted the creature, gaining its attention before backing out of its reach, and when it lunged after Merrith, Kara raced back in again to deliver another blow across the back of the same knee she'd just struck, hamstringing the runehelm. It might not bleed and it might not feel pain, but the creature was still limited by its physical nature; somewhere in its gray flesh its frame was held together with something like bone and sinew, and when those were damaged, its limbs couldn't work. The runehelm floundered to the ground as its leg buckled, but now more of the gray monsters pressed in from all sides.

"Kara!" Sarth shouted. He alighted again, smoke streaming from his cloak. "The runehelms are surrounding you! You must pull back!"

"It can't be," she murmured. She veered around several Shieldsworn working together like a wolf pack to bait and dart at another of the runehelms, and rode clear of the fighting to take stock of how the battle proceeded beyond her own small piece of it. With a sick shock, Kara realized that the sorcerer was right. Despite the desperate efforts of Wester's shield and Larken's too, the runehelms had simply plowed through the Hulmaster soldiers and were turning to one side or the other, systematically cutting down all in their path. The Council Guards following the runehelm assault poured through the breach, shouting in triumph.

For a moment, Kara hesitated. Part of her insisted that by redoubling their efforts, holding where she now stood regardless of the cost, she might yet throw back the runehelms and the Council Guard . . . but her center was smashed beyond repair. If she pulled her army back, she'd lose the encampment at the very least, and the retreat might very well turn into a rout. Without supplies or shelter it would only take a day, perhaps two, before her army disintegrated entirely.

Sarth read the indecision in her eyes, and came to stand at her stirrup. "Kara, there is always tomorrow," he said. "If Geran and I succeed tonight, we will defeat the runehelms for you, but we will need your army to deal with the Council Guard."

"Perhaps you're right." Kara looked around a moment longer, hoping that she'd find some opening or opportunity that would let her salvage the day without abandoning the camp—but each moment she delayed, she knew that she decreased the chances of getting an intact army away from the battle. With a growl, she wheeled and waved her sword over her head. "First and Third Shields, pull back! Icehammers, pull back! Back to the rallying point! Brother Larken, I want the Second Shield to hold in the camp. You're our rearguard!"

The cleric glanced over at Kara, and gave a grim nod. Not many of his soldiers would fight their way free, but if they could slow the runehelms and the Council Guard enough for the remaining companies to break off, their sacrifice might be worth it. Brandishing his mace, Larken turned back to the fray, shouting orders at his soldiers; Kara wondered if she would see him again.

More of Rhovann's constructs flooded forward; Sarth and Kara had to back up to stay out of their reach. All around them, Shieldsworn were yielding ground, an orderly fighting withdrawal through their own camp. "Thank Tempus that we practiced this in maneuvers," she breathed aloud. So many battles ended with one side or the other in panicked flight. "Sarth, see if you can't persuade the merchant cavalry to keep their distance. I don't want our soldiers ridden down as we retreat."

The tiefling nodded. "Will you be able to hold on your hilltop there?"

"What choice do we have?" Kara answered. "We'll hold somehow. Now go!"

Sarth leaped into the air and arrowed off toward the Icehammers as they withdrew before the merchant coster riders. Kara swallowed her bitter disappointment at the outcome of her first meeting with Marstel's forces, and turned her attention to the challenge of extricating her army from the murderous strength of the wizards' runehelms. She'd lost the day, but the war wasn't over yet—the next move was Geran's.

TWENTY-TWO

14 Ches, the Year of Deep Water Drifting (1480 DR)

Dusk was falling over Hulburg as Geran led his horse into the small barn behind Mirya's house and quickly stripped off the saddle and harness. He knew he ought to give the animal a good rubdown and look after it with more care, but he had little time to spare and he doubted he'd need to come back for the gelding. If he needed a mount in the next few hours, he'd borrow or steal one close at hand.

By the time he finished with the saddle and blankets, Mirya was waiting in the yard with a shawl around her shoulders. "Are you ready?" she asked.

He nodded, and they set off for Erstenwold's. It was a little shy of a mile away, on the other side of the Winterspear. From Mirya's lane they hurried down River Street, skirting the Tailings proper. Geran did his best to keep his stride quick but confident, maintaining a cool distance from Mirya. He'd already established for himself that his disguise was good enough to protect him in Hulburg's streets, but now that he was accompanying Mirya, it felt far more risky. Mirya was a known friend of his, of course, and anybody who noticed her going about on the streets when most folk were taking to their homes might wonder why she was dealing with some foreign mage. Worse yet, if one of Marstel's soldiers or spies saw through his disguise, they'd also catch Mirya. She could hardly deny that she was in league with loyalists if they were caught together, and he feared it would go hard with her.

I should have left her safe in her house, he told himself. This is far too dangerous.

They turned on Cinder Way and came to the Middle Bridge. Half-a-dozen runehelms stood guard over the span. Geran steeled himself to walk past them, feigning the same sort of dismissiveness he'd shown before. But Mirya's steps faltered as they drew closer to the towering creatures. He risked a quick glance at her, and realized that she was shaking. Her lips moved softly, saying something he couldn't hear, and her eyes were fixed on the nearest of the clay warriors. She's terrified! he realized with horror. He hadn't expected that, but then again, there was a difference between flouting the authorities with a secret meeting and brazenly walking down the street in his company.

Geran grimaced. It was already too late to go back the way they came without being conspicuous about avoiding the monsters. And even if they did, they'd have to cross the Winterspear at the Lower Bridge or the Burned Bridge to get to the west bank and Erstenwold's, and they'd run into more of the runehelms at the other bridges. He sidled up as close to her as he dared. "Courage, Mirya!" he hissed under his breath. "You've walked past these things a hundred times before. Just ignore them and keep on!"

She didn't reply, and her steps slowed even more. In desperation Geran reached out to take her arm, gently pulling her along and doing his best to ignore the hulking creatures looming around them. Human guards would certainly have suspected something by now, but these were automatons, endowed only with the power to execute the orders they were given. They possessed no intuition, no empathy; they might not notice Mirya's distress or the solicitude of a foreign wizard toward her.

He put his arm around her shoulders and urged her on more force-fully. But as they drew abreast of the first pair of runehelms, she stopped suddenly in her steps. With a dull, sick look on her face, she looked up at the blank visors of the tall creatures, now regarding them both in silence. "Mirya!" he hissed again. "Come on!"

Looking up at the runehelms, Mirya said clearly, "Tell Rhovann that this is Geran Hulmaster. He is here with me."

Geran stared at her in horror. Mirya did not just betray me, he tried to tell himself. But she had. She stood, frowning at the monsters around them, not paying any attention to him at all. And the runehelms were already swinging into motion, swiveling to face him as their massive black halberds lowered.

Somehow he found the presence of mind to step away from Mirya, so that she wouldn't be hacked down by a careless swing of those terrible axes, and drew the shadow sword from its scabbard. If he could teleport out from the middle of these creatures, he might have a chance to elude them—but the monsters were on him before he could even draw breath or seize the calm focus he needed to wield magic. Automatically he ducked beneath the first halberd, twisted away from a second, and lunged wildly at a third. *Umbrach Nyth* gleamed with an eerie purple radiance as it slashed deep into the gray flesh of the runehelm, and this time a great gout of thick black vapor spurted from the cut. The creature sank to the ground as the enchantment binding it frayed and failed under the shadow sword's touch.

"It works!" Geran said aloud, and allowed himself a fierce smile. The runehelms had no instinct of self-preservation, and gave no thought at all to defending themselves from his blows—an acceptable strategy so long as they were nearly immune to injury. But now he had a weapon that could slay them as easily as it would any mortal opponent. He blocked several more halberd thrusts with a flurry of slashes and jabs. The shadow sword sliced deep into gray flesh, and oily black ichor splattered from the wounds. For a moment he'd hoped that a simple cut from *Umbrach Nyth* would be sufficient to unbind a runehelm's animating spell, but he found that the creatures stayed on their feet under his attack—he had to strike deep into their substance to reach the magical essence they harbored, something that would have been a mortal wound in a living foe.

He turned on the nearest of the constructs, trying to draw it farther from Mirya—*why had she betrayed him to Rhovann?*—and sliding in under its guard to bury the shadow sword's point just under the creature's breastbone, or whatever it had in place of one. The runehelm crumpled, and Geran began to hope that he might be able to fight his way free despite the superior numbers of his enemies. He wheeled back to engage the next of the monsters, but a hard-driven halberd blade glanced from his wardings and knocked him off balance toward the others. Then, seemingly out of nowhere, the thick haft of a halberd loomed right before his eyes and struck him a terrific blow across the forehead. The bridge and the town around him turned upside down, and darkness reached up to embrace him.

"Mirya," he croaked. His mouth was dry, and it was difficult to speak. "Why?"

She did not answer him. She didn't even give any sign that she'd heard him. The last thing he saw was her gazing down at him, a small puzzled frown creasing her brow.

It seemed that he flailed and struggled in dark dreams for a long time, somewhere between consciousness and unconsciousness. Full wakefulness hovered just out of reach; it felt as if he'd been buried in warm, thick blankets that clung to his limbs and smothered him in blackness. Eventually it was the throbbing ache in his skull that brought him back around. His forehead stung fiercely whenever anything brushed the crust of dried blood above his eyes, and trickles of warm fresh blood dripped down his face. He was dully aware of being dragged down stone steps, his arms pinioned in the cold clay grip of a pair of the towering runehelms. Then he was stripped and stood up against a rough wall while iron fetters were locked around his wrists. He sagged weakly, held up only by the cruel chains.

"Where am I?" he rasped. No one answered. Slowly he forced his eyes open, and found himself gazing down at a brick floor, covered with a thin handful of straw. The Council Hall dungeons, he realized. He'd been imprisoned here once before, when Kendurkkel Ironthane took service with his cousin Sergen and set out to trap him. Strange to be able to recognize the dungeon he was held in by a glimpse of its floor; clearly, he was spending too much time in dungeons. For a moment Geran was lost in the incongruity of it all, and wondered how long Sergen would be able to have him held here before Kara and Harmach Grigor made the Merchant Council surrender him. Sergen hated him, and he was plotting to seize the throne for himself . . . "No, that's not right," Geran mumbled aloud. "Sergen's dead. I killed him."

With a start, he came fully awake. He was exactly where he'd thought, chained to a wall in the prison beneath the Council Hall. Two Council Guards were making a careful inventory of his clothing and belongings at a table on the other side of the iron bars, leaving him only his smallclothes for his decency. Two of the runehelms stood close by him on either side, their blank helms fixed unwaveringly upon him. His forehead throbbed abominably, and when he glanced up at the small barred window near his cell, the sudden motion made him feel dizzy and nauseated with the blinding white pain. Outside he could see the orange gleam of a streetlamp on wet cobblestones in the gray light—it was after sunset, but not by much. In a few hours he was supposed to meet Sarth and Hamil to venture into the Shadowfell and search out Rhovann's master stone, but Mirya had put a stop to that.

She betrayed me, he told himself again. He didn't want to examine it, didn't want to believe that he'd heard her say what she'd said, but the thing was undeniable. Not only had she told the runehelms who he was, she'd *suggested* that they should go to Erstenwolds, and led him to automatons guarding the Middle Bridge. She'd planned it while they were talking in her kitchen . . . while he was opening his heart to her, and asking her if she would be his wife.

Whether it was the blow to his head or the wound in his heart, his knees gave out again. "Was it all a lie?" he mumbled to himself. Had she allowed him to dote on her all the months that he'd been back in Hulburg? That he couldn't believe. It simply wasn't possible. He'd rescued her from the clutches of the Black Moon pirates and brought her safely back home. At that moment five months before there'd been no doubt in his heart that they were drawing closer again . . . and he'd been exiled from Hulburg before anything more could come of it. So no, her affection for him hadn't been feigned, at least not at the moment when he was driven out of Hulburg.

"Ah, our dreaming prince is awake," one of the Council Guards, a burly half-orc, remarked. He stepped into the cell and advanced to seize a handful of Geran's hair and raise his head fully upright. "Are there any other Hulmaster spies wandering about in Harmach Maroth's realm, my lord? Speak up now, and it may go easier on you."

Geran winced in pain, but said nothing.

The half-orc guardsman tightened his grip. "You didn't slip into town just to pay a visit to Mirya Erstenwold," he sneered. "Who else did you see? What are your plans?"

"My plans are to kill or run off Rhovann Disarnnyl, that fat oaf Marstel, and all the brigands and thugs who call themselves their soldiers," Geran replied. "What else would I be here for?"

The half-orc's face darkened. He stepped back and delivered a jarring backhand slap to Geran's jaw. The swordmage reeled in his chains as his already-throbbing skull filled with hot red pain, and he found himself spitting blood on the cell floor. The Council Guard raised his hand for another blow, but one of the runehelms standing nearby reached out to catch his arm.

The blank visor swiveled down to gaze at the half-orc guard. "Do not damage Geran Hulmaster further," the creature intoned. "I am coming to attend to him soon. Do you understand?"

The guard paled and stepped back. "Yes, Lord Rhovann. We will be ready for you," he replied. "What shall we do with Mirya Erstenwold? She is waiting upstairs."

"Send her home," the creature replied. "She's been of great service to me." The runehelm let go of the guard's arm, and he quickly retreated.

Geran closed his eyes, hoping that would dull the pain. The guards ignored him, and he returned to the question of Mirya's betrayal. He *knew* that nothing could have turned her against him before he was exiled from Hulburg, so what had changed between then and now? "Selsha," he whispered aloud. That had to be it. When he'd returned to Hulburg and called on her at Erstenwold's, Mirya had said that she'd sent Selsha away for safekeeping. But what if Rhovann or his captains had threatened her daughter? That was the only thing that he could imagine to explain Mirya's betrayal. She wouldn't have done it for money—she wouldn't have done it to save her own life.

But if she'd betrayed him on Selsha's account, she hardly would have needed to admit her love for him. Had Mirya lied when she'd said she was a fool to love him, that she couldn't bear to live in doubt of his own constancy? No, he decided, it wasn't a lie. She loved him, perhaps as much as he loved her. But that made the fact of her betrayal hurt more, not less.

Whatever her reasons, Mirya had put him in a desperate situation indeed. In a matter of hours Kara would be moving in on Hulburg, expecting to brush aside the wizard's deadly constructs. If he didn't carry out the strike against Rhovann's hidden source of power, she'd have to fight her way through all the runehelms at the wizard's command. Scores, perhaps hundreds, of Shieldsworn and Hulmaster loyalists would die in that battle . . . assuming they won.

It's up to Sarth and Hamil, he decided. When he didn't show up for their planned rendezvous, they'd realize that he'd fallen into some kind of trouble. They'd understand that somehow they'd have to undo Rhovann's spells without his help—if that was even possible. The black hilt of *Umbrach Nyth* gleamed in its silver-tooled sheath among Geran's clothing and other possessions. Was it even possible to destroy the master pearl without the lich's gift?

With a small groan of frustration, Geran gave himself up to his black despair and slipped into unconsciousness again.

TWENTY-THREE

14 Ches, the Year of Deep Water Drifting (1480 DR)

Some time later, the creak and clang of the dungeon's heavy iron doors roused Geran from his darkness. Swift, light footsteps echoed down the hall, and then Rhovann appeared, dressed in a long, tailored blue waistcoat over his shirt, with breeches of elven graysilk and knee-high suede boots. His wand rested in a holster at his hip, and his silver hand rested lightly on its slender ivory handle.

The elf wizard halted a few steps from Geran, studying him with narrowed eyes. "Ah, now this is a sight to warm the heart," he said softly. "Here hangs Geran Hulmaster in chains. The reckless freebooter and scofflaw, captured by a few words whispered in my runehelms' ears!"

Geran carefully set his feet under him and levered himself fully upright. Standing, his hands were chained at about the height of his head; sharp twinges of pain in his shoulders and wrists brought a wince to his face, but he stifled it quickly. "Enjoy it while you can," he told Rhovann. "No matter what happens to me, your days in Hulburg are numbered."

"Your confidence appears misplaced," the elf answered. "Matters seem well in hand to me. I have you exactly where I want you, my harmach's dealt with your army—with a little help from my runehelms, of course— and soon enough I'll have Mirya Erstenwold help me clean up the ugly little resistance she's been fomenting all winter. I anticipate nothing but success in all my endeavors."

Geran set his jaw in an angry frown. Dealt with the army? He had a sinking feeling that Rhovann wouldn't bother to lie to him as long as he was in his power, which meant that something else had gone wrong with the Hulmaster strategy. Kara was supposed to be waiting near Rosestone; she wouldn't have deviated from the plan they'd worked out. Had Rhovann sent out his army to face Kara already? He and Kara had talked about whether it would be wiser to wait until the runehelms were disabled before bringing the Hulmaster army eastward, and ultimately they'd decided that it would be useful to either lure much of Marstel's strength away from Hulburg or bring their own force within striking distance. But if Rhovann had somehow surprised Kara outside of the town with a number of runehelms, then they'd simply stuck their heads into the spring-loaded trap Rhovann and his minions had readied for them—the worst possible outcome, really.

How many more catastrophes am I going to blunder into today? he wondered. Even though he had no desire to listen to Rhovann's smug triumph, he had to know more about Kara and the Shieldsworn. "I don't believe you," he replied. "Kara trained that army all winter. They wouldn't break."

"I hardly care whether you believe me or not," Rhovann snapped. "Still . . . it seems a pity that you should remain uninformed as to the scope of your failures." The mage turned to study the nearest runehelm, and murmured the words of a spell. With one hand he touched the creature's shoulder, and with his silver hand he extended one finger and tapped Geran between the eyes. "Observe!"

A confusing jumble of images appeared in Geran's mind, and he struggled to make sense of what he saw. It was dark outside, with a cold rain falling. He seemed to stand at the foot of a low but steep bluff crowning a wide hillside; under his feet were bare gray rock and tufts of moorgrass. Dozens of guttering lanterns glimmered in the night, illuminating company after company of Council Guards and runehelms who sought to climb up the rain-slick hillside. Atop the bluff, a large knot of Shieldsworn still held their ground, fending off the runehelms with what looked like pikes improvised from wagon axles and peppering the ranks of Marstel's army with a steady arrow fire. Geran caught a glimpse of Kara at the top of the Hulmaster defenses, shouting for the Shieldsworn to stand fast. Then his point of view swiveled, almost as if he were turning his own head;

Geran realized that he was seeing from a runehelm's eyes, such as they were. Is this how Rhovann can perceive what his constructs perceive? he wondered. With the new perspective, he saw that Marstel's army had the Shieldsworn and the Icehammers fairly well trapped on the hilltop. They couldn't push Kara off the hill, but neither could she fight her way clear.

If they lost the camp, they'll be short on food, water, and shelter, Geran thought furiously. How long can they hold out on a bare hilltop?

Rhovann withdrew his finger, and Geran blinked the wizard's images out of his sight. "As you can see, it is merely a matter of time. Perhaps I will allow your cousin to surrender her army and spare their lives, or perhaps not." He chuckled. "I must admit, I never would have thought to look for you in Hulburg when I observed you riding out to parley with Marstel. A clever trick, that; I owe Mistress Erstenwold my thanks for pointing out my mistake. I shall have to give some serious thought to devising an appropriate reward for her."

Geran scowled. "What do you mean to do with me?"

Rhovann smiled coldly. "I could have ordered your arrest half a year ago when you returned from the black moon. But I would have faced an inconvenient amount of unrest if I'd passed a harsh sentence on you after your incompetent bumblings appeared to save Hulburg from the threat of the corsairs—so instead I permitted you to go into exile, knowing full well that you would inevitably return to challenge me. Now you are a traitor, rebel, and murderer. At last, I can see to it that justice prevails for all the insults and injuries you have given me."

Geran raised his head and looked Rhovann in the eye, even though his head was splitting. "Do your worst, then," he rasped. "But spare me your aggrieved airs and your little show of sanctimony. It's wasted on me, and there's no one else here but your creatures."

"Aggrieved airs?" Rhovann snarled. "Believe me, there is nothing insincere in the grievances I bear you. With the exception of the Years of Retreat, my family has lived in Myth Drannor for almost three thousand years. Thanks to your your fawning and simpering before that soft-hearted coronal, you were permitted to displace me in the affections of a *teu Tel'Quessir* princess as if you were in some way my equal, or hers! Our Houses were ancient and glorious when your inbred ancestors were crouching in squalid huts and fumbling with sticks to make fire! Do you have any idea how much *shame* you brought upon my family, and Alliere's?

"And let us not forget *this*," Rhovann continued. He stepped close and thrust his silver hand into Geran's face. The swordmage found his eyes struggling to focus on it; the artificial member was bound seamlessly to the flesh of the wizard's wrist. Tiny runes gleamed around its base, where it met the stump of the arm. "The Red Wizards provided me with this replacement—a capable enough device, bought at a very dear price, I might add—but not a day goes by that I do not feel the ache of my severed hand and long to *feel* with these cold metal fingers as my living fingers would have. Not a day goes by that I am not constantly reminded of how you maimed me, Geran!

"When at last you'd finally demonstrated the *quality* of a human of your high breeding with your craven, savage stroke against me when I was helpless before you, and even Ilsevele had to admit that you had no place among the *teu Tel'Quessir*, still you ruined me. Your friends at court could not abide the idea of their favorite human pet punished, and so they began to whisper against me, to spread malicious lies and suggestions until all my affairs were laid bare and I was forced to endure the same ignominious fate that had been decreed for you!" Rhovann's teeth were bared in pure fury as he leaned close to Geran's face. "And finally we come to perhaps your most galling offense against me: I, the scion of a House thirty centuries old, was treated like a common human criminal and turned out of my ancient homeland on your account! What for you was the end of a casual visit was for me the denial of everything I might ever have had or striven for! Now, tell me again that I am manufacturing my indignation! Tell me again!"

Geran tried to blink some of the crusted blood from his eyes. He knew that he should choose his words with care, but he was weary. "You brought much of that on yourself, Rhovann," he said. "Alliere's heart was never yours to begin with. You chose to dabble in arts forbidden in Myth Drannor. And when you and I fought, you reached for your wand when I'd beaten you. Your fate is your own doing, and you're a fool if you blame it on me."

A door slammed down the corridor, and Geran heard the sound of heavy footsteps and rustling mail. Rhovann scowled in irritation as a beefy, black-bearded Council Guard officer appeared, flanked by several council soldiers. Geran recognized him as Sarvin, castellan of Griffonwatch under Edelmark; he'd seen the fellow at a distance in his earlier visits to occupied Hulburg. The castellan's face was set in a fierce scowl, broken only by a small snort of satisfaction as he glanced toward Geran in his chains. "Forgive the interruption, my lord," he said to Rhovann. "I have urgent news that cannot wait."

"Well?" Rhovann snapped. "What is it?" Castellan Sarvin glanced at Geran again, and Rhovann rolled his eyes and moved to the far corner of the room, taking the officer by the arm. The fellow whispered urgently to the elf, as Geran strained to hear what news he was bringing Rhovann. He was too far away to make it out, but after a moment Rhovann simply nodded and gave the castellan some answer that satisfied him. With a shallow bow to the mage, Sarvin marched out of the room again, motioning for his guards to join him. Rhovann stood silent for a moment, absorbed in his thoughts, then wheeled around to approach Geran again.

"Ill tidings, I hope?" Geran asked.

"It seems I let Mirya Erstenwold go too soon," Rhovann replied. "The Hulmaster loyalists are arming themselves to rise against the harmach all across the town. And of course much of my army is scattered across the Highfells in pursuit of yours. Doubtless that was not part of your plan, but the timing of it may cause some inconvenience. Well, no matter. Within a few hours the loyalists will be put down. After tomorrow, no one will ever dare to challenge my grip on Hulburg again." He paused, allowing the swordmage to consider what he'd said. "Never fear, Geran. I'll make certain that you live to see the destruction of your House and the final futility of your efforts to unseat my harmach before I allow you to die."

Geran set his face in an iron mask, refusing to let Rhovann see him wince. If he hadn't allowed himself to be captured, the runehelms the elf mage was so proud of would have been sabotaged by now, and the battle for Hulburg already won. But unless Sarth and Hamil somehow found a way to proceed without him, Rhovann would keep his constructs for the foreseeable future. He glanced again at the pile of clothing and gear that had been taken from him when he was brought in. The scrolls of shadowalking and *Umbrach Nyth* were lying with his other belongings on the table by the cell's door. So far Rhovann hadn't thought to make any close inspection of the things Geran had been carrying with him . . . and if there was any hope of striking an unexpected blow against the master stone to which the creatures were all bound, he couldn't let Rhovann guess that he attached any special importance to dealing with the mage's powerful constructs.

"You might pay your mercenaries and build your automatons, but no one is truly loyal to you," he said to the mage. "You trust no one, and therefore no one trusts you. How long can you keep Hulburg under your thumb without allies?"

"Allies come and go; as long as I hold the reins of power in this city, I'll never want for them." Rhovann studied him coldly, and a cruel smile crept across his features. "As much as I might like to continue this conversation, I have to admit that it would inconvenience me to let your misguided loyalists cause any great amount of damage. Unfortunately, that means I have no more time to bandy words with you now. But before I go, I think I'll leave you with a little something to remember me by, and a promise of many more conversations to come."

The mage motioned to the runehelms hovering close by Geran. The creatures moved in to take Geran by the arms and pin him firmly against the wall of the cell, his arms outstretched in the fetters. He drew his wand from the slender holster at his hip, and advanced on the helpless sword-mage. "I am nothing if not a creature of reason," Rhovann remarked. "You brought about my exile from my home; I did the same to you. You humiliated and disgraced me; I will think long and hard about how best to give you the same, measure for measure. But first and foremost, you maimed me. What compensation should I require for that, I wonder?"

Despite his determination not to show any weakness to his enemy, Geran felt his stomach tighten in sudden fear. He pressed his lips together, refusing to say anything.

"No suggestions?" Rhovann raised an eyebrow, waiting for Geran to speak. When Geran kept his silence, he suddenly scowled. "As you will, then," he said. He pointed the wand at Geran's right hand and snarled, "*Aitharach na viarl!*"

From the wand green-glowing liquid jetted forth, a splatter not much larger than half a good-sized mug. It covered Geran's palm and most of his fingers—and instantly began to blacken his flesh, bubbling and sizzling. The acid was appallingly strong, stripping away the skin in mere heartbeats and dissolving its way to muscle and tendon underneath. Despite his determination not to give Rhovann even the slightest flinch, Geran howled in agony as a thousand red-hot needles skewered his flesh and began to chew deeper and deeper. The smell of his own burning flesh filled his nostrils. He looked again, and saw bare black bones emerging from the ruin. Nausea and pain overwhelmed him.

Suddenly his arm swung free from the fetters, and he sagged toward the floor, held now only by the chains around his left wrist. For an instant he thought that somehow he'd slipped out of his manacles and saved his hand—but when he looked at his right wrist, there was only a pocked, blackened stump, throbbing with unbelievable agony, a pain so intense his shoulder ached and his heart hammered in his chest. An animal-like sound of misery escaped his mouth.

"Not so clean or swift as the wound you dealt me, but the end result is much the same," Rhovann snarled. He looked to the runehelms. "Send for a healer to clean and bandage the injury. He is not to die before I permit him to do so. I will return when I am done dealing with the Hulmaster loyalists." Then he wheeled and strode out of the dungeon, his cloak fluttering behind him.

Geran looked again at the charred bones of his wrist, and fainted.

TWENTY-FOUR

15 Ches, the Year of Deep Water Drifting (1480 DR)

Mirya hurried through the lamplit, rain-streaked streets, fleeing the Council Hall and the awful knowledge of what she'd done. Tears streamed down her cheeks, and for once she didn't care who might see them. Near the corner of Plank and Cart Streets, she ducked into a doorway, wrestling with her despair. *Oh, Mirya,* she thought over and over again. *You've killed the man you love. Rhovann'll flay him alive, and he'll die thinking that you were the one that gave him up to his enemies.* She shuddered in pure horror, and a stifled sob escaped her. For a long time she covered her face and gave herself up completely to her tears.

The whole episode had been a strange, dark dream in which she saw herself saying and doing things she never meant to, a spectator inside her own head. She'd fought furiously to awaken as she saw herself leading Geran directly to the spot where she meant to turn him over to his enemies . . . but Geran had taken her silent struggle for simple fear, not understanding that it was Rhovann's dark magic that forced her steps onward. The runehelms ignored her, and the Council Guards allowed her to go after Rhovann instructed them to release her—no doubt believing that she was still under his influence. But she'd emerged from Rhovann's enchantment shortly on the steps of the Council Hall, the terrible understanding of her betrayal crashing down on her waking mind with the force of an avalanche.

Finally she gave herself a small shake. "What's done is done, Mirya," she told herself. "Stop this nonsense, and *think*. There must be something to be done."

It didn't seem likely that Rhovann would kill Geran out of hand, or he could have done it already. The wizard had imprisoned Geran instead. Perhaps he thought that Geran knew something of value about the Hulmaster attack, or perhaps he was keeping Geran alive to serve as a hostage in case the fight for Hulburg went against him. Or maybe it was as she feared, and Rhovann meant to do Geran to death in some truly slow and horrific manner . . . but in any of those cases, he'd keep Geran alive at least for a little while. And that meant it might be possible to plead for mercy, to find someone to intercede, or to rescue Geran somehow.

"Marstel and Rhovann have no mercy to speak of, and I can't imagine who might be able to intervene," she murmured. Perhaps one of the merchant companies, or a temple? The Sokols might help, but she'd seen over the last few months that Nimessa's voice didn't carry much weight in the council. It would have to be a rescue. Somehow she'd have to get into the Council Hall dungeon, free Geran in spite of the guards and runehelms (and likely Rhovann himself), and get him away again.

"It can't be done," she told herself, and scowled in the shadows of the alleyway. Even if she gathered her loyalist cell together, it would be suicide. Perhaps with some sort of magic . . . "Sarth!" she breathed. The sorcerer was supposed to meet Geran at the Burned Bridge, and Hamil too. If they couldn't help her, no one could. Perhaps Geran's friends could undo her treachery before any lasting harm came of it.

Of course, there was the thorny question of whether she could even *get* to the Burned Bridge with the town in the state it was. The streets were crowded with bands of merchant coster armsmen defending their companies' storehouses or stores, shorthanded Council Guard detachments hurrying here and there, gangs of Tailings thugs and bravos roaming in search of chances to loot stores or rob passersby, and bands of Hulburgans gathering in squares to pull on old mail shirts or leather jerkins and pass out spears, axes, pitchforks, any old hoarded weapon or tool that might serve as one. From time to time silent squads of runehelms marched past, scattering crowds and driving gangs into retreat—it hadn't taken long for both foreign gangs and loyalist militia to learn that the mage's creations were almost invulnerable to any weapon they could find.

It would have to be the buried streets, she decided. They'd get her close enough. With a new determination fixed in her mind, Mirya slipped out of her shadowed doorway and hurried for Erstenwold's. The store wasn't far off, only a half block or so, and she hurried around the side of the building to let herself in the back—somehow the idea of unlocking the store's front door while so many ruffians and thieves were about didn't seem wise. She paused to throw the bolt at the back door and hurried to the cellars. Beneath a large square of canvas waited the crossbow and lantern she kept ready for venturing into the old passages beneath the streets. She didn't like the idea of wandering about in the buried streets by night, but it wasn't as if it would be any darker than it was during daylight. She lit the lantern, hoisted the crossbow on her hip, and clambered into the underground maze.

She hurried through the dark and dusty passages, following her usual route to the place she and her band usually met—an old wine cellar beneath the ruins of a wealthy merchant's house in old Hulburg. She paused to consider her way in the shadows of the great, dusty tuns, searching her memory for the right combination of passages and cellars to take her toward the Burned Bridge.

Something moved in the darkness behind her. It wasn't much, only the rattle of a small pebble kicked over the old flagstones by a careless foot, but Mirya's heart leaped into her mouth. Instantly she dimmed her lantern and wedged herself into the darkest, narrowest space she could find, backing between two of the old storage shelves and bringing her crossbow up before her. For a moment, she heard nothing more—then the soft rustle of footsteps reached her ears, and a gleam of light played across the old vault. She released the safety catch of the crossbow. A large, hooded figure entered the room, a lantern held high in one hand and a wicked hatchet bared in the other.

Mirya heaved a sigh of relief. "I'm here, Brun," she called softly, and came out of the shadows.

The young tavernkeeper jumped, startled by the sound of her voice. "Mirya?" he asked. "I didn't expect to find you here—I was just on my way back to the Troll and Tankard."

"Nor I you, but I'm glad to see you. I need your help. Geran Hulmaster's been captured; Rhovann's holding him in the prison beneath the Council Hall."

"The Lord Hulmaster's in the city?" Brun breathed. "We've got to help him! How in the Nine Hells did Marstel's wizard catch him, anyway?"

"Through me," Mirya answered. "Rhovann used his magic to spy on me, keeping watch for Geran." That was as near the truth as Mirya could bring herself. She paused, thinking for a moment about what exactly she wanted him to do. She didn't know if Hamil and Sarth could free Geran by themselves, but even if they could, she simply didn't know if they'd be where Geran expected to meet them, or if they'd be able to divert themselves to the task when they likely had other important things to see to—in which case, it might come down to Mirya and whatever help she could muster from her neighbors. With a small nod to herself, she made her decision.

"Brun, I want you to gather the rest of our cell, or as many as you can find in half an hour's time," she told the big brewer. "Bring them to the cellar under Wennart's storeroom, and wait for me there. It's just behind the Council Hall; it's the nearest safe place to meet up I can think of. I'm going to see if I can find Geran's friends."

Brun thought for a moment—making a list of who he could gather quickly, Mirya guessed. "Aye, I think I can find you at least a few fighters in that time. Nothing else we mean to do tonight would be as important as snatching Lord Geran out of Marstel's talons!"

"Good luck. I'll see you under Wennart's." Mirya took Brun's arm for a moment before she hurried off northward again. Behind her, the brewer wheeled and ran back the way he'd come.

Mirya followed the buried streets as far as she could, and eventually climbed back up to the surface through a rubble-choked cellar near North Street that was bare to the sky. The rain was cold on her face after the underground passages, and she shivered. The neighborhood was one of the old razed portions of Hulburg that had never been entirely rebuilt. A few cheaply built rowhouses clustered close by Keldon Way here, home to more of the poor foreign folk who'd come to Hulburg in recent years; it was generally not a neighborhood that Mirya would have chosen to cross at night. But the troubles and disorders elsewhere in the city seemed to have everyone's attention now, and no one was about in the ruined districts.

She reached the small square at the west end of the Burned Bridge, and hesitated in the shadows. The Burned Bridge wasn't ruined, of course—it was a perfectly serviceable wooden structure built atop the stone piers of the bridge that *had* burned, sometime in the years before the Spellplague. She couldn't be sure, but she thought she could make out more of Rhovann's gray monsters standing watch near the center of the span. "Am I to find them at this end, the other end, or the middle?" she wondered aloud. She certainly had no liking for the last two options; she simply refused to go anywhere near the runehelms again if she could help it.

Mirya looked and listened for a long moment, peering at any place that seemed like it might offer a clandestine meeting spot. Her eye fell on an old ruined mill just a little bit past the bridge. She couldn't see anything in the shadows of its empty walls . . . but each time she looked away, her eye wandered back to that spot. Deciding to trust her intuition, she skirted the square by the foot of the bridge and ventured into the old shell of the building. "Well met?" she called softly. "Is anybody here?"

She heard nothing but the patter of raindrops, and the moaning of the rising wind. Then came a sudden rustle in the debris close by; a big rat scurried over the rubble. Mirya gave a startled yelp and leaped back as the creature vanished down a crevice, heading for the river bank. This was a foolish notion, she scolded herself. What if there'd been a band of ruffians lying in wait here?

She wrapped her cloak closer around her body and picked her way back toward the street—but then she heard another sound. "Mirya, is that you?" Hamil called. The halfling advanced from the darkness at the far end of the mill, sheathing the knife that gleamed in his hand. "What are you doing here?"

"You're truly here," Mirya said with a sigh of relief. She hurried back to meet Hamil in the middle of the ruined building. In the shadows of the far wall she now could make out Sarth's horned silhouette. "It's Geran," she continued. "He's been captured, and Rhovann is holding him in the dungeons below the Council Hall."

"Damn it all!" the halfling swore. He paced in a small circle. "Now what? We certainly didn't plan on this."

Sarth frowned, and looked at Mirya. "How did you find us?"

"Geran came to my house earlier this evening, before he was caught. He mentioned that he'd be meeting you here at midnight. I've no idea what the three of you are up to, but I'm hoping that you can help him."

"Me too," Hamil muttered to himself. He glanced up at Sarth as he paced. "Do we have time to free him and carry on? For that matter, *can* we free him? He's sure to be well guarded."

"Geran had the scrolls, and the sword," Sarth observed. "I might be able to translate us into the shadow, but Aesperus said that we would need *Umbrach Nyth*. Can we succeed without the sword, or Geran to wield it?"

The halfling shook his head, and came to a halt. He looked back up to Mirya. "What happened?" he asked.

Mirya couldn't bring herself to meet his eyes. "I betrayed him," she said in a whisper. "Rhovann bewitched me tendays ago, and I didn't even know it until I turned Geran in. It's my fault."

Hamil stared at her, a hard and cheerless look that chilled her to the marrow. His eyes flicked to Sarth, and Mirya realized that he was speaking silently to the sorcerer. The tiefling studied her for a moment, and shrugged. "It's a clever and ruthless ploy," he said to Hamil. "Rhovann is a wizard of formidable learning, brilliant and unscrupulous. Why should we be surprised that he conceived something like this?"

"Because I hate it when my enemy proves more clever than I thought," Hamil replied. "How do we know that she isn't still under the wizard's influence? He used Mirya to catch Geran, maybe he now hopes to use Geran to catch us."

"That I can test," Sarth said. He advanced on Mirya and peered into her eyes. The tiefling's orbs were the color of hot brass in the shadows. "Be still, Mirya. This will not harm you, but I must be certain. *Zamai dhur othmanna.*" With the last words, he raised his rune-marked scepter and brought his magic to bear; his eyes glowed as bright as candles, and Mirya felt a strange tingling sensation over her skin. She shuddered, but tried not to retreat.

After a moment, Sarth nodded to himself. "No enchantment holds her, but I detect the fading impression of one that was recently upon her. We can trust her."

"That's a relief," Mirya said. "I feared that I was still under Rhovann's spell without knowing it."

"Start at the beginning, then, and explain to us what happened," Sarth said.

Mirya started to speak, and then stopped herself. "No. We haven't the time for that," she answered. "I've a few loyalist fighters assembling near the Council Hall now. Every moment we delay, Geran remains in Rhovann's power."

The halfling and the tiefling stared at her. Then, slowly, Hamil nodded. "All right. Perhaps Rhovann isn't expecting anyone to be able to mount a rescue so swiftly. Or perhaps we'll all get killed. I don't suppose you have a plan?"

She shook her head. "I can get you to the Council Hall unseen. After that, I hoped you'd have an idea."

Hamil replied with a low laugh. "You surprise me, Mirya. You're too practical for this sort of nonsense. Well, lead on, and we'll see what we see."

"This way, then," Mirya replied. She led the halfling and the sorcerer back to the open cellar and its hidden entrance to the buried streets. A distant flicker of lightning brightened the sky as she scrambled back down to the old door, and the raindrops started falling thicker and faster. Her allies paused as she levered the door open again, looking dubiously at the dark passage revealed. Mirya retrieved her lantern and ducked inside; after a moment, she heard Sarth and Hamil following.

"Well, now I understand what you meant about getting to the Council Hall unseen," Hamil said softly as they hurried along. "I never knew any of this was down here. How far do these tunnels go?"

"They lie under much of the new town, anywhere there's been building atop the ruins of the old city," Mirya answered. "They reach to Cart Street to the south, and as far as High Street on the east, but they don't cross the Winterspear, of course. Still, they're useful for smuggling and staying out of sight." They passed through the old wine cellar, but no one was there; Mirya didn't waste time, and simply pressed on ahead at the best speed she could manage. In another hundred yards she passed by the cramped door leading into Erstenwold's cellar, and took a branching passage to her right. It took her one or two false turns, but she finally found her way to a wide but low cellar half filled with old rubble. Old casks, barrels, and trunks were stacked haphazardly around the bottom of an old wooden staircase that led up to a wooden door.

In the dim gleam of a lantern whose shutter was open only by a sliver, she saw several hooded figures waiting by the foot of the stair. Brun Osting raised the lantern and opened the shutter by a little more. "Mirya, is that you?" he called in a low voice.

"Aye, it's me," she said. "I've brought Hamil Alderheart and the sorcerer Sarth. They'll help us get Geran out of the Council Guard's clutches." She quickly introduced Geran's companions to her small group of loyalists— Brun, his cousin Halla, Lodharrun the smith, and Senna Vannarshel, the fletcher. It seemed that they were all Brun could find swiftly; Mirya decided that they'd have to do.

"Will we be enough?" Senna Vannarshel asked. "There might be scores of Council Guards guarding the hall."

"Do not be concerned about them," Sarth said. The tiefling smiled coldly. "Their numbers will not avail them."

Mirya nodded in the dim light. She'd seen Sarth in battle before, when Geran dueled his cousin Sergen on the decks of a warship drifting through the skies of the black moon. The tiefling wasn't boasting when he spoke in such a manner. "Up the stairs," she told the others. "And try to be quiet about it."

They climbed up the steep, dusty stairs. At the top there was a brief delay as Brun had to force the door open against the heavy barrels that had been left in front of it. Hamil quickly slipped past the burly brewer and went to the storeroom's door, brushing a clear spot in one dirty pane of the window. After a quick peek, he opened the door a handspan and stuck his head out to look up and down the alleyway. The drumbeat of rain grew louder, and a breath of cold damp air—cool and clean after the close quarters of buried Hulburg—flowed into the storeroom. "No one's around. Follow me!"

They filed out into the alley and splashed across through the cold puddles, gathering in a knot against a door in the back of the Council Hall—Hamil, Sarth, and Mirya to the left, and Brun, Halla, Lodharrun, and Senna Vannarshel to the right. The halfling gave everyone a look of warning, and then stealthily tried the handle. The door didn't open. "Locked," he whispered. "Give me a moment." The halfling kneeled by the lock and drew a small pick from his sleeve.

"I don't suppose we've any idea of where to find Lord Geran?" Senna whispered.

"In the prison below the hall. I saw him taken there. A guardroom blocks the way to the cells; there'll be Council Guards there."

"There it is," Hamil murmured. He silenced the group with an upraised hand, and carefully peeked inside the door. A dim yellow light shone out into the alleyway. Motioning for them to wait, he slipped inside.

"Remember, we're not here to pick fights. The quicker and quieter we go, the better our chances of reaching Geran and getting out again," Mirya told Brun and the rest of her band as they waited on the halfling. "When the time comes to withdraw, we'll try to find our way back to this door and retreat into buried Hulburg. It's our best chance to lose any who chase after us."

"We'll give away the secret of the buried ways," Lodharrun muttered.

"By tomorrow night we'll have won or lost, and we'll be done with sneaking through cellars," Mirya replied. "If we give it away, we give it away."

"Remember, the runehelms speak to one another," Sarth added. "From the moment we meet one, all the runehelms in the city will know of our presence, and likely Rhovann as well. We must not be delayed."

Hamil reappeared at the door, and motioned for quiet. *There are a lot of Council Guards here,* he said silently, his eyes flicking from one face to another. *I think we can get to the guardroom without a fight, but we'll need a distraction, something to draw Marstel's soldiers away.*

Mirya thought for a moment, and looked at her band of rebels. "What if we shoot a few arrows or bolts at the guards by the front door?" she asked. "Either they'll come out and give chase, or they'll close the doors and fort up, but they'd be out of our way."

Hamil considered it, and nodded. Mirya turned to Senna and Halla; the fletcher was a skilled archer, as one might expect, and Halla was nearly as good with her sling. "I think that'll be work for you two," she said. "Stay well back in the shadows, and move between your shots. If they come out after you, you know what to do. We'll give you a two-hundred count to let you get into position."

"We'll do what we can," Senna replied. Halla bit her lip, but nodded. Together the old fletcher and the young woman hurried down the alley into the rain. Mirya said a silent prayer to the gods of mercy and good fortune that she hadn't just sent the two women to their deaths. She waited with the others for a short time in the alleyway, silently counting off. Inside the Council Hall she could hear occasional footsteps, the sound of voices, the creaking of doors as they opened and shut, but none sounded very close by. Then Hamil motioned to the small band and led the way as they crept in from the rain.

They were in a large kitchen, currently unoccupied. For a moment Mirya wondered what in the world the Merchant Council needed with a kitchen, but then she realized that the prisoners in the cells below and the guards who watched them had to have their meals fixed somewhere. For that matter, the Merchant Council likely hosted banquets here when the occasion demanded. They quietly filed through the room to a servant's hall on the far side, proceeding past several doors opening on either side until they reached a door at the end of the hall.

Here Hamil paused. *Now we wait a moment for Mirya's friends,* he said. *If they get the guards' attention by the front door we should be able to cross the hall outside this door and duck down the steps to the guardroom without being seen.*

Carefully, he opened the door a finger's width to peer out. The voices and movements of the soldiers outside grew louder, and Mirya steeled herself for violence. But then a sharp scream sounded from a short distance away. Cries of alarm and angry curses echoed from outside. Hamil gave them all a quick wink, and darted out from his hiding place. Sarth, Brun, and Lodharrun followed; Mirya brought up the rear, after the dwarf. She risked a single glimpse to her right as they crossed a wide, open hallway. Several Council Guards clustered around the building's front door, some peering outside, others tending to one of their fellows, who was on the ground with an arrow in his stomach.

Then they clattered down the stairs leading to the dungeons below the great hall.

Ahead of her Hamil vanished around a bend in the stairs, knives gleaming in his hands. An instant later another cry of alarm echoed from the room at the bottom of the stairs, followed by the sudden clash of steel on steel. Sarth rounded the bend after Hamil, and she heard the tiefling's rough voice snarling words of magic; Brun and Lodharrun leaped into the fray after the two heroes. With a quick glance back up the stairs behind her, Mirya turned the corner after her friends, crossbow ready for a shot.

The violence of the scene appalled her. One guard was on the floor, vainly trying to staunch the blood pumping out of a murderous stab wound in his upper thigh, and Hamil was systematically slashing and stabbing his way through a second guard whose weak efforts to defend himself couldn't last more than another moment or two. On the other side of the room, another pair of guards sprawled in frozen gore, pierced through by a blast of icicles that riddled them and the wall behind them. Brun Osting and the dwarf Lodharrun attacked the remaining two guards, the big brewer using his axe with his hand choked halfway up the haft, the dwarf fencing with his opponent. From her vantage on the stairs, Mirya had a clear shot at the smith's foe, and before she could second-guess herself, she leveled her crossbow and took it. The thick quarrel suddenly sprouted in the fellow's right shoulder, spinning him half around; the dwarf stepped forward and ran him through while he was distracted. In moments, the room was still again.

Brun Osting looked up from the man he'd felled, and grinned. "Well, that wasn't so bad," he said.

"It's not the breaking in that's difficult," Hamil told him. "It's breaking out again." With that, he seized the keys clipped to the guard-sergeant's belt and hurried over to unlock the door leading to the row of cells beyond.

The Council Hall prison was not a very large one, no more than a pair of intersecting corridors, with perhaps a total of a dozen or so cells. Reaching the intersection, they saw Geran—naked except for his smallclothes—in the cell at the far end of the rightmost passage, slumped unconscious with one hand shackled to the wall. Two runehelms stood watch over him.

The powerful constructs flowed into motion as soon as the loyalist band came into sight, drawing short-hafted maces from their harnesses since there was little space to wield their massive halberds.

"They do not feel pain, and they do not bleed," Sarth warned the others. "But they are knitted together with bone and sinew, and these can be destroyed. Break bones and sever limbs until they can fight no more."

"I think I brought a knife to an axe fight," Hamil muttered. But he threw himself forward, rolling neatly under one powerful mace swing and attacking the construct's knee. Brun and Lodharrun joined in, while Sarth turned on the second monster and blasted at it with a jet of roaring green flames. For a moment the loyalists' assault seemed like it might actually overpower the creatures, as steel bit and clods of claylike flesh flew. But a backhand slap staggered Brun in his tracks, and before the brewer could resume his place at Lodharrun's side, the left-hand runehelm wheeled away from Sarth's fire to hammer its mace down on the dwarf. It missed the smith's head, but crushed shoulder, collarbone, and ribs with an awful sound of crunching bone, smashing Lodharrun to the floor. The smith writhed on the ground with a thin, wet scream before he fell still.

Mirya sighted and shot with her crossbow in the sudden space opened in the fight; the weapon was the wrong tool for the job, but maybe it would distract the creature for a moment. Her quarrel took the first rune-helm square in the middle of its visor, and actually punched through the armor. To her surprise, the monster staggered, drops of thick black blood streaming from beneath its steel-plated face. It reached up to try and dislodge the quarrel—and Brun Osting leaped in with a snarl of pure rage, hewing off its weapon arm at the shoulder. As the creature crumpled, the brewer went to work on its neck, and managed to take off its head with several vicious chops.

"The visor protects a weak point!" Hamil called. "Good shooting, Mirya! Do the same to the other one!"

As quickly as she could, Mirya worked the mechanism of her crossbow, and laid in another bolt for the second runehelm. This one advanced remorselessly on Sarth, shrugging off everything the sorcerer could throw at him until Sarth melted its iron visor with another intense blast of flame.

The creature flailed blindly until Hamil climbed up its back and surgically planted his dagger between its skull and its spine. The runehelm crumpled to the ground without a sound.

Mirya set down her crossbow and hurried over to Geran's side. He was slumped in an awkward position, crumpled over his right arm, his left arm still stretched out above his head by the fetters. "Geran, wake up!" she cried, kneeling beside him. "We're here to get you away from this place." She gently turned his face up to peer into his eyes; he groaned, his eyes fluttering open. His right arm fell away from his chest as he stirred.

His right hand was missing.

Mirya recoiled in horror, covering her mouth to stifle a scream. "Oh, no," she moaned. A simple dressing covered the stump, and around its edges small patches of blackened skin showed around the wound. She couldn't bear to look at it. *This is what I've done to the man I love?* she berated herself. *He trusted you, Mirya Erstenwold, and look what it's cost him! You put him in the power of his enemies, and they've maimed him!*

"By Bane's black heart," Hamil swore viciously. "The bastards!" His face dark with fury, the halfling threw down his knives and hurried up with the sergeant's key ring, fumbling for the lock to the fetters. In a moment he had it open, and Geran fell forward into Mirya's arms as he was released.

"Geran, I'm so sorry, it's all my fault—" she cried. Tears streamed down her face. She buried her face against his neck, and gave herself up to her tears—grieving for the harm done to him.

"What did you think would happen if you gave me up to Rhovann?" he said hoarsely. His face was pale and pinched with pain, but he rallied enough to shrug her aside, and reached for Hamil's hand to pull himself upright. "I wish you'd just told me he had some hold on you. I would've protected you and Selsha from him."

Mirya drew back, mortified. He knew that she hadn't wanted to do what she did, but he still hated her for it. "Geran, I—" she said, trying to find words through her tears.

"Mirya was enchanted, Geran," Hamil said. "Whatever she did was no fault of hers."

"Enchanted?"

"I examined her and discovered the lingering impression of the spell not an hour ago," Sarth said.

Geran met Mirya's eyes, and bowed his head. "Of course. I should have known. I'm sorry that I thought anything else." He reached out to her; she hurried back and draped his arm around her shoulders, supporting him as he shuffled out the cell's open door.

"Can you walk?" Mirya asked him.

"I'll damned well walk out of here," he replied. "Let me fetch my belongings there, and we can go."

Hamil hurried over to grab Geran's clothing, while Brun checked on Lodharrun. The brewer shook his head, and came back to lend Mirya a hand with Geran. Then the small band hurried back out of the council prison.

TWENTY-FIVE

15 Ches, the Year of Deep Water Drifting (1480 DR)

Geran didn't recall much of the next half hour. Despite his brave words, he was hardly steady on his feet, and he wasn't far from simply passing out in pain. His missing hand burned as if he'd thrust it into a brazier full of hot coals and left it there; needlelike jolts of agony raced up his arm with every beat of his heart. In the guardroom Sarth unleashed a hellstorm of shrieking fireballs, scouring the chamber clear of the Council Guards clattering down the stairs to hinder his escape. Mirya ushered him through the corridors of the Council Hall and out into the driving, cold rain of an early spring thunderstorm. Icy water on his bare back and shoulders shocked him into wakefulness as they crossed to the old tailor's shop behind the Council Hall. He caught one glimpse of orange smoke billowing out of broken windows and doors blown from their hinges before Mirya urged him down into the cellars. Brun Osting followed, then Sarth and last of all Hamil.

"Keep going!" the halfling called. "No point lingering here!"

They hurried through the buried streets, passing through several cellars and dusty old passages until Geran was no longer certain of where they were. Mirya knew where she was and guided him along. He felt his legs growing steadier under him as they went along, and when they finally halted in an old wine cellar, he was able to stand up straight and push the pain of his injury to one side of his mind, focusing his thoughts on what to do next. The rest of the band filled in behind him and Mirya; Hamil took up a post by the passage they'd just used, looking and listening back the way they'd come.

Brun brought his belongings over, and set them down. "Your things, Lord Geran," he said.

"My thanks, Brun. I'll remember who came to fetch me out of Marstel's prison." Geran clapped the big brewer on the shoulder with his left hand.

Sarth reached into a small pouch at his belt, withdrew a small vial, and unstopped it. "Drink this, Geran," the sorcerer said. "It's a healing potion. I took the liberty of providing myself with a couple before we left Thentia. It should help a little with the pain."

"I appreciate your foresight," Geran said. He took the vial and drank down the contents. The elixir felt like warm mead in his mouth, sweet but heady. It left a glow in his stomach, and a flood of fresh strength filled his limbs. A deep, vital warmth seemed to gather at his right wrist, almost too hot to endure, and he grimaced as the potion did its work. When the magic faded, he felt much better—still a trifle weak in his stride, perhaps, but he was no longer hunched over his wounded arm. He was tempted to peek under the bandages that swathed the stump, but decided not to; the dressing was secure, and he didn't want to redo it.

Sarth smiled as he saw Geran's posture straighten and some of the pain fade from his face. "I wish there was more I could do," he said.

"Good," said Mirya. "Now get yourself dressed, and we'll see you out of Hulburg. We've a few ways to slip out of town without being seen."

He shook his head, trying to ignore the trembling in his limbs. "I'm not leaving. We still have a job to do in the Shadowfell, and Kara is counting on us to see it through." In fact, based on what he'd seen through the runehelm's eyes, Kara and the Shieldsworn were in dire danger.

"But you're in no condition for a fight!" Mirya protested. "What more do you expect of yourself?"

"There is no dishonor in withdrawing, Geran," Sarth told him. "We will see to what must be done."

"Trust me, I have little stomach for fighting right now, but Rhovann showed me Marstel's army and his runehelms surrounding the Shieldsworn. Destroying Rhovann's hold over his runehelms might be the only thing that can save them. I mean to cross into the shadow and finish what I started—the sooner, the better."

His companions were silent for a moment. Finally Hamil nodded.

"All right. We'll see you to where you need to go, and help you do what Aesperus told you to do. But you're to leave the fighting to Sarth and me."

He met Mirya's eyes. After a long time, she nodded too. "Very well. Sometimes wisdom comes disguised as foolishness, and this might be one of those times."

Geran looked at the bundle of clothes, and frowned. "I'm afraid I'll need some help getting dressed," he said.

"Of course," Mirya said. While Hamil and Sarth waited, she helped him with his shirt and buttons, held the right side of his breeches as he pulled them over his smallclothes, pulled on his boots for him, and then helped him shrug on his jacket. They shared an awkward grimace when he fumbled at his belt before she leaned close to cinch it for him. The difficult part was his scabbard and baldric, which were rigged to ride on his left hip for a right-handed draw. Mirya solved the puzzle by putting the baldric on him backwards, then unhooking the scabbard and turning it around. The sword hilt was a little farther back around his hip than Geran would have liked, which would slow his draw. But then again, he hardly felt like he was up to a duel at the moment.

"I'm ready," he announced. "It's now or never."

Hamil looked at him dubiously. "Can you fight left-handed?"

"A little. Daried used to make me train with my left hand from time to time. Many bladesingers are ambidextrous, or very nearly so, and he thought it was important that I learn as much of the technique as I could. But I'm hoping that you and Sarth can handle any trouble we meet up with."

"I'd better come with you," Mirya said.

"I'm not sure that's such a good idea—" Geran began.

"Nor am I, but I'm coming nonetheless," Mirya interrupted. "You said yourself a few moments ago that you had no certain idea of what to expect. Well, I might very well be able to help, especially if Sarth and Hamil find themselves too busy to aid you with whatever you might have to do. And don't you dare tell me it's too dangerous, when you're set on trying it injured as you are."

I think she has you there, Hamil remarked to Geran.

The swordmage stood his ground, then sighed. "All right. The shadowcrossing will work as well for four as it would for three. Besides, I doubt that there's any place in Hulburg that's truly safe tonight, so I might as well have you where I can keep an eye on you. But you must promise to do whatever I ask you to, without hesitation. The Shadowfell is no place to be trifled with. Brun, you'd better do what you can to gather whatever loyalist bands you can find and avoid any serious fighting until it's the right time to strike."

The brewer frowned. "How will I know the moment?"

"Watch the runehelms, I guess," Geran replied. "Now be on your way, or you may be pulled into the shadow with the rest of us when we make the crossing." Brun gave a sharp nod and backed away. Ducking under a low archway, he hurried off into the tunnels.

"Do you want the scrolls?" Hamil asked.

The swordmage shook his head. "If Sarth is willing, I'd rather save the scrolls in case something goes amiss." After all, if they used up the scrolls and Sarth were incapacitated or killed, they'd be unable to return to the Shadowfell if some other work of Rhovann's demanded their attention.

"I am willing," Sarth said. He indicated the old cellar around them with a motion of his horned head. "Shall I perform the crossing here? We will translate into a shadow analogue of this cellar. You may prefer to be in the streets above when we make the crossing."

"Here is fine," Geran decided. "We might as well stay out of sight as long as we can."

"Then gather close to me, take one another's hands, and be still. The crossing itself is not perilous, but we have no way of knowing what awaits us on the other side." Sarth waited until Geran, Hamil, and Mirya were arranged as he liked, then drew a large vial from beneath his robes and poured black, acrid-smelling ink in a rough circle around them. Replacing the vial's stopper, he took his rune-carved scepter and murmured words of command, pointing its tapered end at the splatter of ink on the floor. Under the influence of his magic, the ink flowed and shaped itself into glyphs of power. Geran didn't recognize them, but that didn't surprise him; he'd seen that Sarth's learning was not the learning of Myth Drannor. As each glyph took its final form, the dark ink shimmered with a violet glow. Sarth chanted softly as he worked, shaping the circle. As the diagram approached completion, the tiefling stepped carefully inside its bounds to stand close beside his companions, and gave Geran and the others a warning glance without breaking the words of his spell.

Mirya stiffened next to Geran, and clutched at his arm. In the cellar around them the light was *changing*, growing dimmer in some strange way that did not change their ability to see. The flickering shadows dancing on the walls and ceiling from Sarth's glowing runes began to take on an unsettling, viscous appearance, sliding and flowing over the brick and timbers like liquid oil. Sarth's chant approached its end, and the tiefling completed the last glyph of the circle surrounding them. The whole design pulsed once; Geran felt a strange lurch or pull on his stomach from a direction he couldn't define, and the circle went dark.

The cellar seemed almost the same . . . but Geran could see at once that the doorways were subtly crooked, the rubble and debris heaped a little higher, the air colder and more still. Mirya shivered against him, and he put his left arm around her shoulder, drawing her close. "What is this place?" she murmured.

"The shadow world," said Geran. "Sometimes called the Shadowfell, or the Plane of Shadow. It's an imperfect echo of our own world, existing alongside us but rarely touching our world. In some ways we're exactly where we were when Sarth began his spell. But if you were in the cellar we've just left, you would have seen us disappear into thin air."

"I see that you are familiar with the Shadowfell," Sarth observed.

"During my days as a Coronal Guard, I was part of a small company sent into the Shadowfell to retrieve an elven artifact stolen by the shadar-kai," Geran answered. "I never mastered the crossing ritual, but I learned what I needed to know about this realm and its perils."

"Perils?" Hamil asked.

"The powers of darkness are very strong here," Sarth said. "This is where the restless shades of the dead wander when they refuse to pass on to their final judgment. And there are old, hateful entities that lurk in the deepest shadows. They are best avoided."

"I can imagine," the halfling muttered. "Well, let's get on with this, then. Where is Rhovann's citadel?"

Geran studied their surroundings, allowing his eyes to become accustomed to the gloom that seemed to press in around them. "My guess is the shadow copy of Griffonwatch. It's the strongest, most secure place in Hulburg, so it stands to reason it would be here as well. Mirya, where's the closest access to the streets from here?"

Mirya shook herself and pointed to the corridor leading north. "There's a door not fifteen yards down that hall that lets you into the cellar of the old Black Eagle guildhall."

"Good." Geran allowed Hamil to lead the way, and followed after Sarth. The door proved to be a little farther than Mirya remembered, but then again, that might have been the disconcerting proportions of the Shadowfell; distances were not as constant here as they were in the daylit world. When they finally found it, the door was stuck fast. It took Geran and Sarth pushing together to force it open. Inside, a rickety staircase led up to the ground level in the middle of a burned-out shell of a building. Through a gap in the floor over their heads they could look up and see a starless night sky above. Despite the lack of streetlamps, moon, or stars, there was a faint gray luminescence that gave them just enough light—or a lessening of shadow, anyway—to see by. Silently they climbed up and made their way out into the street. They weren't far from the Winterspear, at the north end of Fish Street.

"Look at the castle," Hamil said softly.

Geran found that the dim gray gloom didn't hide things with sheer distance the way a normal night might have. Over the ramshackle rooftops and ruined walls of shadow-Hulburg Griffonwatch's black crag towered, noticeably narrower and steeper than it would have appeared in the normal world. He followed its battlements up to the Harmach's Tower at the top, which leaned precariously over the cliff's edge. Pale swirls of lambent light played about the castle's upperworks like a purple aurora.

"Rhovann's defensive wards," Sarth observed. "Interesting. The spells with which he guards the castle are visible in this plane."

"Come on," said Geran. "Kara's waiting for us, and we've already lost hours." He led the way as they turned left and headed north—if such directions had any meaning in the Shadowfell—through the ruined districts on the west bank of the Winterspear. These neighborhoods had been razed long before in the daylit world, and he was somewhat relieved to see that they were much the same here. Wiry tufts of pale grass and thorny brambles grew out of great mounds of rubble, intersected here and there by the crooked silhouette of a surviving wall. Sarth conjured a small, ruddy orb of light that bobbed along a little above him. It did little to brighten the gloom that surrounded them, but Geran decided that it raised his spirits a little, and it wasn't so bright that it would be seen from any great distance. Once or twice as they hurried along the rubble-strewn street he thought he heard ominous scuttlings or whispers from the mounds of debris around them, and he noticed that Hamil kept a wary eye on the shadows nearby. Geran chose not to say anything to Mirya; he didn't want to needlessly alarm her if it turned out to be nothing, since she was unsettled enough already.

They came to the small court where Keldon Way met the foot of the Burned Bridge. The bridge wasn't there. The old stone piers were still where they belonged, but the newer wooden trestle that had been built atop them was missing. "What in the world?" Mirya murmured. "Now how do we cross?"

"It's the nature of the Shadowfell," Sarth answered. "Sometimes things that have come to ruin in our world remain intact here, and other times things that are still whole in our world have been destroyed here. It can be capricious."

"Well, capricious or not, it's damned inconvenient," Hamil said. "We're still on the wrong side of the Winterspear." He looked at the river, swift and dark in the ever-present gloom. "I hate the thought of swimming it. I don't suppose we can fly or teleport across?"

"It's too far for my teleport spell," said Geran. "Sarth, can you carry us one at a time?"

"If I managed you once, I can certainly manage Hamil and Mirya." The sorcerer gauged the distance, and sighed. "Let me begin with you, Geran." He murmured the words to his flying spell; Geran felt the shadows drawing in around them as the magic took its shape, but nothing more happened. Sarth stepped close behind him, locking his arms beneath his, and sprang up into the air. The cold waters raced swiftly beneath Geran's feet, and the broken stone piers of the old bridge reeled by on their left.

Then the two of them landed heavily in the ruins by the riverbank, not far from where the Troll and Tankard stood in the Hulburg Geran knew. Sarth panted for breath.

"Well done," Geran told him. "Bring Mirya next—we don't want to leave her alone in a place like this."

The sorcerer nodded, and rose up into the dark sky again. Geran turned to study his surroundings, keenly aware of his solitude. He'd never been one to take fright easily, but the shadow world was no place for a living human to linger, and he was keenly aware of his vulnerability if something should happen. He could see more of the ancient city wall than he would have expected; it seemed that the Shadowfell remembered Hulburg as the ruined city it had been a hundred years previous, not the thriving town it was today.

A small scrabbling sound echoed through the darkness not far off, a sound like someone or something slipping across the weed-choked rubble. "What is that?" he murmured softly. He set his left hand on *Umbrach Nyth* and drew the sword from its sheath, aiming the point in the direction of the unseen thing moving about in the shadows. Nothing more happened, so he took a moment to perform a couple of simple attack and defense patterns with the dark blade. It was ready and responsive in his hand, despite the awkwardness of using the wrong arm. Without any false modesty, Geran knew he was an excellent swordsman under normal conditions; he'd only met a handful he knew to be better in his years of adventuring and travel. Fighting left-handed, he still had his learning, his knowledge, his footwork, and his swordmagic, but his strength and quickness suffered. He could probably handle a strong but inexperienced opponent, or perhaps a swordsman of average skill and no great natural talent, but he wouldn't care to hazard his life on the outcome.

"I'll get better in time," he told himself. Unfortunately, he didn't see that he had any great need to fight six months or a year from now, but he might very well have to fight in the next few hours—possibly several times. Rhovann couldn't have picked a worse time to cripple him.

The flutter of a cloak in the air caught his ear as Sarth returned, carrying Mirya with an arm around her waist and one of her arms over his shoulder. The tiefling alighted, and Mirya eagerly disentangled herself. "I thank you for sparing me the swim, Sarth, but I think I'd rather leave flying to the birds," she explained. "It's no natural thing for a person to do."

Sarth smiled. "I've come to like it," he said. Then he shot off into the gloom again.

Mirya glanced at Geran, and frowned as she noticed the sword in his hand. "What is it?" she asked in a low voice.

"I thought I heard something moving about. It's probably nothing. A rat, perhaps."

"Are there such things as rats here?" She set the stirrup of her crossbow on the ground and drew back the string as she studied the shadows around them.

He started to shrug—and at that moment the creatures attacked. Several gaunt, gray houndlike monsters bounded from the shadows of the ruined walls and rubble mounds, charging the two humans. Their flesh seemed tattered and dessicated, and bare bone showed beneath; their eyes were sunken, black pits in which fierce pinpoints of crimson burned.

Geran moved to intercept them without a moment's thought. "*Cuillen mhariel*!" he snapped, automatically invoking the silversteel veil to protect himself in the coming fray. Silver streamers of mist took shape and began to flow around him—and Mirya as well, since she was close beside him. Then he leaped forward, thrusting his point straight at the breast of the first of the gravehounds as he spoke another sword spell: "*Reith arroch*!" A brilliant white radiance flicked along the ebon blade as it found the gravehound's chest in midleap. He shouldered the dying monster aside as it slammed into him, evading a snap of its jaws only by jumping back out of the way.

"What are these things?" Mirya cried out. Her crossbow sang behind him, knocking another of the creatures to the ground. It snapped at the bolt in its flank before scrambling to its feet again.

Geran fixed his eyes on the next creature rushing them. "*Naerren*," he breathed, invoking a spell of hindrance that took the form of red-gold lashes streaking around the monster, steering it away from Mirya. Then he ran over to meet the one Mirya had shot as it started after again. Mirya yelped in panic and backed away as it snarled and snapped at her. Geran slashed at it with his sword and managed only a glancing blow from its bony shoulders. The things stank when he came too close; the air was filled with a foul rotting stench, and his stomach—none too steady for a while now—threatened to revolt entirely. He managed to drive it back with a flurry of wild cuts before turning back to the other he'd enmeshed with his hindering spell. The gravehound rushed at him and leaped for him. This time Geran's thrust missed its mark, sinking into the creature's thick shoulder instead of skewering its heart. The impact took him off his feet, and out of pure reflex he threw his arm behind him to break his fall. Instead, he jammed his stump against the ground and screamed as white-hot agony nearly overwhelmed him. Only the swirling silversteel warding saved his life, resisting the monster's vicious fangs as it struggled to find his throat.

"*Kythosa zurn!*" From somewhere behind Geran's head, Sarth's powerful voice thundered in the ruins, and a barrage of golden force orbs hammered into the gravehound pinning him to the ground. The orbs blasted fist-sized wounds in the monster's side, hurling it away from him. Geran rolled to his side and scrambled to his feet. Sarth and Hamil battled furiously against the rest of the pack, Hamil keeping close to Mirya to fend off the creatures darting and snapping at her, Sarth scouring the monsters with one spell after another. In another moment the gravehound pack broke and retreated—not before Mirya loosed another bolt at the fleeing creatures, bringing down one with a quarrel in its spine.

"Geran, Mirya, are you hurt?" Sarth asked urgently, descending to the ground.

"The one tore the hem of my skirt, but I'm all right," Mirya replied.

Geran sheathed his sword and brushed himself off. "Not much more than my pride," he answered. "It would have been much worse if you hadn't returned when you did." In fact, he was fairly sure that the grave-hounds would have killed both him and Mirya. They wouldn't have found me such easy prey if I'd been at my best, he thought angrily. He scowled in the shadows.

"Were those creatures of Rhovann's?" Mirya asked.

"I doubt it. I've never known him to employ undead servants—he prefers to work with inanimate subjects." Geran forced himself to set aside his frustration; there was no point in dwelling on the fact that he'd been caught and maimed. Will this poison me the way it poisoned Rhovann? he wondered. There would be all the time in the world for wishing otherwise later, but now he had things to do. "No, I would guess that the skeletal hounds are simply denizens of this place. We should keep moving before any more are drawn to us. The castle's not far off."

"I don't care for the idea of marching up the causeway to the front gate," Hamil remarked.

"Nor do I," Geran answered—especially since he doubted that he'd be able to help much if it came to fighting their way in. He studied the towering shadow of Griffonwatch's crag, crowned by its flickering curtains of violet light. The spires and battlements of the Hulmasters' castle had a jagged, menacing look to them, stabbing up at the starless sky like a thicket of spears. The lower floors were lost in the gloom, but he could see flickers of light in the uppermost portions of the old castle. It struck him as likely that Rhovann would appropriate the safest and most comfortable part of the old fortress for his own use, and that meant the Harmach's Tower or some part of the castle close by it. "But how to get in without being seen?" he mused aloud.

Mirya glanced at Sarth. "Can you fly us up to the top?" she asked him.

"Possibly, although I doubt I could bear Geran so high aloft. But I do not advise it." Sarth pointed at the flickering aurora around the keep. "We would have to pass through the wardings there. If they were to incapacitate me or suppress my flying magic . . ."

Mirya shuddered at the thought. "Never you mind, then. We're not meant to take wing anyway."

"We'll make for the postern gate," Geran decided. "It's easily overlooked, and Rhovann may not have paid it much attention. If we're careful, any guards that Rhovann's posted won't notice us until we're well inside the castle."

Tugging at his baldric to seat his sword more comfortably, he led the way from the clearing by the Burned Bridge into the shadow of Rhovann's castle.

TWENTY-SIX

15 Ches, the Year of Deep Water Drifting (1480 DR)

Geran and his small band met no more gravehounds or other undead as they made their way through the gloom of shadow-Hulburg. From time to time they heard strange rustlings in the dark alleys or the creaking of floorboards behind dark doors, and Geran felt unfriendly eyes upon them once or twice, but nothing emerged to trouble them. Near the square of the Harmach's Foot they encountered a number of intact buildings— houses and workshops and storehouses—in more or less the same place that they would have been in the living Hulburg. The windows were dark, and no lights glimmered behind their shutters, but Geran sensed that the place was not as empty as it appeared.

Mirya must have sensed it too, since she drew closer to his side. "Who raised these buildings?" she whispered. "Does someone live here?"

"I think that no one built them. Each one's here because someone put up a house or a workshop or a storehouse in Hulburg."

"Do they just appear out of nothing here when someone builds them in our Hulburg? And why is each one wrong in some way?" Mirya pointed at a cooper's workyard as they passed by. "That's old Narath's place, but his front door faces across the street, and there should be a fine old laspar tree in his yard."

"That's the nature of the Shadowfell. It's a reflection in a broken mirror. What it shows isn't the truth of things."

"What of the people? I can feel them nearby. There isn't a copy of me here, is there?"

"Souls wander here," Sarth answered her. "Dreamers drift through briefly, and the dead linger here, sometimes for centuries, before they fade away to the godly dominions. Some know that they are bodiless phantasms, and have no true life in this place. Others do not perceive their incorporeity, and settle into the habits and places they have—or had—in the firmament we come from. And there are also those few who, like us, are here in body and soul at once. Most are travelers who don't stay long, but a few make homes here for reasons of their own. I have never seen them, but I have heard of strange inns and gloomy towns where those who live in the shadows gather."

Mirya shivered. "So the shades of the dead are what we feel around us?"

Geran drew close and took her hand in his. "We don't perceive them because most are already fading from the world. Only the most determined—or most confused—would take a shape we might see."

"What a terrible place," she breathed. "The sooner we're done with it, the better."

They rounded the base of the causeway, and threaded their way into the woods that lay south of the great stone massif on which the castle stood. The small stretch of woodland in the heart of Hulburg was wild and dark even in the normal world, but here in the Shadowfell the gloom beneath the branches seemed physically impenetrable. It took a conscious act of will for Geran to force himself to take the narrow path leading into the trees.

The silence and the gloom settled in around them, even thicker than before. He felt Mirya pressing up close behind him, and even Sarth and Hamil hesitated before following after him. A walk of a hundred yards or so brought them around to the south side of the crag, a towering shadow that now loomed menacingly over them. To Geran's left a wrought-iron fence leaned crookedly, marking off a small space where a flight of stone steps led up to a thick door of iron plate in the side of the crag. He let himself in through the rusting gate and approached the doorway.

"Allow me to examine the door," Sarth said. He murmured his detection spell, peering closely at the postern gate. After a moment, he nodded to himself. "It is warded, but I believe I can suppress it."

"Go ahead," Geran told him. He drew the shadow sword again and waited as Sarth began to incant his spell, weaving his hands in the complicated gestures of his craft. The swordmage sensed his magic gathering, exerting invisible pressure against the magical wardings sealing the portal. With care, Sarth checked his power, keeping his effort as stealthy as possible. Geran waited for the sudden clatter of runehelms closing in from the forest, or the lash of some deadly spell trap . . . but the moment of tension passed, and the postern gate swung open under the sorcerer's power. Impermeable darkness waited beyond.

"I cannot guarantee that Rhovann is ignorant of my work here," Sarth said. "He may have sensed the breaching of his defenses."

"In that case, we'd better not give him much time to react," Geran replied. With the shadow sword in hand, he plunged into the darkness of the gate. Inside, a short passage led to a low, barren mustering hall where the castle's defenders could gather for a sortie or mass to defend against any enemy effort to force the postern gate. Geran half expected to find Rhovann's servants waiting for them just inside, but the hall was empty—evidently the wizard counted on his magic to protect the door. On the far side of the hall a stairway spiraled up through the living rock of the crag, climbing toward the halls and buildings of the castle proper. He murmured the words of a light spell to dispel the brooding gloom, crossed the hall, and began to climb the steps.

The stairway seemed narrower and longer than Geran remembered, another subtle lie of the Shadowfell. His head grew light and his missing hand throbbed as he hurried up the steps. By the time he reached the top, his heart pounded in his chest, and his legs felt weak and rubbery under him. He paused, leaning against the wall to catch his breath. Mirya peered at him, a taut frown across her face. "Are you in pain?" she asked quietly.

"It's nothing I have time for," he answered, and winced. She snorted, seeing through his bravado.

Hamil and Sarth reached the top of the stairs. "Which way?" the halfling asked.

Geran set a hand on the shadow sword's hilt, and reached out for the touch of magic, dark and strong. They stood in a passage that ran beneath the upper courtyard. To the left it led toward the kitchens and storerooms near the great hall. To the right, it met another short stair that climbed up to the chambers built in the cliffside beneath the Harmach's Tower and the rest of the castle's highest ring. The air seemed to shiver with the potency of Rhovann's wards in that direction. "To the right," he decided. He hadn't really expected Rhovann to hide the runehelms' master stone in the kitchens, after all.

He led the way up to the next level of the castle. Now they were just beneath the library and the tower. Here, on the southern face of Griffonwatch, the crag's top had been leveled and excavated so that the foundations of the buildings above had rows of windows facing the Moonsea, and served as an intact and inhabited floor in its own right. Geran reached the long hall with its windows peering out on the dark, endless night outside. Ahead of him stairs climbed up to the Harmach's Tower, but the unseen currents of magic did not draw him any higher. Instead they washed over him from his left, where a large council room and trophy hall stood at the end of the corridor. A pair of runehelms stood guard outside the door; he drew back quickly, hoping they hadn't seen him.

"The trophy room," he whispered to his companions. "Rhovann's device is in the trophy room."

"I sense it too," Sarth said. "Is there any other way in?"

"No doors, I'm afraid. There are a number of large windows, but most look out over a sheer drop. You might manage them with your flying spell, but the rest of us would need a rope."

"It sounds like we're going through the guards, then," Hamil breathed. He crouched by the corner, drawing his knives as he prepared himself for his rush—and there came a loud clatter and rustling from the corridor behind them. Half a dozen of Rhovann's constructs appeared by the postern stair, and charged wordlessly up at Geran and his companions.

"Behind us!" Mirya cried.

Sarth spat an oath in his own tongue and whirled. "*Narva saizhal!*" he shouted, raising his scepter at the towering monsters. A barrage of deadly icicles took shape in the air before him before sleeting through the corridor. Dozens of the icy missiles skewered the leading runehelms, to little effect—there were no vital organs to pierce, no blood vessels to sever. White patches of frostbite spread from each icicle, stiffening the constructs' flesh and hindering their movements, but still they came on. The thin glaze of ice coating the floor and walls after Sarth's spell proved more effective than the hail of deadly icicles; while the runehelms were hard to hurt, they could slip and fall as easily as any human might. Several of the gray guardians briefly tangled up in the hallway, but the two in the lead kept coming.

Geran drew his shadow sword and summoned up the magic for his dragon scales warding. "*Theillalagh na drendir,*" he breathed, conjuring a shimmering field of lambent force that rippled and flowed around his body like a loose-fitting coat of mail. Then he advanced to meet one of the charging runehelms, as Hamil scurried down the steps to engage the other.

"Geran Hulmaster, have you lost your mind?" Mirya snapped at him. "You're in no shape for sword play!"

"I'm afraid Rhovann's monsters think otherwise," he replied. The creature in front of him launched a powerful thrust with the point of its halberd, trying to run him through. Rather than try to parry with his left hand against the heavy halberd and the runehelm's terrible physical strength, he concentrated on dodging and tried to stay away from the halberd point until he saw an opening. "*Ilyeith sannoghan!*" he shouted, invoking a spell of lightning on the sword as he leaped forward past the halberd point. The crackling ribbons of light took on a new hue when *Umbrach Nyth* wore them; on his Myth Drannan blade they'd always been a bright blue-white, but on the shadow sword's black steel they were a deep violet color. With a wild backhand slash he sliced the runehelm deeply through its thick neck. Purple lightning flashed around its iron visor and crackled under its breastplate; the construct jerked and twisted nervelessly as the lightning danced in its flesh, and then it toppled to the floor.

Geran smiled grimly. I'm not so helpless after all, he decided. Of course, the runehelms were hardly skillful opponents. They gave all their attention to destroying whatever was in front of them. He turned on the runehelm battling Hamil, and took it to the ground with a forehand cut to its leg. The creature toppled, but it lashed out with the butt of its halberd at Geran as it fell. The wooden haft caught him on his right hip and knocked him spinning to the ground a few feet away. Before the runehelm could draw back for a strike with the greataxe blade or wicked hook at the other end of the weapon, Hamil and Mirya quickly dragged Geran out of its reach.

Careful, there! Hamil told him. *Mirya will never forgive me if you get yourself killed trying to guard my back.*

Sarth turned another spell against the crippled runehelm, burning it down, but now the others that had momentarily tangled themselves on the slippery ice were working their way free. Worse yet, more heavy footfalls and ominous clanking of armor echoed through the castle halls. "This is madness," the tiefling growled. "There is no point in fighting each one of these guardians. Geran, go and destroy the master stone before we are overwhelmed! I will hold off Rhovann's creatures here."

Geran hesitated, unwilling to leave Sarth, but Mirya caught him by the arm and pulled him up toward the hallway leading to the trophy room. "Sarth is right," she said. "This battle can be won with a single stroke."

"Very well," he conceded. Sarth gave him a quick nod, and Geran turned his back on the fight by the postern stair and hurried around the corner toward the trophy hall and the runehelms guarding its door. Hamil and Mirya followed a step behind him. The door guards perceived the three of them at once; one moment they were standing as still as statues, and the next they lowered their halberds to advance a couple of steps, barring the way.

"Shoot the left one through the visor if you can," Hamil told Mirya. "It seems to throw them off their game. Geran, you finish it off while I keep the other one busy."

"Aye, I'll do it," Mirya replied. She started to draw back her crossbow— and the doors at the end of the hall flew open.

Mantled in the ghostly shapes of powerful spells, Rhovann Disarnnyl stood in the doorway, pure fury blazing in his face. Behind him the old trophy room was filled with arcane apparatuses and more runehelms beginning to stir in the great vats where they were grown. "You have the stubbornness of a troll," the mage snarled at Geran. "You ignorant fool! What more must I do before you comprehend the fact of your defeat?"

"You would've been wiser to kill me when you had me in your power," Geran answered. In the room behind the wizard he could sense the invisible currents and eddies of the wizard's devices and spell artifices, each a subtle vibration of Rhovann's careful weavings. The shadow sword in his hand seemed to quiver slightly, resonating with the power concentrated in the wizard's laboratory. There was a focal point in the center of the room, an irregular crystal of dark purple in which a lambent flame flickered . . . the master stone for the runehelms? he wondered. His eyes narrowed as he studied it, and he resolved that whatever else happened, he'd deprive Rhovann of his toy before the wizard destroyed him. "You sent the Cyricists and their devils to slay my family in Lasparhall—assassins and monsters set loose to murder a frail old man and dozens of men and women whose only offense was their loyalty to the Hulmasters! Did you think that anything short of death would stop me after that?"

Rhovann snorted. "I should have expected no less. You simpleton, the Vaasans ordered the harmach's death. I had nothing to do with it. You've sought out your demise for a mistake."

The Vaasans? Geran wondered. Could it be true that Rhovann hadn't ordered Grigor's death? The elf was his enemy, and no stranger to cruelty, but Rhovann wouldn't lie out of sheer pettiness. It certainly made little difference to Geran now; even if Rhovann hadn't sent the assassins to Lasparhall, he'd set events in motion that were certain to result in mortal peril to Geran's family, and he'd conspired with Sergen Hulmaster before that. "It doesn't matter," he said. "My uncle's death is still your doing, and I mean to see you dead for it."

"Believe what you will. I will now correct my earlier oversight, and you can go down into death with your bitter, misconceived notions of vengeance unattained as you like." The rumble of Sarth's battle magic echoed through the shadowed hall, and the elf wizard sneered. "Did you truly think that I would not take steps to guard my sanctum? Your devil-born sorcerer cannot hope to overcome my defenses in the Shadowfell. You and your companions, even your beloved Mirya there, will never see the sun again."

"I defeated you once before," Geran said. "I wonder if you're hesitant to begin this because you fear that I'm still your better, even crippled as I am." He glanced at Hamil and thought at the halfling, *Cover my back if you can, but above all keep Mirya safe.*

I won't fail you, Hamil replied. *Do what you must.*

"My better?" Rhovann hissed. "We shall see!" He raised his wand.

"*Sieroch!*" said Geran, invoking his spell of teleportation. Once before he'd used the spell to close on Rhovann and take him off guard; the wizard snarled an oath and leaped aside, expecting Geran to appear behind him. But instead of materializing within sword's reach of the wizard, Geran emerged from the icy black instant of nothingness a good ten paces beyond the doorway where Rhovann stood. The purple master stone hung in its iron frame only an arm's length away; Geran hewed at it with all the strength he could muster in his left arm. The black blade bit into the crystal; a white spiderweb crack starred its surface, and small flakes of purple crystal flew. The eddies of unseen magic in the chamber jolted as if a titan had struck a temple bell, roiling in protest. But the iron frame caught the long blade in a jarring blow, keeping Geran from finishing his stroke cleanly.

"You *fool*!" Rhovann shrieked. He leveled a blast of golden lightning at Geran that lashed through the workshop, shattering glassware and splintering wood. The swordmage's wardings held just long enough for him to dive aside, flinging himself to the ground in search of cover. One stabbing bolt caught him in the calf and burned a smoking hole in his leg as he crashed into a clutter of casks and molds beside the vats in which the half-formed runehelms struggled to rise.

Hamil sighted quickly and hurled his dagger at a point between Rhovann's shoulder blades, but one of the intact runehelms next to the wizard simply stepped into the weapon's path to protect its master. The knife bit deeply into its pale torso; the runehelm ignored it. Rhovann glanced once over his shoulder and snapped, "Slay them all!" before returning to his assault on Geran. The damaged runehelm started toward the halfling, leveling its great halberd point first. Mirya took careful aim and shot it through the visor with her crossbow, staggering it, but before Hamil could move in to finish the thing more runehelms surged into the hall behind them.

Geran rolled to his feet and started toward the master stone again. Rhovann rounded the heavy table, lining up his wand on the swordmage. Snarling another spell, he blasted at Geran with a hissing jet of emerald acid, but Geran answered with a lightning-quick spell of parrying. "*Haethellyn!*" he shouted, raising the dark blade in an awkward block. A strange blue sheen flickered over the steel before the acid jet struck the blade and rebounded. With better control Geran might have been able to send it straight back at Rhovann, but instead he only managed to splatter the ground at Rhovann's feet as a shower of droplets sizzled around him. Wisps of smoke from the potent acid started from half a dozen places on Geran's clothing, but also from Rhovann's. With a muttered oath the elf stumbled back from the seething pool in front of him, waving his hand to clear the air of the acrid fumes.

Geran used the moment of Rhovann's distraction to turn back on the master stone, raising his blade for another stroke—but a damp gray hand closed on his ankle and yanked him to the floor. One of the incomplete runehelms had seized him and was trying to drag him away. "Damn it, leave me be!" he snarled, and split its skull with *Umbrach Nyth*. Dark ichor bubbled from the awful wound when he jerked the sword free, but the fingers remained clamped around his ankle, and it took him several precious moments to wrench himself free.

"Geran, smash the thrice-damned stone already!" Hamil shouted from the hallway outside. The halfling darted recklessly from one runehelm to another, dodging halberd blows that splintered the floor and smashed great gouges out of the walls. One of the monsters turned toward Mirya, drawing back its weapon to run her through as she fumbled with her crossbow; with a desperate lunge the halfling bounded over and dug out the back of its knee, sending its thrust aside as its leg buckled. The creature smashed at Hamil with a backhand blow of its great fist; the halfling flew a good ten feet through the air before hitting the opposite wall with bone-jarring force and crumpling. Another runehelm prepared to hew him as he lay stunned, but at that moment a brilliant green ray shot down the hall and struck it in the head. In a bright green flash the iron visor and gray clay disintegrated under Sarth's magic, and the headless construct sank to the floor.

Battered and bleeding, the sorcerer smiled grimly at the top of the stairway they'd climbed. "I think I have finally determined how best to destroy these creatures," he remarked. Then he was beset by the remaining runehelms in the hall, replying with a furious barrage of force darts and flame lances.

Fiery pinpricks burned here and there on Geran's torso and arms where the droplets of acid clung, but he clenched his jaw and made himself ignore the pain. Instead of attacking the master stone directly, he darted clockwise around the great apparatus surrounding it, searching for his foe. Twice now he'd attacked the stone instead of the wizard; it was time to change tactics for a moment. He plunged through a cloud of smoke—Rhovann's lightning spell had started a fire, it seemed—and found Rhovann only a double-arm's length away, coming to meet him. Without a moment's hesitation Geran stepped and lunged, driving his sword point clumsily at the elf's midsection. Rhovann twisted aside with a sudden oath, deflecting the thrust by slapping at *Umbrach Nyth* with his silver hand. Sparks flew briefly as the shadow sword and the rune-marked hand met; the elf survived with a long, shallow cut under his ribs.

"*Damn* you!" Rhovann hissed. He jumped back as Geran recovered from his lunge, and leveled his wand at the swordmage. This time there was no dodging the mage's fury; Rhovann shouted a spell of thundering power that picked up Geran like a child's toy and threw him halfway across the chamber. Worktables exploded in clouds of broken glass and wooden splinters; incomplete runehelms were smashed into shapeless putty by the blast. Geran found himself stretched out on the stone floor, covered in debris and the contents of Rhovann's vats. He groaned and shook his head, unable to stop the ringing in his ears. The room darkened and spun drunkenly as he fought for consciousness.

Slowly, he rolled to his belly and tried to push himself upright. He'd only managed to rise to his hand and knees when Rhovann kicked his sword away from him and leveled his wand in Geran's face. "Now, at last, we see who is the better," the mage spat. "Farewell, Geran. We shall not meet again." He started to form a word of magic—and abruptly broke off into a choked cry, wheeling half around.

A crossbow bolt was lodged high in the back of Rhovann's right shoulder. Geran glanced toward the workshop's doorway and saw Mirya standing there, already working her crossbow mechanism for the next shot. "That's for enchanting me!" she shouted. Behind her, several runehelms whirled away from Sarth and Hamil to charge at her back. She glanced over her shoulder, shrinking from the massive blades aiming for her heart. "Finish it quickly, Geran!"

"*Cuilledyr*!" Geran rasped, pushing himself to his feet. The shadow sword quivered once and leaped to meet his outstretched hand as he staggered forward—not at Rhovann, but instead at the master stone. With a strength born of pure desperation he rammed the chisel-like point of black steel into the center of the gouge he'd already carved from the great purple crystal. The shock of it jarred his arm so hard he bit his tongue as his jaw snapped shut, but a great white crack shot through the stone from side to side, and began to spread. The runehelms behind Mirya crumpled in silence, gray hands fumbling at their visors, halberds dropping uselessly to the floor.

"*No*!" Rhovann screamed. "I will not be defeated by you!" The elf seized Geran by the shirt as the swordmage drew back to finish his blow, dragging him away. Geran struggled to escape his grasp and strike again; in the space of a heartbeat they were grappling fiercely with each other. Geran fought to bring the point or edge of the shadow sword into position for a killing blow, but Rhovann managed to get his left hand on Geran's sword hand and locked his hand of silver in a viselike grip around Geran's throat. The metal hand was horribly strong, and the cold fingers ground into his neck, seeking to crush his windpipe. Swaying and stumbling in their desperate grapple, they blundered into a rune circle marked out on the floor.

A few feet away, the master stone's mortal fracture split, and split again. Now the whole thing was shot through with white cracks, and the lambent flame flickering in its depths guttered and went out. In the instant the stone went dark, it shattered in a tremendous explosion of dark energy, rocking the shadow-Griffonwatch and devastating the wizard's sanctum. The magical diagram under Geran's straining feet pulsed to life, activated by the sudden release of shadow magic from the broken stone; even as he gasped for breath and his sight narrowed into a tunnel stretching longer and darker by the moment, he felt the jolt of magic at work.

Then all went dark as he and Rhovann were catapulted out of the Shadowfell.

TWENTY-SEVEN

15 Ches, the Year of Deep Water Drifting (1480 DR)

Thunder rumbled away to the north over the moorlands of Thar as Kara Hulmaster peered through the cold, steady rain at the lines of Marstel's army encircling the barren hill where she was trapped. The thick clouds overhead hid the approaching dawn, but the night wasn't completely dark; hooded lanterns and watchfires here and there gave a dim orange glow to the battlefield. The Shieldsworn were drawn up along the edge of the short, steep bluff ringing the hilltop; a half mile or so off, she could make out the jagged outline of Rosestone Abbey against the faint lightening of the coming dawn. In the smoke and gloom below her, Marstel's mercenary army gathered to make its last assault against the Shieldsworn, spearheaded by almost one hundred of Rhovann's great gray-skinned guardians. From time to time, when the rain slackened, Kara could hear the distant clash of arms or the roar of angry voices rising from some skirmish or another farther around the hill.

"Where are you, Geran?" Kara murmured to herself. She was supposed to be marching into Hulburg by now, Rhovann's construct warriors dead or incapacitated, the Council Guard broken and fleeing ahead of her. Instead, she'd spent the last eight or nine hours fighting furiously to avoid annihilation as Marstel's commanders threw wave after wave at her improvised redoubt. Only the steep scramble up to the rounded, boulder-strewn top had kept the runehelms from destroying what was left of her army; as the creatures sought to climb the last few feet of the bluff, they could be dislodged by heavy rocks rolled down from above or pushed off by a couple of strong men using a big pole. The constructs took little harm from the fall, but each time the creatures had to pick themselves up and clamber up again. Marstel had allowed his tireless automatons to attempt the task for hours before finally sending living human soldiers against the Shieldsworn at the same time—but Kara's archers had shot Council Guards down by the score, breaking the first general assault. Now Marstel was preparing to try it again.

She glanced back at the Shieldsworn's uneven lines. The Icehammers and the Third Shield had managed to fall back from Rosestone relatively intact, but she'd lost a good third of Wester's First Shield in the runehelms' assault, and only a handful of Larken's Second Shield had reached the rallying point after serving as rearguard for the rest of the army. Larken himself was missing—dead or captured, Kara supposed. Most of the five hundred or so soldiers left to her huddled under cloaks or their own shields, catching a little rest after their night of fighting.

A jingle of mail and a muttered oath in Dwarvish announced Kendurkkel Ironthane's arrival. The dwarf clumped up the rounded jumble of rocks she stood on, surefooted in his heavy boots. His ever-present pipe glowed softly in the darkness, in spite of the rain. "They'll be havin' another go at us soon," he said.

"So they will." She stared down at the enemy companies forming up on the lower hillside. She could see better than most in darkness, and she could see how much the Shieldsworn had hurt the Council Guard. They'd even managed to destroy a dozen or so of the runehelms. But they'd been hurt worse, and the numbers favored Marstel's army all the more now. "They're going to storm the hill from several sides at once, and try to overwhelm us."

"It's no' a bad plan," Kendurkkel admitted.

In the earlier attacks Marstel's captains had concentrated on a narrow, notchlike draw in the hill's eastern face that formed a ramp to the hilltop, but the Shieldsworn had choked it with boulders and overturned wagons, and Kara had naturally concentrated her forces there. Now the threat of a general escalade forced her to spread her soldiers all around the edge of the hill. Kara doubted that she'd be able to stop Marstel this time. Her archers were almost out of arrows, and her soldiers had denuded the hilltop of any boulders small enough to lever over the bluff at the runehelms.

"Have ye any word from Laird Hulmaster?" the dwarf asked her quietly.

"Not yet," Kara admitted. "I should have heard from him hours ago. I fear that something's gone wrong."

"What d'ye mean t' do if he's failed?"

"Fight my way off this hilltop and draw back to Thentia until we find a way to deal with the wizard's gray warriors." Given time to reorganize and prepare, Kara thought she might be able to come up with a few ways to deal with the runehelms even if Geran failed to defeat them. But she knew that it was a thin hope she was clinging to. If she retreated from this place— assuming she *could* retreat, which was no certain thing—there would be no second campaign to liberate Hulburg, not unless another Moonsea power chose to involve itself in their troubles.

The dwarf nodded. "That might not be up to ye," he observed. "Marstel's got no reason t' let ye go. Have ye given thought t' requestin' terms?"

"Yes, I've thought of requesting terms. My life is forfeit, of course, but I'd do it if I thought my Shieldsworn would be spared. Unfortunately, I don't trust Marstel. I think he'd accept our surrender, and then execute every Hulburgan soldier who took up arms against him. It's been done before." She hesitated, and then added. "On the other hand, your Icehammers might be allowed to surrender. I can see if they'll let you leave the field."

"You might've forgotten, Lady Kara, but Marstel said no quarter, asked or given."

"Mercenaries aren't usually dealt with like that."

"Aye, but as you said, I don't trust Marstel or his captains. Besides, you've dealt fairly wi' me and mine. It wouldn't be right to leave ye now."

"You're becoming sentimental, Master Ironthane."

"It's good business t' burnish a reputation for loyalty," the dwarf said. "Unless, of course, it gets ye killed in a lost cause, in which case it's no' so good for business. I suppose I'm not yet convinced that your cause is lost. I've never seen a battlefield leader t' equal ye, Lady Kara."

She smiled grimly at him. "I wish I had just three more companies to match the Icehammers, Master Ironthane. I'd fear nothing from Phlan to Mulmaster."

They stood in silence for a short while, watching as the soldiers below took their places. "Assumin' we're not all killed in the next half hour, how long d' you mean to hold the hill?" the dwarf asked.

"As long as I can. Until I know that he's failed, I still have hope that somehow Geran will succeed in his task," Kara replied. "If he's only been delayed, we might still—" She broke off suddenly, as the soldiers below gave a chorus of war cries and began to surge up the slopes, the runehelms leading the way. She shared one brief look with the dwarf captain, and called for her standard-bearer. "Sergeant Vossen! Pass the word to stand to!" All around her, the Shieldsworn companies stood up, shucking cloaks and hoods and strapping shields into place as they formed ranks at the top of the bluff.

"Good luck to ye," Kendurkkel said. "I go!" He jogged off toward the Icehammers, who held the back side of the hill.

For her own part, Kara motioned for Vossen to follow and headed for the middle of Wester's shield, which guarded the relatively low south face of the hill; the north face was too steep to climb, and Merrith Darosti's shield blocked the draw. Sergeant Kolton and the House Guards joined her as she took up a place in the middle of Wester's shield. There was no reserve left; this was the spot where the fight would be decided.

"Here we go again," Wester said to her. The landowner-turned-captain was tired, and he moved with a bad limp from a wound to his left leg, but his eyes still flashed with pugnacious anger. "Haven't they figured out we're not going to let ourselves get pushed off this hill?"

"It seems not," Kara answered. She motioned to Vossen. "All archers, fire at will! Don't save your arrows now! And don't waste any on the runehelms!"

The thrumming of bowstrings echoed through the damp night air, and once again arrows raked the Council Guard and their merchant sellsword allies. The range was close, and the enemy soldiers made excellent targets as they floundered and slipped up the hillside. Scores screamed and fell under the deadly barrage . . . but Shieldsworn fell as well, picked off the hilltop by the arbalesters in the Council Guard ranks. With a great, angry roar, Marstel's soldiers reached the foot of the bluff in a ragged line.

Runehelms and Council Guards began climbing all around the

perimeter of the hill. Shieldsworn met them at the edge of the bluff, hacking down the Council Guards as they struggled to find their footing and shoving runehelms off the slope with timbers and wagon axles. To Kara's right, several more Shieldsworn managed to lever a large boulder over the edge. It missed the runehelm they'd been aiming for, but it bounded down through the ranks of Marstel's soldiery. The waiting Shieldsworn raised a harsh shout of triumph as gaps opened up in the attacking ranks. Then all at once, scores of Marstel's soldiers swarmed up and over the edge—there were simply too many for the Shieldsworn to stop them all. The runehelms who'd avoided being pushed off strode into the Shieldsworn ranks, their great halberds reaping a grisly harvest. Screams of pain and roars of anger rose above the ringing of steel on steel and the brutal sounds of halberd blades cleaving mail and flesh.

Drawing her saber, Kara joined the fray to lend a hand with the fearsome creatures. Shieldsworn hacked at the monsters' limbs and ducked away from the whistling halberd blades, but the runehelms were terrifying in their power and resilience. Warriors exposing themselves even for an instant to cut at a knee or wrist were hacked down in blinding ripostes or sent flying through the air, broken and bleeding. Thanking the gods of war that they'd managed to delay at least a few of the monsters, Kara lunged close to the nearest and landed one shallow cut to the shoulder before backing away from a halberd blow that could have sheared off a leg. The instant the blade passed, Kara darted back in to strike at the same shoulder, deepening her cut. The silent black visor fixed on her, and the runehelm replied with a straight thrust of the halberd's spear point. She deflected the point past her torso with a hasty parry, but the blow was so powerful that the flat top of the axe head drove her saber back against her and hammered her off her feet. The ranger gasped for air, her breath knocked out of her.

The runehelm that had knocked her down pivoted smoothly and raised its halberd for an overhand blow that she could never hope to avoid. Kara saw her death ahead of her, and raised an arm to fend it off . . . but as the gray monster's halberd started down on its final arc, it suddenly shuddered violently. The magical glyphs inscribed in its flesh all flashed with purple fire, and a wisp of smoke escaped from its iron visor. The thing uttered a high-pitched, metallic scream—the first sound Kara had ever heard one of the runehelms make—and sank to its knees, its halberd falling beside it. As she watched in amazement, the glyphs marking it blurred and faded, vanishing like ink washed away in water.

"Geran's done it," she said aloud. "Geran's done it! He's destroyed the runehelms' master stone!"

The runehelm that had almost killed her started to fumble its way to its feet, but a brawny Shieldsworn stepped up beside it and buried his battle-axe in the back of its neck. The monster collapsed to the ground and didn't move again. Kara picked herself up and looked around; all along the hilltop, her soldiers were hacking the crippled runehelms to pieces and throwing back the Council Guard's assault.

"Are you hurt, Lady Kara?" Vossen asked urgently.

"No, I'll be fine," Kara answered. That wasn't entirely true; she suspected she'd have quite a bruise to show later. Around her, Wester's shield was quickly clearing the bluff of the enemies who'd managed to reach the top.

"There's something wrong with the gray guardians," the banner-sergeant said. He pointed. "Look, they can hardly stand."

Kara followed Merrith's arm. She could make out dozens of the rune-helms no longer fighting their way up the hillside. Some leaned on their halberds, some kneeled on the damp moorgrass, and others were simply motionless on the ground. Without the hulking monsters to lead the way, the Council Guards were already falling back in disorder. Marstel's banner wavered on the lower hillside, and a disorganized knot of Council Guards and merchant company mercenaries dashed back and forth in panic as they realized that their mighty allies were unresponsive. The banner's not that far, Kara decided. And she still had a couple of companies that were more or less intact . . .

"Sergeant Kolton, my horse!" she shouted. "Captain Wester! Form your shield on me! Vossen, signal the Icehammers and Third Shield to follow our charge! We're going after the standard!"

Nils Wester nodded at once. "With pleasure, Lady Kara! Come on, lads—there sits that fat old arse Marstel himself! Let's go give him our opinion of his reign!" The First Shield quickly settled into ranks on either side of Kara, the soldiers clashing blades to their shields and shouting insults at the Council Guard forces.

Sergeant Kolton's men brought their mounts forward from where they'd been picketed, and Kara swung herself up into Dancer's saddle. The big mare snorted eagerly, sensing Kara's mood, and the rest of Kolton's guards horsed themselves as well.

Kara waited a few moments to let Wester's soldiers find their places, then waved her sword over her head. "Charge!" she cried, and spurred Dancer out ahead of her soldiers. In a lurching, skittering slide, she rode down the rocky incline, her guards following after her.

Wester's Shieldsworn roared in battle fury and ran after her, slipping and sliding down the wet stone as they dropped over the bluff's edge to the corpse-strewn ground below. Kara aimed straight for Marstel, steering nimbly around the clumsy runehelms and knots of Council Guards who turned to stand in her path; she trusted Wester's soldiers to deal with them soon enough. The surging Shieldsworn crashed through the disorganized sellswords and the constructs both, sweeping the line of battle fifty yards downslope in a great, confused mass of shouting warriors and silent runehelms. Even as Wester's men left their places, the Third Shield and the Icehammers appeared at the bluff and streamed over to follow. With Marstel's captains spread out to ring the hillside, Kara's charge brought almost all of her strength against only a portion of her enemy's.

Kara galloped closer to Marstel's standard, Kolton and his men guarding her back. Ahead of her she spied the old lord in his half-plate, ringed by his own bodyguards and captains. She drew back her arm, readying a murderous saber slash for the false harmach, but only five yards short of her goal Marstel glanced away from the main press and noticed her closing in on his standard. "Guards!" he shouted, backing his horse away. "To me! To me!"

A Council Guard spurred his horse into Kara's path, blocking her way. With a quick nudge of her knees, she crouched low in the saddle and let the big mare strike the soldier's mount chest-to-flank and overturn the other horse. The guard fell under his mount and vanished, but the impact spun Dancer half around and carried her several strides away. By the time Kara recovered and righted herself, Marstel was out of reach, and the mercenary captain Edelmark stood in her way, mounted on a heavy charger with his sword bared.

"Come on, you spellscarred bitch!" he shouted at her. "I want to see if you're as good as they say!"

Kara narrowed her eyes. Six months earlier Edelmark had led the surprise assault that carried Griffonwatch with the aid of Rhovann's magic, and she'd heard plenty of tales of his brutality as the leader of Marstel's soldiers. He had much to answer for. "Good," she replied. "I was afraid you might surrender."

With a shout, she spurred Dancer to meet him. He parried her first cut, countered with a cut at her face that she passed over her head, and recovered in time to block as she cut at the back of his neck. Then she was by him, wheeling Dancer around to make another pass while he struggled to turn his own horse to meet her again. Kara spurred up behind him on his left, and Edelmark twisted in his saddle with a vile curse to guard his back. His mail shirt saved him from a wicked slash across the shoulder blades, and before Kara could land a better-aimed blow he spurred his horse out of her reach. Once again Kara and Dancer darted up behind him on left, and this time Edelmark turned left in front of her and stood up in his stirrups. He hacked down at her with fury in his eyes as their mounts tangled together in the middle of the press. The Mulmasterite mercenary was stronger than she was; instead of trying to halt his attacks with pure strength of arm she deflected them to one side or the other, ducking away from each in turn.

"Stand still, damn you!" he snarled. Again he hacked down at her, and Kara met his heavy cut with a turn of her wrist, deflecting it to her left. Before he could recover, she flicked her saber's point out in a quick, deadly arc that gashed him across the eyes. Edelmark shrieked and clutched at his face; she leaned forward and ran him through the armpit as blood streamed down his face. The captain slumped slowly over his saddlehorn as his charger bolted away from her.

"Well fought, m'lady!" Kendurkkel Ironthane called. The dwarf stood astride a dismembered runehelm a few yards away, a heavy axe in his fist. "I never had much likin' for that one!"

Kara grinned at Ironthane, and paused to take stock of the fighting. She noticed that she had the taste of blood in her mouth, and her jaw ached; somewhere in the furious play of swords she'd had her own gauntlet bashed back into her mouth and hadn't even noticed. The sky to the east was definitely growing lighter, and the rain had slackened to a gray morning drizzle. All around her, the Council Guard was breaking apart and fleeing in disorder, pursued here and there by shouting bands of Shieldsworn. Without the runehelms to back them up, Marstel's thugs were no match for her own soldiers; the Shieldsworn were better armed, better trained, and buoyed by the sudden reversal. "I didn't think they'd break so soon," she muttered aloud.

The dwarf gave the runehelm at his feet one sharp kick to make sure it was done for, and shouldered his axe. He pointed east over the moors, where Marstel and the survivors of his standard guards galloped back toward Hulburg. "Th' sight o' their lord and master riding for his life was no' so good for their morale."

"Let's not make light of the work ahead, Master Ironthane. We've got a long hard day ahead of us still." Kara glanced around, trying to get the measure of the fight. The Council Guard might be broken, but she'd still have to dig the Jannarsks, the Verunas, and the Iron Ring out of their fortified compounds, and there were the Cinderfists and the Tailings mobs to deal with too. Finally, she'd have to take Griffonwatch, although that was a job best undertaken with the sort of magic Sarth or Geran might command. "It's not over until we've got control of the castle, and Marstel and his wizard are in our pockets."

Ironthane snorted. "Well, I see no wizard at hand, but ye might catch Marstel if ye're quick about it."

"After them!" Kara shouted, and spurred Dancer in pursuit. Wester and Ironthane could manage the business of finishing the Council Guards who didn't flee. Kolton, Vossen, and the rest of her small band of guards and messengers—now less than twenty strong—followed her. It wasn't much, but it was almost all of the mounted troops she had. In fifty yards Kara and her riders broke free of the chaos and galloped onto the trail leading back to Hulburg, only a couple of hundred yards behind Marstel.

Marstel looked once over his shoulder at her; fear and fury flickered across his features, and the old lord hunched lower over his horse's neck and spurred it on. For a half mile or more the false harmach and his guards fled before Kara. But then a company of another twenty armsmen dressed in black armor with black cloaks came up from the east, joining Marstel and his small company. The riders in black quickly surrounded Marstel and the captains remaining with him, reinforcing them.

"What in the world?" Kara murmured, drawing up her reins. The black-clad warriors rode under a dark banner—a banner on which fluttered the gray and gold insignia of Vaasa. At the head of the Vaasan company rode a tall man in plate armor with a crimson cloak and the horned helm of a Warlock Knight. She waited a few moments while Marstel spoke with the knight, her jaw clenched in frustration; as much as she wanted to go straight after Marstel, she simply didn't have the numbers with the Vaasans taking up positions around the old lord and his surviving guards. It seemed that there was something to the reports of Vaasan aid to Marstel after all. Warlock Knights had been involved with the Bloody Skull horde somehow; was this some new plot of theirs, or were they simply taking advantage of the opportunity offered by chaos in Hulburg?

Marstel spared Kara one more glare of fury and contempt, and then he and his Vaasan escort rode off back toward Hulburg, cantering eastward along the trail leading past the old abbey.

"Should we pursue?" Sergeant Kolton asked by her side.

Kara scowled, considering the question. She needed to speak to Geran, the sooner the better; the appearance of the Warlock Knights was not something they'd expected. "Not when they've got more riders here than we do," she finally answered. "We'll send a couple of scouts to keep an eye on them and make sure they're headed for home, and we'll wait for more of our Shieldsworn before we press them."

Wheeling Dancer around, she left Marstel and his Vaasan companions to their own devices, and hurried back to rejoin the fighting around the foot of the hill.

TWENTY-EIGHT

15 Ches, the Year of Deep Water Drifting (1480 DR)

The gray light of morning seemed to rush in on Geran from an immeasurable distance, as if he were falling through pure blackness into a tiny circle of luminescence. He glimpsed the dim shapes of great copper vats and cluttered worktables racing past him; his head whirled with a maddening sense of tremendous velocity when all his reason told him that he *had* to be standing still. Then, suddenly, he and Rhovann no longer tumbled through shadow, but instead stood and swayed in a diagram of silver runes that gleamed on the floor of a cluttered conjury—the old trophy hall of the Hulmasters, now filled with Rhovann's devices and arcane apparatuses. And Rhovann's silver hand was still locked around his throat.

"You reckless fool," the elf wizard hissed. "Do you have any idea what you have destroyed? That stone was irreplaceable, worth more than this whole miserable hovel your family calls a castle!"

Geran opened his mouth to answer, and found he couldn't speak. Nothing but a thin rattle of air escaped his lips. Desperately he tried to find the words for a spell to break Rhovann's grip, but even as the magical sigils glowed and tumbled in his mind's eye he couldn't begin to give voice to them. His chest burned with the ache for a breath, and dark spots danced before his eyes. He felt his knees begin to give way as his struggle with the mage dragged the two of them out of the silver circle and into the nearest worktable, scattering notes and glassware to the floor.

A malicious grin crept into Rhovann's features as the wizard sensed

Geran weakening. "This is unseemly for a mage of my caliber," the elf said between clenched teeth. "I should slay you with my spells, not strangle you like a common murderer. But there is a certain irony to dispatching you with the hand you gave me. It might be enough for me. What say you, Geran?"

Geran could manage nothing more than a thin wheeze. He struggled once again to pull his left hand free or twist out of Rhovann's grasp, but the wizard merely followed his staggering steps before jerking him around abruptly and slamming him into another worktable. The swordmage battled with all his will, his determination, to cling to consciousness, but it was a battle he was mere heartbeats away from losing. With his right hand gone, he had no way to pull Rhovann's hand from his neck, no way to strike back, only an aching stump under a thin, oozing bandage. The wizard bent him steadily back over the table, and Geran's vision swam with darkness . . . but in one brief glimpse he spotted the red feathers of Mirya's quarrel standing out behind Rhovann's back.

He couldn't strike much of a blow with his missing hand—but he didn't need to. Flailing clumsily, he batted at the quarrel sticking out of the back of Rhovann's shoulder. With the hard bone at the inside of his forearm, midway between wrist and elbow, he struck the wooden quarrel and jammed it cruelly in the wound.

Rhovann screamed in agony and staggered back, reaching behind his back in pure reflex. Suddenly the crushing pressure at Geran's throat was gone, and he was able to draw breath again. He raised the shadow sword to strike—but the wizard retained enough presence of mind to seize his sword arm before he could, this time catching Geran with his silver hand. "Bastion!" the elf cried. "Help me!"

By the chamber's door, a great gray creature in a brown cassock and hood swiveled to regard Geran with black, dead eyes. It was almost nine feet tall, taller and more thickly built than even the runehelms were, a golem of dense clay the size of an ogre. The creature reached out with one huge hand, seized a big wooden table that easily weighed a couple of hundred pounds, and flung the table out of its path as if it was nothing more than a wicker chair. Then it strode purposefully toward Geran, its eyes fixed on his face. Rhovann glanced once over his shoulder, and snarled in triumph as his towering minion drew near. "Destroy Geran!" the wizard cried.

Geran looked up at the approaching monster, and his stomach turned to water. While he stood grappling with his old foe, the golem would snap his neck or rip off his limbs, and that would be the end of him. He managed to buy himself a few more heartbeats of life by twisting around the table, moving a few steps away from Bastion's lethal grasp. Somehow Geran found the determination to rip his gaze away from the golem and focus on his struggle with Rhovann. Desperately he sought the clarity of mind to bring a spell to his lips. "*Sanhaer astelie!*" he rasped, speaking the words for a spell of strength. In the next heartbeat he sensed the arcane currents of the room flooding into his limbs, charging his muscles with supernatural strength for a brief moment. Rhovann snarled a spell of his own, and flickers of emerald flame erupted around his silver hand, singing Geran's left arm. But with his strength spell Geran ripped his sword arm out of Rhovann's grip, *Umbrach Nyth* gleaming dully in his hand.

He had time for one backhand slash, a fierce cut that passed through Rhovann's neck in a short, vicious arc. The shadow sword made no sound at all; Rhovann gaped in blank astonishment for an instant before his head tumbled from his shoulders and his body sank to the floor. Green flames danced on his silver hand before they guttered out. Geran stared down at the mage's corpse for a moment, wheezing for breath. "Damn you, Rhovann," he rasped. "Is that what you were looking for?"

The mage's corpse made no answer, but at the last instant heavy footsteps warned Geran of Bastion's charge. He glanced up as the golem hurled itself forward, its huge hands reaching for him. The swordmage retreated two quick steps and sought quickly for a spell of teleportation . . . only to discover that he had no such spell fixed in his mind at the moment. Stumbling backward, he set his feet and managed a fierce cut at the golem's right hand as it reached for him. *Umbrach Nyth* sheared through the clay flesh of the creature, carving off two fingers and half its hand, but the golem seized Geran by the collar with its undamaged hand. Instantly it wheeled and hurled Geran against the windows at the far end of the room.

Geran flew through the air as if he'd been flung by a catapult and crashed into the heavy panes. Leaded glass shattered all around him, and likely would have cut him to pieces if his dragon scale spell hadn't guarded him from the cruel shards. Only the heavy wooden crosspieces that supported the great windows stopped him from sailing through into the dizzying drop beyond, where the castle's bluff fell well over a hundred feet to the clearing by the postern gate, but he paid a price in cracked ribs and a jarring blow to his head that gashed his scalp and left bright stars whirling in his vision. He fell to the floor in a shower of broken glass and splintered wood, shaking his head groggily.

"That's what you get for forgetting about the golem," he told himself. Daried would have been disappointed in him; his old bladesinger master seemed to have eyes in the back of his head when it came to staying aware of his surroundings. Geran groaned and pushed himself upright, grasping the shadow sword's hilt just in time to meet Bastion's next assault. For a moment he held the golem at bay, fending it off with the point of his sword; the towering monster was clever enough not to run itself onto his blade, fighting with grim, silent ferocity to get its hands on him again. Geran limped and hobbled away from the window, finding one new ache or stab of pain after another. Then Bastion swatted his sword point out of the way, and stepped forward to smash its half fist into the center of Geran's torso. The blow drove Geran's breath out of him again and knocked him sprawling fifteen feet away, rolling feet-over-head to end up lying on his belly on the cold stone floor.

Umbrach Nyth clattered across the floor, fetching up by the baseboard ten feet away.

It's almost funny, he thought thickly. I defeat Rhovann, but now his damned golem's going to beat me to death. It didn't seem worth the trouble to keep fighting, not when he was going to be bludgeoned or broken in a matter of moments anyway, but slowly Geran began to crawl toward the place where the sword waited, grunting with the effort.

Bastion studied him in silence; no doubt it was considering the last directions of its creator. The golem wasn't malicious, and wouldn't bother to inflict pain for its own sake. In its own implacable logic it would simply decide upon the quickest and most effective way to carry out his death, and then implement its plan. It would not stop, could not stop, until he was no more. Observing that he was not dead yet, it swung into motion and strode after him. Geran winced and tried to crawl faster.

Bastion's undamaged hand closed on his ankle as his fingers reached the shadow sword's hilt. The golem yanked Geran back, raising him in the air as it reached for his flailing arm with its half hand. Whether it intended to carry him back to the window and force him out, bludgeon him to death against the stone floor, or simply pull his arms and legs off, Geran couldn't tell; he dangled and twisted upside down, held by his foot. But his sword arm was momentarily free.

Stabbing at the golem's torso from his inverted position, he drove *Umbrach Nyth* up under its breastbone. The golem groaned aloud, still holding Geran in its grasp. Then, slowly, its binding enchantment failed, and it collapsed like a broken marionette. Geran had time for one startled cry before the huge creature toppled over on him; his head struck the hard flagstones, and then Bastion's immense weight buried him. He struggled briefly, feebly trying to pull himself free, but then the wounds and exhaustion he'd been fighting off for hours overwhelmed him. Darkness swam up from the laboratory floor to claim him.

He knew nothing more for a long time, drifting in and out of a gray, featureless dream. Somehow he felt that he needed to get up, to swim up through the gray to wakefulness, but he couldn't seem to manage it. A pleasant lassitude held him in its soft grip, soothing his hurts. For a time Geran wondered if he were dying, and if so, why he wasn't more concerned about it . . . but finally the sound of his name roused him—minutes, hours later, he had no idea. A vast weight was crushing him, but then it shifted aside, and he felt hands dragging him out from underneath. A small swallow of something that tasted like warm mead filled his mouth, and he swallowed. With a weak cough he stirred, beginning the long and wearying climb back up to awareness.

"There, the potion's doing its work. I think he's coming around." A familiar voice, somewhere close by.

"Geran! Geran, can you hear me? Are you hurt?" He opened his eyes to see Mirya leaning over him, his remaining hand clutched in both of hers as she looked closely into his face. "Say something!"

"I've had better days," he mumbled. He felt Mirya's hands moving to cup his face, and then she stooped down to kiss him even as he was about to say something more. Tears streaked her face, salty on his lips.

After a long moment, she released him and straightened. "Geran Hulmaster, don't you ever do that to me again! I thought for certain that you were lying here dead!"

"So did I." He sat up carefully, giving himself a moment to find his balance again. The light flooding in the broken windows was still gray with the overcast. The massive shape of the destroyed golem was beside him; he realized that he'd been pinned under Bastion when the creature collapsed. Hamil knelt on his other side, and Sarth stood close by, latching his belt pouch closed again. Geran frowned, trying to make sense of it. "Another healing potion?" he asked.

"My last, I fear," Sarth replied. "I advise against any more serious injuries today."

"That seems a sound idea in any circumstances," Geran replied. The healing magic dulled the pain in his back, his singed leg, his aching throat. There was something strange with the room, though . . . the light was much brighter than he remembered. It was full daylight outside behind the overcast. "What time of day is it?"

"Nearly noon, I think," Mirya replied.

"Noon? It was dawn when Rhovann and I passed through the portal . . ." Geran murmured. He must have been unconscious much longer than he'd thought. What was happening with Kara's army? Or the Hulmaster loyalists in town? "Have you been waiting to rouse me?"

"No, we arrived only moments ago," said Sarth. The tiefling stood nearby, studying the wrecked laboratory. "We could not cross back from the shadow right away. I believe Rhovann's crossing point was disrupted by the master stone's destruction. It took me some time to enact the translation ritual; I am sorry we were not swifter."

"I thought for certain you must be dead," Mirya said. "The last I saw of you, you were grappling with Rhovann, and then the two of you vanished from sight . . ."

"Speaking of Rhovann, it seems you've resolved your difficulties with him," Hamil observed. He nodded at the mage's corpse, lying on the floor in a pool of blood. "Good riddance!"

Mirya looked down at Rhovann, and grimaced. "He's truly dead," she said quietly. "Have we really seen the end of the troubles he's caused us?"

"Almost," Geran answered. "We've still got Marstel to deal with, and the merchant costers that are allied with him." He hadn't forgotten what Rhovann had said about the Vaasans, either. He stood, limped over to *Umbrach Nyth*, and stooped to pick up the sword. He noticed that no blood clung to the dark steel, despite the copious amounts of Rhovann's that he'd spilled on the floor. He ached from head to toe despite the healing potion—his wounded wrist throbbed, his back pained him when he turned too quickly, his chest was sore and tender, and somehow in the beating he'd received from Bastion he'd given himself a good knock on the skull as well as twisting his knee. But for the moment, he was on his feet again. With a sigh, he sheathed the blade.

Hamil frowned. "Now that I think on it, we never seemed to get this far in our planning for the liberation of Hulburg. Did we expect to be dead by now? Or did we imagine that defeating Rhovann's magic would simply unravel the whole puzzle at once? What comes next?"

"We need to learn where Kara's army is and whether the loyalists are fighting still. They might need all the help we can give them. If Marstel holes up in Griffonwatch or the Merchant Council withdraws to their compounds, there might be days more of hard fighting to pry them out."

"Not for you, there won't be," Mirya said. "You've done enough for now, Geran. You need your wounds properly tended, and then a good rest. Others can see this through to its end now."

He gave her a wry smile. "I'm afraid that's up to Marstel, seeing as we're now in the middle of the castle I presume he still holds. Getting out of Griffonwatch might be a challenge. In fact, we've probably delayed here long enough. Rhovann will certainly be missed by Marstel and his captains; sooner or later they'll investigate."

"Geran, have a look at this," said Sarth. The tiefling stood by Rhovann's body. He pointed down; Geran looked, and saw that the mage's silver hand had detached from the wrist. Small, dark runes encircled the replica around the place where it had joined its bearer's arm. "Did you strike it off?" Sarth asked.

"No, I didn't. He nearly strangled me to death with it, but it was still

on his wrist when I took his head. It must have come off after he died."
Geran reached up to rub gently at his bruised throat. He doubted that he
had much more fight left in him, not with his sword hand gone. With
Umbrach Nyth in his right hand instead of his left, he could have carved
his way through the runehelms in the Shadowfell with hardly a scratch,
he could have smashed the master stone in a single stroke, and Rhovann
wouldn't have lived ten heartbeats once he'd closed to sword's reach. Left-
handed, he was less than half the swordsman he needed to be. It was only
a matter of pure luck that his injury hadn't cost him his life in the last few
hours—or, for that matter, the life of Hamil or Mirya. And they might be
far from done with the fighting.

To the Nine Hells with it, he decided. He couldn't afford to be crippled
at the moment. "Sarth, let me see that," he said.

The tiefling gave him an odd look, but he stooped and picked up
Rhovann's artificial hand. He studied it carefully, murmuring the words
of a detection spell as he examined it. "It is a complex and subtle magic,"
he finally said. "I cannot say for certain what it might do. Are you certain
you wish to try this?"

"Try what?" Mirya demanded.

"The silver hand. It served Rhovann as a replacement for his own. It may
work for me as well." Geran used his left hand and his teeth to worry at the
bandages on his right wrist, then began to unwrap them. A flood of fresh
pain washed over his arm as the pressure eased and new sensation returned
to the stump; even after two healing potions, it was far from whole. A faint,
acrid reek—the remnant of the acid, he thought—came to his nostrils.

Mirya shuddered. "Have you lost your mind? How could you think
about wearing that *thing* on your wrist? Who knows what spells Rhovann
wove to bind it to his flesh?"

"I have read of such things before," Sarth replied. "Magical devices that
replace limbs are often enchanted to join themselves to the wearer's body.
It's how they are customarily made, and the experiment is simple enough
to perform. But I still think it is reckless to place your trust in Rhovann's
craftsmanship or intentions. Until you know what he paid for that hand,
or whether it can be removed once you join it to your arm, you would be
wiser to wait."

"Not this day," Geran said. "Lives may depend on me. I can't afford to be crippled, not if I have any alternative." He held out his left hand for the silver device, intending to try it himself.

Sarth sighed, and shook his head. "No, if you insist on proceeding, it's best to let someone else align it. For all we know it may graft itself instantly to you, and if that is the case, you will want to be absolutely certain it is arranged correctly. Here, set your arm on this table. Hamil, hold his arm firmly in place. Mirya, you watch too, and help me to marry it evenly to the stump."

Mirya grimaced, but she did as Sarth asked, leaning down to study the silver device and the blackened ruin of Geran's wrist. As Sarth held it close, Geran realized that the hand was not a perfect match for the one he'd lost; it was a little more slender and long in the finger than his own.

Hamil came up and took Geran's forearm in his own grip, looking up at him to silently say, *I hope you know what you're doing. The last thing this device remembers is that it was locked around your throat. Who's to say that it won't try to strangle you again?*

"Do it," Geran murmured.

Sarth pressed the base of the silver hand to Geran's wrist bones; Mirya reached out to turn the device a fraction of an inch. The metal was shockingly cold against the exposed bone, a jolt of ice that ran up the marrow of Geran's forearm. He hissed in discomfort but held his arm in place. The sorcerer studied the runes glimmering at the base of the device, and spoke the arcane words recorded there: "*Izhia nur kalamakoth astet; ishurme phet hustethme . . .*"

Nothing seemed to happen, and Geran sighed. It had been worth a try, he decided. He started to straighten up—and then the runes on the silver surface gleamed with a flash of purple fire. The silver suddenly grew warm and pliable; Sarth grunted in surprise, but held it steady against the end of Geran's arm. A jolt of searing agony shot through Geran's arm as the silver suddenly *flowed* into the wound where his arm ended. Despite his resolve, he screamed aloud and sank to his knees. Hamil swore in his native tongue, his eyes wide, but he held Geran's arm with both of his and refused to let go. Smoke rose from burning flesh at the end of the stump as the magical device sealed itself to the bones of Geran's forearm and reshaped itself, forming a short, smooth band around the damaged flesh. Geran felt as if the thing were filling his arm with molten metal; the pain was beyond bearing, and he swooned briefly into darkness.

A short time later, he came to in Mirya's arms, who was kneeling behind him and holding him upright. His arm throbbed painfully, but it was no longer unendurable. He groaned and stirred in her arms.

"Geran Hulmaster, you damned fool," Mirya snapped at him. "That's twice in the last quarter hour I've seen you unconscious. Never do something like that again! I thought you were dying under some awful curse of Rhovann's. What was in that thick head of yours?"

He didn't answer immediately. With care he raised his right arm close to inspect the silver hand; it met the flesh of his arm in a metal band only an inch wide, but he could feel by the weight of it that the thing was anchored as firmly on the bones of his arm as his own living hand would have been. For better or worse, there would be no taking it off now. Gingerly he tried to make a fist with the device—and the smooth metal fingers answered to his desire. He could even feel the pressure of fingertips against palm, although it was strangely distant and numb. His wrist still ached, and he suspected it would for a long time yet, but his arm felt whole and sound. "It works," he murmured.

"Best not trust it for sword play until you've had a chance to become used to it," Hamil advised. "Your grip might be different, and it could throw you off."

The swordmage started to answer, but a sudden pounding at the door interrupted him. He exchanged worried glances with his companions and scrambled to his feet. Then a voice in the hallway outside called, "Lord Rhovann, excuse the interruption, but Harmach Maroth said to fetch you right away! Are you well, my lord?"

Geran exchanged looks with Mirya, Hamil, and Sarth. "It seems Marstel is missing his wizard," Mirya whispered. "What do we do?"

"Wait for them to leave," Sarth advised. "We do not want to alert the whole castle."

"My lord!" the man in the hall outside called once again. Then the heavy jingle of a key ring came clearly through the door, along with a murmured conversation.

Hamil glanced at the headless body on the floor, and back to Geran. "Forgive me for saying so," he said, "but Marstel isn't going to be happy with you."

"Of all the luck," Geran breathed. It seemed he'd find out soon enough whether the silver hand would answer his bidding.

TWENTY-NINE

15 Ches, the Year of Deep Water Drifting (1480 DR)

G eran stood paralyzed for a moment more, searching for a way out of the room, and then keys rattled in the lock of the laboratory's door. There was nothing for it—they'd have to deal with whoever was at the door. He nodded at Hamil, who quickly crossed the room to stand beside the door on one side, while he moved to the opposite side. When they were in position, he motioned for Hamil to wait. In his best imitation of Rhovann's elf accent, he called angrily through the door, "Who is there?"

The key stopped at once. Geran couldn't help but smile; apparently the idea of disturbing the harmach's mage in his sanctum was more than a little intimidating.

"Castellan Sarvin and Guard Murrn, my lord."

"What is it?" Geran demanded.

"You are needed, my lord—the Hulmaster army is at the gates, and the harmach requires your counsel. Something must be done!"

The Hulmaster army is at the gates? Hamil observed silently. *Kara must have made the most of her opportunity when we destroyed the master stone.*

Geran nodded. "Something must be done, indeed," he said. He reached down to unlock the door with his silver hand; it seemed to answer his will deftly enough, even though he could not feel the latch under his fingertips very well. "Enter!"

There was a brief hesitation before the door pushed open. Castellan Sarvin—the big, black-bearded officer Geran had seen in the Council Hall dungeon—and his guard stepped inside with some trepidation. They halted in confusion as they took in the wreck of the laboratory, the remains of the golem, and the presence of Mirya and Sarth at the other end of the room. Then Hamil's knife appeared at the throat of the one mercenary, while Geran set the point of *Umbrach Nyth* at Sarvin's belt buckle. The two Council Guards had sense enough—or were simply surprised enough— not to make a fight of it. They froze, keeping their hands well away from their weapons.

"A good idea," Geran told the two guards. "Rhovann is dead, and I'm here to take back my castle. Now, where might I find Maroth Marstel?"

The two guards kept still until Hamil prodded his man with his knife. "The courtyard!" the guard answered. "The harmach is abandoning Griffonwatch. The Vaasans have offered us sanctuary. He sent us to see what was keeping Lord Rhovann."

The Vaasans? Hamil remarked. *What in the world do they have to do with this?*

Geran scowled. He wasn't sure what the Vaasans were doing in Hulburg, but here was a second piece of evidence of Warlock Knight meddling in the space of the last few hours. A year earlier, the Warlock Knights had aided Warchief Mhurren's Bloody Skull horde; he'd dueled a Vaasan sorcerer during the battle at Lendon's Wall. And Rhovann had said that the Vaasans had put Valdarsel up to his murder. Now Vaasans were waiting to spirit away the false harmach? No good could come of that. "How long before they ride?" he demanded.

"He's waiting in the courtyard with the Vaasans now," Castellan Sarvin answered. "We have no more quarrel with you, Lord Hulmaster. All we want is to be quit of this place."

"You should have thought of that before you took Marstel's coin," Mirya replied. "What do we do with these two, Geran?"

"Bind them and leave them here. They answered, and for that I'll spare their lives." He smiled grimly. "After that, I think I'd like to go down to the courtyard and have a word or two with Harmach Marstel and these Vaasans before they depart."

Hamil and Mirya quickly secured the two guardsmen. Geran noticed that the castellan wore a fine pair of light leather gauntlets; he tried on the right-hand gauntlet over the silver hand. He felt more than a little self-conscious about wearing Rhovann's hand at the end of his own arm, and felt like he ought to keep it out of sight. Satisfied with the fit, he nodded to his friends, and they set out into the castle.

The halls of Griffonwatch were eerily quiet as Geran, Mirya, Sarth, and Hamil hurried down toward the lower courtyard. None of the castle servants or clerks seemed to be about; Geran guessed that they'd quietly slipped out of the castle in the last few hours to join loyalists in the streets or simply lay low and wait out events. Nor were any of Marstel's mercenaries at their posts, since the towers and battlements seemed abandoned. They did find a number of runehelms as they descended, but Rhovann's constructs were listless and unmoving. The magical glyphs marking their flesh had almost completely faded, and thin black ichor dripped from beneath their iron visors.

"Should we destroy these things as we pass them?" Hamil asked as they made their way through a motionless band of four gray guardians gathered around the upper entrance to the great hall.

"They are unlikely to pose a threat," Sarth observed. "I suspect that the master stone's destruction erased whatever orders or instructions Rhovann provided them, and clearly Rhovann will provide no new instructions now. With a little time, I might be able to determine whether the rune-helms are crippled, awaiting new orders, or have simply ceased to function altogether."

"Never mind that," Geran answered. "We have no time to waste on the runehelms now—we must stop Marstel's escape."

"I've no reason to think kindly of Maroth Marstel, but does he matter at all now?" Mirya asked. "He was only a figurehead for Rhovann's rule. Without the wizard, he's naught but a drunken old fool."

"That's almost certainly true, but I can't let the Vaasans have him. If the Warlock Knights have someone who can claim rulership over Hulburg in their keeping, there's no end of the trouble they might cause. They might field an army of their own against us on the pretense of restoring Marstel to the throne. At the very least, it would give them a justification to keep up their meddling for years to come." Geran led the way as they clattered down the steps at the rear of the great hall and ran to the doors at the room's entrance. He set his hand on the handle and was about to yank one of the great doors open when Hamil caught his arm.

"Carefully," the halfling said in a soft voice. "Listen!"

Geran paused, and cocked his head. He could hear the hoof stamps of horses and the anxious shouts of a number of men outside. Instead of opening the door, he instead moved to one of the shuttered loopholes in the door, undid the catch, and peeked out. The front of the great hall looked out on the castle's large, lower courtyard. A light rain was falling, and deep puddles dotted the ground. To the left and right stood towers, barracks, and stables; directly across from the great hall stood the gatehouse, where the road climbing up from the Harmach's Foot ended. In the cobbled space, two dozen warriors—some in the red and yellow of Marstel's Council Guard, and some in the black and crimson of Vaasa—stood by their mounts or waited in the saddle. Maroth Marstel sat on a large charger, dressed in a broad-bellied suit of plate armor; beside him a Warlock Knight in a black, horned helm frowned impatiently.

"My lord harmach, we have waited as long as we dare," the Warlock Knight said to Marstel. "Already our path may be blocked. We must leave now, and trust that Lord Rhovann will join us when he is able."

"I don't care for the idea of leaving without him," Marstel answered. He stared up in the direction of the castle's upper towers. "Perhaps I should go speak to him myself."

"There is no more *time*, Harmach Marstel. I am leaving now, with my guards. If you hope to reach safety ahead of Kara Hulmaster's soldiers, you would be well advised to come with us." The Vaasan brought his mount in front of Marstel's. "Rhovann is a very competent wizard. He will have little trouble making his way out of Hulburg, I am sure. But if you allow yourself to be caught here, then you may very well negate whatever effort Rhovann is engaged in. You can aid him best by leaving now."

Marstel grimaced beneath his white mustache. "Very well, Lord Terov. Perhaps you are right. Let us go."

The Warlock Knight—Terov, or so Geran guessed—nodded curtly to his men. With a creaking of saddles and the clatter of hooves on the well-worn cobblestones of the courtyard, the band of riders began to stream out through the castle gate and down the causeway beyond.

"They're leaving," Geran growled. "Quickly, after them!" Before he could reconsider his actions, he pulled open the door and ran out into the courtyard after the retreating riders, drawing the shadow sword as he went. It felt solid in the grasp of his new hand—perhaps a little rigid and stiff, but firmly under his control. Hamil followed after him, brandishing his knives, while Sarth stepped out into the doorway. The sorcerer conjured a ball of sparking green lightning and hurled it spinning into the middle of the soldiers waiting for their turn to pass the gate; with a great thunderclap it detonated, raking Council Guards and Vaasan soldiers alike with emerald bolts. Horses screamed in terror, and warriors tumbled from their saddles as panicked animals reared and shied. Mirya's crossbow sang, and a Council Guard grunted as a bolt punched into his thigh. Some warriors spurred out after the lead riders, some turned to face the unexpected attack from the rear, and others simply hovered in between, torn by indecision.

Geran ran toward Marstel, intending to drag the fat old lord out of the saddle or kill him if he couldn't manage that. For a moment, in the chaos and confusion of the courtyard, he thought he'd be able to reach Marstel unimpeded. But a pair of Vaasan armsmen moved to intercept him, blocking his way. The swordmage found himself engaged by a pair of competent bladesmen who wouldn't simply be swept out of his way; grinding his teeth in frustration, he turned aside from his headlong charge to meet Vaasan steel with *Umbrach Nyth*, falling into the familiar flow of parry and attack. His wrist throbbed with each jolt of steel on steel, but the sword hilt remained firm in the silver hand's grasp, and in a moment he almost forgot that it wasn't his own living flesh that held the shadow sword's leather hilt. "Sarth!" he shouted. "Stop Marstel!"

The tiefling turned his scepter on the usurper. "*Ummar skeyth!*" he intoned. A smoking white ray lanced from the device's end straight at Marstel—but a woman in a crimson veil who sat on a horse near the Warlock Knight drew a wand from her sleeve and spoke a countering spell. The bitter white ray met some invisible shield conjured by the Vaasan witch and deflected upward, blasting a great white patch of ice in the side of one of the towers overlooking the courtyard. Then Terov urged Marstel out of the courtyard, followed by the Vaasan woman with her wand. They galloped out of sight down the causeway, and most of the guards followed them—but not before Sarth knocked two more out of the saddle with another blast of lightning.

Geran ducked under the wild swing of one of his opponents and bobbed up again to bury six inches of his sword point low in the Vaasan's side, unhorsing him. The other guard nearly rode him down as he dodged around the stamping hooves and flashing blades, but Hamil rolled up under his stirrup and deftly cut the saddle strap. The horse spooked away from the halfling at its belly, and the unsecured saddle slid right off the animal's back, taking the second Vaasan with it. He landed badly on the cobblestones; before he could get up, Geran stepped over and kicked him unconscious. The last of Marstel's escorts vanished through the castle gate, leaving six of their number dead, wounded, or stunned in the courtyard.

"Sarth, go after them!" Geran called. "Do what you can to slow them down!"

"Their mage is skillful, but I will do what I can," the tiefling answered. He invoked his spell of flying and rose up over the battlements, heading northward in pursuit.

"Find a mount," Geran told Hamil. He turned to follow his own advice, and spotted a big black charger whose rider was lying on the cobblestones, scorched by Sarth's spells. Trying not to frighten the animal by moving too quickly, he approached. "Easy now," he said in a soothing voice. "That's a good fellow, easy now." The horse snorted suspiciously, but it stood still long enough for Geran to take hold of its reins and give it a few pats on the neck before swinging himself up into the saddle.

"Perhaps you weren't counting, but Marstel's men still outnumber us about ten to one," Hamil observed. The halfling was trying to calm a skittish mare that was a little on the small side, the horse least ill-suited to his stature. "What exactly do you propose to do if we catch them?"

"I'll work that out when we do. Are you ready?"

"Almost," Hamil replied.

"I'm ready," Mirya replied. She'd found a mount of her own and had quickly slit her skirt at front and back to ride with a foot in each stirrup.

Geran frowned. "Mirya—"

"I'll have none of that nonsense now, Geran Hulmaster, not after the daft things I've watched you do in the last few hours," she said sharply. "If

I followed you into the Shadowfell, I can damn well ride with you now."

He hesitated before answering. "Then at least promise me you'll stay well back from any fighting we come to."

"If it makes you feel better." She kicked her heels to her horse's flanks and rode hard through the castle gate. Geran scowled and spurred his black charger after her; behind him, Hamil managed to get himself into the saddle and rode out after the two of them.

They cantered swiftly down the causeway toward the small square known as the Harmach's Foot, the cold raindrops striking them as they hurried after Marstel and his company. From their height, Geran glimpsed a half-dozen thin pillars of smoke rising up to meet the low overcast. He couldn't hear much over the thudding of his horse's hooves on the paving stones, but here and there in the streets below he could see handfuls of people hurrying from one spot to another. There seemed to be a riot or a skirmish by the Middle Bridge, and he thought he could hear the distant clash of arms echoing through the gray morning. To his right, a couple of hundred yards ahead of them, Marstel's company of riders was heading north on the Vale Road; the flash of spells and peals of magical thunder rang through the streets in that direction. Then he lost his vantage as the causeway descended down to meet the Vale Road.

Mirya must have seen what he had, for she turned north and galloped after the false harmach. Geran followed her, and Hamil as well. He leaned over his animal's neck, encouraging it to greater speed. For several hundred yards they thundered madly through the muddy lane, racing toward the outskirts of the town and the partially repaired city wall by the Burned Bridge and the Troll and Tankard.

Not much besides open countryside ahead of us, Hamil called to him. *Perhaps we should follow at a distance, and see if we can sneak up on them later? Or round up a larger company before we set out after them?*

Geran didn't answer for a moment. It was a sound suggestion, but he wasn't willing to abandon the chase just yet. Finally he straightened in the saddle, and began to ease up on the reins, thinking about the best way to proceed—but a sudden skirmish broke out somewhere ahead of him, just over a small rise. More magic flashed and thundered just ahead, and the shrill sound of steel meeting steel came clearly to his ears. He spurred ahead, sharing one quick glance with Mirya as he drew abreast of her. Together they topped the rise.

Just below them, dozens of Shieldsworn ran and shouted after Marstel and his riders, who were galloping madly down the road away to the north. In their flight, Marstel and Terov had run headlong into a company of Hulmaster soldiers. Half-a-dozen Shieldsworn lay motionless on the road or in the muddy fields nearby . . . but just as many Vaasans and Council Guards had fallen too. Sarth sat on the roadbank, a crossbow bolt in one thigh and the other leg stretched out at an awkward angle, while a small band of Shieldsworn waited nearby. Shieldsworn archers started to draw on Geran and his companions, taking them for stragglers from Marstel's band, before they lowered their bows with shouts of recognition. "It's Lord Geran!" they cried. "He's here!"

"I am sorry, Geran," Sarth said from the ground. "I did what I could, but the Warlock Knight's witch put a spell of negation on me and cancelled my flying spell while I was a fair distance above the ground. I fear I've broken my leg."

"That always seemed a significant drawback to the tactic of fighting from the air," Hamil remarked. "That, and the fact that everybody within half a mile can see exactly where you are, especially when you're flinging fireballs and lightning bolts to one side and the other. A good thing the Vaasan witch didn't catch you too much higher in the air. But how did you get that bolt in your leg?"

Sarth scowled. "One of the Vaasans shot me on the ground. I suppose he had some notion of finishing me while I was distracted."

Geran kneeled beside his friend and gripped his shoulder. "You did as much as I could have asked for. A bit of bad luck now doesn't diminish what you've done in the service of Hulburg." He grimaced. "I'm sorry I left you with no potions to drink."

"As am I. I think I'll remember to save one for myself next time."

The swordmage smiled. "I wouldn't blame you." He was about to say more when another group of Shieldsworn with banners flying from their stirrups galloped up from the west, cutting across the fields from the Burned Bridge. Kara Hulmaster rode at the head of the small company; Geran stood and waved. "Kara!" he called.

Kara's mouth opened in surprise as she caught sight of him. She cantered up close and slid from the saddle, hurrying over to catch him in a quick embrace. "Geran! Where in Faerûn have you been?"

"Events didn't proceed as I'd planned." Geran returned Kara's hug. "Rhovann caught me yesterday and threw me in his dungeons. Mirya, Hamil, and Sarth weren't able to rescue me until hours later. We didn't reach Rhovann's master stone until shortly before sunrise."

"I feared the worst until the runehelms began to fall." Kara studied his face and frowned. "By Ilmater, you've had a beating. Are you well?"

"Not as well as I'd like, but I'm still here." He decided he'd tell her what Rhovann did to him and show her the silver hand when they had time for the whole tale; it wasn't something he cared to do in the middle of the road with the Shieldsworn looking on. "What happened to the runehelms when we shattered the stone? And how did you come to be here?"

"The Council Guard and the runehelms drove us out of our camp at Rosestone. We were pushed back to the round, flat-topped hill a little west of the abbey—"

"Yes, I saw."

Kara stared at him. "You saw? How—"

"I'm sorry. Rhovann showed me what his runehelms could see of your stand. He wanted me to know that you'd been beaten."

"We almost were," she replied. "We fought off attacks all night long. Just before dawn Marstel threw his greatest attack at us, but just as the runehelms threatened to overrun us, they suddenly faltered—whatever force that was driving them suddenly failed. That would be the moment you shattered the master stone, I suppose. They were almost helpless from that point on, and without their runehelms, the Council Guard assault failed completely. We came down from the hilltop and routed them. Then we set out for Hulburg immediately." Kara pointed back toward the west side of the Winterspear vale. "We managed to horse most of the Third Shield on mounts we took from Marstel, and I rode ahead with them to throw a cordon around Hulburg and scout out the city. The Icehammers and the rest of the Shieldsworn—those who can still march, anyway—are following on foot. They're probably descending into the vale by the abbey trail right now. I had a mind to send messengers to any loyalists fighting in town and see if we could join forces."

"Send word to the Sokols and Double Moon too," Hamil added. "They'll help."

"Good," said Geran. "The castle's ours—Marstel and his men abandoned it. Send some soldiers to hold it when you can. Even a dozen to watch the gate would be enough."

"Marstel fled?" Kara asked.

"He was with the Vaasans who rode through. They're trying to spirit him away, but I don't see any reason why we should let the Warlock Knights have him, not when he has so much to answer for here."

Kara turned and called out to Kolton, who waited nearby. "Sergeant Kolton, I need every rider you can spare! We're going to run down Marstel and his Vaasan friends before they slip out of our reach!"

"Aye, Lady Kara!" the old soldier replied. He turned and began to bark orders at the Shieldsworn around him. The soldiers quickly moved to gather all the enemy mounts they could catch, while others climbed back up into the saddle and arranged themselves on the road.

Kara turned and caught her saddlehorn, ready to mount up again. "What about Rhovann?" she asked over her shoulder.

Geran gave her a wintry smile. "He's dead."

Kara gave him a grim nod. "Good."

"It seems you must continue without me," Sarth said to Geran. "Good hunting, my friend."

"I'll give the Vaasans your regards," Geran answered. He stood up and clambered back into the saddle, ignoring the tremors of fatigue in his limbs. He could ride and fight a little more if he had to. In a matter of moments, he spurred his horse northward on the road again, racing along the Winterspear's course as Hamil, Mirya, Kara, and fifteen Shieldsworn riders under Sergeant-Major Kolton galloped along at his back.

THIRTY

15 Ches, the Year of Deep Water Drifting (1480 DR)

The sun, weak and pale, broke through the overcast as Geran and his small company thundered over the Vale Road. They raced north for a half mile or more, following the familiar twists and turns through the muddy fields and wooded stretches, the trees still brown and bare from winter. Geran leaned forward over his mount's neck, urging the horse to more speed; the misty air splattered his face with droplets of cold water, and the animal's flying hooves kicked plumes of mud up behind him. All he could hear was the drumming of hooves, the creaking of the saddle, the clash and jingle of the armored warriors behind him.

They galloped into a thick copse that cut off the view of the road ahead, and passed by a motionless horse standing beside a fallen warrior, a Council Guard mercenary who'd evidently ridden as far as he could with the wounds he carried from the engagement by the Burned Bridge. The Hulmaster company sped past the fallen mercenary without stopping. Then they burst out of the woods into the last stretch of open fields before old Lendon's Wall.

Marstel and his Vaasan escort were a scant hundred yards ahead of them, riding slowly northward. The mercenaries and Vaasans stared back in horrified astonishment, surprised by the appearance of pursuit, before they spurred their horses ahead with cries of alarm. Two or three of the riders fell behind almost at once.

"They've got more injured from the fight by the bridge!" Kara shouted to Geran. "We've got them!"

The fleeing lord and his allies realized their predicament as well. They kept up their flight for a few hundred yards more until they reached the spot where the Vale Road passed through a gap in Lendon's Wall, then reined in and turned to make the best stand they could in the narrows. Several worked to ready crossbows as the Shieldsworn raced closer, and a ragged volley of bolts whistled past Geran; he heard cries of pain and the sudden clatter of a warrior falling from the saddle. Risking a quick glance behind him, he saw Mirya and Hamil reining in short of the clash. He was relieved to see that Mirya had sense enough to know that she had no business getting in the middle of mailed swordsmen and swordswomen trained to fight from horseback. She slid from her saddle and began to draw her own crossbow.

That's not a knife fight, the halfling told him. *Go ahead, I'll be here if you need me.*

"Take them!" Geran cried to his warriors, and he led the way as the lines closed. He spied a woman with a veil over her face riding close beside the Warlock Knight; she began chanting a spell, pointing a wand at him. An instant later a bolt of purple lightning crackled across the gap between them, as Geran raised his blade to parry with a counterspell on his lips. The arcane lightning glanced from *Umbrach Nyth* to plow a deep furrow in the muddy ground nearby; a small shock tingled through Geran's arm, but he was otherwise unhurt. Then he was in the middle of a violent skirmish as his horse carried him into the middle of the enemy. Knee to knee with a Vaasan rider, he cut and parried with everything he had left as the Shieldsworn riders hammered into their foes.

"For Hulburg, and the true harmach!" a Shieldsworn shouted. Others took up the cry.

The Vaasan sorceress took aim at Geran again as he was caught in the press. He tried to maneuver into a position to parry her next spell—but suddenly Kara flashed into sight, nimbly dashing through the fight on her agile mare. She took the Vaasan sorceress out of the saddle with a wide slash of her saber; the woman screamed and fell, her wand flying from her outstretched fingers.

Geran's adversary was swept away from him as the Shieldsworn's greater numbers began to tell. He looked for another foe, and spied the Warlock

Knight Terov in his armor of black plate. The Vaasan lord dueled with a Shieldsworn rider briefly before smashing him out of the saddle with a spell that conjured dancing black motes along his rune-scribed sword. Geran spurred for the Warlock Knight, ducking under the Vaasan's blade to stab at the man's neck, but the knight's gorget deflected the stroke. Terov countered with a quick chop at Geran's sword arm, but the swordmage parried as his horse's momentum carried him past.

Rather than follow him, Terov wheeled and shouted at Marstel. "Harmach Maroth, flee! My iron tower is only half a mile farther."

At the edge of the fray, Maroth Marstel wheeled his horse and spurred madly for the open road; the Warlock Knight raced after him. Geran sought to drive his own mount through the press after the fleeing lords, but too many soldiers—Shieldsworn, Vaasan, and Council Guard alike—crowded the gap in the old dike. For the moment there was no opening.

"Marstel's getting away!" Kara shouted over the fighting.

"I know!" Geran snapped. He couldn't get through the press, but he could go around it . . . Before he could reconsider the desperate plan that had sprung into his mind, he slid out of the saddle into the muddy road and fixed his eye on a spot just a short distance ahead of the fleeing lords. "*Sieroch!*" he said, summoning his teleport spell to mind. With one confident step he strode through an instant of icy blackness, reappearing to stand in the road a few yards ahead of Marstel and Terov on their galloping horses. In the moment before they rode him down, he wove his sword through an intricate flourish and unlocked his next spell. "*Nhareith syl shevaere!*"

A bright blue corona of fire sprang into being on the shadow sword's dark blade, streaming an arc of blue flames as Geran's sword danced in his hand. With one final slash, the swordmage flung the fiery blast at his enemies. The horses whinnied and shied from the sheet of fire, losing their footing as they leaped away from Geran and the menace of his flames. Terov cursed and deflected the sword's fiery arc, at least in part, with a counterspell of his own—but the panicked stop of his mount sent him flying from the saddle. Marstel had no such magic to protect himself, and the blue fire seared a black gash through his breastplate that stretched from hip to shoulder. The usurper spilled to the ground as his horse went down.

Geran tried to dodge the tumbling horse as it crashed by him, but it swept through his legs and knocked him down too.

He fell into the muddy road in a great splash, shocked by the cold water that soaked his clothing. The fall knocked the wind out of him, but a heartbeat later he scrambled back to his feet and staggered toward Marstel. The old lord lay facedown in the road, limbs twisted from his fall, a faint wisp of acrid smoke rising from his breastplate. Geran reached him and rolled him over, raising *Umbrach Nyth* to deal the coup de grace to throat or heart.

It wasn't necessary. For a moment Marstel's eyes locked on Geran's as the old lord's breath and blood gurgled somewhere in his broken body— then Marstel's eyes drooped and his last breath wheezed from his lips. "You old fool," Geran rasped. He let his sword drop and looked up to find the Warlock Knight, meaning to deal with Terov next. The Vaasan lord floundered on the ground twenty feet away, gasping with pain as he disentangled himself from his saddle and stirrups. Geran pushed himself upright and started toward him, only to halt in disbelief when a great burst of smoke and wet, bubbling sounds erupted behind him. He spun around in time to see Maroth Marstel's body melting away into a puddle of dark, frothing ooze.

"What in the Nine Hells?" he muttered. He backed several steps away, staring in astonishment.

The sounds of skirmishing behind him diminished as Shieldsworn and Vaasan alike paused, distracted by the spectacle. Kara, who'd picked her way through the fray and was now close behind Geran, peered at the stinking mess. "What in the world did you do to him, Geran?" she asked.

"It was no spell of mine," Geran replied. "That was a thrice-damned simulacrum, not the real Marstel! It must have been!" He was no expert on such magic, but Rhovann certainly was. Now that it was dead, it was reverting to the alchemical brew that the wizard had made it from.

"A simulacrum?" Terov snarled. The Warlock Knight had lost his horned helm in his fall; beneath it he seemed surprisingly ordinary, a man with stern features and steel gray hair. Only his crimson eyes marked the touch of the supernatural in his face. "It was a simulacrum I tried to spirit away? Curse Rhovann Disarnnyl's perfidy! He's made a fool of me, and kept the real Marstel for himself." He finally dragged his feet free of the stirrups and started to stand, pushing himself unsteadily to his feet.

"Whether he did or not, it was little help to him," Geran replied. He turned his attention to the Vaasan lord and advanced on him, setting the point of *Umbrach Nyth* at Terov's neck before the Warlock Knight found his feet. "I have you at a disadvantage, my lord. Yield, and order your men to yield as well, or I'll slay you where you stand."

Terov glowered at Geran for a moment before he sighed and raised his hand to the handful of soldiers still on their feet. "Very well," he said. "I yield. Borys, Naran, you others—lower your weapons. We can do no more here."

Kara trotted forward and dismounted beside Geran. "Where is the real Marstel?" she demanded of Terov.

"I have no idea," the Warlock Knight answered. "If you don't have him, and I don't have him, then I would guess that he is either dead or locked away in some secure dungeon of Rhovann's. This one here"—he nodded at the sodden, bubbling puddle in the empty armor—"has ruled in Hulburg for a couple of months now."

Geran risked a glance at the frozen skirmish behind him. Several Shieldsworn were on the ground, but none of the Council Guards were still in the saddle, and only four of the Vaasans remained. Hamil and Mirya slowly rode forward along the road as Sergeant Kolton directed his Shieldsworn to dismount and disarm their prisoners. Mirya closed her eyes and murmured a prayer of thanks as she saw that Geran was unhurt; Hamil took in the scene with a broad grin, and gave Geran a wink.

Looks like you've got the rascal right where you want him, he said to Geran. *Run him through already, and let's go have breakfast.*

"Not quite yet," Geran murmured. He looked back to the Vaasan. "Who are you? And what is your quarrel with Hulburg?"

The Warlock Knight's face might have been made of stone. "I am Kardhel Terov, fellthane and Warlock Knight. I have no particular quarrel with Hulburg. It is simply not in Vaasa's interest to leave Hulburg in the hands of a weak ruler who might fall under the sway of Mulmaster or Hillsfar."

"You say you've got no quarrel with us, but I don't see it so. Last year on this very spot I fought Vaasan knights who were aiding the Bloody Skulls in their attack on Hulburg. Mhurren and his orcs would have razed Hulburg to the ground if we hadn't fought and bled here to stop them. Now I find that you meant to keep Maroth Marstel as a pawn to use against us whenever you felt like it." Geran narrowed his eyes. "You've caused my family and my people a great deal of blood, grief, and tears, Vaasan. Don't play games with me if you value your life."

"There are repercussions for slaying a Warlock Knight, Hulmaster."

"Which I care nothing for at the moment."

Terov grimaced. "I am not toying with you. We have done nothing more than back the strongest faction in our designs to bring Hulburg within our orbit. Last year the rising power in the Moonsea North was Warchief Mhurren. This year the master mage of Hulburg was ascendant. If your position had seemed strongest to us, we would have approached you, but in fact the survival of House Hulmaster seemed highly unlikely until the last day or two. I would dearly like to know how you ruined Rhovann's construct warriors at a single stroke, by the way. In any event, the grief we caused your family was incidental to your own lack of strength."

"We seemed weak, so what you did to us was justified?" Geran snapped. "Show me your iron ring!"

Terov hesitated, but the shadow sword at his throat did not waver. He drew off his gauntlet and held up his right hand. The ring was surprisingly plain in appearance, a simple band of iron.

Geran shifted *Umbrach Nyth* to his left hand and seized Terov's right hand in the clasp of his leather-gauntleted silver fist. "Swear on your ring that you will truthfully answer the next question I ask."

"That is hardly necessary—"

"Swear it or I'll kill you myself," Kara said from beside Geran.

Terov's eyes blazed with anger, but he nodded. "I swear I shall answer truthfully."

"Did you direct the Cyricist priest Valdarsel to arrange the assassination of my family?" asked Geran in a cold voice.

Terov flinched—not much, only a slight flick of the eyes, but a flinch nonetheless. "Yes," he answered. "But, as I said—"

"Shut your mouth!" Geran snarled. Before he knew what he meant to do, he released Terov's hand and struck him in the face with his right hand. A sharp jolt of fresh pain seared his arm as the damaged bones of his wrist took the impact, and a trickle of fresh blood started from beneath the silver cuff at the end of his arm. But Terov's jaw broke under the weight of the silver fist. The Warlock Knight spun to the ground, spitting blood and broken teeth. Geran strode forward and seized Terov by the gorget, setting the point of his sword at the Vaasan's throat.

"Murdering bastard," Hamil said aloud. "If you don't kill him, Geran, I'll be happy to take care of it for you."

"I yielded, damn you!" Terov snarled through his bloody lips.

Geran glared at the Vaasan, but in his mind's eye he saw Harmach Grigor gasping out the last breaths of his life in Lasparhall, and dead Shieldsworn and servants strewn through the manor. His sword arm almost quivered with the need to take the Vaasan's life. He felt Mirya frown in deep distaste, shrinking from the blow she sensed gathering in him. Somehow he found that he didn't want her to see what he meant to do next; her disapproval held him from striking for a heartbeat as he looked down at the villain helpless under his blade. There was no question that Kardhel Terov deserved whatever fate he chose to mete out, that the blood of Grigor Hulmaster and perhaps hundreds more Hulburgans was on his hands. But slaying the Warlock Knight, however richly he deserved death, would not deter Vaasa from meddling in Hulburg's affairs again.

As a Hulmaster I can justly take his life, Geran thought through his cold fury. But as the Lord Hulmaster, is this the right thing for Hulburg?

"Strike if you think it is right, Geran," Kara said softly. "He has earned it."

Geran's eye fell on the leather gauntlet covering the silver hand he now wore in place of his own. A spot of blood stained the cuff, dripping from where Rhovann's hand joined his arm. Suddenly he felt exhausted, tired of the never-ending circle of strife and suffering he seemed to be caught in. Looking down at Terov, he realized that he didn't hate the man. After all, he hardly knew him. He might hate the things Terov had done, but that was not the same thing. And he knew that a war with Vaasa could end in only one way for Hulburg. "Nothing will be ended if I do," he murmured aloud.

This is why I shouldn't be harmach, he told himself. Compromise isn't in my nature. He sighed, and lowered his blade from Terov's throat. "Can you speak for Vaasa?" he said. "Will the Council of Knights be bound by what you agree to here?"

Terov wiped the blood from his chin and nodded. "Yes," he replied. "Swear to it."

"Damn it, yes, I swear it by my ring. My word can bind the Council of Knights."

Geran reached down and took Terov's ring hand again. "Then swear to me that Vaasa will never again interfere in Hulburg's affairs or support Hulburg's enemies for the purpose of harming my family or realm, and I will let you leave here alive and unharmed."

Terov shook his head. "I cannot swear that oath. Never would make it impossible, and therefore powerless. Five years I could promise you."

"Make it twenty," Kara said.

Terov grimaced, holding his jaw gingerly. "Ten, and in all candor, that is all I can promise without intent of evasion. There are limits to the authority I wield on the council's behalf."

"Ten years, then," Geran decided. "Swear it, and you can go."

"I swear on the part of the Council of Knights that no Warlock Knight or agent of Vaasa shall interfere in Hulburg's affairs or give support to Hulburg's enemies for the purpose of harming the realm or persons of the Hulmasters, to be so bound for ten years from this day."

Geran felt an eddy of magic gathering in the ring under his hand. He released Terov and stepped back, sheathing *Umbrach Nyth*. The Warlock Knight stood up slowly, and regarded Geran for a long moment. The gray turret of his iron tower was a dark shadow peeking through the trees by the shores of Lake Hul. "May we collect our wounded and dead?" asked Terov.

"Go ahead," the swordmage answered. "But I want that tower out of Hulburg's territory by the end of the day tomorrow."

"We will be gone by sunset today." Terov motioned to his soldiers, who quickly gathered their wounded comrades. The veiled mage was sorely hurt, and Geran wasn't sure if she would survive or not, but the Vaasans quickly fashioned a litter for her. They left the Council Guards where they'd fallen or sat wounded under guard, and set off on foot down the road.

"That's done for now, but what happens in ten years?" Mirya asked as they watched Terov and his soldiers march away.

"I have no idea," Geran answered. "But I've got to believe that in ten years we can find a way to convince the Vaasans that we're capable of looking after our own affairs—or, at the very least, are more trouble than we're worth for them." He shook himself, and turned toward Hulburg again. "Come on. Let's go home."

EPILOGUE

11 Tarsakh, the Year of Deep Water Drifting (1480 DR)

A little less than a month later, the great hall of Griffonwatch was as full as Geran had ever seen it. It seemed that half of Hulburg had gathered in the harmach's hall. Bright sunshine flooded in through the windows high overhead, and the smoke-darkened rafters had been dusted, scrubbed, and freshly lacquered. Old banners that had been removed by Marstel's servants were back in their places, repaired and cleaned for the occasion; after all, it had been more than thirty years since the coronation of a new harmach. Geran leaned against a doorway in the back of the hall, watching as his young cousin Natali sat in the harmach's seat, receiving the oaths of allegiance and well-wishing of her new subjects. She wore a dress of rich yellow, and her dark hair was coiffed beneath a slim gold tiara for the occasion. Her eyes looked big, dark, and perhaps a little frightened, but she'd been coached well for the ceremony, and Kara—wearing a fine dress and an elegant coiffure instead of her customary riding clothes or arms and armor—stood right beside her.

"You'll do fine, Natali," Geran murmured, even though he was much too far away for her to hear him. The musicians at the far end of the hall blew a small fanfare of their trumpets. Roars of approval, applause, and shouts of "the Lady Harmach!" and "Harmach Natali!" echoed throughout the great hall. Geran joined in, settling for raising his fist in the air and shouting "Huzzah!" since he'd learned the hard way that it was a bad idea to applaud with his new hand. He hadn't found any way to remove it short of simply amputating it from his wrist, so he simply kept it hidden beneath a thin glove of fine leather that matched his formal coat.

"Well, that was close," Hamil remarked to Geran. He, Mirya, and Sarth watched from beside Geran. "They almost made you king, there. Good thing you picked the wrong chair, but poor Natali!"

Geran answered his friend with a smile and took Mirya's hand, admiring the dress she wore—an elegant gown of a soft rose hue with beautiful embroidery and delicate patterns of tiny white pearls. Where she'd found something like that in Hulburg, he couldn't fathom, but she looked lovelier than he'd ever imagined in it. She read the unspoken compliment in his gaze and smiled softly for him.

"The realm's in good keeping," she said. "And this time I think it will stay that way. You've done right by your uncle."

"I hope so." Geran turned to Sarth, gripping the tiefling by the shoulder. The tiefling still leaned on a cane, but Geran guessed that he wouldn't need it for much longer. "You're looking well, Sarth. I'm glad that you're here."

"It is a great day for your family. I wouldn't be anywhere else," Sarth replied.

"You're staying, then?" Mirya asked him.

"I believe I am." Sarth nodded at the people filling the hall. "Hulburg is one of the few places I've been where my deeds seem to outweigh my appearance. In fact, Kara has asked me to assume the title of master mage; I find that I like my prospects."

"I, on the other hand, have decided that I can't bear the prospect of another summer in a land where it never gets warm enough to kick off your shoes, or lie in the sun, or think about jumping into a nice, cool lake," Hamil said. He gave a dramatic shiver. "I think I'll be returning to Tantras soon. The Red Sails have been without my attention for far too long. If I stay away much longer, I might find that I am no longer a man of means, and that would be truly tragic."

"You'll visit soon, I hope," said Mirya. "Selsha thinks the sun rises and sets on you, you know."

"Well, I certainly can't trust Geran to look after Red Sail business here by himself. I'll be back at least once before the end of the summer to see to a few things. Maybe more than once, if Geran gets himself in some trouble that I have to fix."

Kara appeared at Geran's elbow, having briefly escaped from her well-wishers. She leaned forward to embrace Sarth, then Hamil, and then Mirya as well. "Thank you all for coming," she said. "And my thanks to each of you for what you've done for us. Without your help, Maroth Marstel would still reign in this castle. We couldn't have set things right without you."

Mirya curtsied, and Sarth bowed his head. "It was our pleasure," Hamil replied with a bow of his own. "And the right thing to do, Lady Regent."

"Enough of that nonsense, Hamil," Kara replied. "And you too, Sarth, Mirya. Kara is my name, and I'll be sore if you don't use it. Now, I hope you don't mind, but I'd like to have a word with Geran. I promise to return him soon."

Geran looked at Mirya and his comrades, and shrugged. "Please, excuse us."

"Let's find some fresh air for a moment," Kara said. She led him to the stairs and threaded her arm through his. Together they climbed up to the balcony overlooking the hall and the upper courtyard beyond, the traditional dividing line between Griffonwatch's public chambers and the personal residence of the Hulmasters. The sun was bright and the day promised to be warm for Tarsakh, but the shadows still held a chill; spring in Hulburg was never all that warm.

"Did I do the right thing by Natali?" Geran asked Kara as they walked. "I feel that I've stolen the rest of her childhood by what I've done today."

"At times it will be hard for her, but you shouldn't worry for Natali. I can shelter her for some time yet, and she'll have all of us to keep an eye on her. No one will expect her to be anything other than a lively young girl for a few years, except maybe once in a while when she has to dress up for some banquet or ceremony."

He paused to look down at her. "Thank you, Kara. That eases my conscience."

"Don't thank me yet, Geran. I'm not through with you. You owe me something for chaining me to the throne for the next ten years."

"Owe you?"

"Yes, you owe me. You mean to stay near Hulburg, I presume?"

Geran thought of Mirya and Selsha. No, he wasn't going anywhere for a while—and he didn't want to, either. Hulburg was where he meant to be, and he'd fight to stay here. "I think you know that I'm finally home to stay."

She smiled at him. "In that case, you won't mind taking a seat on the Harmach's Council. I need someone to do for me what I did for Uncle Grigor, a family member I can trust with all my confidences, someone who can see to things I can't see to as the harmach's regent."

"You want me to captain the Shieldsworn?" he said with a frown.

"Not unless you want to. If we need the Shieldsworn in campaign I'll lead them myself, and if we don't, then it's a task that wouldn't suit you very well. No, you seem better at improvising, breaking rules, taking action when others wouldn't—things I've never done well." Kara's expression grew serious. "We have powerful enemies that bear watching: Mulmaster, the Crimson Chains, the tribes of Thar, and soon enough the Warlock Knights. I want you to watch them for me. Think of yourself as the royal spymaster if you like, but if I know you, I imagine you'll rely on your own eyes and ears more than others. Do the things I can't do from the harmach's seat, and tell me what I need to know. Are you willing?"

Geran thought it over for a moment. In fact, he'd been a little worried about what he'd do with himself. He'd assumed he'd busy himself with looking after the Red Sail Coster's affairs in the Moonsea . . . but as Hamil had told him more than once, he wasn't much of a merchant. What Kara was asking him to do intrigued him, and wheels were already turning as he considered the first steps he might take to establish sources of information. There was no reason the harmach of Hulburg couldn't be the best-informed ruler in the Moonsea, and that would be a potent tool to lay in Natali's hands when it came time for her to take her throne.

"I'm willing," he told Kara. "We won't be surprised by our enemies again, that much I promise you."

"Good!" she said. They returned to the stairs leading from the upper courtyard to the balcony overlooking the great hall. The sounds of music and laughter filled the room. "In that case, I think the Harmach's Council is filled. Deren Ilkur's agreed to resume his place as keeper of duties, and old Theron's back as high magistrate. Sarth has agreed to assume the title of master mage, and Mirya should make a fine keeper of keys."

"Mirya?" Geran asked, surprised.

"It was long past time for Wulreth Keltor to retire, especially since he didn't seem to object to staying on in Marstel's service when the rest of Uncle Grigor's council was dismissed. Mirya's got a sharp mind for accounts and she's made a go of Erstenwold's for years in the face of competition from the foreign costers. I think the Tower treasury could use someone exactly like her to put Hulburg's finances in order." Kara nudged him in the ribs. "And I must say that if you didn't know that Mirya and I discussed the question this morning, you're off to a very poor start as my secret spymaster."

"That's hardly a fair test!"

"So you say. In any event, I'm afraid I must return to our guests. I don't doubt that there are a dozen people that I *must* speak to, or risk offending someone I shouldn't have." Kara disentangled her arm from Geran's, and then reached up to kiss him on the cheek. With a small breath for courage, Kara descended the stair and rejoined the crowd below, heading to Natali's rescue; the young harmach and her mother Erna were surrounded by a dozen noble guests from neighboring realms.

Geran paused on the balcony, enjoying the sight of so many familiar faces in the room below—commonborn Hulburgans like Brun and Halla Osting, young Kardin Ilkur, Burkel Tresterfin and his family, and the militia captain Nils Wester, all proud heroes of the Restoration; the secretary Anton Quillon, Kolton, the old chamberlain Dostin Hillnor, and a dozen more retainers of the family Hulmaster; Kendurkkel Ironthane, nodding at the music as he smoked his pipe; Sarth dressed in resplendent robes, laughing softly with Nimessa Sokol as they shared some jest or another; Hamil, who held half-a-dozen children including Kirr and Selsha spellbound with some ridiculous tale as he winked at a lovely halfling woman Geran recognized as a lady-in-waiting to the Marmarathens of Thentia; and there, not far from Hamil and his captivated audience, Mirya Estenwold, her long black hair—unbraided, Geran observed—a river of midnight that fell past her shoulders. As if she sensed his eyes on her, she looked up over her shoulder, and their eyes met. She smiled up at him, a warm and open smile that he'd come to love more than the rising of the sun or the stars in the sky.

He straightened up from the rail and descended into the crowd, never taking his eyes from her, as she slipped through the crowd to meet him.

When they met, he couldn't help himself; he caught her by her shoulders and pulled her close to kiss her soundly. She leaned into him for a long moment before she pulled away, blushing. "Now you'd better stop that, Geran Hulmaster," she said. "Acting in such a way in front of all these good people! What will they think of you?"

"That I'm a very fortunate man, I hope," he answered. In fact they had a surprising moment of privacy in the middle of the revel, as most of the people around them were straining for a look at Natali and Kara, and weren't paying much attention to the two of them. "You've been keeping a secret from me."

"I suppose Kara's told you, then." Mirya glanced at the regent, and sighed. "I'm not at all sure I'm the right person for the job. And I'll have to hire someone to look after Erstenwold's for me, since I can't very well manage the store and look after the Tower's purse at the same time."

"You don't know how strong you are, Mirya. You'll do fine."

She gave him a grateful look. "What are you going to do now that you're not the Lord Hulmaster any longer?"

"Oh, I'll be helping Kara as I can. But mostly I hope to be looking after you and Selsha."

"You think I need looking after?" she asked, and a hint of fire flickered in her eyes.

"I know you don't, Mirya. But I know that I need you." He took her hands in his and gazed into her face, hoping that she could see what was in his heart, everything that was in his heart. "I asked you a question a few tendays ago, and you never answered me. Will you have me for your husband, Mirya?"

Mirya stood still as a statue, staring at him. "You still want to marry me? Even after what Rhovann made me do?"

"Yes, I do," he said. "With all my heart I do."

Mirya tried to speak, and stopped herself. Then, almost as if she didn't expect to hear it herself, she whispered, "Yes."

Geran found himself grinning like a fool. "Yes? You said yes?"

She laughed, and nodded her head. "I said yes!" she cried, and flung her arms around his neck, kissing him deeply.

They stood, lost in each other, until Geran became aware of a tremendous roar and shouts of approval all around them. He looked up and realized that the great crowd had finally noticed the two of them. Commoners, Shieldsworn, merchants, noble guests, all beamed and applauded for Mirya and him. Kara laughed aloud in delight, and clapped along with the rest.

A short distance away, Hamil grinned at him. *About time you got around to that,* the halfling told him. *What in the world were you waiting for, anyway?* "Lord Geran! Lady Mirya!" he shouted, and the crowd took up the cry. "Lord Geran! Lady Mirya!"

Beside Hamil, Selsha jumped up and down in delight. Mirya smiled at her daughter and held out her arm; like a dark-haired bolt of lightning Selsha bounded over and threw herself into her mother's side, hugging Mirya and Geran both. "Mama! Geran! Is it true?" she said. "Are you getting married? When? When?"

Geran glanced at Mirya, and they shared a smile. He reached down to hug Selsha back. "Soon," he said. "Soon, I promise you."

Then, to the wild cheers of the hundreds in the hall, he took Mirya in his arms and kissed her again.

ACKNOWLEDGMENTS

As always, I'd like to say thank you to my editors, Susan Morris and Phil Athans. Susan's been in the trenches with me for almost three years now on Blades of the Moonsea, and she's really helped me to make a better story out of these books.

In January of 2009, just as I was starting on the first draft of *Avenger*, my neighborhood was struck by a serious flood from the White River. An unbelievable number of people showed up to help out. Total strangers whose homes weren't anywhere near the flood turned out to fill sandbags. Home Depot's teams dewatered our crawlspace (and many others) at no charge. A Boy Scout troop cleared debris out of our yard. Friends of ours from church—especially Chris Zabriskie, Joe Hochwalt, Leah Barfoot, Cynthia Schmidt, and Brad Beeman—helped us to pack up an immensely overstuffed and flooded garage and clear it for repairs, and took in our golden retriever for several days. I've never been on the receiving end of any kind of disaster (even a little one like the Pacific flood), and I was just amazed by the energy and enthusiasm of the people who simply saw the need to help. My sincere thanks to all of you!

Last, but not least, it takes about two and a half years of intermittent writing to put a trilogy like Blades of the Moonsea together. For me, that's a lot of evenings and weekends, and the occasional stint of burning some vacation time to stay home and work on it full time. It's a marathon, and there have been times I've felt like I've hit The Wall. The support and encouragement of my family and my friends helped me out more than once. Thanks to everyone who's had my back on this one—especially my ever-patient, ever-understanding wife. Guess it's my turn to do the dishes now.